Praise for De Vries, *Reuben, Reuben*

"Peter De Vries's new novel, 'Reuben Reuben', is his longest, his most ambitious, and his best."
New York Times

"[De Vries's] plots are twisting and ingenious, and he is even funnier in phrasing that twists and shapes a scene."
Commentary

"There is something wrong with the world, and this man . . . knows. He expresses his knowledge not by caterwauling but through farce, parody, language-play, and a kind of commedia dell'arte manipulation of absurd characters and situations."
CLIFTON FADIMAN

"Peter De Vries is a master humorist and literary stylist . . . a vividly articulate master of our contemporary revels and a court jester to our follies."
MILES SMITH, ASSOCIATED PRESS

"Of the few genuinely funny writers at work in America today, Peter De Vries is the most prolific and the best prose stylist."
Newsweek

FIC DE
Reuben

D1267889

350000%

MITCHEL LIBRARY

Biographical Note

Peter De Vries (1910–1993) was born and raised in Chicago. He studied at Calvin College in Grand Rapids, Michigan, and at Northwestern, supporting himself with a variety of jobs that ranged from toffee-apple salesman to editor for *Poetry* magazine. During World War II, he served as a captain in the US Marines and returned home in 1944 to begin writing for the *New Yorker*. He then began using his incredible wit to create works outside of the magazine, writing twenty-three novels and a play, as well as novellas, essays, short stories, and poetry. His most notable works include *The Tunnel of Love* (1954), *The Blood of the Lamb* (1961), *Let Me Count the Ways* (1965), *Reuben, Reuben* (1964), and *Witch's Milk* (1968); some of these have been adapted into films and Broadway plays. Still infamous for his quips and puns, De Vries has been praised as the "funniest serious writer to be found on either side of the Atlantic."

Reuben, Reuben

Reuben, Reuben

A Novel

by Peter De Vries

THE UNIVERSITY OF CHICAGO PRESS

Chicago and London

The University of Chicago Press, Chicago 60637
The University of Chicago Press, Ltd., London
© 1956, 1962, 1964 by Peter De Vries

All rights reserved
Originally published in 1964 by Little, Brown and Company
Paperback edition 2015
Printed in the United States of America

22 21 20 19 18 17 16 15   1 2 3 4 5

ISBN: 978-0-226-17056-5 (paper)
ISBN: 978-0-226-17073-2 (e-book)
DOI: 10.728/chicago/9780226170732.001.0001

Parts of chapters 24, 26, 27, 28, and 29 originally of this novel have appeared in the *New Yorker* in slightly different form.

Library of Congress Catalogue Card Number: 64-10471

Library of Congress Cataloging-in-Publication Data

De Vries, Peter, 1910–1993, author.
    Reuben, Reuben : a novel / Peter De Vries. — Paperback edition.
        pages cm
    "Originally published in 1964 by Little, Brown and Company."—Title page verso.
    ISBN 978-0-226-17056-5 (paperback : alkaline paper) — ISBN 978-0-226-17073-2 (e-book) 1. Man-woman relationships—Fiction. I. Title.
    PS3507.E8673R48 2015
    813'.52—dc23
                                                          2014014264

♾ This paper meets the requirements of ANSI/NISO Z39.48–1992 (Permanence of Paper).

Reuben and Rachel

MODIFIED BY N. H. H.

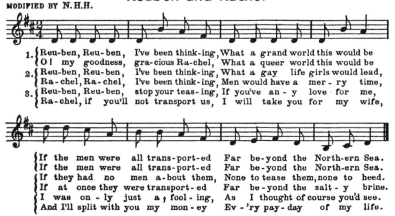

1. { Reu-ben, Reu-ben, I've been think-ing, What a grand world this would be
   { O! my goodness, gra-cious Ra-chel, What a queer world this would be
2. { Reu-ben, Reu-ben, I've been think-ing, What a gay life girls would lead,
   { Ra-chel, Ra-chel, I've been think-ing, Men would have a mer-ry time,
3. { Reu-ben, Reu-ben, stop your teas-ing, If you've an-y love for me,
   { Ra-chel, if you'll not transport us, I will take you for my wife,

{ If the men were all trans-port-ed Far be-yond the North-ern Sea.
{ If the men were all trans-port-ed Far be-yond the North-ern Sea.
{ If they had no men a-bout them, None to tease them, none to heed.
{ If at once they were transport-ed Far be-yond the salt-y brine.
{ I was on-ly just a ₰ fool-ing, As I thought of course you'd see.
{ And I'll split with you my mon-ey Ev-'ry pay-day of my life.

NOTE: Reuben and Rachel may be used as a duet number, the girls or women alternating with the boys or men through the several verses. The number may also be used effectively as a canon, in which case the first verse only would be used, the second part entering after the first part has sung two measures.

From The Golden Book of Favorite Songs, Copyright 1915, 1923, 1946 by Hall & McCreary Company. Copyright Renewed 1951 by Hall & McCreary Company. Used by permission of the publishers, Schmitt, Hall & McCreary Company of Minneapolis, Minn.

CONTENTS

SPOFFORD

one

GIVEN A LITTLE MONEY, education and social standing, plus of course the necessary leisure, any man with any style at all can make a mess of his love life. And given these, plus a little of the right to self-realization that goes with modern life, a little of the old self-analysis, any woman with any gumption at all can make a shambles of her marriage. Statistics show it every day. Romantic confusion, once the privelege of a few, is now within reach of all. Even of me, a chicken farmer. I'm not going to say "mere chicken farmer" like you might expect, because in the first place I lack the humility for it, and in the second there's nothing mere about running a poultry ranch in Connecticut, as they now call them there. Nothing could be less mere, as the facts will show.

I was born here in Woodsmoke, but not this Woodsmoke. I no longer recognize the place. I'm that most displaced of all displaced persons, your native son in a modern town. My father was the last of our line to live his life out without being made an alien in his birthplace by immigrants turning it into a tentacle of New York. Good thing he went out with his time, as he would of had strong emotions on the subject — The Losing of the East. We were not taken captive into Babylon — Babylon came to us — but our harps hang on the willows just the same.

My father was a man of feeling who always wanted his family to show their feelings for each other too. That was why he started a sociable little custom we observed every morning without fail. We always shook hands at breakfast. None of

3

your half-hearted shakes neither, but firm grasps to show how glad we were to see one another again after a good night's sleep. "Morning, Ma. *Good* morning, Grace. Luther." The hearty pumping went on across the steaming victuals till everybody had shaken hands with everybody else, and then we sat down. In falling in with this we three children were naturally following the example set by my parents whenever they met, like at a railroad station or bus depot. They always shook hands warmly.

"I don't hold with reserve. Reserve is for Scandinavians," my father said. "If we can't express the emotions God give us then we don't deserve them. We're only on loan to one another, so let's show our feelings while we can." These were orders none of us would dream of disobeying, as the other main way he had of showing his feelings was to bust you one in the jaw. He busted more guys in the jaw than you could shake a stick at, and the rest he shook a stick at. I mean the heavy hickory cane he always carried on the walks around town that became more and more familiar a sight as my brother Luther and I got old enough to pitch in on the farm.

My father always wrung the chickens' necks to induce death, but after he passed on hisself my brother and I modernized the farm somewhat. We used axes, together with one them automatic plucking machines. Now days they have an electric knife for the small phlebotomy there's still no substitute for, but the automatic plucker is still in operation. I can hear it humming away downstairs as I sit and write this. After Luther left to go into insurance in Hartford, I ran the farm myself until I was in my fifties, when my wife died. Then I passed it along to my son George and his wife Mary, who I now live with in the same old farmhouse, occasionally waiting on trade in the salesroom off the kitchen. At least they think I live with them, though a glance at the property title might show its the other way around. So they try to tolerate me, except when I think of it first and tolerate them. Anyhow. I hope to sell parts of this that I'm batting out to some magazine before it becomes a book, preferbly the *Yale Review*, as Yale would of been my alma mater if I'd had any choice. I hadn't even finished grammar school when my father was snatched away (very suddenly, through the medium of pneumonia) and I had to pitch in on the farm. Luther finished high school by taking evening courses in Bridgeport, eventually bettering himself into insurance. My sister Grace and her husband live in Akron. I never enrolled in nothing again except for an evening class in creative writing, also in Bridgeport, some years back. I wrote a theme for the class describing my father:

"My father was a rangy man with a long face and the brightest blue eyes you ever see, so it was a shame they were not better lined up than they were, for in that department he resembled Ben Turpin. One eye was always gazing at the other in wrapped admiration. That and wiry hair that stood up straight, like a fright wig, give him a look like one them drawings that are done by disturbed children in your better schools, that are suppose to show conflict."

The teacher of this composition class said my tribute to my father was touching, and that the style was certainly a relief from all this writing that is so polished but dead? He seemed to think it might ruin my individuality if he started giving me pointers, a responsibility he didn't want to take. "Get out of this class and stay out," he said, "flee for your life." There was nothing more he could do for me.

I bad farewell to literary pursuits until in my sixties, when I am taking it up with a vengeance for many reasons. One is that with the farm being run by my son and daughter-in-law I have some leisure time at last. Another is that there is now in our Woodsmoke a multi-million-dollar correspondence school for writers. Its a booming industry called the Successful Writers School, and I figured I would give them a chance to help me over the hump like they claim they can in their ads, else let them mfr. pool cues. But the main reason I take pen in hand is that now I have something to say. My message in a nutshell is the one I have hinted at the very start: I am a D.P. in my own back yard. What's more — and this is the essence of what I've decided to try and put down — I got displaced by staying put.

I stayed on at the old homestead and saw the town where I was born grow from 1800 neighbors to 20,000 strangers —

strangers who regard me as the outsider. I'm the foreigner, ever hear the beat? How many miles does the average commuter clock up in a lifetime without going nowheres? Seventy-five thousand? The equivalent of three or four times around the world? Well if I'd pulled up stakes in my prime and plunked down in the middle of Belgium I wouldn't be half as uprooted as I am right now sitting in the bedroom where I was born, gazing out the window — at what? One church, so modern they're thinking of making divorce a sacrament — or so the story goes. And why not? As Mrs. Punck says, you only get married the first time once. One superette (you got it, a regular size grocery store). One repair garage with the slogan "We specialize in American cars." I realize the humor of that ain't unconscious — the proprietor is a satirist I'm just letting do a little of my work for me. You can picture for yourself the imports whizzing by the farmhouse now, the high-powered sports jobs that sociologists tell us are status signs and psychologists claim are sex symbols. You know all that, and how it goes. Men used to shoot jaguars now they drive them, sometimes fast enough to kill deer on the Massachusetts Turnpike. They are also whizzing past the real supermarket where the food is so sanitarily packaged after being sprayed with various and Sunday poisons. Out there are also the subdivisions named, by God, after what the contractors had to eradicate to build them — Birch Hills (named after the grove bulldozed away preparatory to laying the foundation), Vineyard Acres after the rows of Concord grapes plowed under to make way for them. Of course old Mrs. Ponderosa's corner vineyard still stands, visible to me from another window, but that also overlooks a development called Punch Bowl Hollow. Last but not least, there is this writing mill that I am banking on to get me off the ground, else let them go into billiard equipment. The stock of the school, which also boasts a twin factory for turning out artists, is now traded over the counter and may go on the Big Board. It has the largest building in town, a huge modern plant with a warehouse for incoming and outgoing lessons, up-to-date furnishings and a spacious lounge where lecturers come to speak on different subjects like "The Decline of Fiction" and "Whatever Happened to Style?" to supplement the courses.

A smattering of persons comes to mind who aren't commuters but who are part and parcel of the culture the term stands for and I must try to come to grips with. Like the art teacher in the local school who is so highly thought of because she don't have the kids draw; the piano teacher who instructs them through playing cords that certain colors remind them of; and the architect who designed the new church where they're thinking of solemnizing divorce after being inspired by a snail shell. And the Lesbian psychiatrist now living in the old Abernathy place who has written a best seller called *Symbolism in Everyday Life.* I have come to know her well. She has flat heels, her hair skun back in a bun, and a standing week-end order — one capon.

You will recall how the ancient Romans of old use to feel around in birds insides for omens about what the future held in store? Well thats the business I been in for forty years. For forty years I been rummaging in chickens interiors while the shape of things to come walked in the front door to buy what I had killed and was now dressing. I should say for half of that time really, because I can seem to remember the exact day, around 1940, when the cast of characters began to change, the exact hour even. Suddenly instead of the bakers and cobblers and carpenters wives we Spoffords had been selling poultry to since the turn of the century there began coming in the door the kind of women who put "ish" behind everything and "sort of" in front of it. "What size fowl did madam have in mind? How many pounds?" "Sort of fivish." Then the chaps who shop in pairs, that know only too well how to cook what their buying. And on Saturday mornings generally the husbands of the ish women, men in tweed jackets that the elbows of are libel to be vulcanized.

Now Woodsmoke has been called the appendix of Madison Avenue. Those are the birds who made it that — the last mentioned. They go to town every day and back carting one them leather reticules to offices where they sit thinking up slogans to make us buy the kind of bread that when you squeeze

7

it it stays squeezed? That you'd as leaf eat cotton battin? Am I coming in loud and clear? Well at noon they'll knock off for one them exhausting three hour lunches at restaurants with names like Villanova and The Forum of the Twelve Caesars, that give you the absolute creeps along the lines above suggested, as you think, Well the Vandals are at the gates all right, we're beginning to decline if not yet fall. Are you reading me out there? Am I coming in strong? Not to mention the fact that you and I pay for those banquets since they are tax deductible. What they do over lunch I don't know unless its think up some more slogans like "From the depths of a tranquil monastery comes the secret of a superb relish" to be run under a picture of some guy from the model agency praying in a ski parka with the hood well up around the ears for extra reverence and his hands folded. Or maybe firm up a variety TV show containing, oh, a girl with a song on the Hit Parade, a juggler, and one them cerebral comedians they call them. You know, the far out kind who impersonate linoleum and lint, Monday and Denver, while the Russians get ahead of us in everything.

It don't impress me none that the new element here are professional New Englanders. Professional New Englanders are all from the Middle West, the South and New York, ever see one from Maine? So hence I'm not impressed that they buy houses with Revolutionary bullet holes in the front door and collect pewter mugs with glass bottoms that legend has it are glass in order that American troops could see the enemy approaching while they kwaffed their ale in taverns, and maybe even open restaurants theirselfs with menus in olden type saying Roaft Thankfgiving Turkey with Mafhed Cheftnuts and Prime Ribf of Beef with Yorkfhire Pudding and Horferadifh Fauce $8.50. I juft get a little fed up if all. And a little anxious when I realize with a jolt that this culture to which I'm a D.P. must suddenly be regarded as the one into which my granddaughter was born.

Suddenly its her what-do-you-call-it. Milieu.

two

GENEVA WAS ALWAYS a quiet girl, who like most quiet people could periodically come out of her shell to raise worse hell than you get from people who make a general practise of asserting themself, like me. (I'm tall and angular as a carpenter's rule, with a lantern jaw and eyes the color of grass stains. Well thats over with.) Geneva was always strong and sturdy, with hips that swayed like a bell when she walked, and big round eyes the color of butterscotch. Her gold hair fell to her shoulders, when it wasn't tucked up inside one of her father's cloth caps, because she could not abide braiding it or her mother bear to have it cut. When Geneva was twelve her mother did agree to having it cut off, first braiding it into one thick plait which now hangs framed behind glass in her mother's bedroom between the picture of Jesus driving the money changers out of the temple and the famous photograph of Teddy Roosevelt where the light is bouncing off his glasses?

Geneva was looked down on by her peers as they call them now, but not then, the other farm folk and grocers wives and daughters, for wearing dungarees. Till the New Yorkers began moving in and dungarees become shiek. It was the ish women I first see come into the salesroom for chickens wearing pants, sometimes with a mink coat on too. I never stood in aw of them no matter how they showed their superiority, upside down or right side up. One of them, admiring the look of the farm one fine spring morning, started quoting Tennyson at me. Which got my goat, as I knew she thought she was talking down to a clodhopper. "Reading Tennyson," I says with a air of aphorism, "is like drinking liqueur. Your likelier to get sick on it than drunk." Then I stuck my tongue out at her, just before she turned around from the window out of which she had been gazing. She started to chat about her daughter Lila, only yesterday a waif in pigtails bicycling up to the farm to fetch the week end's order, now a graduate of Carnegie and through acting school and working in a famous Broadway producer's office. "She'll be directly under Mr. Slatkin," the woman said. "Most of the time anyway," I thought to myself, knowing them New York producers all right. This mother likes to brag how helpless the girl is, she's so artistic. "She can't cook, she can't sew, she can't type, she can't nothing," the woman says, and I says, "Well that's talent."

Geneva always pitched in with the chores, even the slaughtering. My wife and I use to kill only once a week in the old days, when we had a small trade. (I lost my wife very quickly, through the medium of ruptured appendix. I don't glorify the old days blindly — the fact that there were no antibiotics then ain't one of the things that make me hanker for them.) With Woodsmoke solidly a suburb of New York, business tripled and now George and Mare kill twice a week. While we disliked on sight the new element that could make a curio out of a 1st family like us, we knew that to expect Geneva to be unaffected by what was now her environment would be folly and bucking progress. So I said nothing. But I sure thought a heap when the girl I only yesterday dandled on my knee come home from high school one afternoon when I was stretched out on the parlor sofa taking a snooze and sat down on my stomach. It was the new sophistication. She had so much makeup on her eyes she could hardly keep them open. Which no doubt give her the sleepy siren look no doubt intended by all the calcimine.

"Tad Springer and I have got charge of panel discussion in Social Slops tomorrow," she said, in between eating an apple. "The subject is 'Preparation for a World of Strife.' "

"What will you do?" I asked as well as I could with the weight on my middle. "How will you handle the meeting?"

"Probably throw hot tar on the kids. That ought to prepare 'em."

My heart went out to her. I knew she was playing a role, trying the new sophistication on for size. That it didn't fit by a mile only added to her appeal — which I hoped in the end the right man would see behind all the camoflage. She kind of rolled those butterscotch eyes away, using the bored manner to cover up the embarrassment she was really feeling at the way she was acting. Our Geneva was as ripe and yellow as the Grimes Golden she was sinking her teeth into. I thought to myself, You'll go far baby, provided you just stay where you are. This brittle stuff ain't for you. It ain't your speed. The squeeze on my gut finally made my nose bleed, bringing the discussion to an end.

But I remember something odd. I remember a sensation I had then, of wanting to know more about the tendencies that were infecting our Geneva. It come from nowhere, as those inspirations often do. According to a story I read in a newspaper column, Thornton Wilder claims he got the idea for *The Skin of Our Teeth* while watching *Hellzapoppin*, a show I never saw but which apparently had a lot of shenanigans with the audience. Anyhow when somebody come down the aisle and laid a chicken in his lap he said to hisself, "Wilder, your going to write a play." When Geneva sat on my stomach eating an apple and talking about throwing hot tar on the kids in Social Slops I says to myself, "Spofford, your going to write a book. Your going to take a closer look at this society that made you a D.P. in your own back yard. You may even get mixed up in it. Your going to eat of the fleshpots of Egypt." Which struck me as odd, as I have always believed in plain dealing.

The name of Tad Springer come up next when Geneva arrived home from school the middle of that December to announce that she was going to the Senior Dance at the country club with him. Our sensation was definitely in the sweet-and-sour category. It give us a turn as well as a thrill, because the natural pleasure of having a daughter asked to the big Holiday do by a boy whose family *belonged* to the country club was tempered by doubts how she would fit in with that society, which in turn remember we took a dim view of. You could pick no better example of the culture that made us D.P.'s in our home town than the Springers.

"Well well," Geneva's mother says on hearing the news. "We've never met Tad of course, but I know his mother very well. She patronizes us."

"You can say that again," I says.

No cigar. What burns me is the way George and Mare never read a book, never watch anything on television except junk, never look up a new word when they come across it, let alone make a *point* of learning one new one a day as I have now for thirty years or more. Thus they never get fine points. Subtleties go by them like the Jags past the farm. Bad habits are nothing but quicksand in slow motion, and George's and Mare's is to let what brains they have rot. George has one virtue, he's modest, and the edge is taken off that by the fact that theres no point in his being anything else. I couldn't even get him to high school — he preferred to quit school and settle down to work on the farm, where he's been content ever since. As for Mare, if she ever reads anything besides the local newspaper its a True Confessions magazine. I told her once in a fit of peak that she was bovine, and she only give the grateful grunt she always does when acknowledging a compliment crouched in big words. She automatically thinks a big word is flattering. I tried once to see just how far I could go with this game that I played with her, and with her mother too, Mrs. Punck. One day when "execrable" was my new word I says to her at dinner, "Your cooking is always execrable but tonight you've outdid yourself." She give the grateful grunt, looking away, and George nods too, turning the pages of a bowling catalogue. Of course I wouldn't of said that if her cooking *was* that, not being a monster, but I think I have the right to chastise rotting minds when I have to live with them. The amusement I got out of these games is bitter.

Anyhow Geneva give me a smile for my quip, but when I developed the point, airing some anxieties about crossing social lines, she said, "Oh Gramps, don't be absurd. That kind of Is she our sort? business went out with Marquand."

"Did it?" I says, not knowing whether Marquand was a man or a substance but making a mental note to look it up in the dictionary, and if it turned out to be a man feeling reasonably certain I didn't need him to fill in the gaps in my knowledge of human nature, which I can study for myself where I have always found it, right under my nose.

Well Tad Springer called again after the ball, as I was positive he might, picking Geneva up in a blue Fiat convertible which we caught glimpses of only from the upstairs bedrooms to which Mare shooed all of us, herself included, so Geneva's suitor wouldn't have to meet us. Mare was grooming the girl to be ashamed of us — her test for the education we scrimped and saved to give her, which next consisted of Wycliffe College for women, up in Massachusetts. Tad Springer, a handsome beanpole over six feet tall, went to a college in London. He stayed abroad the next summer too, so the romance died down, but the summer after their sophomore year they both spent hacking around Woodsmoke, and it all flared up into something serious. Geneva was a radiant creature now, her fair skin glowing with that light that seems to shine from inside healthy young girls, her butterscotch eyes giving her face the kind of goofy beauty it has always had. When a set of white teeth adds its wattage in a burst of laughter the general effect is almost too much, as she seems to sense herself, because she has a habit of closing her eyes when she laughs, and of looking away from you when she isn't. There is something at once shy and hostile about her. When she was home, that summer of swimming and speedboats and what not with Tad Springer, she generally kept to her room, hiding her bliss. Then suddenly she kept to it to hide something else. Because the bottom fell out of the affair — or rather was knocked out of it by the Springer clan, as we later heard. It was quite a crisis I can tell you. They called in the local minister to talk to her, some stroke of diplomacy! It's been my experience that most ministers aint as bad as they sound but since all you can do is listen to them what the hell good does that do you? Lucky for Geneva she soon had Wycliffe and another college year to distract her, and I think she got over it in time.

No so her mother.

Mare had always been a hostile woman. Now she was one mass of grievance. You may of observed to yourself that sour people often are not selfish, while "nice" ones are often the most egotistical? I give you a moment to go down your list of friends and acquaintances . . . Through? Now back to our story. Well

Mare would give you the shirt off her back but never a kind word. Not caring a fig for herself, she was a Tartar for her daughter — and now the Tartar burst into full bloom. She had enough family pride to be poisoned to her roots for the rest of her life by a snub like that. She now lived for one thing — to see Mrs. Springer come in that salesroom door in her superbly tailored dungarees and ask for a couple fryers. Just once. Mrs. Springer would of gotten a earful that would of scorched her to a cinder where she stood. But Mrs. Springer didn't come back and she didn't come back, clearing up any remaining doubts who put the kibosh on the romance. I often wished she'd show up one last time and give Mare the chance to get out of her system in one big scene what was poisoning her very blood. But summer passed into fall and fall into winter and no Mrs. Springer, only the wound festering deeper and deeper inside my daughter-in-law.

The only way she had of venting her spleen was to take it out on the commuters who *did* continue to show up. She identified them as a class; they stood for the Springers and the Springers stood for them. She was curt with them, disobliging, finally making plain to them what she was frustrated from making plain to Bobsy Springer, that they could take their custom elsewhere. The cold war on the class that had wounded one of us Spoffords became a hot war — she refused point-blank to sell chickens to commuters and advised George and me that that had better be our policy too. We were suddenly up to our ears in a Grade-A feud. By this time Geneva had probably forgotten her jilting, but her mother was just hitting her stride in a way that began to alarm me.

"In other words," says George one evening after we heard Mare tell an ish woman we were fresh out of something the cooler was full of, "we don't sell to commuters period. That the size of it?"

"That's the size of it. Leastways in any house I'm intended to stay a working member of."

"What about eggs?"

"Eggs neither."

The woman was sick. Or it was a case of saying more, or

going further, in a passion than you really meant to and being stuck with what you blurted. You know the experience. Maybe it was a combination of the two, complicated by her time of life. I don't know. I wouldn't care to say. We all see to it that out troubles are shared, and Mare in this case got to treat me as a member of the family before I could think fast enough to treat her as one, and made it clear that she was laying down the law to me as well. I would see to it that the embargo against the snobs was enforced while I was on duty too if I expected to find any dinner on my table at night. The point was not negotiable, as they say in diplomacy these days. Her scalded pride wouldn't let her back down, or us off the hook. We were all stuck with this blockade of the enemy and the war was total. George give me a combination shrug and look of holy terror that was a sight to behold as he up and beat it to his haven of refuge — the bowling alley.

That was how matters stood when I gathered together what I have written so far and showed it to Flahive.

three

FLAHIVE IS ONE of the teachers at this Successful Writers School. He sits at his desk all day correcting articles and stories that are sent in and giving the scholars pointers by return mail, which was the gist of the objection he raised when I phoned him about a look at some stuff of mine. "We're a correspondence school, you know, Mr. Spofford. The proper procedure is for you to enrol in the course and get your instructions by post." I had an answer for that one which he probably antisipated without looking forward to it.

Flahive writes himself, or tries to. He's had one novel published that the New York *Times* called derivative. I was impressed till I looked the word up — my word for that day — and even then remained a little impressed considering the heap of reading you have to do to get to be what the word means. "He owes a lot to Faulkner," the critic wrote. Well he don't owe Faulkner no more than he does me. I let him run up a bill of thirty-four smackers for fryers out at the farm when he was writing *Mauberly's Wobble*, evadently a tender fictionalized memoir of his father, a ex-alcoholic. Flahive himself is a potential ex-alcoholic, if you get my meaning, who use to turn up in his cups at the farm lamenting how tough things were and softening me up for a little more credit. He knew exactly what afternoons George and Mare killed and I was on duty in the salesroom. He would complain how badly the book was going. "Why don't you take a course at the Successful Writers School?" I finally says one day. "Maybe they can get you out of the bunker." He drew himself up to his full height, such as it is, and says, "Nothing worth learning can be taught." A principle that apparently don't hinder you none on the dispensing end, because next thing I knew he had a job teaching there hisself while he wrote on the side. Now that he had an income he still didn't seem in no hurry to discharge his debt, which I gently hinted as much over the wire. So it didn't take much pressure to make him agree to have lunch, on me, and read what I had so far.

We went to Indelicato's. Its an Italian joint in the wrong part of town that I used to go to a lot but was frequenting only seldom at the time because the suburban element had discovered it and made it shiek. Its an old house in the upper floor of which Indelicato hisself lives. I've known Angelo for years and introduced my friend to him.

Flahive is a born Irishman. He has your Irishman's taste for public drinking, sentimental one minute pugnacious the next, but always *sociable*; buttering you up when he isn't telling you off, but always *company*. Flahive put away two whiskies while he appreciated the interior, running his eye around the silk paneled walls, the bah relief above the fireplace and the old-fashioned teardrop chandelier which I admire too but would rather not sit under as it stirs old memories of *The Phantom of the Opera*. The place was a rich man's residence at the turn of the century, and Indelicato wastes no money on cleaning and restoring, hence the seedy elegance that draws the disserning. I was surprised Flahive had never been there before.

It was filling up rapidly with ish women and sort-of men. When Flahive started to make mystical signs in the air with his empty glass for the benefit of the waiter I hinted there would be a bottle of Chianti to go with the veal Parmagiana we had both ordered, and he took the hint. He put his tongue in among the ice cubes for the last drop of whiskey, like a bee in quest of nectar, and set the glass down. When Indelicato himself had hobbled over with the wine and poured us each a glass, I reached into my pocket and passed the manuscript to Flahive.

"Ah, my reading for tonight."

"You can read it now. Its the only copy I got."

As he read he glanced at me from time to time over the horn-rim glasses he had to put on to do so, his pink nose twitching like a rabbit's, a sort of tick he has, and the wine glass rarely out of his hand. By the time he had finished three or four pages our veal Parmagianas were steaming in front of both of us.

"You've got something in your craw, Mr. Spofford," he said, continuing to read with the manuscript flat on the table now, so he could eat at the same time. "That's as good a motive as any for a work of art of course," he added quickly.

I sensed that I was going to be worn thin. His way of beating around the bush in generalities without giving no opinion of the work in question caused this, in large part. He said vaguely, describing circles in the air with his knife and fork, that I seemed to have an animus. I didn't know what that meant, but it sounded dirty. "What Auden calls a catharsis of resentment," he explained, making it no better fast and shedding no real light on anything. All I seemed to be getting out of this was my word-for-the-day for a month in advance. I tried to grab them out of the air and stack them up in my mind as they went by.

All the while Flahive talked he kept flipping hot little amounts of veal around in his big mouth to cool them off, with short hissing and gasping noises that didn't add much to the occasion either. I could see that he was stalling. He rolled his eyes to the ceiling and made faces as he burned his tongue. Finally he put his knife and fork down and seemed to be trying to push himself away from the table, as though he was sitting in a wheelchair and wanted to bolt. He sat farther and farther back in the chair, till at one point he was connected to his lunch by one strand of melted cheese running between his plate and his mouth. Riled as I was by this incompetence, I felt at the same time a keen interest in all these details that I wanted to hurry home and put down on paper before I forgot them — how Flahive's green eyes rolled around in his bald dome, the hot food, the gasping and hissing, the single frail string of cheese sauce connecting him to his veal Parmagiana — in other words all the living, breathing essence of a work of art.

"What about the writing?" I says. "What about how good that is? The texture of the prose and all."

Flahive's eyes threatened to disappear up into his skull as he leaned back even farther in the chair, the single strand of cheese sauce thinning out alarmingly now till it was ready to snap. He fought off this cobweb with both hands as he said: "The spelling. That's of course out of the question, but of course it can be corrected. Lots of good writers don't know how to — but the mistakes aren't even *consistent*. I mean they *vary*. Just as your grammatical constructions do, I notice. They keep changing from page to page. One place you have it hisself and in another himself. And how the apostrophes come and go!"

I remembered a English teacher Geneva had in school who commented on one of her themes that she sometimes spelled the same word two different ways in the same paragraph, thereby showing spontaneity. I wondered if Flahive was sharp enough to spot the same element at work here. Not that it was any skin off my back; he was on trial here as a teacher, not me. Flahive made odd humming noises, as though some kind of kettle was starting to boil inside him, or some kind of engine generating ideas that nobody would be sure of their validity till they came out. He seemed curious himself about what he was going to say next, some teacher!

"Your work needs discipline," he said, and closed his eyes. He put his head back *past the top of the chair*, as though against some invisible wall he wished he was behind. I felt my hackles really rise now, thinking to myself that if his parents had of administered a little of what he was talking about at the age when it does some good he might not be sitting there dishing out impertinences to somebody twice his age. Just because he wrote a novel that was derivative didn't make him the world's leading authority. I could of done as well myself if I'd had more of a chance to read.

"And what you've got can't seem to make up its mind what it is," he went on with the same crucified look as he took a gulp of his Chianti. "Is it a novel? Is it a reminiscence? Is it a book of loosely strung together observations about life? Of course I'm only going on a very small sample, too little to form a fair judgement. I'd have to read a great deal more."

"I aim to see to that," I says with a look intended to add by way of reminder, Thirty-four clams worth to be exact, pal.

When I finally drove him back to the Successful Writers School he was in a heavily oiled condition, thanks to a few brandies he had with the coffee, and I in a thoroughly foul humor. It was while we were sitting side by side in the car rather than facing one another that he really opened up. "The thing is your too close to the subject. You lack the objectivity necessary to really pin down this society you've got in your crop, even satirically. By all means write. Scribble away, put everything down that comes into your head. What I mean wells up. But then let it cool off. That's the important thing. *Don't show me anything again for six months at the very least.*"

He lit a cigar and threw the match out. He didn't have to roll down any window to do so as the Ford is an open runabout.

"I think you ought to put this car in the book. Tell why you keep it at all. Why you tool around Fairfield County in a 1926 Model T with a license plate reading SCAT. Why do you?"

I thought the question self-explanatory, but I explained it to him anyways.

The 1926 flivver was an answer to the sports cars, Rollses, Bentleys and Cadillacs with radios and even phonographs whizzing by at speeds that may sublamate sex but also endanger children on bicycles. I mean I'd rather have the children endanger me. The SCAT was my razzberries to the whole kit and kaboodle, but spesifically to the custom introduced by the commuters theirselves, whose personalized letters-instead-of-numbers license plates made my teeth ache, especially when they are cute things like CLEF, which declares the owner to be a composer, or WNBC, that he is a net exec. But most of all the letter combinations which are the inishles of husband and wife cunningly intertwined. They gave me the worst belly ache of all because one out of three of them are going to get divorced anyway and then who gets custody of the plates? Its an interesting question. I gave prolonged thought to the four-letter word I would hurl back at them, like my exhaust, settling for the stiffest the law would allow. I showed the clerk at the Dept. of Motor Vehicles a list I had made and he shook his head at all of them except SCAT and he hesitated at that a little.

"You sure hate the sheepherders, don't you cowboy?" Flahive says. "But this Lizzie is wonderful. Where did you ever get it?"

"I never got it. I just kept it."

Here Flahive doubled over and liked to perish with such a fit of coughing I thought the cigar had done him in, but it turned out to be amusement. Laughing like hell he said, "Wonderful. Like Proust and the woman he asked where she ever got her hats and the woman answered, I don't get them, I just have them." Here he had another paroxysm and I thought if he choked to death the Renasonce would really be on in Connecticut, but no such luck. He says, "Well let's do this again sometime," for we had come to a halt in the parking lot behind the Successful Writers School. I stopped with a jerk, and I can say that again.

Flahive asked me to pull in behind as he wanted to sneak in the rear door so as not to have to explain where he was two and a half hours for lunch. "Lets rip a chop again soon. I'll give you a ring. And I do mean take your time with the book. Let it marinate for a while. Don't be in any rush." He hesitated and took me in. "I seem to have irritated you. Please take what I've said in the spirit in which its meant — constructive criticism."

He started to walk toward the door of the building. Then he suddenly came back again and put his head in the open flivver. "There is no great art without compassion," he said. He had to patter alongside the car to get in this postscript, because I had thrun in the clutch and started out the driveway, to hell with him. "And what do you really *know* about these people you're attacking? I mean *as people*. You don't know enough about them to hate them, let alone love them."

"You jist said I was too close to the subject," I says without turning to look at him, and picking up speed as I bounced out onto the road, Flahive galloping alongside the car. "Having a little trouble making up your mind which it is? A little trouble diagnozing my work, Flahive?"

"Too close emotionally while being remote from it in fact, is my point," he says, jumping onto the running board like a cop commandeering the car, or a crook. "It's a question of authentisity. You haven't the slightest idea how these people live. Don't go away mad, Mr. Spofford. I don't mean any offense." I told you he was a born Irishman, now acting on the Irishman's instinct to keep a conversation going no matter what. We were now in the thick of traffic. Flahive kind of squatted down on the running board, holding onto the top of my door with both hands, his coattails flying and his tweed hat nearly falling off. "I didn't say you had no *talent*. There are primitives in art, why not in literature? You could be above sentence structure like Joyce, you have Lardner's anti-sophistication, and you're mean as O'Hara. Greater praise in my book there isn't."

I brought my fist down on his hands with all my might. I kept banging first one of them then the other, as he kept pulling one off then the other, grabbing hold again with the first, like a survivor in the water trying to climb into a lifeboat there isn't room for and having his knuckles rapped by an oar held by who's boss.

"Be careful who you call names," I warned him. "I don't take abuse from nobody, especially when their half my age." With that I slammed on the brake for a red light, flinging Flahive around in a half circle so that his rear went to the front and his face came into view with mine. He lost his balance, getting his footing again in the street. He grinned nervously at me under the tweed hat, which he straightened with one hand. "Your wonderful," he said. "We been through all that," I said. We waited for the light to change, our situation becoming dreamlike. His lips twitched in a grin that was a combination of charm and despair.

"So then is it to be a novel we're going to have, a memoir, or a volume of loosely connected pungent observations?"

"None of your beeswax."

Just then the light changed and I put the car in gear and started off. I could see him in the rear-view mirror, standing there in the middle of the street, looking at my vanishing license plate.

I had made the mistake of consulting the enemy.

four

WHEN I GOT HOME I found my daughter-in-law and her mother, Mrs. Punck, sitting in the kitchen. They had the look of women waiting up for a man rolling in at three A.M. instead of P. There was that air about them. Mare had on the battle dress — George's fatigue jacket from the Korean War — with which she waits on trade. I had driven around for a ½ hour cooling off, and trying to give honest consideration to what Flahive had said. I might even of dropped in at the libary to get acquainted with some of the authors he said influenced me — if I was going to be derivative it was time I got started on my reading — but I was miles past it by the time I cooled off. Now I felt the anger flaring up again. It was touch and go who would strike the first blow, that is who would tolerate who first around here. Of course in the last analysis all that was as broad as it was long — which I will throw in as a quick description of Mrs. Punck.

They were drinking tea, I now noticed, and she had on a striped black and white dress that had been made out of some kind of material, a hat with a veil, now turned up to sip the tea underneath, and a string of blue beads. She nearly had gloves on.

"I thought you was going to take Ma to the Golden Age Club," Mare said. The chip she has on one shoulder for her daughter is balanced by one on the other for her mother. Like epaulets. I had to remind myself that she had none on either for herself.

"Oh that's all right," said Mrs. Punck. "Don't worry too much about it, Frank. We know how things slip our mind when we gallivant around." She beamed at me, and I could hear her corset creak as she turned in her chair to follow my movements across the room to the cabinet where I keep my bottle of bourbon. "You were probably at the libary pestering Ella and the other ladies behind the desk. That it? Nature will out. Of course what you forget is that if its women you got your mind on, theres a much wider selection at the Golden Age Club."

"The ones in the libary are wide enough," I says. I'd be damned if I'd explain that one, cackling like Walter Brennan on television to drive the point across. And if they'd laughed I'd probably resented that as some more domestic coziness I wasn't in the mood for. Coziness was coming from enough directions as it was. Because watch what now happened.

Having finished her tea Mrs. Punck shoved her chair back and reached for a basket of mending. She always did a batch of darning or some other household chore for Mare when she came to set a spell — ostensibly for Mare but really for my benefit, as she was a widow. Nobody wasted no time on subtlety around there. The first garment she pulled out to strike a domestic note with was my pajamas. I swear it. I poured myself three fingers on a cube of ice as she sewed a button on it. I was rewarded with a glare from Mare, but Mrs. Punck said, "Having a relaxing cocktail? Louie always liked his and I always encouraged it. Our system needs a bit of alcohol at our age."

I stood behind both of them and copied Flahive's cornered look by leaning my head against the wall between the sink and the old water boiler, now no longer used. I fluttered my eyes, rolling the balls up into my skull almost as far as he could, though of course he's had more education than me. After sewing the button on the coat Mrs. Punck apparently picked up the pants, because she give a jolly cluck and says, "So we've pulled the cord clean out of our waistband again." Mrs. Punck was famous for knowing how to work a string back through your waistband. You don't worm the cord itself back through the loop as that would take all day, you fasten a safety pin to the end of the cord and work *that* through, pulling the cord along after.

While working she favored us with a running monolog about what a rewarding life she'd had with the late Louie Punck, a most uneek individual who liked his three squares a day, forgot to mail letters that he was given and would of been elected to the state legislature if he hadn't of been defeated. The happy home she maintained for him awaited any other man shrewd enough to recognize a bargain when he seen one, was the implication. Which was right. Which was why I had to put myself on guard. She *was* a catch for the right man. Many a side testimony was tossed in by the fruit of that union, who was openly matchmaking. With Geneva away there was more than enough room in the farmhouse for all of us to live together in peace and harmony, not to speak of the money that would be saved when Mrs. Punck no longer had to pay the rent for the cottage she lived alone in behind the Ponderosa vineyard.

I hardened my heart. Not against Mrs. Punck or even Mare, but against a part of myself — the part that cottoned to the notion. I was of course alone myself, really, and all too keenly aware that man cannot live that way. I had strolled to the window, and looking out of it, drink in hand, I could see the lilac bushes my wife and me had planted, the hawthorn, the apple trees we had tended and eaten the fruit of. We had gardened together, always. I could see the doormat on the back stoop. It was so old and filthy there were violets growing in it. It was years now since I'd had a wife nagging me to pick it up and slap it against the side of the house, and I did not intend to shake from its rich nap what I now decided was Mrs. Spofford's favorite flower. She had always stoutly defended the violet against the view that it is a weed, commonly held by the ish women who do their gardening in Madras shorts and kneeling beside open manuals that they have to consult while they dig and plant, as they do cookbooks in the kitchen. I could see one or two now in Punch Bowl Hollow, just beyond our back stone wall, cultivating measly little strips of tulips and iris that don't look like flowers but like decalcomania pasted against the house and garage, their colors unreal too, like the paint jobs on the houses and station wagons. Change and decay in all around I see! I thought, gazing at the spanking new stuff. I thought what more could anybody want than flowers that grow like weeds for God's sake? So I never wiped my feet on the mat when I came in the house, or did so sentimentally. Lashed to the back of the flivver, above the SCAT license, was a flowerbox in which it would soon be time to plant a few geraniums again. Martha always liked geraniums too — and so does Mrs. Punck.

"A good man is hard to find," said she.

"You mean like they tell wives every day at the Missing Persons Bureau?" I says. As attractive as she was plump, as even-tempered as she was neat and able around the house, Mrs. Punck had to be resisted for a very good reason — lack of affinity. We just didn't seem to me to have that basic rappaport that is so necessary to a union. We just didn't see eye to eye. My tastes didn't run to Golden Age Clubs and other functions at the Y and the church she would of dragged you to. On the other hand she might stop going to these functions herself once she had a man to stay home with. It was hard to say. She was only medium set in her ways, as those things go, and I knew already from this kind of familiarity what some of her habits were. Like reading the obituary page first when she picked up the newspaper. Martha did that too. I suppose all women do. They have this emotional connection with Things. They're custodians of Life, hence the beeline for the death notices to see who passed away lately. But other than the newspaper all Mrs. Punck ever seemed to read was a corny anthology of poems that had been in her family for generations, whereas I was at least trying to continue my interrupted education on my own. Still there she was, well dressed and well meaning, often giving people a membership in a splendid organization for Christmas.

Just as she worked the safety pin through the other end of the waistband with a triumphant "Ahh!" a car stopped in the driveway and a customer got out. Mare quickly joined me at the window, and seeing Mrs. Beauseigneur spring out of her blue Jag she said, "I'll go wait on her." Mrs. Beauseigneur was an ish woman, very slim and pretty and bright, of the kind I liked to stop and chat for a few minutes with before saying we were fresh out. Mare had me spotted as an appeaser, you see, a collaborator with the enemy. She shouldered past me and made for the door to the salesroom before I could. She closed it behind her as she went down the two steps leading into it.

Now I was alone with Mrs. Punck. But nothing very friendly went forward between us, because I stood at the closed door straining to catch the conversation beyond it, and unable to for Mrs. Punck's attempts to keep the ball rolling here. It irked me no end.

"The difference between success and failure is often so slight," she said, sewing away at something else. "Two hundred more votes and Louie'd been elected. And maybe alive today, as I think it broke his heart."

"I voted for him twice," I says.

"But he only ran for Assemblyman once."

"I felt his kind of integrity should be supported in every way possible by the decent element."

"Well there's many a slip betwixt cup and lip," she sighed.

"Betwixt cup and what?"

"Lip."

"That was very neatly put, Mrs. Punck. You have a turn for phrases." Mocking Mrs. Punck about her everlasting maxims was one way I had of reminding myself of our incompatibility, and one as to which I considered myself absolved of cruelty since she didn't know she was being mocked. She didn't seem to realize any more than her daughter did when she was being ribbed. She twisted around in her chair to see what I was doing. Finding me standing with my ear to the crack she said, "Mare giving somebody a hard time?"

I got another ice cube and then walked to the cabinet to pour myself two more fingers.

"Since commuters were two-thirds of our business, it don't take no Einstein to figure what this retaliation is costing us. Talk about cutting off your nose despite your face. Boy. Not to mention the chicken we have to eat ourself to keep up with the inventory. I don't appreciate it running out of my ears just because we can get it wholesale."

"She'll get over it, Frank. Give her time. She's been hurt, and she's a girl who don't heal easy. And remember it's not on her account she's doing it — for herself she don't care. She's never wanted anything for herself. Give credit where credit is due. You'll find in life that people's virtues are often mixed up with their vices. We must be patient with her."

"And for variety we can always eat the laying mash."

"Why don't you come to dinner tomorrow night? Over to the cottage. I mean just you and me. I'll fix you a roast of beef and Yorkshire pudding."

Sipping my whiskey at the window, I see Mrs. Beauseigneur come out of the salesroom empty handed and walk toward her car. She was blonde, in her early forties, with trim bare legs showing under a gray tweed coat. As she sprang in behind the wheel I drew the lace curtain aside and the motion must of caught her eye. Because her red mouth popped open in a smile, her teeth like white seeds bursting from a pod, and she waved at me through the windshield, ducking her head a little to see me. Then a peculiar thing happened I must say. A kind of crazy pantomime went on between us. First she shrugged and spread her hands as though to say, "No dice again." I shrugged back *against my will*. Then a series of expressions was rapidly exchanged — raised eyebrows, nods and smiles, as though some secret understanding existed between us that the treatment she was getting here wasn't my doing, and that she would probably be back in the hopes of better luck next time. It was all over in less than a second. She backed the Jag out of the driveway and then we could hear Mare returning.

"Well what about it, Frank Spofford?" says Mrs. Punck quickly in a low voice, doubling the air of conspiracy I suddenly found myself up to my ears in. "You can bring along a few cans of beer for yourself, if that's what you want."

"I don't mind if I do," I said, knowing full well that whichever way I answered I would of wanted to kick myself.

five

I WAS THE FIRST one of the clan to see Mrs. Springer again. It wasn't at the farm of course, since she never came there any more, but in town.

I was walking down Main Street when I ran into her. It was a balmy day in May, a day that made the artist in me's heart leap. Masses of creamy clouds sailed across a blue sky, blown by a breeze that also ruffled your hair as you went around bareheaded and lifted the skirts of young mothers wheeling perambulators, or stopping to chat in the sunshine. In the distance a jet plane climbed, leaving a long trail of smoke behind it, like a white eel in the sky.

I was carrying a book under my arm. I had just been to the libary to get a novel that had been recommended to me by Joseph Conrad, called *Al Mayer's Folly*. But they didn't have it, naturally. I stopped to rib Ella Shook, a maiden lady about my age who runs the place, about it. "We're getting more select every day," I says. "Pretty soon there won't be nothing on the shelfs." She says, "Its one of his lesser known novels. Have you ever read *Lord Jim?*" I took that. I had to get on with my reading if I was ever going to be derivative.

I paused at the desk after checking it out for a few words with Ella, waiting every time she was interrupted to take care of another customer, with ever an eye for the sweet young things. Once I turned around to watch one go out the door. "You can't resist a pretty ankle, can you, Frank?" Ella says, and I says, "I've got my mind on higher things." She clucked and shook her head, which was just what I wanted of course. She never seems to tumble that a man talks that way to *get* a rise out of her. Ella's easy game.

After that I dropped into a chili parlor that had recently been opened by a Mexican named Carlos, who I had gotten to know and rather like. Carlos wasn't doing very well. His food was too tame somehow. Mexican food should taste like a mouthful of bees — washing it down with cold beer just when you feel the roof of your mouth peeling off is part of the pleasure. I think he thought it should be toned down for American palates — a mistake, for neither the suburbanites nor the workmen from across the river came to eat there. Even his chili con carne left something to be desired. What gives the chili in large-city parlors that extra something is that they use condemned beef. But today I only dropped in for a cup of coffee and to say hello to Carlos. He was out to the bank just then but his snappish little waitress Lily was on duty, so I crossed swords with her in the usual skirmish that every conversation with her seems to become. You had to be on your toes with her.

"Haven't seen you around for a while, Pop," she said. "Did they just let you out?"

"They *threw* me out. Out the Marines that is."

"Oh? What for?"

"I was rotten to the corps."

"I figured you were discharged because your jokes were overage."

"Well I wanted something appropriate to go with this here coffee. It and the gag are contemporaries, you know." I laughed and said, "I ought to insist you brew up a fresh pot for this month."

"Try and make me."

"I understand the young fellows can do that without trying."

After that I felt better, and resumed my walk down Main Street with a spring in my step. That was when the bounce went out of it as I suddenly recognized Roberta ("Bobsy") Springer up ahead.

I shouldn't say suddenly because it took me a second to do so. In the first place she wasn't coming toward me but was walking up ahead in the same direction I was, and when she paused to look into the window of a store I saw her in profile.

Even then I was only sure she was someone I knew, not who she was. That famous phenomenon of not being able to place shopkeepers away from their post of duty works both ways you know — sometimes we have trouble recognizing you customers on the street, especially if we've only seen you once or twice, as was the case with Mrs. Springer. But after a second I realized who it was who had stopped me cold.

She was wearing narrow black slacks with a crease you could of sliced cheese with, and tapered down to loops that go under the feet. She had on a fingertip length red coat, open, her hands in the pockets. Her hair was short, worn with that ruffled feather look, and dyed a streaked silvery blonde. You may or may not have noticed something I have, in the course of a lifetime of studying human nature. Women with flat backsides lack warm natures. The curve is missing from the temperament too, the fulness lacking there as well. I followed her at twenty paces or so, stopping when she did to window shop, remaining two stores behind, watching her out of the tail of my eye. When she turned into the Gourmet Bazaar I went in after her *against my will*.

You know what a Gourmet Bazaar is — a grocery store that don't carry much. Most of the foods in here were only to flavor other foods, herbs, condiments, and the like. But there were also utensils, including a counter full of teeny little pots and pans just come in from France, in different color enamels. I browsed the way Mrs. Springer did, a little distance off. Then I saw, or rather sensed, her turn and look at me. She opened her mouth to say something but quickly closed it again, either because she changed her mind about speaking or because she was having that trouble recognizing tradesmen away from their place of business.

Just then some beaded curtains at the back flew apart and a woman with pink hair said good morning and asked if we were together. We both said no, one with vigor, the other with a musical laugh that went up the scale and down again. The owner's eyes went up and down the lady customer, with respect and admiration. She was of the ilk of the woman psychiatrist with the standing order for capons. I thought they would make a fine pair. They would be very happy together and give the cats clam dip. She wore a skirt and a shirt, even a necktie, but it was conservative. Yet along with her masculinity — or maybe just neutrality, who knew? — she had a certain sweetness lacked by Mrs. Springer, who is *hard but all woman*, if I make myself clear. Mrs. Springer was obviously fresh from a couple of weeks in some place like Nassau or Jamaica, her tan being too rich for here at this time of year. You could see where it ended just above her silk blouse and her natural pallor began. That fine white line was like a razor edge drawn across my vitals. At that moment my hatred for her was sexual. I pretended to consider some kind of jars of candy called humbugs that came from England — everything was terribly imported here — while Mrs. Springer appreciated the junk from France. I browsed my way gradually back to the door, and while Mrs. Springer was wavering between something on the counter ducked out.

I went into the nearest bar for a quick shot. Gone was my pleasant mood of the morning. Instead I could feel myself smoking inside, like a poked potpie. When I had finished the drink I went straight to the parking lot beside the river where the flivver was, climbed in and tooled for home.

Mare was on duty in the salesroom, and I could hear from the hum of the plucker in the back room that George was busy alone there, so I offered to spell her if she wanted to go help him. She got into her rubber boots and disappeared. I settled myself on the high stool and opened the copy of *Lord Jim*. But I couldn't screw my attention into it, so instead started flipping through a copy of *Harper's* that I had there. One or two customers came in, old Woodsmokers of my time, with whom I exchanged the usual bits of gossip and talk about the weather. Then, just as I got set over an article, I heard the smooth growl of a car I knew before looking up would be a sports job. My nerves went oddly tight inside me at the sight of Mrs. Beauseigneur springing out of the open blue Jag.

She walked up to the salesroom door slowly though, and peered through the glass pane first to see who was inside, shielding her eyes with her hand and squinting. When she recognized me behind the counter she gave a grateful smile, but I was ready for her. "Great whore of Babylon and mother of abominations," I says in a undertone, to steel myself.

I have said she was about forty, but late thirties seemed more like it today. Her light hair and the silk scarf around it caught a flash of sun and wind as the door opened. She had that air of — how shall I put it to establish the idea of class that I want to here? That air of being at loose ends that is effected by women of her rank, like reality is too many for them, they are frail vessels. It is in the way they are always saying, "My nerveless fingers," and stuff like that when they can't strike a match or fumble something. It was in the way she now tucked in under her scarf loose ends of hair that the wind had blown, in the way she fought the door. "Absolute shambles," she laughed, with some more tidying up stabs at herself. She was one them lucky women whose crowsfeet turn out to be assets by adding a certain twinkle to the smile? Yes. The creases at the corners of the eyes lengthened toward the temples like star rays, and I believe I have already likened her teeth to white seeds bursting from a scarlet pod.

"Mr. Spofford, no less. How nice to see *you*."

"Afternoon, Mrs. Beauseigneur."

She advanced toward the counter, opening a big straw bag, and the old rigamarole commensed up again.

"I'd like two fryers please."

"Fresh out. We had some this morning but they've all been utilized up."

"Oh dear." Tragic pout. "Broilers?"

"No ma'am, I'm sorry. We're out of them too just at the moment."

Her attitude now changed very subtly as she turned her baby blues slowly toward the row of white coolers on her left and my right. Her features twitched in a little smile, in which was a flirting hint that this was a game we were playing, admit it, that any minute she would drop her mask and there would be nothing for me to do but drop mine too. "Fowl then? Something nice and plump to stew?"

When I said we didn't have no stewers neither, Mrs. Beauseigneur laid her bag on the counter and her hands on top of that, in a getting down to brass tacks manner.

"Look, my husband only rides to Stamford," she said. "He doesn't go all the way to New York."

As Jehovah might smile at a mortal pleading some technicality before the bar of Judgement — as though hairs could be split over Original Sin — I must of smiled. "I don't cal'late that's likely to put any chickens in the icebox that wasn't there before you raised the point, do you?"

This was laying it on. "Cal'late" is not natural speech with me, as it would not be even with somebody living *deep* in New England any more, let alone this shirttail end of it. It went with "fust" and "mebbe" and "up the rud a piece" and all the other folk talk no longer in regular use but very helpful in playing the hick to people you are laughing in your teeth at. In caricaturing myself I was secretly mocking them. At least that was the idea. Though with Mrs. Beauseigneur slipping down from her late thirties to more like her early, as she seemed to when turning on the charm, I wondered if she understood what she was hearing. I wondered, with a sudden twinge, if she understood my license plate. Was SCAT before her time or off her beam? Maybe I should have chosen something more universal, like NUTS.

She batted the baby blues again and said, "May I take a peek?"

"He'p se'f," I says, "though of course anything you find in there is likely to be reserved."

"Of course." She shifted her eyes back to me. "May I reserve some for the week end then?"

"We have all we can do to supply our regular customers ma'am. We just can't seem to take on any new ones at this time. Perhaps if you leave your name —"

"Oh Mr. Frank Spofford, you know my name perfectly well! Now may I make a suggestion? May I suggest that we stop this hanky panky and lay our cards on the table?"

"Why ma'am, I reckon you'll always find us ready and willing —"

"Oh come off that reckon and cal'late! An intelligent man

33

like you with your *Harper's* and all. Have you ever thought of those icebergs banging around up there through the long Arctic night? Of the stars boiling away at ten million degrees Fahrenheit? Of giant redwoods standing silent since before the birth of Christ? How they mock our petty unrealities, our shabby little shams and chickaneries. Mr. Spofford, not a word you've said since I came in here has had any connection whatever with the truth."

I felt the same flash of hostile lust I had with Mrs. Springer in the fancy food store. This woman had come in here to beard me, to stand for no double talk, and sensing her gumption I became uneasy. She spread her hands on the counter and looked me square in the eye. "Do you think it right to discriminate against a minority?"

"Minority?" I says with a snort, and in snorting delivered myself into her hands.

Amusement at the idea that the group she referred to was in any shape manner or form underdog implied that I knew very well which group she meant and that I held it in contempt, whereas the official farm policy was to play *dumb* about all that — simply refuse to sell to commuters without no mention of the word, and if it come to an argument justify the quarantine on the grounds that we couldn't handle the volume of business and had to cut down the easiest way we could. Now I had made a diplomatic blunder. The woman had me like the detective has the suspect who has said something the detective can answer with, "Murder? Who said the crime we're talking about is murder, Carruthers? How did you know it was that? Shall we go to headquarters and talk about it a while?"

"Why is it always and only commuters who get turned down here, Mr. Spofford? May I ask that?"

"Been comparing notes among yourselves have you, Mrs. Beauseigneur?"

"You bet! This is the only decent poultry farm around here. Little indignation meetings sort of spring up at parties that would make your ears burn. Did you know you Spoffords were the chief subject of cocktail conversation?"

34

"Here I thought you only engaged in idle chatter. Accept my apologies."

"You haven't answered my question. Why only commuters?"

"It's a convenient line to draw, like the 38th Parallel acrost Korea. I don't say its a perfect solution, I don't deny its arbitrary —"

"Ah! Then you admit its us you discriminate against. As a class."

Here she opened her handbag wide and took out a small magazine she didn't let me see the name of right away but held against her, like a gambler playing his cards close to his vest. "I think a reader of *Harper's* is up to fairly meaty stuff. Soo . . ." I tried to get a look at the cover, but the woman clearly intended to make a few introductory remarks before letting me.

"The bane of modern life," she began after inflating herself with a long breath, "is the habit of letting words do our thinking for us instead of using them to express our thoughts. Do you follow me?"

"Puffectly."

"Stop that! This thinking in blocks — Republicans are so-and-so, Jews are such-and-such — has got to stop. It pollutes our reason at its source. It corrupts all communication."

"Well we are suppose to be in the capital of that industry here, ain't we?" I says. But I was disturbed by how I was *watching her talk rather than listening to her*, taking in the red lips rather than the wisdom that was issuing from them, if any. That part remained to be seen. Feeling myself weaken I pulled myself together by thinking about a painting I had seen reproduced in *Life*, which showed a nude emptying garbage into a grand piano at twilight. No, you had to be firm with these people.

"There is no such things as Chickens."

"There ain't?" I says softly.

She shook her head slowly from side to side, the baby blues closed.

"There is only chicken A, chicken B, C, and so on. So there are not Commuters. There is only commuter A, B, C, and so on. Tell me *which commuter you mean*, the wise man says, and I will tell you whether he is good or bad, rich or poor, kind or cruel — or deserving of chickens."

She now laid the magazine, face up on the counter. Without touching it I cocked my head around to look, and seen that it was a pocket-size semantic quarterly of Non-Aristotelean thought called *But*. On its maroon cover was featured articles with titles like "The Linguistic Constants in Prejudice"; "Word Hashes in the Congressional Record"; "The Ceremonial Hour: the Wittgenstein-Fabrizio-Shuv Hypothesis of the Coffee Break as Neo-Ritual"; and "The Sub-Verbal Dynamics in Shooting off our Mouth".

"We don't need no magazines today," I says.

The woman stamped her foot, swiveling away a quarter-turn in despair.

"There you go doing it again!" she cried. "Instead of giving me a chance to *be myself as a neighbor in the context of having come to give you something you might find of interest* you simply lump me in with door-to-door salesmen as a Class, thereby falsifying what you see and abolishing all hope of communication between us. Do I make myself clear?"

"Yes. You come here for chickens, and not getting none, pull out this here periodical —"

"Oh, dear God. I am no longer the Woman Who Came in Here For Chickens," she said, now lowering her voice to a whisper that was twice as effective as talking shrill had been, "I am now somebody else. Let me have my identity please." I thought she was going to bawl. "We are different things to different people at different moments — being able to do and be that makes us what we are, all told. Pirandello — No, never mind that now." She sighed and resumed: "I am now a neighbor offering you this magazine, in this context, that of the block thinking which we happen at the moment to be deploring. Forget about chickens for the time being, please. Blot from your mind the fact that they exist. Think only that I want you to read this. I think it may help break up certain rigidities in your thought patterns which are making you as well as the entire community miserable. Not to mention releasing the intellectual potential you have obviously got. Maybe it will help you see the world with new eyes. I know it has me. All this either-or, black-and-white dichotomy has got to go. We've got to apply in everyday life the Relativity our philosophers and scientists have discovered for us. We've got to purge Aristotle from our system."

"I've never read him so why do I have to purge him from my system?"

"It's proof of his grip on Western Man that he dominates the thinking of people who have never heard of him. So will you give *But* a hearing? You need it desperately, believe me. You won't sell me fryers because I'm a commuter, when the fact is I haven't been on a train in six months. Its my husband who commutes, and that only to Stamford as I've been trying to tell you. Secondly how do you know I haven't given you blood or something in the past when you needed it most? Did you look on the bottle to see where it came from? Of course not. You don't make distinctions. Blood is blood. And that's *all* it is."

"But you just said —"

"You're in terrible shape, believe me. All this thinking with our glands."

I put on my specs again and paged through the magazine for a while, reading snatches of this and that to please her. Finally I closed it and put the specs back in my pocket.

"Well I ain't much for big words, like hypothesis and Wittgenstein —"

"Now you're being the tiniest bit dishonest with me, admit it. Anyhow this looks deepish but it actually isn't. It —"

The door of the slaughter room opened and Mare stood in her rubber apron and hip boots watching us. A wet cigarette end smoked in one corner of her mouth. It went out while we all stood there. She closed the door without taking her eyes off us, cutting off the sound of machinery and running water, and tramped forward, the boots going *whuppery-whuppery* on the linoleum.

"Yes?"

"Mare, this lady wants us to read this magazine that claims

37

we shouldn't be so positive. Lumping everything together. That theres good and bad in all classes and that we shouldn't let our thinking get gummed up by letting words do it for us. That about it, Mrs. Beauseigneur?"

"Thats it exactly."

Mare disposed of the cigarette butt by spitting it out on the floor. Sometimes I wished she would be more refined and gracious, not necessarily mincing and artificial like the women we were having the war on, but something in between. But no, none of her mother's ways had rubbed off on her — she was herself. She didn't come no closer to the counter or to us, pausing I'd say, oh about six feet from it. "We don't need no magazines today."

Mrs. Beauseigneur showed the wear and tear of having her identity narrowed down to a door-to-door pedler twice within five minutes and having to buck it twice. But only for a second. Because for the time being anyway she decided to abandon the missionary approach of bringing semantics to the heathen and take Mare on in terms of the technicality. She moved a step to the right, bringing herself at least in line with her opponent though no closer otherwise, and says again, "My husband gets off at Stamford."

The seed fell on stonier ground than with me, but at least she was pleading her case — the battle was joined. She stood before Mare like all the ish women did through all that period of the quarantine on snobs, that is like a wretch before a stern tribunal, but she made her pitch. "And I'm sure you'll agree you can't call that commuting. I mean not *really*."

"Occupation?"

"Investment adviser."

"Firm?"

"He works for Merrill Lynch, Pierce, Fenner —"

"We haven't got all day. Branch of the New York firm, isn't it?"

"Why yes, but —"

"Place of residence."

"Punch Bowl Hollow. We're neighbors!" The woman realized *her* boner the minute she made it — New Yorkers crowding in on us was part of our animus (the word Flahive sprung on me and which I had of course looked up)—and added with an apologetic little laugh, "I know we're making it a bit crampedish for you, but anyhoo . . ."

Mare shoved a pencil deeper into the knot of hair it was generally stuck in, like a bone in the bun of a savage in the *National Geographic*. I guessed she was debating with herself just how far to go toward admitting who the enemy was and naming them. But she wouldn't, like me or maybe George, be lured into it—she would decide on that herself. But all this showed a change in the wind. The woman went on:

"You see Lester telephoned me just now to ask could he bring a friend, a classmate home for dinner." She rolled her eyes and smiled at Mare as though to say we women know this habit of men. "I thought Gawd, the house is an absolute shambles, and I'm *not* a short order cook. But maybe if I could frickasee a few— As I say he works in the Stamford office, and if you ever need any advice on business matters—" She played one last card. "He's thinking of driving in on the Thruway. Not taking the train at all!"

Mare glanced at the coolers herself now. I could feel hope rising in the other woman, that all them qualifications with which her own status was hedged around might entitle her to a few fryers just this once. But I knew better and felt sorry for her. I knew it was part of the pleasure Mare took in prolonging the torture of these women with their open Jags and their absolute shambles. It was a extra dividend. I figured maybe she was bleeding me a little too for suspicion of collaborating with the enemy (false as you know). At the same time I noticed how Mrs. Beauseigneur had been trapped into stating her case from presisely the premise she had a moment ago knocked me for and with which by implication she had no truck. She was O.K.'ing the block against commuters by the very act of pleading her case in terms of her husband not being one, even adding to the semantic mess we were all sinking deeper and deeper into by dragging in the mode of transportation used. It may of been this sense of her rapidly deteriorating position that brought tears to Mrs. Beauseigneur's eyes as she whimpered when Mare finally didn't relent, "Then can I have a dozen eggs?"

"Large or small?"

"Small."

I was surprised to see Mare take a carton from the open cooler and slide it across the counter, not a giving in or concession but one them arbitrary acts of mercy by which the despotic sertify their power.

"There's something sinister in this house," the woman sniffled in between fishing in her purse for the dough. "Something spreading like a poison everywhere. It would be far, far better if you dropped the pretense and hypocrisy and just admitted you *hate* us as a class instead of all this fiddle faddle about the 38th Parallel." I was grateful for the glance at me here as it told Mare, with whom I would be left in a minute to deal, that I hadn't been collaborating as she suspected and wasn't on the verge of treason when she come in at all. "That would be honest though still sick. For I do not hesitate to use the word. Sick do you hear! And so, so in need of therapy."

"You really should go home and lie down," Mare says. That made the women pull out another stop, one she probably never dreamed she would, as it put the one card on the table that was just too much and should never of been openly mentioned.

"I didn't jilt your daughter. *My husband* didn't jilt your daughter. Yet you make us drive clear to town for chickens and those only frozen because somebody else did."

With that Mrs. Beauseigneur, looking as startled as us, grabbed the eggs which Mare made a move to snatch back, and skedaddled. She knew she better because she had blurted out more than she had intended, but in skedaddling emptied her gun. "Isn't that sick? Isn't that paranoid? Oh your in terrible shape. Talk about intensional orientation! Talk about guilt by identification! Talk about linguistic symbol-hash! Read all about it, right in there."

Mare picked up the *But* and thrun it at the woman, who would of caught it square on the coco if she hadn't closed the door on herself just in time so that it hit the framework next to the glass pane and fell to the floor. Mrs. Beauseigneur with eyes streaming opened the door again a second to say, "Believe me, Mrs. Spofford, I'm sorrier for you than for myself and the rest of this community. You need help. I just hope it isn't too late. Because you're a — dangerous woman!"

Mare looked ready to refute that charge with an egg she had in her hand from another carton, ammunition better than the magazine that missed, but the woman closed the door again and ran for the Jag and blew, scattering chickens before her, if you can call it before you when you are backing out the drive at high speed. She disappeared up Vineyard Road in a cloud of dust.

Mare stood at the cooler a minute, tidying up the stacks of eggs. I watched her broad back. Mrs. Beauseigneur had left us a pretty load of embarrassment to deal with indeed. I didn't know whether to wade right in and have it over with or kind of sidle around it in hopes it would disperse of itself. I stalled by picking up the morning's mail which was lying on the counter and shuffling through it. "Gynecocratic goddam community," I said.

"You don't have to swear to show how limited your vocabulary is."

"Mare, your getting very bellicose lately."

"I ain't as young as I use to be and it stands to reason I can't be as slim around the middle no more neither."

Over her shoulder I could see a garden rake. Standing upside down in a corner, I wondered what it was doing here anyway. I dropped the mail and decided to wade in. I waited till she had her back turned, the point being a very ticklish one, and said: "Crazy woman, talking about jilted daughters. Why, I don't believe for a minute that's generally gossiped around here as our trouble, do you? Mare?"

I knew it was a tender spot I was probing — proud flesh is a good term for it as pride was the main element at stake here, family pride, which is keener than personal — but I didn't realize how tender. Mare didn't reveal so much as a flicker of emotion. Her face was blank as she hung another fag in it and set fire to it. She went around the counter, her boots making that awful *whuppery-whuppery* noise, to where the copy of

But lay on the floor. After slapping it on her thigh to dust it off she come around behind the counter again reading it. She stood thumbing through the pages, her face slanted away from the smoke curling from her cigarette. Without a comment she dropped it into the trash bin under the counter. Then in an idle way, as though she was doing no more than remarking on the weather, she says, "If you let them have any they'll only cook them in red wine."

"Or sour cream."

Though I meant what I said about mucking about with perfectly good food, at the same time I hated myself for the degree I was cozying along with Mare, as though I was too scared of her to make a stand at the point where I thought this thing should stop. I wasn't scared of her — I just wanted to keep peace. But I resented the concessions I had to make to get that in what was damn well my own house. I had a chance to recover the offensive in it soon enough on another ground.

"You'll be late for the Golden Age Club if you don't get to washing up," Mare says.

"I wasn't aiming to go."

The air began to tense with the threat of another storm. The probably unnecessary sharpness of my answer was intended merely to keep reminding her that I was my own boss and not to be ordered about, but Mare took it as a slight of her mother. She took my curt refusal to escort Mrs. Punck to the Golden Age meeting at the Y.M.C.A. as a slap at Mrs. Punck as such. No such slap was intended — only the reminder that the property was still in my name.

I watched Mare finish her cigarette and spit it on the floor as she had its predesessor, this time grinding it out underfoot. "Ma's going and would appreciate a lift."

Christ, we not only sold eggs around here, we spent ½ our time walking on them! But I met her gaze evenly a minute. That wild autumnal hope, mine intended to say, that wild autumnal hope that your mother and me might get fixed up and close ranks around here is all well and good, but let me think of the idea myself, maybe on windswept nights or so, not have it rammed down my throat by matchmakers. I says, treading the very narrow line between courtesy and independence that I had drawn for myself on this matter, "I can give her a lift to the Y and maybe I can fetch her back. But I don't aim to stay for what's in between."

Mare reached under her leather apron and pulled out of a pocket of her jeans a partly eaten Oh Henry candy bar. She bit off an end of it, like a man biting off a chaw from a plug, and stuck it back in her pocket again. She bit it off with her side teeth, which worked mightily in me as a call to patience and compassion. "They get the most interesting speakers there," she said.

"I've heard 'em. The last time I went it was a man discussing insects that benefit mankind."

"There's a famous woman traveller lecturing today."

"What on?"

"Christmas in Many Lands."

"I was thinking I might go set a spell with Harry Pycraft."

"That won't lift you up none."

"It won't let me down neither."

While she watched me in silence I carried the aggressive one step farther. The last thing I wanted to do was read anything left behind by sheepherders, but neither did I want any inlaws fancying they were doing the censoring for me. So I stooped to fish the copy of *But* out of the trash basket, dusted it off against my leg and started for the door to the kitchen. There the pendulum swang back the other way, just a little. Feeling I had plenty balance in my favor as far as the independence was concerned, I paid back a little of it by one consession (which again really upped the independence a notch by showing it was mine to make). I turned at the door and says, "I'll take your ma back here for supper if you'd like. We owe her a meal."

She snapped up the puck and started skating back with it.

"I'm going to say something you may not like, Pa Spofford, and that you may think is none of my business. You're not an old man. You're vital. You could have another marriage yet, a married life of your own. Companionship for your declining years and all."

"Your ma can be verbose in fewer words than anybody I ever see." Mare give the grunt of thanks for the compliment on her mother's be½. "She talks in nothing but platitudes exclusively," I pushed on, only upping the gratitude. It was a losing game.

"Well I'll go wash up then," I says and hurried upstairs, not quite sure now where we stood or just exactly how the balance of power shaped up. But I did do one thing before I cleaned up. I went into my bedroom and chucked the copy of *But* in my *own* wastebasket.

six

AFTER DROPPING Mrs. Punck off at the Y for her meeting I turned around and galloped back toward Harry Pycraft's motel — gallop being the illusion the old Lizzie and bad roads between them could impart. Probably another reason why I kept the Ford was it reminded me of the chestnut mare, Nellie, I used to ride through this countryside, of which I again now took angry inventory. For every subdivision my memory supplied the ghost of some birch grove or cornfield cut down to make room for it. All that remained of the landscape was the old Ponderosa vineyard, and now by God if *that* wasn't threatened.

Mrs. Punck had just broken the news that Harry Pycraft, who owned the cottage she rented, had notified her to vacate as it had been sold. Who to? The contractors known to of been lusting after the Ponderosa acreage? Was the last idyllic spot left in Woodsmoke (outside the chicken farm) then doomed for another subdivision? No builder would of bought the cottage property without at long last having wangled from old Mrs. Ponderosa the vineyard it stood behind. Between the two parcels there was land enough for another score of split levels — and another hundred sheepherders.

In spite of myself I fancied that term of Flahive's for commuters, with which the cowboys had expressed *their* contempt for the intruders of yesteryear. By an odd twist of the facts the term applied literally to a family whose house I just tooled past. The Dalrymples kept sheep, or at least *a* sheep, which a collie nipped into line along the property edge. There was the sheep as I shot past, looking as usual not all wool at all but 40% orlon, dacron and other sinthetic fibers. Dalrymple was one the leather handbag toting boys in gabardine. I see him often strolling through town on Saturday morning, trying to look peerless.

This what-do-you-call-it, nostalgia for the bygone and the earthy on the part of people at the farthest pole from it fascinated me — as it fascinated other old timers that it also riled. Old timers who came *out* of the past the commuters now collect — coffee grinders, pewter and wagon wheels. The people who settled this land had hearts of oak. Leaving myself out of it, there is Ned Bradshaw, who broke this soil from dawn to dusk behind a blind plowhorse; Ebenezer Jennings, who once kept a lighthouse and who singlehanded rescued three men from drowning in a howling storm off the Cape; and Mrs. Punck, who takes a few drops of iodine every time she feels a cold coming on.

Harry Pycraft I had my reservations about. As I galloped toward his motel I reflected on what a lot of loyalty he took. The motel would of forfitted any claim to my friendship whatever had it not been on the Post Road, a total loss anyway. Nothing you built there could spoil it any more. Besides, the motel was an expansion of an old inn Pycraft had tried to preserve the spirit of in the motor courts he built around it. Neon signs blinked out its name, but the name remained the same — Dew Drop Inn. Eggs Benedict and lobster thermopane appeared on the menu, but that was in chalk on old Puritan slates — in this case legitimately as Pycraft is not a professional New Englander. He is a New Englander. I know some people think he's crooked as a ram's horn, but I have never found any evidence of that. He's just a slippery and rather lewd tightwad sonofabitch who happens to be the last drinking crony I have left. Harry will do anything for you except a favor. I know. But he does read. Lately he's been reading the modern nihilistic philosophers who consider life meaningless, writers who knock the universe without having no alternative to offer.

I found Pycraft in the Period Room as he called it. I once asked him what period and he gave me a blank look. The subject had never come up before. "Why I don't know," he said. "Just period." It was a bar and adjoining restaurant with heavy panelled walls, mirrors in fancy gilt frames and bow-legged tables and chairs, also fancily carved. He was consulting with an electrician over some repairs and eating a peach. He generally kept a little fruit around to put in the rooms of celebrities, which he often got from the local theatre, a former summer playhouse which now runs 8 mos. of the year.

It was after we had left the Period Room and were walking toward the front office that I quickly broached what was on my mind. I wanted to get the unpleasant part of the visit out of the way so we could settle down to our chat over the bottle.

"I hear tell you sold the cottage, Harry. To them real estate speculators did you, Harry?"

Pycraft made occult figures in the air with the peach, taking a couple seconds to swallow what he had in his mouth, which give him time to transfer his discombobulation to the trouble he was having with the dripping fruit. "Mrs. Punck tell you about it, Frank? Jesus, I hated to put her out, but I was strapped. I have to clean up a loan coming due on this place. But I ain't got any money in the subdivision, if that's what you're thinking, Frank."

"So it is a subdivision."

"Don't tell me this is the first you heard of it. But I swear I'm not in on that. I don't like the way things are going any better than you, Frank, but its the way they're going. And they were the only takers for my property. Which I needed the money."

"Why did you give Mrs. Punck notice instead of them? To keep them behind the scenes? So there won't be no Zoning Board appeals till after the power shovels have got the place half dug up, Harry? Friend of my childhood?"

"No, as a kind of courtesy they asked me to extend her. Though I can see what's going through in your mind, and now I think of it, I wonder if you could be right. Hmm." He stroked his chin thoughtfully while he struck the pose of a misused innocent. "Those bastards! They want to keep out of sight as long as they can, because they know the minute the plans are filed all the bleeding hearts in town will come down on the Zoning Board like a ton of bricks. All them hypocrites that spoiled the rest of the landscape and are always loudest about not letting any more like theirself come in here from New York and New Jersey and finish the job," Pycraft said, acquiring the offensive with his usual flewency. This was his most familiar method of attack in an argument: to shift the ground from a beef between you and him onto a beef you shared toward a third party, if not the world in general. We marched shoulder to shoulder down the long mulberry carpeted corridor while he warmed to his subject, taking the play away from me. "All these bastards that talk about preserving the rustic ways, but would they soil their lily-white hands by doing all the pruning and tying a vineyard calls for? No! They just want it to lay there looking pictureskew, while Mrs. Ponderosa goes blind from failing eyesight and can hardly move with arthritis no more either, never mind the income she needs from the land. Well anyhow, all as I'm saying is I sold the Americana Builders my patch, yes, but I'm not in with them. Hell, I'm spread thin enough as it is, Frank. So I swear I'm not making a nickel on the deal, just getting my money out even steven. I swear it before God Almighty!"

"I thought you was the village atheist."

Gobbling the last of the peach, Pycraft thrun the stone into a nearby sand-pot and wiped his hands on his pants, to indicate thereby a certain integrity, something always trustworthy and dependable. He was gesturing before his mouth was quite clear to speak. "We're not a village no longer, Frank. This town is growing, and we've got to grow with it. In another five years we'll be a city, mark my word. So let's not hear any talk about village atheists."

Marching into the office we probably looked remarkably alike. Both the same height and weight, both rangy and lantern-jawed, with shocks of graying brown hair parted on the side. Only Pycraft's looked as though he sometimes wiped his hands on that too. We had in common a certain muscular restlessness that went quickly into gesture, resulting in part no doubt from living for years without a woman. But I believe I lamented my wife while Pycraft merely wanted another. Pycraft had had two in fact, the first of whom died and the second he divorced after three years, on the ground that she was "a cold compress." He told me once, "When I put my hand on her knee she would *pry it off*, the way you pry an abalone off a rock out west."

Pycraft dug the bottle from his desk drawer and sighed with pleasure as he poured us drinks, communicating thereby the relief, the enormous peace and well-being to be derived from the simple sense of loyal friends in a world of greed and trechery. After a neat sip or two we leaned back in our chairs and Pycraft began to generalize on his favorite theme, the decline of the breed. Here I played another of my games, similar in spirit to my plaguing of Mare and Mrs. Punck in that I done it with a straight face, but different in form. I would question or even deny what Pycraft said, to egg him on into painting in all the more lurid colors the scene of change and decay around us. I agreed with him that everything was going to the dogs but pretended not to, and even argued with him, to see how fast I could make him carry the ball in the direction I wanted to see it carried.

"The young fellows today are all homosexual," Pycraft stated after a drink of his whiskey.

"Oh come now," I says, settling back to hear the theme developed.

"There's no doubt about it. Statistics show it. They're no use to a woman no more, not ten per cent of them." He put his feet on the desk and grunted contentedly, basking in the implication that him and me had more virility in our day and still did. From there he rambled on to a related subject, the frigidity of women, passing over eventually to the question dearest to his heart — the growing promiscuity among school-girls. "Of the, say, five hundred girls in Andrew Hiller High here, how many would you say are pregnant right now? This very minute as we sit here."

"None?"

Pycraft's eyes narrowed dangerously. He did not like sacred

subjects frivolously dealt with, or his cherished illusions made light of. He never seemed to catch on that I was mocking him behind my blank eyes and straight face. "Let's not make ourselves ridiculous, shall we, Frank? Why, probably fifty are in trouble, on the average. O.K. Which comes to about ten per cent of the total. That's an alarming statistic, ain't it?" he said, smiling a little now. "Ain't it alarming? I have no idea where it will all end."

I settled back in my chair and said: "How can it all begin if the boys are all homos and the girls are all cold as cods?"

Pycraft looked at his guest's glass and saw that it needed refilling. He glanced rather acidly at me too, as though to ask why anybody having a perfectly pleasant afternoon visit would want to spoil it by picking flaws in the conversation. He poured a dash of whiskey into each of our glasses. "The ones who get into trouble are the *normal* ones," he explained patiently, "and if that's how high the rate is among them, why, God help us is all I can say. So in other words fifty percent, not ten, of those with any red blood left in them are promiscuous." Having pulled this very satisfying figure unexpectedly out of the maze of contradictions through which he was groping Pycraft paused contentedly again, and the 2 of us sat looking out at the streams of traffic on the Post Road while we sipped our bourbon. "As a country we're through," he observed cozily after a minute. A bellhop in a plum-colored getup entered and dropped several newspapers on his desk. Without moving his feet Pycraft reached over and skilfully jerked a New York tabloid from the bottom of the pile without disturbing the rest. He read the headline which conserned the murder of a Philadelphia socialite which he was following. "No evidence of rape found," the streamer said. He threw it back with a grunt of disappointment, even disgust.

"Some of the things I could tell you," he said, to restore our spirits. "Anybody who runs a hotel or motel could. They're a cross section of the human race. What they call a slice of life. Well between you and me and this desk, some of the kids have got nothing on these grownups. I name no names, not that the ones you get off the register mean anything anyway.

But I know faces when I see them. There's a woman comes here every few weeks to meet a man. He registers as something different every time but I happen to know he's a business wheel from Greenwich. I see his picture once in the *Herald Tribune*, when he got promoted to something. The woman is from around here. She pretends to meet him only for a drink in the Period Room, all open and above board. Then they say goodbye, and give my love to so and so and all that, and then she comes around the front and meets him in his room. There's another local woman, very attractive and high-toned, who meets a fellow staying here now. Quite a different breed of cat from the business wheel. He's a poet. I see his picture in the Woodsmoke *Gazette*, where he was lecturing around here somewhere. Odd gazebo. Reminds me of a grizzly bear. When he's three sheets the resemblance gets uncanny because it looks exactly like he's just learned to walk on his hind legs and has trouble making it, but will get it down pat some day. And a funny smirk on his face like he's got some other tricks he can do too besides walking on his hind legs. Kind of roly-poly, with mussed brown tweeds is probably what gets the wooly bear picture going in your mind. There's certainly no accounting for tastes. Here's this smart, cultured woman — Course this egg's a artist and that gets them I expect. When I tumbled he was so famous I had some fruit sent to his room but he never ate none of it. It just rot. They say his recordings of him reading his own stuff sell like hotcakes. He's from, now, Scotland. That's it." Pycraft took a drink and give that lewd grin that often presedes one of his jokes. "I guess he's getting in a little international good feeling."

Suddenly I get depressed. What a way to spend an afternoon! The level that conversation with Harry Pycraft always sank to was bad enough; much worse was the realization that Pycraft was the only friend you had left. To the old the world gets to be a pretty small place, I can tell you. But was there nothing left in mine but a snort or two with this gink and tea with Mrs. Punch? Was that my choice?

The blues, the real blues that are beyond singing about, had their hooks in me as I walked outside to my car, Pycraft chattering on in the above vein by my side. But I was about to be shaken up by something worse than the melancholy I seen myself as spending the evening in, and so maybe for that reason the shock was welcome.

Pycraft was tucking in some last-minute assurances of the regret he felt on Mrs. Punck's be½ and of the pains to which he would of gone to prevent matters from taking their lamented turn had it been within his power to do so. He tried to give me some idea of his integrity and value in a pinch. Suddenly he broke off and grabbed my arm. He wheeled me in a 45 degree angle to the left of the direction in which we had been strolling across the parking lot toward my flivver, and with that began gesturing toward some excavations under way for a swimming pool behind the motel. So that to an onlooker we might be 2 men discussing the installations in question. "That woman getting out of the roadster," he says out of the side of his mouth. "She's the one I told you about. Who meets this poet."

We stood stockstill on the lot facing the construction work while a sharp feminine footstep drew near behind us and passed on our right. So that without turning my head to speak of I could see out of the tail of my eye this slender figure in a smart tan suit march on high heels across the hardtop to the back door of the Period Room — the cocktail lounge part of it. Brown slippers of some reptile hide matched her bag that she clutched to her as she walked on past us, trying to hurry without hurrying if you get the picture. In order to join the dancing bear who materialized in the doorway, a misbehaving smile under his heavy but pointed nose. She had to turn slightly to the left to go around the door he was holding open for her, so that I had a clear view of at least her profile.

"There," said Pycraft when she was swallowed up in the dim lounge, "ever see her before? Know who that is?"

"No," I says.

Why did I lie? Because something made me want to hoard my secret. Because I had again recognized Mrs. Springer, mother of the boy whose family was too good for mine.

seven

THAT NIGHT AS I swam into my pullover pajama top, my emotions still at sixes and sevens over the afternoon spent by Mrs. Springer in the arms of the waltzing bear, I remembered Mrs. Beauseigneur and the magazine she had left. I fished it out of the wastebasket and climbed into bed.

I put on my specs and began to flip through it, pausing over this and that: a pie chart showing meaning variables in the word baby; another giving the relative filth-quotients in selected English epithets and their European equivalents; then a chart of the kind in which statistics are represented by sillowettes resembling refinery tanks of different heights, in an article contrasting legal verbiage in divorce cases with the actual causes of divorce. "Down boy," I says and shut the organ. As I done so the title of an article sprang at my eye: "The Semantics of Gardening." I opened it again and began to read.

"How many a plant or flower is not doggedly uprooted, mowed or sprayed to death simply because it bears the name of weed, while another no better is patiently cultivated because the way has been semantically paved in its favor. Take the lowly chickweed which we hound from our lawns like a common criminal. Suppose its white-flowered variant were called something like 'mist of morning', its blue, say, 'Mary's eyes', while the pachysandra now preferred as a ground cover bore the name of packweed. How the latter would be plucked up with sweat and curses, while we trod carefully over the grass lest we trample the newly sprung Mary's eye or mist of morning."

Of course. Presisely what my missus and I always said about violets and daisies, and what I use to tell her about dandelions and chickweed, without much luck, at least as far as any letting up about my "getting at" them was conserned. How I wished she was alive today so I could show her *But.*

The next article went beyond what Mrs. Beauseigneur had said — that any group is composed of single members to be each taken on his own merits — to point out that any individual so abstracted *himself* ain't no fixed entity. "In the course of a single day Mr. Doe is one thing to the wife he kisses good-bye in the morning, something else again to the boys on the train, still a third to the secretary he may take out to lunch, a succession of Protean façades to as many salesmen as call to solicit his business, and finally something perhaps completely unpredictable to the wife he again kisses at the door on his return home in the evening."

I paced the floor, reviewing my own day in that light. How many things had I not been to as many people! To the donator of *But* a crusty old geezer (how about that for role-playing!); to Mare a father-in-law showing who was boss; to poor Mrs. Punck the exact opposite of what I had been to Mrs. Beauseigneur, namely a snob to whom *she* was provincial. And finally to Harry Pycraft I had been something completely different from all the rest, a identity quickly thrun together out of elements in my nature which Harry Pycraft drew to the surface.

"Then who at the age of 64 am I?" I says pacing the floor with mingled dismay and excitement. In my fear I felt a certain elation. If this at long last was semantics, open the window and let it in. Let it blow the papers around the room and rearrange the furniture. Let the curtains wind up flat against the ceiling and the rugs on the wall, in the name of fresh air and a new start. Stimulation like this was always ½ rage that I never had no more education but had to school myself whenever and however I could. I got out the quart of bourbon I always keep in my dresser drawer and took a drink, as is my want when in my room. I had a couple more, dropping the empty bottle into the wastebasket with a very satisfying clunk, very rewarding in the answering creak which it drew from the next room. That would be Mare sitting bolt upright in bed, alert to my shenanigans. I assumed still another identity and became a man stealing downstairs to the alarm of others in what was damn well his own house. "Watch out, you are putty in your hands," I says to myself with a nervous chuckle.

I sat in the dark parlor with a drink in a glass, in which I periodically rattled the ice to renew consern overhead, studying over what I had just read in terms of something I had recently learned about Relativity from an article in the *Saturday Evening Post*. I had a kind of grasp of it all now. Time is a dimension so matter is an event! The stairs up which I would presently go back to bed were not the same as those I had just crept down — too much was happening. They existed in time and in my mind. I would rise from this chair a different Spofford from the one who had sunk into it. The chair was altering subtly under me, so was Mare over me, her puzzled head alertly cocked on the landing I had heard her scuffle out onto in her big bare feet, her fat braid coiled like a trained snake around her neck. I give the cubes in the glass another rattle, following this with a soft duck quack, very skilful and true like some of my barnyard imitations, to deepen the current of mistification running creatively through this house. Plowing us over you might say. Because I now had a feeling that exactly that was going to happen to me.

"What are you doing down there?"

"Drinking and thinking and stinking."

Every word has a meaning slightly different from what it had the time you used it before, they shade off in exquisite newances. No word has any meaning apart from the context in which it is used, no getting around that. Relativity. There ain't no Absolute.

On fire, I got a flashlight from a kitchen drawer, clattering the other utensils around unnecessarily, and stole outdoors in my own bare feet. I could smell as I trampled it the thyme growing between the flagstones. I walked across the cool grass behind the beam of light to the hawthorn tree, to which I had neglected to make the daily visit I always do when it is in bloom — a slip in the day's devotions. I drew a branch down and examined it by flashlight, flipping the specs, which were still on my forehead, down to my nose, to study the pink clusters which were at the height of their flower. How like little tiny boquets of carnations they are, ever look at one closely? For shame if you haven't. I sniffed, though of course they had no fragrance except that of the night. Then let the bough spring back.

I picked my way back to the house, laughing hilariously at the gravel under my bare feet, then again the thyme between my toes. On the grass near the house I paused and snapped the flashlight off to look at the world by moonlight. The beauty of the night by no means drained off my mood of frolic. I snapped the light on again and mischieviously shot the beam upward to the second floor. There sure enough was Mare standing at the bedroom window, a white oblong between two oblongs of white lace curtain. She stepped back out of sight. Poor Mare. Tomorrow I would try to explain the principle of eternal flucks, how each of us so far from being a clod — even old George snoring away up there behind her — is an infinite succession of variations each born from the death of the last, like one them kaleidoscopes wanting only a nudge to acquire fresh pattern and color.

I had given both Mare and myself nudging enough for one night, so I called it a night and sat in the parlor some more. There my thoughts took a serious turn, once the excitement and the effect of the booze began to wear off. In fact my exilleration ebbed away and a vague sense of uneasiness began to invade me. I failed or more likely refused at first to recognize its source. Then I admitted it. I had decided to return to Mrs. Beauseigneur the copy of *But*, and in so doing set foot for the first time in the enemy territory known as Punch Bowl Hollow. Why should I want to return what was obviously given intending to be kept? Because, I realized with forboding, I simply had to see that woman again.

She was easy enough found, kneeling in the yard in the bright morning sunshine. She was weeding the lawn, pulling up chickweed and what not with a will, looking very trim and pretty in yellow and green Madras shorts and a white I think they call them Basque shirts. Her legs were encased in them things that are like the knee guards worn by basketball players, and she was doggedly stabbing at the turf with what looked like a letter opener, or paper knife, very slim and silvery, of the kind with which she might, an hour earlier, been found slitting her morning's correspondence. She raised her head and under her floppy straw hat squinted at the figure coming up the walk, me, unfamiliar in the seersucker suit I had on. Then she recognized me and rose with a smile, dropping the letter knife and waddling forward with difficulty in the elastic guards binding her knees. She pulled off the one gauntlet she had on and extended that hand, wiping her brow with the one clutching the glove. "Shambles," she said with a laugh.

"Morning, Mrs. Beauseigneur. Got you working bright and early."

"Weeding this *waste*land. Absolutely take *over* if you don't keep up with them."

"I've brung you your magazine," I says, drawing it from my coat pocket. "I thought you might not of read it all."

"Oh, that wasn't necessary. There's a new one already, and then everything else to catch up with. I guess it just can't be did." She seemed to have recovered from the evangelical lather I last seen her in, but she did eye me sharply and say, "How did you like what you read?"

I says, "Most interesting," mocking her with the "most" which was the way her kind talked to take the curse off conseding anything to the enemy. "Of course its like with anything new thats any good. It only makes us see what we always knew all along but never realized."

"Realized," she echoed, nodding with that kind of midwifery with which women help you bring your sentences into the world, by antisipating the ends of them, or finishing them along with you — ever notice that? I remembered this from my lamented missus and also now Mrs. Punck, who was a great one at chiming your sentence ends along with you. Women *were* all sisters under the skin as Mrs. Punck would of said. That thought was a flicker of loyalty to her and our kind, and hostility to Mrs. Beauseigneur and hers. I was behind enemy lines, but only as a scout patrol.

Mrs. Beauseigneur had turned around to stroll by my side toward the patch of lawn she had been working and that I wanted to inspect. It was a shambles all right. Pock marks surrounded the basket in which lay her harvest of dug out blooms. Or not a basket so much as one them cunning wicker trays with a large looping handle suitable for pine cones or other dry arrangements in homes aiming at a casual grace.

"What if I told you those were called mist of morning?" I says. "That you been gouging out the ground?"

"Oh, dear. They are?" Her eyes were wide with naughty alarm as she brung a hand to her throat; as though she might in a fit of remorse and despair over what she had done tear also from its chain a tiny gold locket hanging there and toss it into the basket as a kind of pennants. "What has Pussy done?" She was pleasantly older than she seemed last time, the bright sunlight revealing that time had been doing a little scrimshaw work on her face all right, bringing the delicate features back over into the forty territory. I must learn as soon as I decently could whether she knew what scat meant. "What I need is a gardener," she wailed prettily. "I'm absolutely ignorant of everything. And my husband is no use at all."

I felt a joint work loose inside me, like a beam in an old house of whose materials no least flaw had hitherto been suspected, but now it was settling faintly out of plumb. Sensing that I was being appraised I put my shoulders back without moving my eyes from the sod which I was myself giving a critical going over. I rubbed my chin. "In case you ever hear of someone . . ." She stooped to toss a loose weed into the basket. "I mean it would only be part time. A day a week at the most."

I took a step sideways toward her, to recover the odor of some advertised perfume against which I was struggling. This made the woman a Jezebel, or so nearly so as to deserve what I now spake against her kind and all that it had wrought in Woodsmoke unto this day, even unto the altar to Baal which King Ahab himself had reared up.

"If there's anything I don't understand, if you'll excuse me ma'am, it's people moving here to the country and then proceed to not learn or care to learn the first least thing about the No. 1 thing the country is for — a piece of God's good earth. I mean why do you come out here at all?"

"I know. I know. Keep it up." She stood with her hands folded tightly under her chin, which rested on the clustered nuckles, her eyes shut tight as though to keep back the tears. "Show us no mercy."

Spofford closed his own eyes and drew a deep breath of the spring air, its natural fragrance tainted with a boughten smell that made his senses reel. "There ain't a man left in this town, this former farm community," I said, thretening to totter back on my heels onto the soft turf, "who knows what to do with a seed or a bulb." I looked at her to see her nod mutely, acknowledging the justice of my thunderbolt. "Look at where you've planted them tulips. Where the sun won't get them an hour a day, let alone right along a wall practically guaranteeing the varmints will eat the bulbs before Thanksgiving. The ten or twelve I see blooming there indicates well enough the hundred already devoured — by what?" I says, like throwing her a question in a catechism. I had decided to give her a test quiz. "What may eat bulbs if you plant them along a wall?"

"I don't know," she says, shaking her head in that pretty despair.

"Mice. They live in the walls in winter, coming out to feed at this cafeteria you provide in the form of a row of tulip bulbs. But there are some things you *can* plant along a wall. What are some?"

"I don't know. I just don't know."

"Narcissus. The narcissus bulb seems to poison the mice, or at least is poison to him, because he leaves them alone. Next rhododendrons. Do they like sun or shade?"

"I don't know."

"That one over there out in the open. Is it a hybrid or a regular?"

She now only shook her head dumbly at my remorseless catechism. Which I continued:

"Then you don't know whether it should be in sun or shade. Next ilex. Why is yours planted there, smack by the marker showing where the well is, which God in his heaven knows its only a question of time till it will have to be dug up and done over right. For he knows the builder, as I do, and that you're going to spend three hundred dollars doing over right what he's skimped ten dollars on materials on. Such as a galvanized metal pump terminal instead of a copper one. Do you know why the terminal will rot, is rotting as we stand here talking? Because the interaction between it and the copper tubing sets up a kind of electrolysis, which rots the lesser metal. Does your husband know that? That the ilex should be moved while its little?"

"Oh, if I only had you!"

I prowled closer to the house looking for defects, devouring them like I was devoured. Something dreadful and delicious was lapping at my loins. I could hear her in my wake, softly on the ground, like a cloud following me through the warm day as I knocked the shabby construction apparent to even a casual eye — the cheap wooden roof gutters, poor window seals, a corner of the building already settling due to hasty and superficial fill-in under the foundation, let alone the mangy lawn resulting from the cheap seed aimed at getting a quick show of grass to impress a client as green as it. Her feet whispering in the grass behind me were encased in delicate little scarlet and gold slippers with pointed toes as sharp as the letter knife. She could of weeded the ground with them. She sighed and said, "Maybe we should landscape with gravel more, like the Orientals."

I turned and glared around. "Well if I was stuck with a place like this I wouldn't let no grass grow under my feet getting a decent lawn under way in it."

She heaved a smiling sigh, like a small breath of adoration that kind of yielded the owner's soul up to you. "I'll dine out on that," says silly, pretty, sweet-smelling Pussy Beauseigneur.

Instead of gouging the turf with the letter knife, or even with the proper weeding implement uncovered in the garage, I preferred a commercial spray like Weed-B-Gon, which one of us would have to run down to the hardware store to fetch. I doffed my cap to scratch my head and squint off toward the chicken farm where I had left the flivver. Watching this the serpent whispers on my left, "Have you ever driven a Jag?"

I laughed through my nose as together we walked to the sleek blue convertible standing in the drive. The look of arrogance I had so long resented in those driving around in these machines come to me naturally as I slid in under the wheel. I give another snort as she explained the shift, because hadn't I driven enough stick shifts in the Buicks and Dodges my in-laws had before automatic transmissions? My cloth cap gave the final degree of appropriateness to the figure I cut behind the wheel probably. I slouched down for autobiographical reasons as I purred past the farm, averting my face from the house as I went by because if anybody had accidentally glanced out the window and seen me they wouldn't of understood.

The beast throbbed beneath me, obedient to my hand. Maneuvering her through the suddenly lot denser traffic of the Post Road I thought of something in my own ancestral past, my pedigree, that give me the right to be doing this. To be doing something soft just because we weren't soft. I remembered a great grandfather on my mother's side who was known to have guided a whaler into Gloucester in a storm that swept nearly everybody else overboard. We got documents. Well I had an impulse to turn into the motel and surprise Harry Pycraft but checked it till I understood more clearly myself just what was happening to me. For the time being I kept in mind the idea of the rather intrepid one-man patrol behind enemy lines already touched on. I slipped the Jag with contemptuous ease into a parking slot at the shopping center where the nearest hardware store was and bought a can of Weed-B-Gon with the two bucks Mrs. Beauseigneur had given me, putting the change in a coat pocket separately from my own. Within 10 minutes I was back weeding the lawn the way I damn well was going to do it myself.

I worked out a system that seemed to me better than spraying, and for that reason had bought no spray. I had found in the garage a discarded billiard cue, which become my main tool. I would dip the pool cue in the Weed-B-Gon and dab the offending plant with it. Then I would dip the pool cue in the Weed-B-Gon again and dab the next, and so on, poisoning in this manner everything in my path that was not grass. I spared neither mist of morning nor Mary's eyes on the one hand nor dandelions on the other, for what kind of semantics would it be that hesitated to eradicate something just because it bore the label of flower? I mean it works both ways. I worked standing up, in systematic rows the length of the yard, with my coat off.

At 4 o'clock sharp the French windows opened and with a gay tinkle Mrs. Beau stepped onto the terrace holding a tray of drinks. She was fresh from a bath I had heard her running through an open window and wore another outfit: yellow pedal pushers tied with teeny bows at the calves and a jockey shirt of red and white silk. "Iced tea?" I remembered both to put on my coat and remove my cap before approaching, but done so in a secret parody of menialness. For I had had a hardening of my heart out there on the lawn and decided to keep Mrs. Beau in her place. The technique I used as I shuffled like a rabble of low degree toward the terrace was that by which such characters are always portrayed in plays. The actor holds his hat or cap against his chest and turns it slowly like a steering wheel, kneading the brim in both hands in the case of a hat. Whoever does that in real life? Yet it is the method by which the serving class is illustrated on the stage.

"What is the name of that flower out there by the Wilcoxes gate?" she asked after we had been sipping iced tea and munching little frosted cakes. I think they're called petty fours. She turned and pointed to a row of tall stem plants not yet in bloom. I was absolutely amazed. Didn't the woman know what hollyhocks were? There are times when ignorance should be punished. "Why that's what they call Gabriel's Horn," I answered, saying the first thing that popped into my head.

Then I felt sorry for her and had another petty four. The sprig of leaves floating on top of my iced tea stuck to my nose when I drew a deep breath once. I removed it and put it back. "This is mint," I said like I was identifying some more foliage for her. Then I felt sorry for her again and popped a third petty four into my mouth as I said, "Where do you get it? The mint I mean. There's none on your grounds that I see."

"I snitch it from Mrs. Wilcox. I just sort of put my hand through the fence?"

"Don't let her give you none to plant. You'll never get rid of it."

Mrs. Beau sipped her tea and eyed me with the same look of speculation as that morning. "Could you take on somebody else? Because Pussy — by coincidence Mrs. Wilcox and I have the same nickname — is looking for somebody a day a week too, or even half-days she'd appreciate. Her mother's been staying with her and things have been just absolutely ghastly. She has these perfectly murderous migraines."

My research of these people had begun in earnest. I took mental note of a couple more things in rapid succession. One, everything with these women no matter how trivial was ghastly. Or hideous or gruesome or some equivalent, probably to heighten the suggestion of theirself as frail creatures easily crushed by reality and too good for this world. It would be interesting to know what they would call something that was really ghastly or gruesome, like the sight of their husband laid out flat after they had seized a shotgun in an argument, as had happened once or twice recently. Two, families were by common consent an evil. At best a nuisance. Instead of being glad to see kin as I believe we were in our time, women folks now days are felled by migraine at the first threat of an approaching blood relation, especially mother. A college mate of my granddaughter Geneva once defined a mother as "a wad of contributing factors." I thought of my own parents, and of our family shaking hands at breakfast, then of my son George growing up and marrying Mary Punck, of the first baby they had, born dead, finally of Geneva herself, not nearly so brittle as she tried to pretend, whose jilting had touched off this ridiculous chain of events landing me on a terrace in Punch Bowl Hollow in the middle of May with a woman called Pussy next door to another woman whose friends called her the same damn thing. That much I had already picked up eavesdropping on a telephone conversation by an open window I was weeding next to. Mrs. Beau had called this neighbor and *told* her about me, not gotten a call from the neighbor asking about me at all. No doubt this was a rather charming hypocrisy. The pendulum of my feelings about these people kept swinging violently back and forth. Now in a spurt of righteous anger at them all I said, "Tell Mrs. Wilcox I'm not a handyman, and I have things to do at the chicken farm and all, naturally, but that I'll see what I can do."

"Oh would you?" and the pretty little hands come together in wrapped adoration again.

We chatted some more about gardening, I telling her all the things I had grown and liked to grow on the farm, in such room as we had in the back yard. I told her about my small rose garden which I'd cultivated for years, and this got pretty technical, and I noticed her mind wandering. Then the telephone rang and she shot back through the French windows to answer it.

Alone out there, I strained to catch what she was saying but couldn't make it out, so I turned my attention to the magazines on the wrought iron and glass cocktail table on which our tea things were spread. They were arranged in a neat row in such a way that you could just read their names, all new to you. Feeling a little like a man picking the card from the pack the parlor trickster wants him to, I reached out and took a literary quarterly called *Griffon*.

After paging through it at random I turned to the back, where my eye was caught by some pictures of the contributors. One jumped off the page at me. It was the dancing bear all right, grinning in a turtleneck sweater against a stone wall with the sea in the background. His name was Gowan McGland, and that rung a bell. Wasn't he the poet Geneva had a recording album of, reading his own stuff? I found his contribution in this issue and read it. It was called *Materia Medica*.

From black tracheal trunk to bronchial tips
Wherein one cardinal like a blood clot sits
The winter maple dominates the lake
Whereon my skating townsmen swirl
Like microbes on a slide. Eventually the moon
Like a pale medicinal lozenge —
                    Enough. I cough
Like a sick sheep and wait for June, when all
These liquid lakes and brooks unlocked and chuckling in the sun

Will lure me out of doors, my singular and pleural woes put by,
Wool mitts and muffler sloughed like scabs in Tweedsmuir's hell,
By blue Scamander wobbling thrice, then aw faw down . . .
A ram into her thicket gone will hymn my season's favor in her arms
Where we together all the green-groined summer lie.

I felt my cod itch, and squirming noisily on the wicker chair
wondered if this was now the accepted aim of poetry. More than
that I wondered this: if, no longer able to shock us bourgeoisie,
artists had nothing left but to befuddle us. In cases like this you
seemed to been flung back into the raw materials of poetry and
had to shift for yourself from there, like with the Jag. I tingled
with vexation I could almost hear, like all my nerve-ends was
rasping on one another like a chorus of katydids rubbing the
undersides of their wings together in mating time. The very
comparison seemed to me an act of poetry on my part, a notion
I would like to air with His Nibs himself over a beer. He must
like it, judging from the foaming stein he held in the picture.

Mrs. Beauseigneur stepped back through the French windows.

"Take that if you'd like. We've finished with it. Why, that
was Pussy Wilcox again. Pussy sees you from the kitchen and
just can't get over you. Of course she's absolutely green with
envy. I mean trying to get anybody decent in Woodsmoke!
Well I told her I couldn't answer for you definitely, and I
didn't want to disturb you just now, but that she might make
bold to give you a ring at home herself. Was that all right?"
Mrs. Beau bit a nuckle in that imitation of a little girl who
might of done something naughty.

Clutching my new reading matter I lit out for home. I had
been gone all day! How would I explain my absence there?
Then the usual head of resentment built up inside me at *having*
to do so at my age, driving out the nervousness.

Mare and George were waiting for me in the kitchen all
right. They had finished dinner and were just sitting there,
two people sitting up for someone. They watched me, waiting
for my explanation.

eight

"WHERE IN GOD'S NAME have you been all day?" Mare asked. "Dinner's been ready an hour. Finally we didn't wait. Not that we could eat much."

"We were worried sick. For fear something happened to you," George said.

Espionage was a development so new to me, by which I had been so taken by surprise myself, that instinct made me conceal the fact till I had more clearly studied out its nature, scope and purpose, as well as made some estimate of its dangers. Also I resented the fact that all that ever varied their attitude of toleration was anxiety: they worried about me in between hollering at me. So I said:

"Maybe I spent the day at Harry Pycraft's."

"You mean you walked all the way to the Post Road and back?" George said. "Your legs must be killing you."

"My dogs are barking," I agreed. I went to the icebox for a beer. "Well lets have a scuttle of suds. It looks like an absolutely ghastly summer."

I could feel the tension generating behind me. I knew they were watching me — if not looking at each other. What I had said was not our talk, it was *theirs*. I had done it deliberately, on an impulse coming from I knew not where. I had been seized with a sudden desire to mock my own kind with sheepherder talk just as I mocked the sheepherders with our kind. It was the same drive, itch. Of course Mare thought the expression just slipped out by accident, betraying where I'd spent the day. "I don't know what you two are so hairy about," I said, watching them as I stood leaning against the sink after taking a pull of beer from the bottle. I let them have another, then another, a mad sort of thrill going up my spine as I baffled and unstrung those dear to me. I took another swig, and then watching them wilt under my eyes I said, "I don't see why we eat at this grotesque hour anyways. I mean isn't it sort of ungodlyish? I mean I couldn't eat a bite now," I said, and walked into the parlor with the beer. "I've got to unwind."

My fascination with the enemy, especially their women, grew. Of course it was with the women that I spent most of my time. What a miraculous thing language is! I supposedly spoke the same one as the Pussies Beauseigneur and Wilcox, yet on their lips it was something to be learned all over again, a foreign tongue. How the most infinitesimal shift in tone or gesture sorts women into classes divided by the thinnest of membranes that are yet walls a 100 ft. thick. I played mental games. Putting a single word of Pussy Beau's into Mrs. Punck's mouth, like I done in fancy, was weird fun. I whiled away sleepless hours in bed imagining such switches, different scenes based on them. Like I made Mrs. Punck say into the telephone "My dear we must shove along. We're frightfully late for dinner as it is," and felt a shiver go through me. It was just as crazy to reverse it and imagine Pussy Beau saying what Mrs. Punck would, and did, "I've had a lot of troubles in my life but most of 'em never happened." It made my flesh creep even while I hugged myself with laughter, there in the dark. But all through the sport I realized the sober point of it. It was I who was being split down the middle.

While I befuddled and pained my kin with the new expressions I picked up in Punch Bowl Hollow, with the residents of the latter I continued to play the rube. I laid on with a trowel the rustic terms that I knew to be not native to these parts at all but they didn't, or so it seemed. To Mrs. Wilcox — one of the 3 I decided to give a day a week the better to spy on them — I said one time, "I've got nowt left in the back to do, so if you haven't summat that wants tending to in the front I think I'll be moseying along." Nothing in that sentence but mosey was even American, the rest was English north country talk that I gleaned from a novel I had salvaged from a pile of discarded paperbacks to which she had invited me to help myself. And so on.

Playing both ends to the middle in this way kept me in a state of moral and emotional balance — for the time being.

66

Having made fools of my family I would set out to make fools of the fancy. And having spent the day doing that I would hurry home to make fools of my family again and whoever else I might find there — sometimes Mrs. Punck if I was lucky. She was often a dinner guest after a day spent with a real estate agent looking for a new place, and getting back too late to cook for herself. Sailing into the kitchen an hour late for supper one evening in June I found her and Mare and George at the table. In keeping with their policy to humor me "while I went through this phase" instead of laboring with me, they invited me into a conversation I knew damn well my arrival had just put a stop to. "We're talking about the birthday party for Ma next week," Mare said, "and were wondering whether we should invite Maggie Klumber."

"Oh Gawd," I said heading for the icebox and beer. "I mean her stories are longer than Lent." I waved the suggestion away with a airy gesture copied from some very flossy guests Mrs. Wilcox had had on the terrace that day, a interior decorator and his wife whose talk I was also copying. Because all this was essentially my old nack for imitation put to new use. I had often regaled Mrs. Punck and them with my impersonations of local characters, like the minister and the First Selectman, backed up by what they now call total recall. I could reproduce whole conversations like a phonograph record. The different thing about the new development — that both tickled and frightened me like I say — was that I had the odd feeling of becoming what I was reproducing.

They set looking neither at me nor at one another. They had put down their forks and were staring into their plates. They were beaten animals.

"I mean this is sort of effing the ineffable," I continued as I opened the bottle of beer at the sink, "but if Maggie Klumber wants to be the news behind the news she's got to learn to stop being all exposition, for Christ's sweet sake." Mrs. Punck brushed a tear away. I pushed remorselessly on. "And the absolute end is those travelogues about members of her family. Gawd," I says rolling my eyes up. "I mean if she wants to do the ill-met-in-Timbuktu sort of thing, she'll need better than relatives who are always sort of being transferred to Cleveland or winning cruises on TV shows, for the living love of God."

I leaned back against the sink, beer in hand, drinking them in. They were a sight, disintegrating there. In my other hand I held a slice of freely sweating Swiss cheese I also dug out of the icebox and on which I munched as I took them in. George had a hand on either side of his plate, into which he kept on staring. He wore an expression often seen on the faces of cattle that don't understand what is happening to them. Mare pressed the oilcloth tablecloth outward from her plate with both palms. Mrs. Punck worried in her round little paw a handkerchief that she took from her dress pocket. Otherwise no one moved. I took a loud gulp from the beer bottle and walked on into the living room.

Coached by a frown from Mare into taking a firm line George called out. "Ain't you going to eat, Pa?"

"Not on an empty stomach," I says and laughed out loud.

I would clip and mow near terraces or around swimming pools where guests were gathered and conversations going on, every chance I had, picking up something new in the way of a word or a inflection almost every day. It showed again how fast people can learn if they have to or want to. I would pause ostensubly to mop my brow or adjust the mower, my ear cocked and my brain a sponge. Or pruning shears in hand I would eavesdrop at open windows on those long telephone monologues from which I learned even more, practising in the privacy of my room or my automobile what I picked up, sometimes standing in front of my bureau mirror to rehearse gestures and stuff in mocking, yet magnetized, detail. Was an infection getting into the farmer's bloodstream or were the farmer's horizons being legitimately widened? Well may you ask.

Early one afternoon, as I was trimming privet for Pussy Beauseigneur with an electric clipper she bought me, I heard a cry from the garage. I dropped the clipper and hurried over.

She was standing in the middle of the garage pointing to a great big copper kettle on the floor. In it was a white semi-liquid concoction I didn't recognize. It was bubbling faintly. "It's a fish stew I fixed last night so I wouldn't be rushed today. I'm having a dinner party tonight," she wailed. "It's sort of a bouillabaisse. I didn't know it would turn this hot. Look at it. Just look at it."

As we watched, the contents of the pot seemed to be slowly boiling, or as we both knew very well, fermenting. "It's spoiled all right," I said.

"And I have ten people coming. What'll I do? I can't take a chance. Probably poison them all."

Mrs. Beauseigneur moaned and flung an arm upward into the air and gave a half-spin of despair without actually leaving my side, or turning away from me. I shifted from one foot to the other watching the bubbles rising lazily to the surface of the stew. It looked like lava. "What'll I do, Frank?"

Now she did move away, walking out of the garage onto the driveway. When I joined her there she was standing forlornly on the gravel, looking off vaguely into the distance, but unmistakably in the direction of the farmhouse. The second story was just visible above the line of willows marking the edge of the Hollow. I stood by her side, my hands sunk to their thumbs in my hind pockets, saying nothing.

"If I had just half a dozen, say, fryers. Or even broilers. Harriet could manage it in time I think. But I'd have to have them right away."

I pulled out my watch and glared at it. Two fifteen. I climbed into the Ford — I generally took it to work now — and drove slowly home. I muttered inarticulately under my breath that I hoped nobody would be in the salesroom.

The quarantine on snobs was still in affect you realize. I simply had no stomach for taking Mare on where that subject was concerned, no less touchy for Geneva's spending the summer in Brazil as a cultural exchange student. In fact there were people who said she couldn't bear to be in Woodsmoke with her broken heart, not convinced that she had won a scholarship and was living happily with a South American family, in keeping with the purpose of those international educational swaps. Mare herself suspected that Geneva had applied for the scholarship for the above romantic reasons. Anyway the war was still raging.

My heart sank when I pulled into the driveway. There were four cars lined up in it, including an MG and a Mercury station wagon. That many to once probably meant an indignation committee of women come to slug it out with Mare.

I recognized them instantly when I walked into the salesroom. They were a rather pathetic little splinter group whose point was that their husbands commuted the *other* way, away from New York and toward New Haven, where (except for one who worked at a silver factory in Wallingford) their connections with Yale University and its adjunks give them a status in direct opposition to the New York advertising crowd under blockade.

"My husband is engaged in research at the laboratory there," a woman in a dirndl was telling Mare across the counter. "Not just medical, but general scientific research. How do you know efforts of his haven't resulted in improved laying mash for your hens?"

"Next?"

A back door opened. Not the one to the slaughter room but one leading downstairs to the cellar, where George had spent the morning mending the sump pump. His fleshy face, acquired from his bygone mother and fattened up by 20 yrs. of married cooking, appeared in this doorway at floor level, as though washed up from the basement by rising flood waters.

"Mare?"

"Yes?" without turning around.

"Could you come down a sec when you're finished waiting on trade? I want to show you something."

He started to withdraw, or I should say recoil from the solid falanx of assembled females, a little like one cancelling an agreement to let balls be thrun at his head in a circus sideshow after a glimpse of the customers out front there. "Come here young man!" says one of the appelants, a tall woman with bobbed hair who was next in line. She stepped closer to the counter with an air of importance.

"I'm entertaining U.N. Personnel." By means of a sign over her shoulder she drew from the other women a kind of insurrectionary scuffle, so that they closed ranks behind her as their spokesman for issues larger than the mere purchase of poultry.

"They are members of a delegation from one of the still un-committed nations, but how long my brother, who works for the U.N., my husband and I can guarantee their neutrality let alone hope to gain their loyalty for the Western camp I just don't know, once they get wind of how minorities are dis-criminated against in a so-called democracy. Time is running out. I warn you." She emphasized the point by rapping the counter with her nuckles. "Here is the question. Are we or are we not going to show at least some intelligent grasp of the challenges posed by the world in which we live, and *live by our reason instead of our prejudices?*"

"Hear! Hear!" someone behind her mumbled, and the rest of the women took the mumble up too.

There being no answer from the high tribunal but the deep, satisfied drags taken on the cigarette burning steadily toward Mare's lips, the woman spoke more directly to George, whose head had remained obediently on the threshold wearing a pretty wretched expression you may be sure.

"Would you come up here please?"

The woman crooked a finger at him, as though luring him into some rite that didn't have anything to do with pure logic at all. The head floated up off the floor to reveal a body after all, and he shuffled in, overalls caked with grease, and stood beside Mare to form the meeker ½ of the high tribunal.

"Sometimes men are more independent in their thinking than we women," she says to what I knew to be a hundred and eighty pounds of good natured pulp. I myself remained in the background, wishing they would go away so I could begin my raid on the icebox for a woman in so much direr straights than them. I had come to appreciate George's dread of these women, still I wished the boy had more grit. But see-ing how miserable he was, and for my other reasons, I shoul-dered my way in behind the counter to put an end to the episode that wasn't going to net nobody nothing anyway, with a vigor that I knew would please Mare. Frankly I was nervous about the way she was holding her fire where my consorting with the enemy was conserned. I wondered what her game was. I suspected, on the basis of past experience, that she was waiting for some chance to turn my guilt to real account — to catch me in some direct treason which she would then use to get a favor out of me. Up to now she had no grounds for saying my gardening jobs were anything but what I said, spying on the enemy.

"Look," I says, facing the women, "there's no stronger supporters of the U.N. than us, or stronger believers in the value of scientific research, but that don't put no chickens in the icebox. Now we've heard your case and we'll take it up *as a family,* which is how we decide who is justly entitled to the limited quantity of chickens we can butcher, pluck and dress here for sale on these premises. Now will you please trust us to do that? You will have our decision in due course. Thank you one and all. And now good afternoon."

That was how I shooed them all out the door and into their cars. George went back downstairs, followed after a few minutes by Mare.

Spofford flew to work like a thief. Jerking a cooler door noiselessly open I was greeted by a substantial stock inside, but all wrapped in brown paper sacks with the names of customers for whom they were reserved written on them in black crayon. I closed that door and opened another. Luck. A jumble of fryers met my eye, freshly dressed but unwrapped — all open stock. I looked hurriedly around for a carton in which to put 6 or 7 but there wasn't any. I could hear Mare downstairs consulting with George about the sump pump, or whatever it was he had wanted to show her. Then saying something about calling the plumber, in a way that suggested she might be on her way back up any second. I reached in and begun to load fryers on my arm like kindling wood. When I had several I shoved the icebox door shut with my knee and shot away on tiptoe, hearing Mare's tread on the stairs. As I plowed through the swinging gate in the counter on my way to the door a couple of the chickens fell off my arms. I snatched them up off the floor by the necks. Just as I rose again and was turning the knob of the door I heard Mare's voice behind me. "Have you got a minute to spare, Pa Spofford?"

"What is it, Mare?" I smiled over my shoulder without turning around. She came through the counter gate with outrageous leisure. Reaching me, she leaned against the wall beside the door-jamb, facing my left side. I stayed facing the door, one shoulder hunched up to hide my burden. She glanced down at it once. Pretending to of seen nothing out of the way cradled in my arms she said, "It's about Ma."

"Yeah, Mare?" Another chicken was sliding off the mound and I tried to hitch it back up. In the effort they all got dislocated and began to tumble to the floor in a general jumble. I laughed. "Absolute shambles," I said. I stooped to retrieve them and rearrange them in in a more systematic stack in my arm. Then I straightened again. "What about your mother, Mare? What about Mrs. Punck?"

"She has to vacate the cottage by the first of the month and hasn't found a thing. As you know. That kind of rental don't grow on trees. And I won't have my mother in a rooming house."

"Of course not."

"So the only thing I can think of, is it all right with you for her to move in here with us?"

"Oh, sure. For a while."

"Then we can all be together."

"In one moist heap," I says and ran out.

Through the door pane she watched me chuck the fryers onto the seat of the flivver, then shove them all aside and climb in behind the wheel. I backed out of the driveway but I didn't immediately hightail it to Pussy Beau with the fryers, urgent as her situation was. My own affairs were too uppermost in my mind, namely what exactly my family were thinking about me, what they were saying about me behind my back. Now was the time to get an earful, when they only thought it was behind my back. I stopped at the side of the road just past the driveway, where the car was hidden from the house by a clump of evergreens, got out and stole over to behind the salesroom where I could listen crouched under an open window. Sure enough Mare had summoned George out the basement and I could imagine him standing there as she briefed him on the latest developments.

"Well we've solved the problem of my mother. Now the question is what are we going to do with your father?"

"Now what's he done, Mare?"

"He's a chicken thief."

"Who's chickens has he been stealing, Mare?"

"Ours."

"That would be partly his."

"That makes it any saner? That he's burglarizing his own coolers and taking the products you know where — them whores in the Hollow!"

"You act as though it ain't just the hobnobbing now. That there's something more serious. Something wrong with him?"

"There is, and I think I know what it is."

"What?"

"Geriatrics."

"What's that?"

"Its something that happens to old people, and it must be whats ailing him. Its a new word. Of course its not for anything that never existed before, but today more people are living long enough to get it. I don't blame him for what happens in old age. But we still have to keep an eye on him — more than ever. It remains to be seen whether he goes beyond the odd jobs and the hobnobbing, and does something to really disgrace himself and us. Or even how far the hobnobbing itself might go for that matter. His talk is getting funny. You know that. He copies these people in his ways. Of course with my mother coming to live with us, as he's agreed to, he may have another steadying influence. Maybe keep him home more. Or it may be just one more of us to disgrace. Who can tell. But thank God Geneva ain't here to see her grandfather take up with the sort that broke her heart."

Geneva was feeling no pain, as her letters showed, and I wanted to yell through the window at Mare, "Don't be bazaar!" Geneva was in South America with a schoolmate of hers, a girl named Nectar Schmidt, from Pennsylvania — the same one who had defined a mother as a wad of contributing factors. Real far out, and ergo ideal to get Geneva out of her shell. "What the girl needs is a bad influence," I says one night, and oy-oy-oy the looks saying, "That's about enough of them worldly epigrams." I was writing her regularly, giving her hints about the new life I was leading. Once to show my new influences I had cooked us a chicken in red wine at home. Mare had looked up from her plate and said, "This cooked in wine?" I said yes. She rose and scraped hers into the dog's dish. Things like that I wrote Geneva, little homey touches about every day life back in fair Connecticut.

I ran silently back to the car, doubled over to keep out of sight, and took poor Pussy Beauseigneur her much-needed chickens. "These are a special breed that were developed in a monastery," I says dumping them on the kitchen table. "There called Dominican Fryers." I guess she had her mind on her problems because it laid an egg. "Well they have to be cut up. I believe we've got a cleaver here?" My left eye begun to twitch, a tick I was developing.

The worldly associations to which I now freely bared myself did not by any means include the "idleness of frivolity" we at home had always cursed as characteristic of them. Spofford had never been busier. From gardening I took to doing all sorts of handyman odd jobs, including a little carpentry work, which I was glad to get my hands in again. Then a sudden new development, which broadened my horizons by leaps and bounds.

I was climbing into my flivver, one evening after a day's work at the Wilcoxes, when Mrs. Wilcox run out the house after me with a cry of distress — just like Mrs. Beauseigneur when the bouillabaisse fermented. "My sitter has stood me up!" she wrung her hands. She was dressed to kill, in a long green dress. Behind her I could see her husband in a tuxedo at the window. "We've just absolutely *got* to get in to this dinner. Its important. Are you by any chance . . . ? I mean could you . . . ?"

Now I was inside the citadel. Now began them long, nocturnal rambles through the houses with the children snug in bed. The houses soon yielded to me those final secrets I hadn't been able to learn from my outside work, though I could gather plenty from even such contacts. Servants know everything. I read mail, new and old, combed files and glanced into a few desk drawers, showing in all this, I think, a decent interest in other people's troubles, till I sometimes knew more about the owners than their best friends did. I knew their salaries and their debts, what analysts they went to and how long they had been going, and sometimes why. I knew from yellowing scrapbooks what housewives had dreamed of being singers and dancers, and from where the entries ended when the dream had died. Pussy Beauseigneur was an actress *manqué*. Women who never made it as actresses are always "on" in real life, if you've noticed, and Pussy is no exception. She had the lead in the college play — Wellesley — a few bit parts in road shows of Broadway hits — and then nothing. The rest of the scrapbook was blank. The rest was marriage. I knew what television serfs still secretly plugged away at That Novel or That Play, and even dipped into one or two — for my sins! I knew from unfinished oils on corner easels which housewives still dreamed on a little, or resumed it again after a child or two. In a wall photograph I seen a slim young dancer, poised on point they call it, the thickened ruins of which had hired me for the night — Lucy Wilcox herself. There was another of the husband in goggles and a long duster standing beside a Stutz Bearcat. An old car buff he was, or rather use to be, because there was no Stutz Bearcat around the premises to my knowledge. A sheaf of legal correspondence in his desk indicated that divorce action had once been contemplated and then dropped — little wonder as the poor fish was paying two hundred bucks a week alimony to one squaw already. Probably why he sold the Bearcat. So it went. My God, I thought closing the checkbook and putting it away again, if this is what sitters do then why does anybody have them in the house?

I would hurry to my own at 11 o'clock or midnight or sometimes 3 or 4 in the morning, my head as full of secrets as a Dickens lawyer. Them split levels and sinthetic Cape Cods standing dark and mute in fields I had once plowed, what beasts lay chained or faintly stirred in their owners brains, what dogs ate their sleeping hearts? I would lie in my own bed breathing like a stoned ox as I reviewed in aw what I had learned in secret, or digested in terror the truths I had fed on in my idle amusement. Because I knew now what was happening to me.

The joke had backfired. The mockery boomeranged, and the more I wrote down what I learned the less likely I was ever to be able to publish it. But write it down I did, every night a little, in the form of a diary or journal now. Flahive was clean forgot, that is as anybody to whom I would ever show anything, though I did see him turn up on the terraces once or twice, nibbling canopies and knocking back the Old Fashioneds.

But I had not seen the last of what people were like. The time came when I found myself in the innermost room of the castle. You know it. Punch Bowl Hollow had its own psychiatrist, of the several in the town itself.

The Wolmars were nearing their forties, with a boy of five named Rolf. I couldn't wait till the lad was asleep, to creep downstairs to the basement where Dr. Wolmar had his office and resume the final phase of my research: the notebooks from whose secrets one would ordinarily have shrunk, but which the obligation to look further into the lives of people I had enough on to hang, to see what extenuating circumstances might have made them what they were, made it my duty to examine. I had to give them the benefit of the doubt. No man is an island. So anyhow, the casebooks were easily accessible, neatly stacked in deep double drawers of a steel desk, though the spidery German scrawl they were written in sometimes made them hard to decipher. But there they were, the skeletons in all the cedar-lined closets all around the town. He drank because she bitched because he wenched, jepardizing a job doubly important now that the children would need straightening out at the best schools. Boys set fire to fathers discovered with cooks, girls hated mothers who sought refuge in the arms of other men seeking refuge from other wives who bitched or sculped. And so on. They were so bad, they so overwhelmingly documented the contempt Spofford had set out to document that his contempt vanished. It changed to compassion. All this muckraking was regrettable. It was too bad. But I realized how deep I had gotten into it by an experience that also abruptly snapped me back to its original cause and purpose. I encountered in Dr. Wolmar's casebooks many familiar names, but one shot off the page like a firecracker.

Thaddeus Springer. Tad. The boy who had wounded our Geneva.

Now for the first time that night the sitter really sat — glued to his chair. Or rather Dr. Wolmar's chair, a padded gray steel swivel to match the desk, well never mind that: I hitched it closer up to the desk, adjusting the gooseneck lamp over the casebook. I would of liked to light a cigar as I settled down, but I knew where not to leave my spoor.

"Room of his own," I made out in that spidery scrawl. "Since age of four has consistently sucked eggs . . ." I bent over a word I couldn't decipher, some foreign probably medical polysyllable the length of a scorpion I couldn't identify near enough to determine its deadliness. I skipped it and my eye met "stole it because —" Here I heard a noise behind me. I turned my head without moving the rest of my body. Little Rolf was standing on the stairs in his pajamas, watching me. I smiled over my shoulder.

"Aren't you in bed?"

The boy shook his head in the negative. At the same time he took in the office, or what he could of it in the choked light from the gooseneck lamp bent almost down to the desk. He had a riot of black curls, which his mother was always postponing the cruel harvest of, and a pink pulpy mouth which he worked wetly about as he watched. He wore a sleepy charming expression reminding me of the old trademark for Fisk tires, without holding a candle.

"You want a drink?" The boy shook his head again. "Well I'm writing a letter Rolfie. Ain't that something?" My hand felt for and found a loose sheet of paper and pencil before I rose. Keeping myself between the boy and the desk I walked over to him, turning back once to put the paper and pencil down after making sure he seen them. I took him by the hand and led him upstairs. "You want me to tell you another story. Well O.K., I'll finish my letter later."

As we made for the bedroom overhead I was struck by something funny in Rolf's gait that I had vaguely noticed before. The kid marched along on his heels, keeping the rest of his bare feet clear of the floor. The result was a series of oddly disturbing thuds. My heart still galloped as I tucked him back under the covers and sat down on the bed beside him with a book, for I had decided it would be better to read than to try to tell a story tonight.

"There was once a duck who could see through his wire fence into the forest where the fox lived who longed to eat him up . . ."

I raised my eyes uneasily from the page, to meet his. I was being watched rather than listened to, or as much. He worked the muckle mouth as he studied me.

"Then one dark night just as . . ."

At last the gazing eyes drooped and Rolf reached under the covers for something. It was his own foot he drew up, and poked into his mouth. That explained why he walked on his heels when barefoot. He wanted to keep his feet clean because he sucked his toe instead of his thumb.

Something told Spofford he couldn't read any more about Tad Springer when *he* was a little lad like that. There was a limit beyond which it wasn't any of my business. The bowels of mercy, as the Apostle calls them, melted. Surprised to find my now pretty crusty old self capable of being touched by such a scene, I tucked Rolf in and stole downstairs to set the office to rights. A pleasant warmth lapped me as I put the notebooks away and turned off the desk lamp. I laid down on the living room couch with a book, and was soon in dreamland myself.

Then someone was bending over *me*. I awoke at 2 a.m. to the sight of Mrs. Wolmar's fat face smiling down, like a gashed old canteloupe. She still had her coat on and was holding a wad of money as though I was trying to take it away from her. "I'm so sorry zat we got back so later zan we figured," she crooned maternally, "but so glad you get some sleep on ze job. Eight hours, two of zem overtime, is seven dollars ten cents, please?"

Clutching my money without bothering to count it, but confident of its accuracy from the dime I could feel through the bills in which it was wrapped, I hurried out into the cool night. I didn't have my car, as the way home was quicker crosslots over the stone wall. The wall was in back of the property and to get to it I had to pass an open bedroom window. I was stopped cold in my tracks by the voice of Mrs. Wolmar coming through that: ". . . could kill you."

One of the things Spofford had observed about people on this level — though its probably true of all walks of life — was how much of these marital pugilistics occurred after a gay evening. Why? Is it because at parties the gaieties are individually enjoyed, that is the husband and wife for an hour or two slip off the matrimonial yoke which must then be promptly assumed again? Husband and wife are of course separated for the evening at dinner parties, free to air in fresh company impulses long neglected or denied, only to have them snapped abruptly back into the cage again. Dynamite, them identities allowed to sprout for an hour then to be stamped out within the four walls of a bedroom, or of the car for that matter, because this had the sound of an argument resumed after a brief interruption. Mrs. Wolmar still had her coat on, as I could see, for your correspondent had his snout on the sill the better to give them the benefit of any doubt there might be in witnessing with the eye what might sound unnecessarily bad to the ear alone. The aim to publish this as well as write it down was momentarily revived, but that was always happening, to as suddenly vanish again. The doctor was saying?

"Symbollically you do kill me. But I stand not for myself when you murder me but for Heidelberg, so do not worry. Which in turn stands for . . ." Here his words were lost in the groan from the bed onto which he sank to remove his shoes. Wolmar was heavy, not fat, heavy, bald but with thick silver gray eyebrows like 2 sardines. His mustache was like still another sardine. "My feet are killink me too," he grunted humorously.

"Why did you spend all evening digging up Heidelberg with Rosa? Do you wish you were back there with her now?"

"Now?" Wolmar laughed as he drew off his trousers, still sitting on the bed across the foot end of which the woman raged with her arms folded and her teeth clenched. She might of rushed in to have it out not just before locking the house up but before leaving it altogether — such was her manner. "My dear, ull tall you why you do these things. Ull tall you why in a nutshell. Because you know it irritates me."

This bald man was revealed on disrobing to be extraordinarily hairy. I was amazed, there at the window, where I remained alert to every shift and turn in the scene, not to judge them without all the evidence. Sometimes the way people look makes what they say not half as bad as it sounds; a mitigating expression or gesture, a twist of pain across the face. Because what life does to all of us in some measure excuses or explains what we do to each other. Or I hope so! But nothing I seen ameliorated anything I heard that night.

Wolmar turned his pants upside down, clamping the cuffs under his chin while he lined up the legs at the creases, preparatory to slipping them over a hanger which he had ready on the bed. "You are like, my dear, a child that runs its fingernails deliberately over ze blackboard to get on ze teacher's nerves. *Nicht wahr?* It knows it grates on ze teacher's nerves. Dot's mature?"

"There are times when I'd like to run zem down your back," Mrs. said, exhibiting the red talons referred to. "Till I've torn every shred of skin off your hide."

"*Natürlich.*"

"Once in Stuttgart —"

The man had started to pick up the hanger with the same calm he had shown so far throughout all this. Now with a sudden motion he dropped it back on the bed again. Then, drawing back the trousers in a wad, he let fly and hurled them into the woman's face with all his might.

"— Woldenheim," she finished with a dying growl, like a phonograph suddenly deprived of its power.

It was the last your correspondent heard of these night cries. He took off across the grounds to the stone wall dividing the subdivision from the chicken ranch. Scrambling over that, he made for home through the back door. The light was on in the kitchen. Mare was sitting at the table.

With something of Wolmar's calm in the first part of the scene, I was disturbed to note, she wet a finger and turned the page of a newspaper spread out before her on the oilcloth. There was an empty coffee cup at her elbow. That trifling detail, of wetting the finger before turning a page, announced a return to another plane of sensibility altogether, as surely as a stone or a blade of grass marks a passage into another kind of country than one has been in. These things always struck the now keyed up farmer with a terrible clarity, the overwrought farmer. It was the little things, the tiny details, that identified the two different cultures he kept being alternately dipped in and out of, like going from hot to cold and back to hot again. Mare looked not at me but at the green banjo clock on the wall beside the framed Currier and Ives print entitled "Awful Conflagration of the Steam Boat Lexington."

"Half past two," she says.

"Let's not be chintzy."

"Do you want to ruin your health?"

"I can sleep till noon."

"Like them!" She swung in a 45 degree arc and pointed in the direction I had come. When I asked her how she knew where I had been she answered, "We've got eyes. We can see where you go."

"So, spying on me! That's what you've come to. I'd be ashamed to admit I had nothing better to do with my time than that. I seem to live with a bunch of Meddlesome Matties."

"No I'm not a Meddlesome Mattie, Pa Spofford," she said, lowering her tone again. "God forbid it. I'm only interested in all our welfare. All of us together, as a family."

I could do one of three things. I could whistle "Where Is My Wandering Boy Tonight?" thereby squandering where it was not appreciated my hard-earned sense of irony. I could pound the table in such a way as to remind her that what she was sitting at and what I was pounding was my own, bought and paid for before she was born. Or I could stroll to the icebox for a beer while I evolved some suitable middle course between those two extremes. That was what I done.

"They don't sleep till noon, darling," I drawled pleasantly, opening the beer bottle. I could sense her alarm at the new menace in that word. "In fact I doubt whether very many of them sleep much at all."

"What do you mean?"

"You've heard your mother's old clinker about how if we all

of us put our troubles in a pile and looked them over with a chance to take our pick, we'd each of us make off with his own again. It's a rather trite little wheeze but it has its point."

"You mean the enemy's human too?" Mare said, as though the roles were reversed and she was sneering at the kleeshays.

I poured some beer into a glass, walking around in the large kitchen behind her. "As far as I'm concerned, darling, you're just running your fingernails over the blackboard because you know it irritates me."

"What?"

"We don't all speak the same language. That's the whole thing in a nutshell. O.K.? O.K.?" The repetition in no way qualified my terseness. I was just being laconik twice. Well I stood watching the back of her head, the thick braid hanging down the collar of the flannel bathrobe she had on over her nightie. I rolled the glass in my hand like I had seen done on terraces, leisurely and suave. "Go on to bed now. You're the one who has to get up early."

Of the 2 impulses at war within me, I was about to obey the one prompting me to say nice things to the after all rather sad Mare when the sight of George, unhappily descending the stairs in nightdress, followed by Mrs. Punck in same, revived the exquisite pleasure I took in being a misfit here. It was Mrs. Punck's first night under our roof, though her stuff itself hadn't been moved in yet. Their faces were such a comical blend of anxious inquiry and plundered sleep that I had to laugh. Mrs. Punck spoke, continuing with the reasonable bit.

"You use to go to bed with the chickens, Frank."

"Did you read about it in Krafft-Ebbing, darling?"

Oh you're rotten, rotten clean through their eyes told me as I paced in my tweed jacket and beret not yet removed. Your calling us darling is no consolation, using it in the way *they* do, dismissing you more than being warm really. Nothing is sacred. That was what their eyes said.

"You're cruel," come from Mare.

"No you are," I swung around. "You've the makings of a born sadist, did you know that? Pussy Beauseigneur and me are both worried about you. Have you read that magazine yet?

No, because it'll put you onto yourself. How your a prisoner of words, still harping on that one 'commuter', and your heart and soul all locked up in it though the daughter because of who you got into this mental bind and intend to go on hating people the rest of your life for it, she's long ago forgotten about it. She's not even in this country! She's in a foreign climb woman! And you probably won't rest till she's married somebody from that class *anyway*, though he'll be from like Boston or Philadelphia instead of here. That'll be the only difference. It'll have that label instead of this. Your an interesting case all right. Oh-ho baby doll you are. Your so full of defense mechanisms you squeak. I say this for your own good, baby. Your a paranoiac."

She looked modestly into her lap at the rain of big words, though making it clear again that she would not be bought off with flattery.

"We call the minister for you, Pa?" George suggested.

"He's a wet smack."

"Let's all go to bed now for heaven's sake," Mare said, rising. "If we can still manage to get into them before its time to get up."

"You all run along. I'll finish my nightcap. I have a thing about nightcaps."

Mrs. Punck had one on! A lace thingamajig with a silk band running through it and alternately visible, like a belt through pants loops. Under it she watched in consternation while I hung up the beret on a peg by the door and carried my beer into the living room. Where I settled down in an armchair with a book Pussy Beau had lent me. After a while I raised annoyed eyes to the trio watching me in the doorway. Mrs. Punck was in the middle, like a perfect piece of stage direction, her moon-face between the other two. "Well?"

"What are you reading, Pa?" George demanded, on a nudge from Mare aimed at calling him back to his filial duties.

I finished a sip of my beer and set the glass down. "New novel by John Wain."

"Gosh, he write books too?"

"No, no, no! Not *that* John Wayne! Not the actor for

Pete's sake. This is a British writer. One of the Angry Young Men. So toddle along now, all of you. I'll be right up."

They shuffled sadly off to bed, to be followed soon enough by Spofford. I had forgotten what I had down on my appointment calendar for tomorrow, and wanted to see. I was anxious to get back to my own sort.

Yet a lingering sense of perfidy haunted the farmer in me's conscience. I would feel pangs of remorse at looking down on my family. I would think of Geneva, and wonder what she was doing down there in South America. What would she be like when she got back home the end of August? That would be next month, for we were well into July now. Maybe this experience that was happening to me would take a new turn before then, or develop an unforeseen crisis.

The development that did occur was immediate, and one I should of foreseen. Perhaps you have. It was certainly natural enough. In the circles in which I was now moving, it was only a question of time before I stood face to face with Mrs. Springer herself.

nine

IT WAS AT PUSSY BEAU'S, where we find me in still another guise that I must pause a moment to explain.

Pussy had come running out the house that afternoon when I was working on the grounds, stringing up Japanese lanterns for a lawn party she was giving that night, to moan this time that the little Lithuanian who helped her maid Harriet out when they entertained had stood her up. "Do you have a white coat?" she asked. "Yes," I fibbed, and hightailed it to town to buy a flannel jacket to wear with some blue surge pants I had. I guess I misunderstood what she meant. She was talking about a waiter's linen jacket, not the white summer dress coat I got me. Anyhow, I was indistinguishable from the guests that night, and so was launched on a career a little beyond that of extra waiter. As I was dressing upstairs in my room I could hardly wait to get to the party. There was a rumor Cyril Ritchard would be there.

Everybody else was, looking very handsome in full summer fig under the colored lights I now took pleasure in having installed. The guests were 2 doz. strong, and they all seemed to arrive at once, so Harriet and I were kept pretty busy pouring champagne out there on the lawn. (It turned out Mrs. Beau had a whole extra couple doing the catering, but we were all needed.)

This was the first time I had ever handled champagne but under Harriet's instruction I quickly learned how to wrap the bottle in a napkin and how to pry the cork off and how to pour without spilling. My only mishap was with Mrs. Springer, I was so startled to find myself serving her.

It was her who had promised to bring Cyril Ritchard but had arrived instead with a ½baked set designer in tow that nobody had ever heard of and who she promptly cast adrift. "I told Cyril if he played Captain Hook on television one more time I'd scream," she was telling another woman, at one lick explaining the actor's absence and making her seem even more familiar with him than at 1st suspected. Her husband, who they called C.B.S., was tied up in town with a television production of his own, and would be along later. Her yellow eyes in their thick black lashes reminded me of bees glutted with honey, but behind their lazy superiority you sensed the lust behind all snobbery, the drive, the social and physical appetite. She was lean and hard, with thin lips and a smile like a twist of lemon peel. The purr with which she spoke was that of a cat with claws ready for use at an instant's notice. She wore a pink stole that was soft as cotton candy, intended no doubt to bathe in a rosy glow a neck and face of whose beauty pride and desire and no doubt pleasure (cultural affairs) had took their toll. At which Ambition, maidenly and then motherly, had also et like acid. This was the adulteress who had ordered her son to discard the chicken farmer's daughter. But at the moment the farmer was studying her as a student of local tans. There are 2 kinds, those acquired lying in the sun and those acquired working in it. I had noticed that these women most obsessed with turning brown (there are some who literally dedicate their summers to it) did not seem to realize that whats called the law of diminishing returns operates here as well as everywhere in life; that theres a point beyond which more sun cracks and dries rather than beautifies. "Your beginning to get that cowchip look," I wanted to warn her. I was disturbed by the note of compassion creeping in again. And of course there was that faint line where the brown ended and the white began, that was like a razor edge drawn across my vitals.

"Whoa!" she laughed, drawing her glass from under the cataract pouring down like a cascade.

"Sorry ma'am."

"That's perfectly all right," Mrs. Springer said, not looking at who was embarrassed. I left her the napkin off the bottle to wipe herself with and beat it, hearing her friend remark, "Extra measure for the guest of honor."

Standing behind the icebox in the kitchen I drunk my first champagne, gulping the dregs straight out the bottle as I watched the couple from the caterers and Harriet bustling about under the Japanese lanterns. So the arch enemy was not only here, the party was for her. Her birthday I found out later. Still wasn't it fearless of me and not traitorous to be stalking the enemy right on their home ground? And why enemy when you finally got down to the brass tacks? Hadn't I rightly insisted to Mare that what drove us Spoffords on was not our hatred of this society really so much as our wish and determination that in spite of her first rebuff our girl would finally one day make good in it? What were we scrimping and saving to educate her for to begin with if not that? Yes, that was my vow for her now in this environment where, in some way not yet clearly revealed, I might at this moment be running interference for her. Geneva would not only be asked again by some educated boy to meet his family. *This time she would pass mustard.* I promised myself more than that. I would run her interference by damn well passing mustard in that society myself.

That night I dropped forever the rustic ways by which I had

been keeping these people rather priggishly at a distance, I suppose, and tuned myself even more finely than ever into their ways. I kept my ear twice as cocked for words and inflections, my eye twice as peeled for gestures, mannerisms and attitudes, tirelessly observing, rehearsing, copying.

Well during a breather after the first of the dinner service I stole around the high paling which bordered the Beauseigneur grounds on the other side from the Wilcoxes, where the Kidderminsters lived. The Kidderminsters were spending the summer in the Orient so the house was dark and nobody would see me there. I found a knothole rather close to the ground, and squatted down to peer through it at the guests, a short whiskey in hand. I found myself not four feet from a table at which were seated Lester Beauseigneur, Mrs. Springer, Pussy Wilcox and a eminent dentist named Haxby who had capped the teeth of several actors. I won't mention them by name though I know. I can't stand name dropping, as I once told Bea Lillie. Mrs. Springer was lamenting her failure to bring McGland along any more than she had Cyril Ritchard, to maybe read for them after dinner. "Gowan has gone up to Harvard to cut a new recording. Some of his later things," she said. Evidently failing to have celebrities in tow was her fort. A sharp tap on my shoulder made me turn, revealing the tap to be from a nightstick held by a uniformed policeman.

I rose, recognizing the cop in charge of the evening's parking, who had walked over to make a routine check on the Kidderminster premises. They had their name on the police list as vacant while they were in the Orient.

The glass in my hand give me the inspiration for my answer. "These parties," I said. "Wouldn't you say its a little early to be throwing them over the fence? It's the shank of the evening." I pretended to look around the lawn for others. This seemed to satisfy the cop. He even squatted down to peer through the knothole himself. "What's that they're eating?" he says, and I says, "Something Provencale." That seemed to reassure him even more, and he presently moseyed back to the front road to watch the cars, swinging his stick. I went back to the kitchen to help pass seconds around.

At midnight I was leaning against a porch pillar having another breather with a cigar. The tray on which I had just passed a round of highballs was on a table near the kitchen door. The caterers and Harriet were cleaning up inside. Mrs. Beau was at the other end of the garden with a group who were singing discordantly under the stars. A stocky man in a Madras jacket strolled up to the porch. "Haven't I seen you somewhere before?"

"That could be. Your face seems familiar . . ."

"Now I remember. The Model T with the flowerbox behind. And the SCAT. I *love* your SCAT. Just the way I feel about the new cars myself. Tell me, what year is she?"

" '26. Tell me, what do you drive?"

"Apperson Jack Rabbit '21. Remember the Jack Rabbit?"

"I do indeed."

He turned around and beckoned another man over, much taller and thinner. "My name is Gromler. Hopwood here has a Stutz Bearcat," he chatted. "You may have seen a picture of it in *Life*. I don't believe I caught your name."

"Spofford."

"Yes. Hopwood and I were just saying how ridiculous it is we don't have a gymkhana here when towns half this size put them on every year. How do you feel about that, Spofford?"

"I couldn't agree with you more," I said, trying to make a mental photograph of the word in order to look it up later, though its meaning as a term for some kind of tournament or display was clear from the way the talk was going. Hopwood, a man with a red wisp of beard and a curved pipe, nodded agreement as Gromler went on to say, "There must be a good thirty of us around here with traps worth showing, and once these gymkhanas get established as annual events, they pour in from miles around to enter. Look, why don't we go as a committee of three to the country club and ask for the field some Saturday? Hopwood's game I'm sure. How about you, Spofford?"

"I'm with you 100%."

"Let's drink on it. Where's that jackanapes who's suppose to be serving?"

Thus in five minutes I had changed from a man who had just kept his Ford, like the woman in Proust who kept her hats, to an old car buff — very nearly the innermost circle in Woodsmoke as far as outward status symbols was concerned. Beyond us lay only that small, final band of snobs who grind their own coffee and suck on pellets of bitter licorice.

Seeing Mrs. Beau in the distance shooting frowns of investigation around I excused myself and ducked into the kitchen. Under Harriet's watchful eye I prepared a fresh tray of highballs and brandies which I managed to pass among the crowd without being recognized by either of my fellow car buffs, who were in any case at a table making a list of other car buffs and the make and year they drove. My rounds again made, I put the tray down and mingled some more. I was particularly fascinated by an amusing little group who were being malicious about friends not present, on whose fringe I hovered nursing a leftover whiskey and soda. A man was describing a young woman they knew as "an aging Lolita." That was exactly the sort of thing I would like to do, and listened closely in order to get the hang of it. The problem was to refine into more sophisticated, or brittle, talk the humor that in some small degree at least I possessed. The glances of the speakers making the quips began to include me (proof again of my point that nobody ever looks at a waiter when he's serving them). From there I concentrated on the next stage, making some contribution to the conversation myself. This made me both keyed up and a little apprehensive. The talk presently turned to the perenial subject of college choices and chances. A young man was mentioned that I happened to know. "Jimmy's interested in comparative religion," a woman said, "and his mother was wondering if he might get into Yale Divinity School."

"He hasn't got a prayer," I cracked, and took a swig.

They all roared. The woman said she would dine out on that. I took another generous slug of my highball, at the same time melting a little closer into the group so as to keep out of sight of Mrs. Beau. The conversation turned to another youth who wanted to write, had, in fact, published a novel about this very section of the country. "It's a good external picture of exurbia as such," a man said, "but there isn't a single character in it who's three dimensional."

"Ever meet anybody around here who is?" I asked.

Now they began to ask who I was, whispering among each other in subdued hums when I left, as leave I prudently did when I seen Mrs. Beau on the prowl looking for the help. They repeated what I had said to fresh arrivals, as I could make out as I stood behind a porch pillar near the group. Harriet stuck her head out the kitchen door to ask was I having a good time; if not I might pitch in with the cleaning up. I was about to go in when over the heads of the crowd I caught sight of Mrs. Beau again, this time beckoning me definitely down. She came toward the porch, pulling along with her none other than Mrs. Springer.

I was waiting for them at the front of the porch steps when they arrived, my heart in my throat.

"Frank, I've been telling Mrs. Springer you're the man in town who knows everything there is to know about roses. Mr. Spofford, Mrs. Springer . . . Mrs. Springer has this fabulous rose garden and nobody to help her with it. I know you're busy and I shouldn't have mentioned it, but once I had she insisted on meeting you." Mrs. Beau run on in this vain for a few minutes, then excused herself to make another of her sallies among the guests.

Mrs. Springer looked slightly less fresh than when first seen, and was rather badly treated just there by the colored shadows thrown by the paper lanterns, which prove that soft lights are not automatically flattering if they hit you wrong. She looked like a member of a darker though not necessarily more primitive race. I figured she probably looked better lying in bright sunlight coated with one or another of the exotic variations of Crisco women use preparatory to broiling theirself in summer.

"Can I get you a drink?" I says, seeing her roll an empty glass between her palms.

"No thank you. I'm fine."

"How is Tad?"

"Oh fine. You know my son?"

While deciding whether to seethe or snort I tried to find in her face some clue as to whether she was playing dumb or had really not tumbled to my name. My face I could write off as probably rendered as unrecognizable by the lights as her own. Could she so lightly have sluffed from the Springer memory the incident that still rankled in the bosom of the Spofford? I decided she was insincere, and to draw on my own resources for orneriness. She give me plenty of opening by transferring her attention from the tumbler she was still rolling between her hands to me and saying, "Haven't I seen you somewhere before?" I struck the stance in which she would of seen me at Harry Pycraft's motel, if she looked; I turned my profile and hooked a thumb into my pants pockets while gazing off into the distance, or what there is left of it in Conn. I accompanied this with a vague mumble about the Dew Drop Inn. Then I give her memory another malicious jog.

"I heard Gowan McGland was coming to read. I'm disappointed he didn't show up."

"You like his work?"

"I admire his artistic — well is gall the word? I mean he does get away with murder."

"Well he takes chances. Any genius must, don't you think?"

"Of course."

She knew by now which was which in the cat and mouse now in full swing, and smiled nervously. She said, "Would you like to meet him? He's moved into our guest house for the summer you know, to get some writing done. He's always leaving his desk to wander about the grounds. He loves flowers, and anybody working out there would be bound to get to know Gowan."

"And to know him is to love him."

"We have this old Bradshaw place, you probably know it and all those roses old Mrs. Bradshaw nursed along for so many years. I can't seem to keep anybody, and it's tragic to see it go to rack and ruin." She dropped the sparring manner — or her end of it — and laid a weightless hand on my forearm. "A day a week? Please?"

"There's only seven in a week, and God himself needed one to rest on."

"Mrs. Beauseigneur says you've got the greenest thumb in

Woodsmoke. Never mind me. Think of the roses. Or old Mrs. Bradshaw. My husband is no use." This was far from the first time I had heard that cry around here. Spofford grew tense as, across a vast, cold tundra of his mind he saw flash off and on in red neon letters the word "nymphomaniac".

"What about your son?" I said. "How does he spend his days?"

"Trotting around the roads in shorts and a sweatshirt. He's going out for track next year. He's taken a vow to do the four-minute mile. I mean we're all glad for these obsessions, but where do they come from?"

"Maybe he's running away from something."

Mrs. Springer raised her hand so suddenly I thought she was going to paste me one. After removing it from my arm, though, she laid it flat across my chest, as though she was going to shove me backward onto the porch steps. Nothing of the kind. Instead a look almost reverent in its appreciation come into her face as she said, "I wish I'd said that. May I steal it?"

"Help yourself." I shifted my weight a little and looked down, pinching my nose. "Don't you have another boy? What about him?"

"Married and living in Waltham. *And*," Mrs. Springer added, slightly increasing the pressure of her palm against my chest, "about to have his first baby." Now she removed her hand and hung her head like a debutante. "I'm about to become a grand-mother."

I nodded. "Well maybe I can come Tuesday and at least have a look at your roses. Maybe give you some advice."

That I didn't need to commit myself any more definitely to these women than that was I guess part of my snowballing what-do-you-call-it. Vogue.

ten

I FOUND MRS. SPRINGER lying face down on a diving board over the swimming pool behind the house, as was her want in the heat of the day. She was wearing shorts and a halter. One arm dangled down to the water, in which she was writing with one finger. My footsteps, the last few of which were accompanied by coughing, brought her to her knees, peering at me and bobbing slightly on the board. Her eyes were enclosed in thick goggles which confused the metaphor to which she give rise — the rich marinating theirselves in bland oils — with pictures you had seen of women laborers operating acetylene torches in Soviet factories. "Oh it's Mr. Spofford. So nice of you to come."

She walked to the edge of the grass where I waited, not coming no closer to the poolside, knotting the strings of her halter behind her neck. "It's just a slingshot with two stones in it," I told myself, without conviction.

"There they are over there," she said, pointing to what was certainly a riot of foliage if not of roses, running in a wide semicircle across the back of the property. I laughed. "Have they been dusted?"

She lifted the goggles to stare at me with a come-again look, the white rims of her eyes exaggerating the look of astonishment to a degree that nearly made me laugh again. "Sprayed. For pests," I explained. "Horticulture, you know, is nine tenths destruction."

"*Love* that. You see, we moved in here in the spring, actually. We used to live over in Punch Bowl Hollow."

"I know." I stood in a dizzying swarm of emotions. Mrs. Springer's hot brown body seethed with the summer itself. The air around her shimmered in a way that set my brain to dancing like a pan of boiling water. I welcomed the diversion that suddenly checked our movement toward the rose bower.

I have described that as encircling the back of the property,

94

but visible through an arched white gateway in the middle of it could be seen a guest house nestling in still more untended greenery of its own. It was a frame cottage with scaling white paint and a chimney that listed over the doorway with an air of managed suspense, as though the figure now emerging from the door would of deserved the ton of bricks about to come toppling down on his head. The wooly bear came forward smiling sheepishly at the shrill rebukes of a maid behind him. There was the famous hair curling in untidy scrolls down his brow, like wood shavings from a carpenter's plane; the bulging eyes like black grapes; the cigarillo burning in one corner of his mouth. Seeing him as a stranger on the street you would of wondered, as Harry Pycraft said, whether he was a clean poet or a dirty business man; but the puzzle uppermost in my mind now was whether he was an old boy or a young crock. I wouldn't have bet a dime on his age except that it lay somewhere between twenty-five and forty. He was dressed in a blue shirt under the flapping tails of which appeared at last a glimpse of the shorts you were afraid might not be there. Straight as a pine though round as a barrel he advanced toward us.

"I want you to meet Gowan McGland. This is Mr. Spofford, who knows all there is to know about flowers."

A poet, I thought, shaking his hand. Why, he looks just like anybody else. In fact, worse.

As we shook hands a kind of pistol shot rang out, to wit the screen door snapping shut behind the maid, who came down the flagstone walk with a tray of lunch dishes, scowling daggers at the guest. She handed him a dish of yellow pudding with a spoon in it as she went by. "You didn't eat your dessert," she said, and made for the main house.

"Warm today," McGland said, gazing vacantly around at the day, still not shut of the silly smile that was at once hang-dog and mischievious. He had the look of a scolded schoolboy. "Yes," Mrs. Springer agreed. She folded her hands before her, as though she was going to lead us in prayer. The screen door of the main house contributed a second gun shot, or slap in the face. We now all worked our way slowly out of the hole in which we found ourselves by means of a series of physical actions that had nothing to do with the cause and none of which antisipated the next, but all of which together resembled a kind of rite for the exercism of human embarrassment.

First, Mrs. Springer knelt down on a huge striped towel, as though that was a prayer mat and she really was going to pray. Instead she picked up a pack of cigarettes that had been lying on it and drew one out. Then seeing McGland making motions in the air with his pudding she took it from him and placed it on the towel, on which he then knelt by her side, as though now ready and willing to confess his sins, with the pudding to be offered up as a sacrifice. At the same time his carnivorous gaze come to rest on Mrs. Springer's halter. She meanwhile started to get her smoking paraphernalia out of a wicker bag. She twisted the cigarette into a long black holder and then picked up a book of matches. McGland tore the book from her grasp and a match from the book. When he held a flame to the cigarette at last the holder wobbled in her teeth, so he had to steady her hand with one of his, dropping the matchbook again to do that. Everybody was breathing heavily.

By the time this part the rigamarole was at an end the two of them were more or less sitting on the towel, sideways on one haunch, leaving Spofford still standing, as though a place had not yet been found for him in the scheme of things. Mrs. Springer squinted up at me against the sun and said, "The cottage is cool from away back. Maybe from the days when it was used as an ice house." She was smiling tightly. "I suppose you remember all these local . . . local . . ." I guessed the word she was resisting was landmarks, and felt the hackles of satire rise into position like cannons being drawn up. I wanted to wound her. "Any how the Bradshaws converted it."

"And others are letting it backslide."

Mrs. Springer threw her head back and laughed out of all proportion. She was grateful both for deliverance from the jam and for this local tidbit she could throw her distinguished guest, some little pleasure addressed to another side of him than the sexual gluttony on which his fame was half founded, I later learned. If he had not cut such successful swaths down the eastern seaboard on two previous visits to this country he would probably not be here for a third, at this house in particular. McGland had already forgotten the maid and was turning on Mrs. Springer's buttered flesh the attention that it deserved. Not so much however as to of missed the joke. From deep in his throat come an amused grunt far more satisfying than Mrs. Springer's laugh, the kind of glowering mirth that was his own regional ware. I later came across a description of that laugh in a magazine: "It had the Scotch-Welsh sea rumble of a mixed blood, a heritage at once rich and unstable, jovial and brooding. Falstaff prowling among the winding towers of Elsinore would be McGland." He rolled his bulging gaze at me and then down at the pudding, which had somehow found its way between his bare feet. I instantly caught the difference between the two. Mrs. Springer was being democratic, McGland saw no need to be — what was unusual about yokel wit? Mrs. Springer's response was the overappreciation of those silly intelligent women of her sort to whom everything was "wonderful". I moved quickly to exclude her from the conversation, in a manner that also made hay in another way.

"I've read your stuff, McGland," I said, "but my granddaughter tells me the thing is to hear you read it in person. She did at Wycliffe. Remember when you were there? She also *saw* you reading a magazine at the railroad station there. Anyhow it's good to see young people with other heroes than rock and roll singers."

"I like rock and roll." However McGland changed the subject with remarkable speed back to himself again. His need for praise was second only to his sexual craving. He fed on every fresh reminder of the vogue that put both within his reach, and turned this country into one vast playground for him. He suddenly looked not like a young crock but an old baby, reaching blindly for the teat of flattery. "What's your granddaughter like? Maybe I remember her. I remember waiting for the damned train."

"Geneva —" I paused to let the shaft enter Mrs. Springer. Her mouth hung open for a moment like an idiot's and then closed. I took the aluminum folding chair at which she fired a apprehensive look and sat down on it. This kept the demands of respect in ratio I figured. As I'd of had to remain standing while they were seated, I could sit down while they laid down, or nearly did. At the same time it brought me halfway to the lounging position that would of made me one of them. They were now lolling over on one elbow on the towel.

"Geneva's a sturdy girl with fair skin and blonde hair but brown eyes."

"Always a stunning combination," said Mrs. Springer.

"Especially if it's natural," I said, looking away from her fine thatch in a manner that was the equivalent of a direct glance at it. "Her eyes are big and round and she's always got a surprised look, like she just swallowed her gum. And often looking down, as though not quite sure of herself or of the world. A wide, well shaped mouth that's pink without lipstick."

McGland had been making peculiar humming noises, like a seashell — or maybe water starting to boil. "I think now I remember someone like that selling tickets to some benefit or other in the station," he said. "She was shaking a can like a tambourine. Does she wear her hair in bangs, like a row of question marks?"

"That's our Geneva!" I got down off the chair to set fire to McGland's cigarillo. Now I was on my knees, nearly on a level with them. Oh, I was climbing fast! One more move and I would be one of them, lollygagging on one elbow beside a swimming pool.

"Where is she now?"

"In Brazil on an international exchange scholarship. She's due back any week now. She said she did her damnedest to get a look at what you were reading. Something deep probably."

McGland frankly laughed through his nose at this. He said he generally picked up a true detective magazine in a railroad station and regaled us with an account of the unsolved murder he had whiled away that journey back to New York with. At this point Mrs. Springer come to. She told of having seen the same crime dealt with in a television series on vintage crimes. During an exchange between the other two about this, while they weren't looking, I slid down all the way onto the towel. I leaned over on one elbow also, my head propped on my palm. Now I was one of them — worldly, effortless, delinquent and suave.

Mrs. Springer shot a glare in the direction of the garden. Before I could be ordered to my feet I sprang to them. "I've come to look your roses over," I reminded her sharply.

We sauntered in loose formation toward the bushes, McGland tagging along with the dish of dessert at which he now poked with the spoon. He showed interest in the spoon. Mrs. Springer explained the carving on it as dating it Pre-Revolutionary. McGland told us that in Wales spoons had a definite folk significance. "They're a courtship symbol," he said, and jammed his suggestively into the pudding.

With that I understood his poetry. Double meaning. Everything is sexual whether people know it or not, whether the authors themselves know it or not sometimes. Emerson sleeps on his hill without the faintest idea. Wordsworth and Tennyson didn't know what they were talking about ½ the time when they talked about Maypoles and steeples and flowers opening, any more than the yokels in the Welsh countryside knew what they were giving the girls when they gave them spoons to stir their tea with. These birds did, birds like McGland. It was all very exciting. I might even try my hand at a little poetry myself I thought. "My love has a red, red rose," I would write, and barricade myself in the house and defy the cops to come and get me.

Just then the screen door of the house flew open and a human colt dressed in white shorts ran past us with the easy lope of the long distance runner and disappeared up the footpath leading past the guest cottage and into the woods beyond. He give the impression of having run in the front door and straight through the house out the back. "Tad," Mrs. Springer called, "don't forget to —" but he was gone, his long legs flickering out of sight among the birch trunks. I remembered having learned what his full name was from Dr. Wolmar's casebook, Thaddeus, and wondered if that was what he was running away from. Hiawatha would of been a good one to change it to based on what we had just seen. McGland watched the clean-limbed spectacle vanish with a pang of envy, of sorrow almost that I could read in his face — what was that tosspot of a god always pictured belching under a tree's name? Silenus? Him catching a glimpse of Mercury — and drew his own shorts up about his pudgy middle. Mrs. Springer gave a helpless laugh and said, "His daily workout. Yesterday he left with his lunch strapped to his back. Today I suppose it's berries in the woods. Well here are the roses, or I should say the rose *bushes.*"

"That's because they weren't pruned when they should of been," I said. "Too late now for this year. You can't prune anything when it's flowering, though we can cut off some of the dead stuff here." McGland and I both bent to smell a rose which Mrs. Springer seemed to be holding invitingly toward us after sniffing it herself, inhaling instead a mad chord of odors consisting of soap, suntan lotion, perfume, powder and broiled female skin. McGland licked his lips like a baby, watching his hostess.

"Spring flowering shrubs," I says, calling the class to order, "are pruned after flowering. For instance that spirea and weigela could use it now. Anything that blooms after June goes under the knife when its dormant. Now this Doctor Van Fleet here," I said leading the way to a rosebush staked on a trellis, "should of been cut along about April, so as to leave three to six buds. Three to six buds," I repeated for the benefit of one pupil whose attention was wandering again. McGland nodded, the spoon upside down on his tongue as he gazed down at Mrs. Springer's bending form. I wanted to lash them both with a switch cut from the nearest tree. "That is on the strong shoots. Weak shoots should be cut clean to the base. Get rid of them! What you've got here," I cried with a wave of my hand, "is a mess of greens."

McGland snickered though still intent on the contour changes in Mrs. Springer's constant shifts in position and posture. I turned my fire suddenly on the poet: "Don't you care about flowers?"

"Very much. Very much indeed. Wild flowers." McGland had now licked even the dish clean, and he set it with the spoon in it on a nearby stone bench. "Now here's a real favorite of mine. Dusty miller. Nobody asked it in here. Nobody invited it. It's a crasher. It just climbed over the wall and stayed."

Taking over as lecturer now, McGland led us to a small clump of flowers he had noticed, a deeper, yet at the same time softer, more velvety, crimson than any of the roses. They were nodding on their tall stems in a patch of phlox among which they had taken root. The dusty miller is an anarchist all right. I stood while the other two knelt together to inspect them, in a picture of nature worship and appreciating beauty that was a sight to behold. But McGland's obvious interest in her rather than the flowers give me a chance to recover the initiative as lecturer.

"No, nobody plants this particular *variety*, because they don't have to — women would more than likely pull it up for a weed, like a violet. It's a wild type that just drops in and makes itself at home. It don't need pampering. It'll always make out. Reason I've always liked the dusty miller myself." I had no doubt I would stoop to anything to take the play away from McGland, for I have become very cynical about human nature. "A point about wild flowers that you may miss, Mr. McGland, is that they're often flowers that have *escaped* from gardens in the *first* place, and have only gone back to where they started. So who's to say who's the rightful settler?"

"Where do they get their name?" Mrs. Springer asked.

"Look at the stems," says both lecturers in unison, but Mc-Gland, kneeling beside Mrs. Springer, had the advantage. He put his hand to one of the silvery gray stalks just as she did, so that their fingers grazed. From above I could see them touch, and gave a grimace that I guess is characteristic of me in moments of exasperation or stress or mental pain. I swing my head away and click my teeth together, like an old dog snapping at flies. "So it comes down to a question of semantics really," I said. "Don't pull something up just because it's called a weed."

"Called a weed," Mrs. Springer echoed.

Then Mrs. Springer too finished sentences with you just like any housewife, and there was no need for the pang of superiority to Mrs. Punch and to Mare or to your dead missus for that matter. There all sisters under the skin when it comes to chiming along, in what is probably a oral form of backseat driving.

"I'll get to some of these bushes now. The ones that are through flowering." I glared critically around. "This place looks like an unmade bed."

All through the hot afternoon I plied my shears among bushes from behind which, pausing to mop my brow, I could peer through the foliage at the swimming pool, ringed with its ever-changing succession of callers. Mrs. Heist the attorney's wife was there, Mrs. Wolmar, Lucille Haxby — Mrs. Springer's sister-in-law and wife of the Greenwich dentist — and the Pussies Beauseigneur and Wilcox. And Cora Coit, the artist who painted with an electric toothbrush. Some wore floppy straw hats, some sat at a table with a parasol, but most of them worked at their tans. Occasionally one would go in for a dip, climbing out again to sun herself among her fellows, like seals sporting the summer afternoon away. They sipped long drinks and nibbled canopies the maid brought out. McGland kept wandering in and out the guest house, sometimes pausing to chat with me and at last even offering to help with an extra pair of shears he had found in the toolshed. He seemed restless. Once or twice he looked as though he was going to charge the female congregation but he never did, either because he was self-conscious about his figure by contrast to most of theirs and would of looked even more foolish dressed fully to join them at a pool, or (what might be a point of psychology I wouldn't vouch for out of my limited experience) your Casanova who chases women singly is ill at ease in a whole group. I enjoyed his company but he was little use as far as the work was concerned, being unable to grasp the distinction (as even some practicing gardeners can't) between pruning and shearing — the latter being simply what you do to a privet to shape it. "Every bush is different," I explained to him patiently. "Now this baby seems to like to put out extra shoots. So if you want to, you can get down there and cut away the dead wood from around the base." McGland stooped to his work, then knelt, then finally laid down on the ground to do it, his legs sticking out from under the overhanging boughs of the weigela in question like the legs of a garage mechanic from under a car he was repairing. The sound of the pruning shears was heard briskly at first, then more slowly, then stopped altogether, till at last there was only that of McGland's regular breathing, deepening at last to the contented snore of Silenus asleep under the summer shrubs.

About five o'clock a new car was heard coming to a furious stop among the several parked in the driveway, with quite a spray of gravel, and a red-faced man clutching a leather reticule marched into the house with but a glance in the direction of the swimming pool, and that sent there like a shot. Instinct born of experience told me to get ready for some fireworks. Because Mrs. Springer seen him and, excusing herself to the other seals, hurried into the house. I shot around to the other side where I could stand clippers in hand near an open bedroom window. The sound of cars being started up and driven off in rapid succession was heard.

"You mean I drove them away," C.B.S. said, crow-hopping around the bedroom on one foot as he drew off a pair of seersucker pants. His coat and shirt already lay on the bed. He was a dark man with smooth hair and handsome if thickening features, as well as a tire or two above his boxer shorts.

"You said it, I didn't." Mrs. Springer began to fiddle with the knot of her halter with quiet deliberation, probably tightening it.

"Oh hell! I mean a man breaks his neck to get away early once, as I specifically said this morning I would make a point of doing, to get away early once and have a drink *with his wife alone* — remember that word, alone? — and finds the same goddam thing he always does instead of a home to come to. And what he has to put up with week ends. To wit: a lot of goddam women sitting around looking as though they're going to swim the English Channel. Is that all they've got to do is sit around with grease jobs an inch thick on them?"

"You mean is that all *we've* got to do? Meaning I've got to do."

"If the shoe fits."

"I'll take a shower," she told him, softening her mood with an effort noticeable to the casual onlooker, if not to Carl B. Springer. She began to caress her sides. "Then you can see where I'm tiger lily and where I'm Easter. You could now if you'd look. Don't let's fight again. Please?"

"Well I mean come home to a wife looking like a pig turned loose at a church picnic," C.B.S. muttered, hopping on the other foot.

"I *said* I'd . . ." Her temper flared up again, meeting his coming down.

"I mean define your terms. Let's define our terms. What do we mean by a Relationship, which you were discussing so glibly the other night. Let's get together and try to establish *contact* with each other, shall we? To talk *with, not at,* each other. I mean I'd just like to know what you mean by it and where you think I've fallen down. Me," he said, poking himself in the chest and as though appealing the case to an unseen listener to the conversation, who might be more amenable to plain reason, "after slaving all day over that idiotic show to *keep* a place — Christ, I nearly said place in the sun — a place like this to find it overrun by, I mean a quiet drink, let's, you said yourself if we had more of those I wouldn't hit the bottle so much myself. You know — quiet drink?" CBS said, his face twisted into a hideous exaggeration of Good Will. "Remember?"

"Oh my God, Carl, don't tell me we were happiest when we didn't have a dime."

"I warn you not to twist my —"

"Half the lines you throw at me in these arguments you wouldn't stand for in those scripts you produce."

"You mean *even* those scripts. Say it. I immerse myself in bilge to the ears to pay for this. I spend the day buried to my chin in manure to maintain someone in the style —"

"Don't. Argue intelligently or don't argue at all."

"Well now, there's an idea. That's a switch. Don't argue at all." C.B.S. had slipped his trousers over the rod of a coat hanger, which he now stood holding. History seemed to be about to repeat itself. I remembered the Wolmars, and my obligation to miss no detail that might extenuate these people's guilt. But the danger passed. Or no, wait. After slipping the coat on the hanger C.B.S. looked over at his wife, who stood framed in the bathroom door now, one hand on the jamb, in an attitude of royal ease, ready for her bath but waiting a moment. "Oh, baby," he said, "let's hole in together tonight, alone again. Just the two of us. We'll take a shaker of martinis and a bottle of wine with some supper out to the guest cottage."

"Oh, uh, well . . . he's still in it, you know."

"Who?"

"Gowan."

"I thought I said for him to go."

"I thought you said for him to stay."

Tightening his grip on the hanger, wearing a look of lunatic deliberation, C.B.S. swung coat and pants in the air over his head three times in a wide circle, like a comedian imitating a helicopter on one of his own variety shows, then slammed them down on the bed with all his might. "And I'm in communications," he said.

He was talking to himself. His wife had vanished into the bathroom, closing the door behind her. From inside came the sound of running water.

"I'm in the business of making contact with people on a large scale," C.B.S. babbled to this invisible third person, "for Christ's sweet sake. To establish *connections*. To *communicate*. On a *mass scale*. I can't even communicate with my own wife. I can't make a simple thing clear around here. Himself he cannot save," he said, rolling his eyes upward in a tragic manner. "All channels have broken down between us. Neither any longer knows what the other is talking about." He struck his breast another blow. "To say nothing of that ultimate aim, *communion*." He stared distractedly at the bureau, as though accusing it of being something other than a piece of furniture, something in league against him too, like everybody else. "I guess we can start drinking on that note."

I shook my head sympathetically and turned away. I was rapidly reaching a crucial point with these people. I was emotionally involved with them, and the point I was again reaching was when you see how completely entitled you are to contempt — which is the point at which you waive it.

I heard a rustling behind me and began busily clacking the shears in midair, doing so until I reached the nearest bush which I proseeded to barber briskly. It was McGland, looking refreshed after his snooze under the weigela and spoiling for action.

"Look, is there a pub in this town?" he asked, flourishing a new cigarillo as he hove into view. "Not a cocktail lounge — a pub. A saloon. Someplace where the tablecloths are never changed, and cockroaches the color of these women march steadily across the walls."

I thought a moment, revolving in my mind what the town had to offer in the way of them rather exacting standards. "Indelicato's" I said finally, which would be the closest. "Not the upstairs dining room, but the bar down in the basement. If we want to eat we can get either fancy Italian food or a plain pizza or hero sandwich. How does that strike you?"

McGland nodded, looking around as though at surroundings whose elegance had begun to pall on him. There was a sound of footsteps and panting nearby, then the human colt crashed through the brush and burst into view. He looked hot but was running easily, his long legs moving like pistons, his fists at his sides. He ignored us and ran straight for the pool, into which he dove head first, swimming its length and hauling himself out on the other side, pulling his dripping trunks up around his wiry loins as he jogged for the back door of the house. The same pitiful look passed across McGland's face as he watched the vision of clean-limbed Youth vanish.

"That your car out there?" he asked.

"Yes but I'll have to go home first and change. I can pick you up about seven or a little after. How's that?"

"I'll be waiting on the road."

eleven

GALLOPING HOME IN the flivver I could see the attic turret on the farmhouse blazing in the evening light. The sun was far from setting, but the low glazed octangle on our rooftop gave back its rays in a dazzling band of gold, behind which I seemed to catch a distinct other flash. Mare was watching my return from the Springers with a pair of binoculars.

The innocent expression with which she pretended to be tidying up the salesroom when I entered through it was a howl. Feeling good, I picked up the cat and threw it in the dog's face. "I shan't be home for dinner," I announced.

"Why not?"

"I'm going to dine out with Gowan McGland."

"Who's *that*?"

"A poet."

"One of them." This was another three-minute boff. By them she meant not artists but commuters, with which she lumped in all intellectual and literary life, a pretty wobbly identification. To equate McGland with the sheepherders was really something. I paused briefly for station identification and then said, "This man is from Scotland."

"Where did you meet him?"

"Oh around town. He's a famous poet. Geneva reads him in college. She's got his records."

It went against my grain to use terms like "famous poet" which, I now knew, never crossed the lips of people in whose circles famous poets were to be found, any more than among the truly cultured and sophisticated you ever heard the words cultured and sophisticated spoken. I was onto all of that.

Who was sitting at the kitchen table but Mrs. Punck, surrounded by her luggage. Viz: 3 wicker suitcases and various cartons tied with cord — all her wordly goods outside her furniture and a few other things she had sent to storage.

"Ah, moved in for real are we?" I said.

"Hello, Frank. I didn't want to ask Harry Pycraft to take my things all the way upstairs," she said, giving her back hair a pat, "being as how he was kind enough to haul them here for me in his car. Being as how everyone else seemed to be busy."

"Its the least he could do considering he kicked you out of where you were. Well that's progress."

"Besides I don't think it proper to let a gentleman all the way into your bedroom."

"Well Harry Pycraft is no gentleman, so don't have no qualms on that score."

Determined to welcome Mrs. Punck, the handle of the largest suitcase hung by one hasp, so I picked it up like a young stevedore and swung it onto my shoulder, with such a will that it sailed clear on over and landed on the floor behind me with a crash. The snaps flew open, scattering the contents across the linoleum, viz: one hot water bottle, a flannel nightie embroidered in tiny rosebuds, and a large, armor plate corset. "Thank you," said Mare, stooping to collect these and other objects.

Clucking apologies, I knelt to retrieve some myself, only to have Mrs. Punck, blushing like a bride, get down beside *me*. Making the second time that afternoon that people got on their knees to deal with embarrassment. "If this is hospitality," says Mare, giving me a look.

I liked this criticism. I ate it up. It was a necessary part of the revitalization going on in this whole house. I welcomed it even when it was imported, for instance by the minister. Because they had asked him to come to the house and labor with me. He pretended it was just a routine pastoral call, not to set my back up too much. They didn't realize the to-do tickled me pink.

"Haven't seen you in church in some months, Frank," he had said scratching himself behind the ear with his pipe stem. "I wish you'd come and worship with us again soon. And do come to the spring social next week, even though you haven't been to services. We want you to feel a member of the congregation."

"Fine!" I said. "Who is she?"

He told them not to despair, it was just a phase lots of people went through and come out O.K. on the other side without permanent harm. I had stood at the head of the stairs listening to them whisper together in the front hall when he left. He said a young divinity school graduate was coming as his assistant, who had training in psychological counseling they were giving theological students these days, and that he would send him over the minute he arrived. Or he might call the local rabbi in for consultation. He was very good at these things. "But we're not Jewish," Mare said. "I know," he said. "It's very hard."

As I started away again with the closed suitcase, this time carrying it by the handle, Mare detained me with a hand on my arm. I instantly sensed some more of her strategy, her trick of wringing another concession from me when she had me deep in the doghouse, like the time I was caught red-handed stealing chickens (my own!) which she had used as a lever to get my permission to move her mother in.

"What are you doing tomorrow, Pa Spofford? George has to go to Bridgeport and can't take Ma to the Golden Age Club. We were hoping this time you'd *stay for the meeting.* Meet some real people."

"Oh, not that!" I says, and give my "rotten" laugh.

The instant I set the grip down in Mrs. Punck's room I shot back downstairs on tiptoe to hear some more criticism. I stood on the second step from the bottom, just around the corner, and listened. They were talking in whispers.

"It isn't just the fast crowd he's got mixed up with," Mare was saying. "It's everything. The way he acts and talks. Like what he said just now about real people. I think his mind is effected."

"I don't think he hears very well," Mrs. Punck whispered back. "He couldn't have understood what you said, because his answer just didn't make any sense. Have you had his ears examined lately? I find he has trouble understanding the simplest things, like proverbs and sayings."

"No, it's not that. He knew what we said, and he was being — what's that word I'm thinking of? Oh, it's on the tip of my tongue. It starts with a 'd'. *You* know. For this type of wickedness among the high-muckamucks."

Mrs. Punck didn't seem to know the word, but I did, and I wanted her to hear it. I wanted this criticism very much. So much so that I was willing to pay the price for it, namely admit that I had been eavesdropping.

"Deckadent?" I says, coming into the kitchen.

"If the shoe fits," says Mare.

I made for the next suitcase.

"We were just talking about the kind of people you get thrown in with to do the jobs you seem to like now, Frank," Mrs. Punck took up, with that patient reasonableness that was one of her more disturbing attractions. I had to harden my heart against her again. "Well money makes them that way I guess. Success. It's an attitude toward life human nature seems to get into when it develops in a certain direction. I think it's behind all the loose morals and the divorces too. The more you get the more you want."

"Want," Mare chimed in. What an echo chamber the place was going to be with two women in it! "Want," I threw in for good measure, striding between them with a grip in either hand. "Yes, scratch a commuter," I says disappearing, "and the dollars will take care of themselves." Garbling proverbs was a special form of befuddling them that I had been refining. I left them sitting there, with their cattle patience.

After smashing the last of Mrs. Punck's baggage I stayed upstairs to take a shower. I rummaged around in Geneva's phonograph records, but though there was some poetry in it there was no McGland that I could find. I wrote a few pages of this Journal, then dressed and went down. Mrs. Punck had tied on an apron and was baking a cake to show how she was going to pitch in around here and be far from a burden. I put up my guard.

"Got your glad rags on, eh Frank?" she greeted me cheerfully over her shoulder from the sink. "When are you going to meet this Mr. Gland?"

"Sevenish."

She mixed the cake batter standing at the kitchen table, and I sat a minute to watch. I felt a flicker of corruption in the light I now viewed Mrs. Punck in — like something in a Currier and Ives print, which I now took in on another level. I had come to see her as I was myself once seen, a bit of human bric-a-brac. Yet as she bent over the table I could note the straight line of scalp down the middle of her parted hair, a clean scalp, always smelling of soap, as I knew from coming near her accidentally or otherwise, like at teatime at my table or hers. I pursued a parallel between Mrs. Punck and her cozy domestic wares. Not only was she round and plump as her favorite tea-pot — now visible on my own shelf — with eyes as blue as its glaze, but there was about her a general ora testifying to a lifetime of propinquity to herbs. A woman like that around the house was a pleasure well remembered. I jerked up my guard again, giving myself a fresh reminder of the gulf widening between us daily, a sort of booster shot on that.

"Thanks for taking my stuff up. Its just that I mustn't do too much lifting on account of my back. Don't want my disc slipping out again, do we? Look," she says, lifting out a glop of the batter to test it for consistency, "don't feel too badly about Mare. She tends to make a mountain out of a molehill."

"Out of a what?"

"Molehill. *Mole-hill*," Mrs. Punck repeated, shaping the syllables exaggeratedly for my benefit.

"That's neatly put, Mrs. Punck."

"Call me Eunice. You mean you've never heard that expression before?"

"No, I can't rightly say I have."

"Well its very common." She went to the icebox for a drop more milk. From there she continued cheerfully, "But at the same time, watch out about getting in too deep where you don't belong. That leads to heartache. Getting in a rut is bad, but far worse is landing in the ditch because you swerved out too far too suddenly. I needn't say any more than that to Frank Spofford. He's an intelligent man and knows that a stitch in time saves nine."

"Saves what?" I said, wondering in my own mind just how far this pastime could be legitimately carried.

"Nine, *nine*." She held up that many fingers.

I watched her pick up the wooden spoon set down in order to

do this, and then beat a little more milk into the batter. After a minute I says, "Nine what?"

She dropped everything and heaved a sigh. "Stitches of course! What else? Are you deef? Don't you think you should see a doctor and have your ears examined?"

"Oh I see. Your using the term in a figurative sense."

Just then the banjo clock on the wall struck seven and I rose and got under way.

Galloping back to the Springers to pick up McGland I toyed with the notion of showing *him* what I'd written so far, and promptly vetoed it. I now looked on my Journal less as something to be published (either now or fifty years hence when all concerned are dead) than as a means of getting something out of my system for its own sake. Thats the purpose of all art anyway, we now know — to exercise the ghost of something. Be it an unhappy childhood, a tyranical father or a dominating mother — the artist is always exercising its ghost. Like there's a Broadway playwright who is suppose to always portray women as awful bitches and battleaxes because with each such characterization he gets to exercise his mother. My ghost was the need to belong, somewhere, somehow, with something, and since I was exercising it daily with what I slapped down on paper, sometimes at white heat, why, publication was not of the essence. That being the case why the hell revise? Why the hell bother about consistency in spelling, use and construction, and all the other things Flahive had had kittens about at Indelicato's that time? Of course I spell words differently at different times, sure I write a number out in letters one time and dash it down as a numeral or a fraction the next, depending on the heat of the composition. Generally I say "would of", though I realize "would have" is the preferred usage. Grammarians say a double negative makes a positive, yet if I want to be extra positive by using two negatives are they with me as having achieved that end? In any case the whole thing will have to stand as it is, to the point where I bring it, which God alone knows. The very thought of writing a whole nother draft gives me a headache.

I thought McGland would be curled up like a dead rhododendron leave with a book or a drink at the back of the house, but he was waiting and watching for me on the road in front. He had the usual cigarillo smoking in a corner of his mouth. He pitched it away before climbing into the Ford.

"Is that all they have to do around here is devote themselves to getting brown?" was one of the first things he said.

"I haven't seen a white woman in six months," I said.

McGland gave the mirthless snort I remembered about him. He never patronized anybody. He never called anybody or anything wonderful, and he didn't the flivver either as he turned his attention to it, asking about its vintage, model and condition. He had on unpressed green slacks and the brown tweed coat between the lapels of which hung a stained tie, that he presently clawed loose from the shirt collar. He quizzed me about American life, asking me how long people here had been wearing plastic clothes, and whether they were really spun out of soybeans and flu germs; whether it was true that flowers bought at the supermarket were guaranteed; whether he had heard correct that we had developed supersonic dry cleaning, where you *bombed* the dirt from clothes by vibration, and that we had a vacuum cleaner nobody had to operate — you just set it in the middle of the room and it drew dust from the remotest corners by electronic suction. I said I hadn't heard of some of those things but I shouldn't put it past us. He turned the vacuum cleaner idea over in his mind with a kind of lazy amusement. Mightn't it suck the bobby pins and small change off the bureau top and little Dresden figurines off the whatnot? Then he became serious again and asked whether all American couples slept in twin beds. I said I couldn't answer that but they all seemed to in the ads, when they weren't laying wide awake in them.

Suddenly he fell silent and took something from his pocket and began to fiddle with it. Curiosity got the better of me and I turned my eyes without turning my head. He was holding a jackknife with more attachments than I had ever seen before, all of which McGland picked open. It really bristled with gadgets when they were all unfolded. He held it out and contemplated it. "Is crime in this country really as bad as people say? Juvenile delinquency and gang wars and all that?"

"You're not likely to run into that much out here, but I guess it's bad enough in the big cities. Isn't that a Boy Scout knife?"

"Yes." He held it toward me so I could see it better. The attachments included a nail file, fork, spoon, bottle opener, corkscrew and screw driver, besides, of course, the knife blades. He closed them all again one by one, being very careful not to injure his hand, and pocketed the knife.

"Are you carrying that around for protection?" I asked. "Because of what you've heard about this country?"

"Well it isn't only this country of course."

McGland liked Indelicato's even before we got inside. I took him directly into the downstairs bar by the back door. It had the pleasant quality of a root cellar McGland liked a bar to be, intimately cool and humid he said, condusive to quickly sprouting friendships and dankly flowering thoughts. He breathed a grateful "Ah!" as we entered. I introduced him to Indelicato who happened to be there at the moment and not upstairs. He had to look at me twice, or pretended to, making off he didn't recognize me all spruced up. And indeed McGland the cultural star looked more at home in this joint than me the chicken farmer. Evidently this business of crossing class lines was trickier than you thought — or easier than you imagined. But pouring us our martinis I could see Indelicato was waiting for McGland to come to focus too. He didn't have him quite. I think he put him temporarily in the Miscellaneous pigeonhole reserved for strangers who were neither Italians from the riverfront or Bridgeport Hungarians on the one hand, or commuters slumming on the other. Upstairs in the main restaurant it was more conventional; here in the bar (with its ½ dozen dinner tables too) the mixture was complicated. He watched McGland view with approval the single couple eating spaghetti by candlelight, then walk with his martini to an electric bowling game standing in one corner.

"This place reminds me of my favorite pub in Glasgow," McGland said. "Stone foundations four feet thick and that damp, damp smell. Gives you the feeling a drinker wants."

"What's that?" Indelicato asked, who after twenty years tending bar didn't know.

"That he's a mushroom." McGland abandoned the bowling machine and came over and patted a stool preparatory to sitting on it. "Ever notice how barstools are unconsciously made in the image of a mushroom? The drinking soul is that, sensing itself sprout deliciously and damply within itself." I watched Indelicato for the effect of this, identifying myself with it. "Those of us who drink seriously belong to this class of thallophytes: mushrooms, molds, mildews, rusts and smuts, characterized chiefly by absence of chlorophyll (no sun, just electric light) and by subsisting on living or dead organic matter." He laid a hand on my shoulder with unexpected joviality. "How's that? You tell me about roses, I'll tell you about mushrooms." But he didn't give anybody much chance to tell him anything that night, or ever, once he was under sail, as I was about to learn to my regret. "Fungus: a spongy morbid growth, as proud flesh formed in a wound. Poetry: same thing."

Was he one them lushes, off and galloping on one? An academic question, because the first martini was followed by a steady parade, so that by eight thirty he had had six or seven to my own slowly nursed two. A kind of lazy, loitering smile, as though some secret humor was playing inside him, became fixed on his lips; his black eyes seemed to recede, but back in their depths, under the bulging brow, they glittered watchfully, alert to every woman in the place. His speech, which God knows was burred enough to begin with, slowed and thickened some more as though his tongue was collecting a nap of some sort, maybe that thallophyte spoor itself. What worried me most was the watchful eye on other pastures behind all that Scotch *gemütlichkeit.* "Let's eat," I said nervously.

McGland didn't eat his spaghetti exactly — he inhaled it. Forkfuls of it vanished like objects into that electronic vacuum cleaner we were just talking about. Meatballs disappeared intact, interrupted by swallows of Chianti or pauses to use a napkin in which often as not his necktie was entangled. I had purposely ordered a small bottle of wine, soon gone. When the waitress brought over another I said, "We didn't order that." She said, "Compliments of the next table."

There were four people at it. One man was a handsome Sicilian bandit type with a blonde girl, the other a young priest escorting what looked like his sister. The priest smiled and raised his glass to us. McGland rose and went over to their table where he stood a minute or two in a hum of flattery. Admirers. The priest was a teacher at a nearby Catholic college who had recognized him and said he looked forward to hearing him read on the campus in the fall. He did the introducing, courteously twisting in his chair to include me but I turned it off with a that's-all-right shake of my head. McGland wore his flustered boy's smile, while gazing down at the sister in a manner that caused her to draw her stole around her shoulders.

One by one I noticed the drinkers at the bar begin to take the scene in, till almost everyone in the small taproom was listening. Through this gawking I sensed a faint undercurrent of hostility from the three punks who had taken positions at the end spot vacated by McGland and me when we went to our table. They were obvious regulars here, young lugs probably fresh off trucks or construction gangs or factory lines, scrubbed and dressed for the night with clean sport shirts of which they wore the collars spread out over their coats. Once I thought I heard them mutter the word "commuters" in resentment, as they glared at us.

You've often read in fiction passages beginning "Desmond had no idea how he got to a telephone," or "Carruthers could never afterward reconstruct the events of that night." That's bunk, the fakery of authors shirking their obligation in a pinch. Desmond knew perfectly well and Carruthers would never forget. I could always afterwards recall the chain of events climaxing that crazy night with McGland despite the semi-fog I was now beginning to share with him. Because I took advantage of his absence to quickly send down my own gullet most of the complimentary bottle of Chianti to keep it from going down McGland's. So I was in a fair way to get as fuzzy as him, hardly a solution to the problem. But we were sobered up quite abruptly.

"Tell me," the blonde woman was asking, her hand at her own neckline in loo of a shawl, using the excuse of toying with some beads, "how long are you going to be around?"

"I don't know yet," McGland said. "No definite plans after September. It depends. I'll see what I'll see."

"Tell me, where are you staying?" the other girl asked, a short dark girl who bore an unmistakeable family resemblance to the priest. The tallest of the three lugs at the bar was heard to mutter "Tell me, tell me," in a comical aping of this upper-class speech. His friends laughed. I hadn't realized how nasty waiting for a place at what was probably an old hangout of theirs had made them. With a few under their belt they were prepared to be ugly.

"I'm staying at the Springers."

"Oh yes, Bobsy. I know her well," said the blonde.

Here a definite snicker was heard from the card at the bar, followed by "Who doesn't?" McGland and his fans didn't hear it but I did, and I turned and glared at the guy, who acknowledged hisself author of the remark by returning my gaze with cool insolence. There was no mistaking its gist. It was suggestive and he meant it to be.

I got up and walked the eight feet or so to the bar, trying not to be conspicuous. But Indelicato noticed the menace sprouting there and leaned over the bar and said to the trouble-maker, "What's the matter, Joe? Had one too many already?" When Joe said nothing Indelicato looked at me. I said, "Some of us here would thank him to keep his voice down, or better yet watch his tongue."

"Who'll make me, Pop?" says Joe.

"Look," I says, "I've knocked the ears off bigger than you in my time, and maybe I can do it yet."

"Care to try?"

"All right, all right you guys," Indelicato cut in, "let's knock it off. Everybody back to his own kind."

A more apt choice of terms could not have been imagined — or more unfortunate. By putting his finger on the problem he put it on the guy's gripe, touching thereby a tender nerve. It was exactly the sense of being crowded out of an old-time neighborhood joint by a cultural set discovering it that rankled the regulars. Their underlying resentment had pretty well boiled to the surface by the time McGland, sensing the ruckus behind him, turned from his admirers to me.

"What's the trouble?" he asked, coming over.

"He spoke disrespectfully of your hostess, and I took exception," I said.

"I see."

McGland's face was a sight to behold. He enjoyed the role of gallant, but that of knight was something else again. He had no stomach for that. Moreover the defense of a woman's honor by one who had compromised it was one for the book, though precisely therein may have lain a kind of rye justice. And of course there were other members of the fair sex looking on now, including some very fetching acquaintances of the lady love in question, to wit the ones he had just been buttered up by as their hero. All these factors, together with the confidence that the church would surely intervene before any blows were struck, emboldened our McGland. Giving his belt a hitch he says, "Well in that case we'll have to ask for an apology, won't we?"

"Here or outside?" says the jackanapes.

The two of them stood glaring at one another, breathing heavily and swelling up like blowfish. It must have seemed to McGland an unconscionable time for the sound on which he had been banking to materialize, namely the cloth scraping back his chair and coming over to make reason prevail. McGland managed a finely timed threatening motion, cocking back his arm for a blow in a way that looked fearless yet made it convenient for the priest to grab and restrain him. Which was what happened — for the moment.

"Now isn't this a ridiculous way for grown men to behave? May I suggest we all go quietly back to our food and drink?"

"Father," the guy called Joe smoothly answered, "that's just the thing we can't do here any more. You know when church members can't find a seat on Christmas and Easter because they're crowded out of their pews by people who never go the other fifty weeks of the year? That's how we feel here — only we're crowded out *all* the time lately. Bars like these are our bars. We helped build them up. They were meant for our kind. We shouldn't be frozen out of where we belong by people who think they're slumming."

"I don't feel I'm slumming," said the priest, "though you tempt me to that conclusion."

"A cigar for that one Father!" Indelicato barked. "O.K., that's all now, all!"

It might have been had it not been for McGland. Confident that the danger was now past, he got more truckulent. Sure that restraining hands had ruled out hostilities encouraged him now to press for the demands of chivalry. "All right, but I'd still like to hear a word of apology for what was said. That much the case calls for."

"I think he's right there," I put in, "on general principles."

"What ails you guys?" said the jackanapes. "You must of misunderstood what I said. What are you so touchy about this for, Pop?"

"Because it concerns a lady," I says, now irritated more by the succession of Pops than by the aspersions on Womanhood to be frank about it. "And a friend of ours — mugg!"

"She has lots of friends, was all I said. Everybody knows that."

"How do you?"

"I use to deliver oil there."

It probably suffised as satisfaction without striking a note of nuckling under to us. After all nobody could *prove* any slur or offense was intended by the remark, or that it had been accompanied by a snicker. In fact if he was shrewder he might accuse *us* of casting a shadow on Bobsy Springer's name by taking it the way we had — or the way I had. Maybe my reaction had a significance of its own, there being fire where there was smoke because of what I knew and read into the remark. In view of all this I said "That's better," to up the amount of apology that could be read into his explanation, and with an extra glower at the jackanapes as I took McGland by the arm myself and drew him away. But now it was the jackanapes who had to make a little final display of masculinity. He was still smarting under the priest's rebuke, of which he probably resented the adroit phrasing as much as the content. Anyhow as a parting shot he threw at me, "And after this watch who you call a mugg — dodo!"

I let him have one across the chops. Though it was with the back of my hand you could hear it clear across the bar. The priest, who had started to sit down at his table again in the belief that matters were resolved, rose again with a groan. He never penetrated the malay though. The jackanapes knocked me backward over our table, not socking me but pushing me with the flat of both hands. Then he whirled sharply, antisipating action from McGland. McGland's face was a sight to behold again, but probably not quite on the same scale. Confident again of intervention from the cloth, he cocked his two fists in a manner at once menacing and scared. He kept one hand near his mouth, I noticed, as though favoring his teeth. "So you'd hit him, would you?"

"I didn't hit him. I only pushed him out of the way, and in self-defense. But in your case I'll make an exception. Care to make something out of it? Why don't we step outside and finish this?"

"I'm perfectly willing to finish it here," McGland said, not taking any chances on the church failing to tag along and intervene. But the church had more important concerns than stopping the battle either indoors or out, to wit the wounded and dying. Back on my feet again, I was feeling under the back of my coat. My hand come out red. In falling onto the table I had overturned the wine bottle, which lay in a widening stain on the tablecloth. I had drunk the majority of the wine but the dregs were enough to make quite a vivid blot. Now in its straw covering you didn't know but what the bottle had been broken, and the red soaking my shirt and coat was blood. That was what worried the priest, who lifted my coat, pulled out my shirttail and had a look. "It's all right Father," I said, and he said, "I'm not so sure. Looks like a little cut there." He examined the bottle and found it was cracked. "Better have it tended to," he said. "You might have tiny bits of glass in there and never know it. You'll do that now, won't you?" I promised him

I would. No use pretending I was unmindful of the worried gazes of the two beautiful young women.

McGland and Joe were now definitely committed to a fight. No blow had as yet been struck, but they were circling one another in the prescribed fashion in the space cleared for them, and in a style from which there was no drawing back. They crouched lower and lower, till they looked like wrestlers about to grapple rather than boxers weaving for the first punch. Both were breathing heavily. The dance went on. After a minute or two Joe's hand moved cautiously upward toward his pocket, or seemed to, in a motion that McGland at any rate thought he understood. Quick as a flash his own hand went to his pocket and came out with something. It was the Boy Scout knife. At the same time backing off just a shade, crouching low, not taking his eyes off his opponent, therefore not looking at the weapon in his hand, he slowly opened one of its attachments. It was the spoon. This at the ready, he circled with a cautious but formidable air, always keeping the weapon at belt level like he probably seen members of street gangs do in American movies, never taking his eyes off the other guy's hands. Joe had seen the wicked glitter of what McGland brandished, with a split-second downward flick of his eyes. "Oh, so that's the way it is?" he said. Turning his head, he gave his two companions some kind of signal. Then *they* began to circle and weave, trying to maneuver around behind McGland. They obviously intended to jump him. It was here that the priest stepped between them to put a stop to it at whatever risk to himself. But it wasn't necessary. At that moment the front door burst open and two policemen entered with drawn pistols.

Someone, it was never discovered who, had slipped into a phone booth at the very first sign of trouble and called the cops. A prowl car patrolling the vicinity had been given the message by short-wave radio of course, and been on the scene in two minutes. It was all over in three more. One of the cops pinned McGland's arms from behind — to McGland's considerable relief I might say — while the other struck the knife to the floor with the barrel of his pistol. The second one picked it up, closed and confiscated it.

By questioning a few witnesses, mainly Indelicato and the priest, the police realized it was just another barroom brawl with nothing very serious about it except, from their point of view, this desperate character carrying a knife which he seemed ready to flash at the drop of a hat. This rated a little questioning at headquarters.

"How about him?" McGland said, pointing at Joe.

"He wasn't wielding a knife," one of the cops answered, "so as far as we're concerned he's just another tavern loudmouth. I've taken his name in case we want to ask him anything later, but I think you'd better come along on a charge of armed assault. We'll take your friend too for some first aid."

I sat in the back seat of the squad car, leaning forward with my coat in my lap and holding my shirt up under my arms while one of the cops applied to the oozing cut a dab of Mercurochrome from a first aid kit they carried. It was the same cop who had found me peering through the fence at the Beauseigneurs party from the Kidderminsters yard, the night I first began catering. "You certainly get around, don't you?" he said. McGland rode in the front with the driver.

"Can I have my Boy Scout knife back?"

"No, sir."

When the cop with me finished dabbing the cut he closed the kit and settled back with a sigh. "This has been some night," he said.

"You can say that again," the driver said. "Personally I'm glad I'll be sixty in two more years. I'll welcome retirement. Not that I aim to sit around and rot. I want to do something, but something peaceful."

"Like what?"

"Oh something that's not work but isn't puttering either. Something in between? Pleasant and relaxing but still productive. Know what I mean? What my wife and I have been thinking of is maybe moving a little farther out in the country and settling down on a little chicken farm or something. That ought to be one place where a fellow could get some peace."

twelve

McGLAND GOT THE BRUNT of the questioning but I stayed in the room where Sergeant Lawson, the driver, took down his statement in an arrest report. A Band-Aid was all my cut turned out to need. The cubicle we sat in was so tiny that McGland's and the Sergeant's knees touched under the desk they faced one another across, me at the side with my chair straddling the threshhold. McGland had his as far back against the wall as he could get it. He was hot and sleepy and thoroughly out of sorts. I could read his thoughts. He was beginning to wish he had never come back to America to repeat his first and second triumphal tours. What a nuisance for a visiting poet, which was how he represented himself as to occupation when asked that, me adding "of international repute." He gave a Welsh address, naming one them Welsh towns of gag length. It *was* a gag as a matter of fact; his home town was one in the north of Scotland, but he preferred to give the law a hard time with a name it had to write out with sweat and blood, and which it finally gave up and just put down Wales. We were both determined to keep his local hostess's name out of it. When it came down to it we said he was staying with me.

"Now you had an argument at the bar which developed into a fight," Sergeant Lawson said, hiking up a pants leg and writing in the arrest book. McGland muttered inarticulately at this opening with which, for sheer meaninglessness, you could have no quarrel. We stared at the moving pencil, our thoughts hostile yet curiously inert, like a hive of numbed bees that neither outrage nor amazement could seem to rouse to life. This was a little truer of McGland than me, probably. He should of gone to the south of France and then on down to Italy and Spain, he told me later, instead of returning to the States for triumphal tour No. 3. His head went down slowly till at last it came to rest on the crook of his arm on the desk.

Cradled in which position he had to roll his eyes up into his skull to look at the cop.

"O.K." The cop took a long drag on a cigarette and studied what he had written down. He returned the cigarette to an ashtray. McGland was hypmatized by the fan of blue smoke fluttering upward from its burning tip. He followed it with drooping eyes, a few inches from the ashtray. He adjusted his head on his arm as you do on a pillow. He seemed to go to sleep. "Then as the fight grew in intensity, you pulled a knife."

"Spoon," McGland reminded him listlessly.

"As it turned *out*." The cop raised a finger to emphasize the delicacy of the point. "*You* thought it was a *blade*. That was what you intended to pull out and do business with. So to all intents and purposes that was what you pulled on him. That made it assault and battery."

"Battery schmattery," said McGland, using an expression he had picked up on some of the college campuses where he had read. "Knife, fork, spoon. It was a Boy Scout Knife."

"That's the one thing in your favor — that you weren't carrying a switchblade, or anything longer than four inches. But you did pull a knife."

"Spoon."

"Knife."

"Spoon." McGland raised his head and pulled a face. We felt he might be going to come to life after all. "All right. I pulled a knife, fork, spoon, corkscrew, nail file and bottle opener," he said. "Let's get it all in there."

"All right I will." The sergeant was getting testy, and I give McGland a warning poke under the desk, which brought a look from the sergeant so cramped were our quarters. I must of poked him.

"And that I acted in self-defense," McGland said. "Put that in the record too. The other bloke was going to pull a knife on me first. He put his hand in his pocket, or moved it toward his pocket, obviously not to get out a handkerchief and blow his nose. My friend here will corroborate that." I did, with a nod. "So why shouldn't I defend myself in the same way?"

"But he didn't pull any knife. He didn't even have any on him. We frisked him."

"But I *thought* he was. I thought it as much as I thought what I pulled on him was a blade instead of a spoon. You're the one who keeps insisting it's motive that counts. Is it any disgrace to be quicker on the draw than your opponent?"

"You've been seeing too many movies."

"I've been living in London too long. We have teddies there, you know. You're not the only country with juvenile delinquency."

"No but we have more here than any one else. We lead in it."

"Are you an America Firster?"

"No but I have a feeling for my country." The cop put his pencil down. "So your English. I thought your accent was different but I couldn't quite place it."

"No, I'm Welsh, and I think, if I may, that I would now like to make a telephone call." McGland rose, and I did too, to make room for him. "As I believe is my right under law?" he added.

McGland could come to life with miraculous suddenness from the most profound funks, under certain circumstances such as giving public readings or pulling a hoax. He now spoke with a tone that made the sergeant nervous. The sergeant said yes, he would be permitted to telephone someone if he wished. Whom did he wish to call, his lawyer? "No, the Welsh Embassy. As a citizen of Wales," McGland said, looking at the telephone booth in the main room. "I have a friend who's an attaché. I rather think he'll put a stop to this nonsense in short order."

Now definitely anxious, and throwing a worried look toward the main desk where the captain was sitting, the sergeant said, "You going to phone New York?"

"No, that won't be necessary. He happens to be staying at a local motel here with the Welsh delegation to the United Nations. They're here for a reception being tendered them by the governor of the state."

The sergeant was in a huddle with the captain before Mc-

Gland was in the booth. As I sat on a bench taking the scene in, I turned over in my mind a puzzle about McGland. It was a mystery a number of writers touched on, that I later read. How could a man who mumbled so in ordinary conversation read with such ethereal magic on the public platform and into phonograph mikes? Did I seem to recall that he was once a professional radio actor with the B.B.C.? That only doubled the mystery — how could a mouthful of marbles read *and act* so beautifully? His physical appearance was the same as his diction in real life — sloppy. He slouched around in soiled tweeds and mumbled at you, he slapped and snickered about like a naughty schoolboy. How could such a person be transformed into an angel when publicly required? The act of performance itself must galvanize him into it.

It was a performance he put on now for the law. It had its effect. I heard words and phrases like "famous poet" and "international incident" exchanged in whispers between the sergeant and the captain, who both looked worried now. The sight of McGland emerging from the phone booth with his stomach in and his chest out, rather than the other way around, striding over like an important American businessman, made the officials nod and hastily agree to something.

"You two can go now," Sergeant Lawson said. "We'll overlook it this time."

"Can I have my Scout knife back?"

Lawson shot an uncertain look at the captain, who shrugged. "All right," he said, and went into the anteroom to get it out of a desk drawer. "But be careful where and how you take it out," he warned McGland as he handed it over to him, "or next time you may get into serious trouble."

It was cool and pleasant outside the police station. I was for making the cops drive us back to Indelicato's for my flivver but McGland said his friend, who was on his way over, would take us in his car. He laid down on the grass with a grateful groan to wait for him. I followed suit, asking him what this was all about. "There ain't no Welsh Embassy, is there?" I said. "Ain't it part of Great Britain?"

"Go to the head of the class," McGland said. The lazy smile come into his face as he gazed up at the stars and wondered aloud when the police would tumble, if they ever did. "I thought I owed them that sporting chance to see through the hoax. I think that's the trouble with most practical jokers, don't you? I mean why they seem cruel? They seem cruel because they don't give their victims that sporting chance, most cases." He took out a tin of Between-the-Acts, offering me one. We both lit up. Then he filled me in on the guy we were waiting for. "This bloke I telephoned is English, with a really fruity accent, as well as an actor — I used to know him in the old B.B.C. days — and he'll do a State Department attaché to a T. I let him in on the jape, so he'll be breezing up presently with his bowler on, swinging a briefcase. Spats. The works. He's a real jessie."

"What's he doing here in Woodsmoke? And how come you can rout him out of bed at half past twelve?" I asked. The courthouse clock had just struck that.

"He's over here writing a book about the English artist in America and all that. Cultural cousins stuff. Why he's chasing me around. He wants to pick my brains badly enough to do me a favor like this. Now I'm almost sorry we got sprung so easily. It would have been a joy to watch him strut his stuff. You'll see what I mean."

We didn't have long to wait, but I filled the few minutes we did picking McGland's brains myself a little — about his previous tours, where he'd read, articles that had been written about him that I might look up. It got a little deep for me, and I said so. "I don't get it all but my daughter would." I laughed at the blunder. "Granddaughter."

Here McGland opened one eye. For a fleeting moment he resembled one them barnyard villains you see in movie cartoons, foxes and dogs that are always on the prowl and are always foiled by the smaller animals. There was something about him at once beastly and begiling, unscrupulous and devoted. I knew he liked me as he knew I liked him. But he was a rogue and we both knew that. Amoral is I guess the word for it. He closed both eyes again as though he didn't want to think about anything and said, "When did you say she was expected home?"

"Any day." I turned on one elbow and watched his face while I said, "I guess your pretty famous." This was a ornery measure to make him simper and look silly. It's how a compliment makes any of us look, of course, but McGland more than most. I didn't have long to enjoy the results though. A black Volkswagen like a hurtling turtle turned into view off Main Street and came to a stop on the station-house drive in a spray of gravel. The most dapper figure I ever saw or hope to see popped from the door like a slice of bread from a toaster, slapped the door smartly shut behind him and strode toward the steps swinging a briefcase.

"Mopworth!" McGland called, getting up.

Swiveling on the sole of one foot the newcomer made a right turn, like a soldier in answer to a military command barked at him, and marched across the grass toward us. He wore a natty double-breasted seersucker, white shirt with a collar pin and a Navy blue tie. "I say, Gowan!"

He didn't have spats on but he didn't need them. He was so British I thought he was kidding. He was also almost ridiculously good-looking. I thought I saw the same look of suffering envy pass across McGland's face at the sight of this sapling figure, brown eyes and gleaming smile as it did at the sight of Tad Springer's athletic beauty. McGland spanked the dirt from his thick flanks and introduced us. "Delighted," Mopworth said, with a bow from the waist that wasn't a bow from the waist so much as a nod with the entire upper half of the body. He seemed to *gesture* with his body too, as though he had at one time taken ballet lessons and was using in real life all the techniques he learned there and paid good money for to express himself as a muscular whole. At the same time all this was mixed up with the peculiar impression you couldn't get out of your mind, that the bird was engaging in a military drill. Maybe he had done a hitch in the armed forces and was using all that physical discipline too in real life. When McGland had told the story of the evening for about ten minutes, making no secret of how highly he appreciated the ingenuity that had enabled him to end it on the note he did, I broke in to remind them that my car was still at Indelicato's to be picked up. Mopworth pivoted on one foot and pointed at his own with his head, to indicate it was at our disposal. McGland climbed in back, I beside Mopworth in front.

Once he had been filled in on the events of the night Mopworth made no secret of his relief at not being called on to impersonate a chap from the Embassy after all. "I mean you put it to me out of a sound sleep, Gowan. Tooling down the Post Road I got to waking up and thinking isn't this a bit sticky? What if they ask for my credentials?"

"You could say you left them in London," McGland mumbled from the back seat. His voice had that low buzz into which it dropped whenever he was about to settle into hibernation, but he did say something about a nightcap. To which the jessie echoed "Rather!"

Indelicato was just closing up when we got there. Through the locked door I could see him inside tidying up for the night. I had gone over myself to try the door. Now I heard the jessie behind me.

"See here," he said in a whisper, "I'd like to know more about what this fracas was all about tonight. Gowan may have told you I'm doing this book. More than a bit of Boswelling about Gowan, mind you, but in any case he may clam up or have forgotten most of it by morning. So I'd like to talk to you if I may, so if you know somewhere else where we could have that nightcap. I mean I don't want to be an albatross, but I did roll out for you chaps."

I laughed nervously, not understanding much of what was said but sensing this was literary history in the making and glad to be in some way mixed up in it. I could hardly breathe, the credit this give me. There was also just a dash of justifying yourself to the family along with surprising your family when I said, "Let's go to my place. It's only down the road. You follow me." The jessie turned on his heel and marched back to his own car. "There shall be cakes and ale, yes, and ginger shall be hot i' the mouth," he promised as he tramped toward the Volkswagen and I made for the flivver.

I chuckled nervously to myself as I led them down the backroads, but as we approached the farmhouse I began to have actual qualms. There wasn't just the usual kitchen light left on: the whole house blazed with them. Were they waiting up for me on that scale? Was something wrong? Was someone sick?

I took my friends in the side door, which is really the front door as it leads directly into the parlor. We always let company in that way. Through the lace curtains behind the oval pane in the door I could see Mare and Mrs. Punck and George, all of them, sitting there. They seemed in good spirits. At least their faces didn't suggest trouble. The reason was soon evident. A fourth person walked into the parlor, laughing. Our girl was home!

"Geneva!" I said, leaving the two standing out on the porch.

"Grandpa!" She ran into my arms.

"We didn't expect you till next week."

"I cancelled my steamship passage at the last minute and flew home. I telephoned from New York — I figured that was enough of a surprise. I took the ten thirty home. I only just got here myself. Oh, it's good to see you, Grandpa."

She drew back, seeing the two figures outside. They were both grinning and waving their arms in a cloud of moth millers swirling around them in the porch light and flitting into the house through the screen door one of them, the good-looking one, was holding open.

"I want you to meet two of my very good friends," I said. "Mr. Gowan McGland — you've probably heard of him — and Mr. Alvin Mopworth of London. Gentlemen, my granddaughter, Geneva Spofford. Come in and meet the rest of the family."

thirteen

THERE WAS A couple of reasons why Geneva may not immediately of noticed the change in her grandfather. The first was that the change was only one side of a split personality that still had its other old side, between the two of which he constantly shuttled back and forth. But mainly Geneva had been undergoing transformations of her own. She was my granddaughter more than she was either of her parents' daughter. At Wycliffe she had met girls from Ohio and Chicago and even farther west who were more "eastern" than she, and had surrendered willingly to their influence. Uppermost among the girls whose spell she was under was this Pennsylvania classmate named Nectar Schmidt, who had been with her on the Latin American exchange fellowship. Later when I met Nectar I realized how much Geneva was modeling her speech and manner on Nectar's, in one them copying crushes young females of that age have. The fact was that I first noticed the change in *her*.

What the boys noticed was a strapping girl with hair like ripe wheat and rousing breasts, standing in sawed-off denim slacks and bare feet at which they must of promptly in spirit knelt, moaning her name whilst their arms in fancy encircled thighs that were like the pillars of a temple. There is after all no aphrodisiac like innocence. The southern sun had baked her arms to the color of peaches, and to sink your teeth into that flesh must be, you thought, to taste the juice of bleeding fruit. She had one defect, if in the long run it can be called that. (Stendhal reminds us that a flaw may multiply a virtue by ten, like a zero behind a integer.) The slight pop to her brown eyes give her that look of just having swallowed her gum, but they also light her face up with that staring, rather goofy beauty. I think it was the knowledge that her eyes bulged that made her constantly lower them, especially on meeting men, in a gaze at once bashful and hostile. Now to this may of been added a slight touch of self-consciousness with which she used the still unfamiliar vocabulary soaked up from the likes of Nectar Schmidt and a host of other ventriloquists lurcking in the background.

"There you were," she said, smiling at the floor as she recalled for McGland the time she had seen him pacing the railroad station at Wycliffe, "with a worried look on your face like those men — those men in ads, you know, who sort of wonder if they've invested wisely? Or think to themselves if

I'd only had a checkup six months sooner? And this is not good."

"I was afraid the train would never come, and I'd have to go back to that inn you have there."

"The Ethan Allen!" I says. I had stayed there. "They have a rope hanging out the window for a fire escape!" I cried to all collectively, even George and Mrs. Punck, not to mock and pain them so much now as to invite them to learn this light sophisticated talk, show the hang of it. "Talk about professional New Englanders!"

"And the menus on slates," said Geneva. "And that fussy cooking, sort of like *bride's cooking*? It's a place where they serve you *portions*?"

McGland was wide awake again. He took both the highball I gave him and the chocolate cake Mrs. Punck handed around, coffee to follow presently. Mopworth sat notebook on knee firing questions at McGland about the night's events. He was a shrewd cookie who knew that when McGland had a girl for an audience was the time to put him on. Mare wandered from room to room stalking the moth millers that had got into the house with a upraised copy of *But*. She had that look of udder indifference to the conversation that meant acute attention to every word of it. Mrs. Punck sat on the settle with her lap spread much too wide for this part the country, nodding and smiling at what was said and occasionally contributing a maxim of her own or a bit of vital statistics. She knew all the Indelicatos and when they had been born. George sat in the adjoining "small" parlor with a bottle of beer, bored enough for a man with degrees from 7 colleges. We all had our coats off. It was so muggy the potato chips made no noise when eaten.

"There I was, you see, with the three of them having at me, and only this knife." McGland, who had risen to act out the scene, exhibited the Boy Scout knife.

"I didn't even have that," I said, putting my beer down after a gulp.

"He didn't even have that. So there I was . . ."

McGland began to weave about the room in a humorous portrayal of combat, impersonating his assailant with swipes of his thumb across his mouth, to which the assailant had not been given but which muggs do in American movies, of which McGland was an addict. He danced around the parlor lightly on the balls of his feet. The jessie's pencil flew, taking down not only what McGland said but what he done. "Suddenly he reached toward his pocket for something, and I pulled out my knife and opened it — to this." Geneva laughed as the spoon came out, and McGland laid a hand on her shoulder as he wove on by. "The payoff, you see, was that I didn't *know*. I thought I was armed."

"What was the argument all about?" Mopworth asked.

McGland looked at me and I at him. I got to my feet, picking up my glass of beer. "Oh, those hoods were talking about some woman or other. We didn't even get who. But it makes no difference."

"Of course it doesn't," McGland said. "No man is going to sit idly by while someone, no matter who, is publicly called a tramp."

"Speaking of tramps," said Mrs. Punck, returning from the kitchen just then with the pot of coffee, "we rarely see those around here any more, though last year we had one going from door to door asking for handouts. I hadn't seen one for years. Hung about town for quite some time too. He probably got off a boxcar. But he did *not*, contrary to the popular notion, put a mark on the gate for other hoboes. Coffee, Mr. Gland?"

Most everybody had coffee, which we watched Mrs. Punck go around pouring. It was Mopworth who spoke up. "By the bye, Gowan, I don't want to switch the subject, but before we disband I do want to hear you out about this whole commuting business. Mrs. Punck speaking of the boxcars brings it to mind and I don't want to forget. I mean we don't in England have all this hoopla about a special cultural class, all those anthropological treatises and one thing and another. What say about the commuters? Any special thoughts on them, Gowan?"

There was another of the many reports from the small parlor. The copy of *But* came down on another moth miller, the mashed remains of which Mare flicked daintily from the magazine with her finger.

"Why, I read a rather interesting comment the other day," Geneva said. She fixed her butterscotch eyes on the floor at the first sign that she was again the center of attention. "That men commuting really enjoy the hardships they have to put up with on the New Haven railroad because it appeases their sense of guilt. They'd really like to ride in boxcars if they could."

"Guilt about what?" said McGland, stranded in the middle of the room with the knife in his hand and his story dangling unfinished.

"About leaving their wives home with a pack of kids and a sinkful of dirty dishes while they sit in air-conditioned offices and take clients out to three-hour lunches on expense accounts. Late trains and sitting in the broiling sun or freezing coaches with bedbugs in the seats gives them back the sense of being men again. Sort of the last pioneers?"

McGland nodded, absorbing this with a kind of roofful boredom. Then he looked down at the knife he was still clutching. "Well, there I was . . ."

"Gowan." The jessie took a swallow of his coffee, frowning. McGland was not sintillating on the subject of commuters. He must try another. He put him on with something related but different. "Gowan, do you find the *home* the American commuter — or subway rider for that matter — rides back to any different from the British? Let's talk about the home and what's happening to it."

"I'm not interested in the home," McGland said, closing and pocketing the knife as he sat down again. That kind of naughty-boy smile came to his lips. "I consider the home an invasion of privacy."

McGland showed off in this fashion for a good ½ hr. or more. But as he expanded under everyone's laughter, especially I suppose Geneva's, I began to notice a subtle change in Mopworth's attitude. I think that after so much of the star hogging the limelight it began to get to him. Of course I am only speculating, but there was a sudden shift in the kind of questions he asked. Those up to now had been of a kind that gave an intelligent fellow a chance to be witty. Now he seemed to feed him questions so hairy they could only elicit hairy answers. Like "Gowan, what's your opinion of the American woman?" or "Would you say that as a civilization we are getting soft?" I heard McGland murmur "Jesus" at the last one as he sank back in his chair and returned the jessie's look. But why would masculine jealousy over a woman enter into it if he was a jessie, as McGland gave me to believe? I didn't know. Maybe professional jealousy was at work here. Maybe the need to take McGland down a peg had suddenly become more important than an evening's harvest of quotable stuff for the book. McGland was a sight to behold as, crossing his legs and puffing at a cheroot with his eye on the ceiling, he drummed his fingers on the arm of his chair and tried to maintain the pose of a wit and deep thinker after Mopworth's hack-kneed question were we getting soft as a civilization. It hung in the air like a Damoclean sword as we watched and waited. He now looked like the man in the ad reading, "Are you sick of batteries that don't last?" Mrs. Punch's voice was the next one heard.

"People who have everything lack something," she said.

McGland shot his shirtsleeves back and wiped his brow with his fist, moving it across it once from left to right. He shifted his gaze from the ceiling to Mrs. Punch, who he scrutinized with prolonged interest, as though to say he had partisipated in conversations in the best New York and London drawing rooms but he had never heard the beat of this. He watched again as though hypmatized while Mrs. Punch rose and went to the sideboard where the chocolate cake was, cut him a second slice and laid it on his plate while he downed the last of his highball.

"Freshen that for you?" I said taking his glass. "I didn't know we were going to entertain no angels or I'd gotten some decent bourbon. This is just everyday stuff."

"It's the only time I drink."

We got on other aspects of this culture including why young girls take up horseback in such quantity, ever try to figure that one out? Someone give the psychological explanation, that they subconsciously admire their father through the stallion principle. So I says no, I think they are riding their mother, who was a nag, but I was a voice crying in the wilderness.

The jessie frowned at what he had wrote in his notebook, which seemed to be what Mrs. Punck said last, in a version he would probably never know whether he got right. He held his knees very tight together and he sat very erect in his chair. "How do you find journalistic standards here? Mary McCarthy said that writing about mass culture for a mass audience is the mirror on the whorehouse ceiling. What do you think of that?"

"I think that's quite a reflection," McGland says.

"Things are looking up anyways," I says, "since the face on the barroom floor."

But at last there was enough culture for one night and the guests got up to leave. At the door McGland said to Geneva, "I hope I'll see you before I go. Look, my hostess is giving a sort of do Saturday night. Why don't you come?"

"That's sweet of you, but if you're a house guest . . ."

"It's me the party's for. She's asked if there was anybody in particular I'd like to have. And there'll be so many people there nobody'll know the difference anyway. I've already asked five others." McGland laughed at this, deploring hisself as one deplores faults you're still trying to keep some tolerance and sense of perspective about. Charm plus irresponsibility won the day as ever.

"Well all right. Where are you staying by the way? I thought you were both at the motel."

"No, just Mopworth. I'm staying with the Springers."

Geneva flushed a deep red and dropped her eyes. "Oh. Well in that . . ." She clasped her hands behind her back like a child embarrassed at a social function, or stuck in the middle of a recitation. "I mean I'll have to see. I'm not quite sure about the date."

"I'll give you a ring."

When I had seen the callers out I turned from the shut door to see Mare standing alone in the parlor. George had run upstairs, Geneva into the kitchen to help Mrs. Punck with the cleaning up. The clock behind Mare said twenty minutes after two. She was watching me with an air of stern thought.

136

"Well! Wasn't that nice?" I says queasily. "Two English gentlemen, well one of them's Scotch, that I brought home for her to meet the first shot out of the box when she gets home! Hah?"

"I see your little game," she said, ignoring the testimonial to my own prowess as a social bushwhacker. "I see now what you had up your sleeve all along."

"What?"

"You want to get her back up there with the quality. For another chance."

"I'm glad to see you're getting around to looking at things my way," I says, and I was — glad that what had all along been bucked in theory was freely accepted now that it had begun to pay off in actual fact. It was a sweeter moment for Mare than for me, even, the knowledge that her snubbed daughter would return to the wrong doers in triumph on the arm of their guest of honor. "I'd like to see their faces," I said, reading her thoughts.

"Well you won't," she said, reading mine. "In case you've got any notions of being there in the garden passing out or dervs or what not. This one you'll keep out of sight. You've done your bit. You've paved the way for her, if that really was your bounden aim. Now you'll keep out of sight, mister man."

"Oh all right," I said, pleased enough to be justified at last in my own home again. It was reward enough. I turned to the hum of voices in the kitchen. "What if she won't go?"

"Leave that part of it to me."

By the time Geneva joined us in the parlor she had learned from Mrs. Punck what she hadn't earlier in the evening, about her grandfather's summer's didoes. She seemed to admire the aparent ease with which I moved in these new circles, but doubted that she could carry the day herself at the Springers. She didn't want no return match. She would not go.

Here Mare stepped in. Planting herself squarely in front of the seated girl, she laid down the law to her like I never heard the law laid down to anybody in that house before. The contest of wills was not a long one. The same timidity that had made Geneva lose heart at the prospect of going to the party caused her to crumble under the mother's determination that she damn well was going there. She was going to rub it in, but that wasn't all. There was a more positive, more constructive side. "You'll meet lots of nice boys there," Mare said to the girl, who sat with her great eyes lowered and wearing the shy and hostile look. "And I don't mean Tad Springer, nor Mr. McGland either for that matter. Just boys. Lots of them. Learn to *mix* more!"

"Oh well, I guess I have nothing to lose," Geneva said. The rebellion in her nature made her try to state as her own the decision into which she had been cowed. She rolled her eyes up. "And maybe Grandpa'll be there?"

"He will not."

"Mother, you act as though I should be ashamed of all of you."

Here Mare became actually menacing as she made a bludgeon of the *But*. She stood there tapping it in her palm like a billy.

"Now look here. We're scraping good money together to send you to college, penny by penny and dollar by dollar, and we aim to get our money's worth. What do you think we're educating you for if not that you should wind up above us? What good have all our sacrifices been if you can't manage to look down on us at least a little? Yes — feel ashamed of us!"

"Mother, there are times when you're positively schizoid."

Mare gave the modest grunt, grateful for the compliment and for her flesh and blood talking over her head, but at the same time with her old implication that flattery would get you nowheres. She was still laying down the law when I went upstairs to bed. The last thing I heard, listening on the landing with my toothbrush in my hand, was Mrs. Punck saying, "And there'll be Mr. Gland to make you feel to home, dear. You tell me he's suppose to be such a goat, but I don't know why you say that. He couldn't have been nicer to you."

fourteen

THE SEX LIFE AIN'T isolated any more than it is constant, but is so intimately bound and tangled up with other forces vying for the upper hand in the network of human emotions that elements remote from it may suddenly bring its sluggish stream to life, or reverse its course entirely, turning negative currents into positive, making a millrace of obstacles and grist of hostility. During the week in which Geneva's approaching party date promised the climax to a summer already like none we'd ever had, an overstimulated Spofford drove Mrs. Punck to the Y.M.C.A. for her Golden Age Club meeting and found hisself kidding her in a totally unaccustomed manner.

"How would you like a mink coat?" I suppose the relief at being out of the doghouse and vindicated in my summer's shenanigans snapped the windows of my spirit open, and flung my shutters wide.

"Goodness," Mrs. Punck says straightening her bonnet. It was a straw rig with a single flower that swayed on its wire stem as we bounced over the road to town, like the geranium in the box behind the car. In her lap lay her coat, pocketbook and minutes of the last meeting, for she had been voted secretary-treasurer of the outfit. "How would I ever get one of those?"

"How do women usually get them?" I repeated a off-color story I had heard at one of the better class parties I'd been to, to illustrate the point. "There, that draw a picture for you, darling?"

"What will people say?" said Mrs. Punck with a giggle.

"We can find out."

"Well I won't sleep with you," said Mrs. Punck who prided herself on her modernity where using expressions like that was concerned, and her ability to go along with japes and didoes that required broad-mindedness.

"Well then I'll send you one if you *don't*."

"What do you mean?"

"And jewelry and flowers and what not," I improvised in a sudden turn of fancy. "So you'll be compromised in the eyes of the world. I'll pay your rent, I'll be a sugar daddy in every manner possible. There's only one way you can avoid all that."

"How?"

"By living in sin."

"I get it now. You're switching it around to blackmail. You mean you'll threaten to give my life the appearance of evil if I don't commit it. In other words," Mrs. Punck went on, revolving the notion in her own wooly noddle, "to save my reputation I have to take leave of my virtue." This was pretty spry on the uptake for someone as rich in limitations as Mrs. Punck, and I made my appreciation known by answering smartly, "You got it, baby."

"What if I don't? What else will you do?" she says, wriggling with pleasure.

"I'll leave everything to you in my will. You see how that would disgrace you for the rest of your life the minute it got out? You'd have to leave Woodsmoke. There'd be no place to hide from wagging tongues. So if you want to hold your head up, start hanging it in shame. I'll give you a week to think it over. That's my last offer."

"You really are a devil, aren't you?" Mrs. Punck laughed, shaking her head as she gathered up her junk to get out, for we had reached the Y. "Won't you come to the meeting, Frank?"

"I've got something to tend to. If I'm not here when the orgy's out, meet me in there," I said, pointing across the street to the public libary.

"Its Reverend Biddle speaking on Self-Reliance."

"God help you one and all."

I hoped to find Ella Shook the libarian on duty alone when I arrived, as I was eager to maneuver her into a discussion of McGland if I could, and get her point of view. I happened to know that was what she dreaded most, being engaged in conversation with me alone. My widening intellectual horizons and ramifying interests made me "a pest and nuisance" she had said, according to reports that had reached me, but that was easy to see through. It was that my reading put her on her metal.

Luck was with me this time.. Not only was her assistant still out to lunch and the time a good hour off when the high-school student who acted as busboy with the returned books was due; there wasn't a soul using the libary. Ella stepped quickly behind her desk when she seen me enter, removing my tweed cap and walking with a brisk stride except for a slight limp in one knee. "Afternoon, Ella."

"Hello, Frank."

She drew up a chair and bent her head to her clerical tasks. I sauntered over to the magazine rack to look for a recent number of a literary review that McGland told me he had a group in. I found it and sat down at a reading table from where I could see Ella every time I looked up from the page and over my specs. I read the group through and then studied one the poems that particularly took my fancy. It was very quiet in the room except for when Ella cleared her throat, or I scraped my chair or turned a page. A fly buzzed against a window pane. I read for about fifteen or twenty minutes. Then I glanced up and found Ella watching me. I smiled and said:

"I see Gowan McGland has this new group in here. I wanted to catch it."

"Oh yes," said Ella. She continued her work, humming to herself.

"Have you read it?"

"No I haven't."

"He told me about it." I hooked an arm over the back of my chair and crossed my legs into the aisle. "The other day."

Ella rose and carried a book to a back shelf, walking up the aisle so that I had to move my feet out of the way. She looked down at them at first, and glanced at the magazine as she went by. I turned to watch her put the book on the shelf. She stayed there with her back to me, running a finger across other titles there at a length that didn't seem entirely convincing. She turned her head slightly to look back at me over her shoulder. Seeing me watching her again she said, "You know him?"

"Gowan? Yeh, he's in town for a while. Quite an amusing guy, and a hell of a swell egg. Like me to bring him in sometime?"

"Oh I think not. We don't generally . . . I know he's all the rage right now —"

"I like this group." I picked up the magazine from the table. "Especially this one called *River*. Just let me read a few lines."

"I'm really quite —"

"Goes:

> *How deep your warming stream my storkleg knows*
> *Who measures true, a ruler in your bed,*
> *Wherein the halfmoon rolls, traditional and wan,*
> *Who recks the hospitable ease and ooze of love . . ."*

"Stop, please!" said Ella, who had turned around and was looking at my legs, which were crossed even farther into the aisle than they were before. She had her back to the shelfs, as to a wall.

"Why?" I says. "We're alone."

"I know but someone may come in."

I set the poem down and removed my glasses. "Then I guess you understand what the poem's all about."

"Of course."

"What?"

"Wildlife."

"You're not kiddin'!"

She stared at my feet. She seemed to be weighing the alternatives of either leaping over them, to get back to the safety of her desk, or go out by the back door, around through a Chinese restaurant which ajoins the libary building, and come in again by the front. I put on my specs again to consult a line. "See, it's one leg, not two. That makes his symbolism clear," I says. "The ruler in the bed has this other meaning, of not only something to measure with, but who's boss. King you might say. Them are all clearly phallic implications." I pulled back my feet when she looked like she really was going to jump over them, and she scuttled on past me back to her desk. "How do you know?" she said, running.

"We realize those things today. We know more than we did a hundred years ago."

She got behind her desk as though back into a stockade while I continued keeping the conversational ball rolling with my analysis of the poem. "Of course the halfmoon makes it clear that by bed he means not the riverbed but —"

"Get out of my libary," she said, "you dirty old man."

"What for?"

"Go on get out."

"Now look." I rose and stood leaning against the table with my arms folded. "Can I help it if he brings a whole Scotch village to life with double meaning? Can I?"

"*Double* meaning. Huh! That's a good one."

"And if your afraid of a little literary criticism, then all I can say is you belong in Mrs. Hooton's dry goods store, not here."

She stamped her foot and squealed, "You beast!"

"Listen, I'm a taxpaying citizen of this town, and I guess I can drop in here on a hot day if I want and discover the beauties of poetry. So don't you beast me or I'll report you to the town council for not being able to appreciate nothing since Longfellow." Here there was a pause, and I picked up the magazine again to make another point. "Take like this passage here:

The ewe alone knows the ramifications of sex —"

"Out!"

At the height of this discussion the front door bust open and somebody did come in. It was Mrs. Punck, running at a trot and puffing like a steam engine.

"Reverend Biddle has been taken to the hospital with mononucleosis!" she said. "I've got forty-five people sitting there and no one to talk to them. Ella, could you?"

"Me? Oh no," she said, shrinking away again. "I couldn't. No public speaking for me."

"Then read them something. *Anything.* Just grab a book and *come.*"

"No. I simply cannot go in front of an audience, Eunice." She looked so terrified at the mere thought that Mrs. Punck knew it was no use. While she stood wringing her hands and Ella cringed against the wall, I walked past them both to a telephone on one end of Ella's desk. I looked up a number in the book and dialed it.

"Who are you calling?" Mrs. Punck asked.

"McGland. I can have him down here in ten minutes *if* he's home."

But he wasn't. The Springers maid had no idea where he was either. After hanging up I stood a moment in thought, taking in the joint spectacle the two women made. "I'll do it," I said.

"You mean speak?"

"Well, read a few of his poems and comment on them, like he does. It won't be no formal speech but it'll be better than leaving the poor old things sitting there in the lobby playing checkers. Come on, they've been waiting long enough."

I picked up the magazine and went out. Mrs. Punck, looking if anything more frantic than when she come in, trotted in my wake.

"My fellow Americans," I began, "this is unexpected, and only to fill in. All I claim to be is better than nothing. I see many familiar faces and a few snickers that seem to doubt even that, but anyhow. The question is what to talk about, and since I stand before you with no preparation, I'm just as eager as you to find out what I'm going to say. I have to take it potluck too. Well all joking aside, it seems to me that the most logical thing to talk about would be what I happened to be thinking about when the first notice of your predicament come to me about five minutes ago, over there in the libary. When Mrs. Punck found me there I was deep in poetry. The latest group by a Scotch poet who happens to be stopping here at the moment in our fair city. I tried to reach him before throwing myself into the breech, but no go. So the fact is I'm substituting for two people, a minister and a poet. Pretty good for one afternoon."

There was a laugh, which gave me a moment to look my audience over. I recognized many familiar faces, of course, most of the men and women being old timers like myself, and even one or two cronies. I spotted Charlie Keeley, a retired truck gardener I hadn't seen for a couple of years. I use to play checkers with him in front of the firehouse. One of the firemen too, retired Lou Haley. They were sitting side by side, leaning forward with an ear cupped. Mrs. Punck was less nervous, and smiling.

After reading the group from the literary magazine, three in number, I launched into a brief analysis of their content and technique.

"They're love poems, but you might not know it at first," I says. "Because instead of beating around the bush with fancy talk and highfalutin words, like the old time poets, he comes straight out with double meaning."

After five or six minutes I see that I had pumped myself dry and was sucking air. I had exhausted all I knew about that element in art, and found myself branching out, or I might say taking off, from there into sexual symbolism in everyday life in general, drawing heavily on articles I had read in *But* and other advance thought periodicals, as you can imagine.

"Take these high-powered cars the American men go in for. Seems they serve as symbols or what they call substitute releases of masculine power, though the public in general don't realize that yet, leastways the fellows that preen theirselves on them . . ." Having elusidated the theory with all the examples I could remember from my reading, I was thrown back on private speculations of my own to stretch out the main thread of the discourse as far as possible and give them their money's worth so to speak. "Take our national pastime," I says. "It's obvious what the baseball bat represents, not that we always think of it consciously in those terms. Of course we may dream about it, but I don't want to get into surrealism here. The ball is the egg to be fertilized. The nine innings . . ."

"Louder!" someone yelled. It was Charlie Keeley, leaning forward in his immaculate overalls till his chin was nearly on Mrs. Meserve's shoulder, his hand behind his ear.

"The bags . . ."

A woman with a mouth as straight as a razor slipped out the back door and returned almost instantly with a policeman. The cop stood against the wall just inside the door listening, the woman beside him, watching his expression while her own got primmer and grimmer, occasionally whispering a word in connection with what was being said. Explaining the explanation probably, as I believe Byron put it.

By this time I had run out both of facts *and* inspiration, and rounded out what was about a fifteen minute talk by reading one of the poems over again. Since I had no more comments to offer, wishing only to leave my hearers with the effect of the poetry itself fresh in their minds, I thanked them and sat down, to quite a brisk round of applause, as well as a few whistles from my cronies. The cop shrugged at the woman and went out again.

The woman must have pursued him, explaining the explanation as they pattered down the Y steps, because the cop was waiting for me there on the sidewalk when I left the building. The woman herself was nowhere to be seen, but I fancied I saw a gray head bob in and out of sight behind the window of a drug store across the street, watching.

"There were some complaints about your speech," the cop said. "What I heard seemed perfectly O.K., nothing objectionable, but they say the first part of it was pretty rough. Before I got there. What did you talk about?"

I was not even looking at him. A man walked by just then, dropping the celophane wrapper from a pack of cigarettes on the sidewalk. It was well within sight of a litter bin reading "Keep Your City Clean." I called after him, "Hey mister." He turned around. "You dropped something," I says, stooping to pick up the wad of celophane, and handed it back to him. "I believe this is yours." The guy looked at what he seemed to have in his hand, went "Chsssssss," to the cop, as though to say what characters don't you have to put up with these days. But he dropped it in the trash box before he marched off, the double lid of the box swinging behind him. I too give the cop a look, as though to suggest law-enforcing chores he might better be busying himself with than meddling in the cultural life of the town.

I had told Mrs. Punck where the flivver was parked. She was sitting in it when I got there, straight on the seat, her stuff piled neatly on her lap, her straw bonnet in place.

"You were superb."

I nosed into the late afternoon traffic and headed up Main Street for the country road and home.

"You'll have to help me make out the minutes of the meeting, though," she said after a bit. "A short summary of what the speaker said has to be included, and I really don't have too clear an idea what you were talking about some of the time there. Especially the explanations of the poem, though I do get the general drift. Now I like poetry — second to none and more than most — always have, as you know. But this modern poetry I don't seem to fancy. I guess it's one of my bald spots."

She backed out of the flivver with her things while I waited in the driveway with the motor running, having something else to do before supper. I promised I'd help with the minutes that night as she insisted, while what had been said at the meeting was still relatively fresh in my own mind.

I hurried over to see if McGland was home. I was eager to tell him about the lecture, and how it had gone. I parked the car on the road and slipped along the driveway past the Springers house to the guest cottage. As I neared it I heard Bobsy Springer's voice coming, not loud but with considerable animation, through the open window. Since I couldn't help overhearing what was said, I crouched under the window in a clump of cedars which screened the place from the main house.

"Is it simply that you don't know where to draw the line, Gowan? Or that you don't care? Do you refuse to accept that there are limits to what we can get out of life, even as a sexual anarchist, but must go on grabbing, grabbing and again grabbing?"

"At everything in skirts?"

McGland's voice was flat, without contention or irony, and he spoke, as you could imagine even though you couldn't see, with that dull nod with which he responded to just reproaches. He was helping her grope for the moral bromides that he had coming to him, not being sarcastic about the bromides themselves that it was a mistress's unpleasant task to dish out to him. Bobsy went on.

"Are you completely amoral, Gowan? We used to have a phrase, moral imbecile, you know, but I will spare you that, using the one that has taken its place in more tolerant times. What is it about you? I wish I knew. I mean I dearly and sincerely wish I could get inside your mind and makeup just for once to see what makes you tick. What are you trying to prove? Or is it something else, at once simpler and more hopeless? Are you simply a sexual glutton? A child always reaching out for another piece of stick candy?"

"Always lining up for another ride on the carousel?"

McGland's voice was toneless in the way it could suddenly become after a burst of animation. Maybe he had shot his bolt in the argument, if argument it could be called with McGland echoing and even amplifying the diatribes against him. A better guess was that he never had anything to say in his defense. This went on for some time — till my knee began to bother me actually. Something in the location of their voices assured me that it was safe to raise my head up to the level of the window, at which, in any case, the Venetian blind was down, not quite to the sill. Under its bottom slat I could peer into the room.

Mrs. Springer, in a bathing suit, her skin well buttered with the eternal summer grease, gleamed as she paced across the foot of a bed on which McGland lay stretched out full length, in an unbuttoned shirt and white clam diggers. The general effect was at once jaunty and exhausted. His spine was flat straight up to his head, which was propped on a wadded pillow at a very nearly right angle, like the head of a hockey stick to its shaft. He wore a look of unutterable boredom. A moist stub of cigarillo burned toward his lip, neglected, forgotten, as though, seized in a fit of contrite renunciation of all fleshly habit, he had dropped even smoking midway one cigar and would puff on it no more. He stared at nothing while Mrs. Springer talked on and walked on. From time to time she twirled a pair of sunglasses vigorously on their bows. McGland must have seen her only when she came into his line of vision as she paced like a sentry across the foot of the bed, and sometimes even then his eyes drooped shut.

"I mean my own sister-in-law. My husband's sister. What must we think of you who have given you our hospitality, fed and even clothed you? Those are C.B.S.'s things you've got on right this minute. C.B.S. is jealous enough, but Lucille's husband would kill you. I mean it quite literally, Gowan. He'll kill you if he finds out."

"He's a dentist, isn't he?" McGland asked without inflection, the dead butt flapping in a corner of his mouth. He looked like an old dog that has learned to smoke and even talk.

"Yes and one of the best, I warn you. His moral standards are as high as his professional ones, and they're the highest. Go to him and see. I mean he'll bash your teeth in if he finds out you've been making a play for Lucille, he'll tear you limb from limb. I happen to know what he did to another man who tried. Maybe C.B.S. would too. I just don't know. I don't think he suspects, but you should hear what he called you just for making passes at Lucille."

"What did he say?" McGland asked, a flicker of curiosity bringing him momentarily to life.

"He called you a lying, cheating, wenching, swilling drunken son of a bitch."

"And what did you say?"

"I said, 'Oh I think he's a good deal more than that.'"

"Then what did he say?"

Mrs. Springer spun around once, pushing her hair up with both hands, so that she looked for the moment like a debauchy in an orgy. "Oh I don't know! How should I know? Just listen to what I say and take it to heart once."

Here I felt again the stab of compassion for her, sharper than ever. As for her round heels, styles change. The standards for immorality are getting progressively steeper, for life and art both. A hundred years ago Hester Prynne of *The Scarlet Letter* was given a A for adultery. Today she would rate no better than a C-plus.

The sharp twang of a screen door and the sight of the maid coming out the main house sent me back into cover. Through the evergreens in which I squatted I watched her carry a tray of drinks toward the swimming pool on whose blue surface, now, I minded also the long form of Tad Springer floating on his back, his hands folded on his breast. He would have been running all day over secret footpaths known perhaps to Spofford's boyhood, pretty dim now but rediscovered on the verge of their obliteration among what remained of oak and maple and birch. The variety and amount of glasses and bottles on the tray indicated he would be joined, no doubt by the two in the guest house, so Spofford crept from his lair and vamoosed across the grass beside the drive back to the flivver, picking up his heels and wishing Mrs. Springer would press her lips to his for once while again the line dividing dark skin from white ran its razor edge across his longsuffering cod. His mulled blood sent up a howl for himself and all the uselessly roused, and for the well understood McGland of whose villainy Geneva was well aware, had told *us* had she not, and therefore against which she was perfectly well on guard who knew perfectly well how to take care of herself, could she not, maybe a little too much so, while out of that still undishonored Garden blew the clear pipes calling, "It's so she'll impress all the *other* lads around the pool, and their mothers too, that we want her arriving on the arm of the poet, not the poet himself necessarily." "That's right," I said.

We worked on the minutes after dinner that night in Mrs. Punck's room, because the parlor was jumping with a crowd of girl friends Geneva had in to celebrate her homecoming. The sound of the phonograph music beating like a tide under the floor keyed me up still further, flooding me with a urgent melancholy. About 10:30 Mare brought us coffee and a plateful of the cookies the girls were nibbling with their Cokes, using her best silver service. She was in better spirits than I'd seen her for years, this nagging woman who wanted nothing for herself. And so was I, despite the undercurrent of melancholy. I fortified myself with a few belts·from a bottle I had taken into Mrs. Punck's room, and was soon in the soaring dumps. I mean that mood you get into when you kind of *revel* in the blues? I began not to care what I did or said.

"Well what about it," I said to Mrs. Punck when Mare had gone, "give any more thought to that fur coat? You ought to sublimate all this energy you devote to civic stuff. Pour it into sex."

"You always were a devil. I mind how at picnics you use to chase women and tickle them." I denied it. "Yes you did. I remember once you and Charlie Keeley got Ella down on the ground and tickled her till she couldn't stand it."

"That reminds me. I must return that magazine." I sat in the easy chair while Mrs. Punck perched on the high brass bed finishing her coffee. To shock her I said, "Why don't you have your hair cut off?"

"I was thinking of it."

"What, cut off all that hair? There use to be a story you could sit on it."

"I still can."

The music throbbed in the floorboards, vibrating in my feet and churning up emotions. "Let's see you do it," I said in a low voice, wretched.

I watched her stand at the dresser and remove the tortoise shell pins from the thick brown braids she wore at the back of her head. They dropped into the tray with intimate ticking sounds while the plaits disintegrated and flopped in a soft veil down her shoulders and back. When it had all been shooken free, she sat down on the bed again by way of demonstration and said, "There, you see?"

"Well only just." I watched from the chair with my legs crossed, the coffee cup balanced on one knee, trying to affect an air of worldly depravity while my throat tightened. "Still it's beautiful hair I must admit. Amazing there's no more gray in it."

"I get it from both sides of the family. Neither my mother nor my father lost their hair or ever got to have much gray in it. And I take care of it. A hundred strokes every night. I might as well do it for tonight, now that it's down. Unless you want to do the honors. It gets to be a chore. No you take it, Frank," she said when I extended the plate with the last cookie on it. "You're getting to be a cumpulsory eater." She was picking up from me the same expressions I picked up from the commuters.

I took the silver-backed brush she then passed to me and began to run it through her hair, causing her to emit squeals of pain as I plowed roughshod through the rats and snarls, then more gently. The hair crackled faintly, fluttering upward as I brought the brush away for the next stroke, the ends hanging momentarily suspended in midair and catching glints of light from the lamp burning on the dresser. The music had stopped.

"Are you —?" I began and got a hitch in my throat. "Are you counting or shall I?"

"We won't bother tonight."

"Did we ever chase you at picnics? Keeley and me?"

"I'm not ticklish."

"We'll see about that."

A jab in the brisket with the brush was intended to put an end to the spell cast by brushing her hair. What it did was set in motion another mood which was far less easy to stop, in fact impossible. It caused Mrs. Punck to rise with a little squeak of delight and run around to the foot-end of the bed. With this ritual under way, I was stuck with it. It had to be let run its course. Mrs. Punck could not be left capering around the furniture, making dancing starts away from me as though great mirth was afoot, without me holding up my end of it. So I began to chase her, chucking the brush on the bed. "You," she said as I come half-heartedly forward.

It was stylized, and very taxing. Your amorous red tape. Just beyond the bed was the upholstered red and white striped chair in which I had only a moment ago sat in peace. This Mrs. Punck scooted around, getting up steam for the idea that I was a caveman in hot pursuit and she had to keep something between us. The small table at which we'd been working on the minutes was next to that, forming a cool de sack. In the other direction was the 3 ft. corridor between the far side of the bed and the flowered wall, in which she no doubt banked on being trapped. That would be the climax of the rigamarole. She wore a green silk kimono, which from time to time she paused to tuck up around her throat to suggest that the romp was getting wilder, her face flushed and smiling. Gritting my teeth, I made a couple perfunctory lunges to which she responded with corresponding galvanized shuffles of her feet, or what was oftener the case, made darts in response to hers, sustaining as best I could that I was inaugurating them. I was glad when the music resumed downstairs, where they might otherwise have got engrossed in interpreting the noises overhead; now they were being drowned out. Though on the other hand the music stirred Mrs. Punck up further.

At last I jerked the chair away, causing Mrs. Punck, deprived of her last bulwark, to scuttle into that narrow alley beside the bed. It ended in another wall of course. There she stood with her back to it, her hair in wild disarray and her face a glowing pink, panting like an abandoned woman in a revel. She rolled her head from side to side and her eyes in her head. "Now don't go raising sand." I advanced along this passage with as much show of frolic as I could, hunched over like an incoming wrestler, my arms out. This brought us full circle to the original question that had touched off the romp, whether she was ticklish. Mrs. Punck contracted with a preparatory giggle. When I reached her I began dutifully to rummage in her ribs.

She doubled over in my arms, with shrieks of laughter and hilarious warnings that her disc would come out again if I did not control myself. She dropped over onto the bed, me after her. I fumbled at the sash around the kimono till the robe flew open and both jolly old bosoms spilled out, like two sacks of flour. The music on the phonograph was now a shrill clarinet chorus which licked up the stairs and down the bedroom hallways like a long, spreading tongue of flame. Between it and Mrs. Punck's continued squeals of delight neither of us heard the rap on the bedroom door. It had been closed but not latched shut, and now it swung open as a result of the knock, revealing the face of Mare and the percolator held up in smiling inquiry whether we wanted any more coffee.

"I'm tickling your mother," I said, looking over from the bed.

Mare nodded, coming into the room just long enough to refill the coffee cups before backing discreetly out again, shutting the door behind her. We had got to our feet by now, and stood watching the closed door. We were both breathing heavily. I turned and walked to the table where our steaming coffee awaited us. "You're a devil," said Mrs. Punch with approval, pulling her kimono to rights and tucking the assets back into place.

Once at the table I made a firm point of getting this thing back on the track and no nonsense about it. "I mean this Charlie Keeley sort of thing went out with sleeve garters and trombone solos in church, for God's sake." I switched to the snobbish drawl and airy gestures. I put a lump of sugar in both our cups. "Well Charlie Keeley got the idea somewhere that he was a character, you see, and went to work at it. Not just a character but a *character*, with overalls and a bandanna and a foxy look? The whole bit. He played a mouth organ yet. I mean Cheerist! Well he looked sly and he chuckled sly, and his eye roved sly above the harmonica as he played it, you see. And he remembered to sort of flutter his hand around the harmonica when he played? All that. But he forgot one thing."

"What?" says Mrs. Punch, already sad at the switch in manner.

"He forgot to wipe the harmonica on the seat of his pants when he finished."

I did the la-de-da sort of thing till I saw Mrs. Punch's jaw fall to a level where I knew it was conclusive. The cruelest was the kindest, there was no doubt about it in this instance. When Mrs. Punch presently found occasion to say, "Least said soonest mended," I said, "Soonest what, pie? I don't believe I've ever heard that expression."

Nevertheless I found myself gravely disturbed by the position into which I had let myself be drawn. I had compromised myself. More than that, I had lost ground, precious ground; all the ground I had so painstakingly gained that summer. One fit of provincial behaviour had tumbled me back to where I started. Worse than my relapse was Mrs. Punck's advance — the encouragement in her of impressions I had known all along must be scrupulously guarded against, must be brutally squelched. How far the situation had deteriorated I was given to realize from an exchange at breakfast between her and Mare, the morning after the bedroom lark. I overheard it coming downstairs. It indicated that the nature and extent of my interest in Mrs. Punck were being wildly exaggerated and grossly misconstrewed both as to quality and quantity. I took the first opportunity to pull myself together and set matters straight, once and for all. It offered itself late the following morning, two days before the big blowout for McGland.

fifteen

GEORGE AND MARE were in town, shopping and looking in at the bank about some business matter. Geneva was at the beach with her friends. I was once again minding the salesroom. It was pleasant. I sat on the high stool behind the counter reading a book.

After a bit I heard the door to the kitchen open and Mrs. Punck come down the two stairs into the salesroom. I grit my teeth. We had of course seen each other in the house that morning, so no greeting was necessary. I didn't even look up from my book.

I sensed her circling behind me, pausing just long enough to glance down over my shoulder to see what I was reading — *Vanity Fair* by Thackeray. She didn't speak but puttered helpfully about, which was even more of a cross, tidying the cartons of eggs, checking the paper bags on the counter and replenishing them from a supply in the back bin. Out of the corner of my eye I saw that she was wearing a blue and white polka dot dress. It looked freshly ironed. She spoke at last.

"I'm sorry Mare dropped all those hints about people getting fixed up," she said. "They weren't even sly. But Mare ain't got it in her to be sly."

"They were hardly on the subtle side, were they?" I said dryly. "Not as deep as a well or as wide as a church door, but you got the idea."

"Church door, so that's what's on our mind this morning. Well."

I closed the book and shoved it aside. The time had come to spell things out.

Spell them out I did, as bluntly as I could without being unkind. I said that I had nothing against her personally — indeed she was one of the most personable women I knew and a splendid catch for the right man — but I wasn't that man. We simply lived in different worlds. We no longer spoke the same language. That, in a nutshell, there was no true rappaport between us, and the union would be a disaster within 6 mos.

"No true what?" she asked.

"Rappaport. You see? I would be explaining every other word I used. It just won't wash."

Mrs. Punck, who had hoisted herself onto the stool I had vacated to pace the floor, shook her head in a unhappy daze. "Those two for a quarter words. I thought you were talking about that new doctor that just moved into the Hollow. I believe he's a Jew."

"No, no. It's something that exists between two people. Means the same as affinity. Or compatibility. Or being soul mates, if you understand that term better."

"But Frank," she protested, "don't you think you may be exaggerating something two people can rise above if they really put their minds to it, and want to make a go of it? I think you are."

Having been made somewhat self-conscious by the nature and importance of what we were discussing, Mrs. Punck left the stool herself, got a broom from the corner and began busily sweeping the floor. She worked at arm's length so as not to soil her dress. "And you think you might find this companionship more with some — the time is past for mincing words — some woman of the sort you've been hobnobbing with? Are you getting notions, Frank?"

"It's not a question of notions. Notions are what we're trying to squelch. But I suppose you could say something has rubbed off on me, yes," I said, walking to the window, where I stood looking out. "If it comes to that."

"If I may say so, I don't think that at your age you can afford to go on the idea that a rolling stone gathers no moss, Frank Spofford." Using both names indicated a lecture. "Do you know people are talking about you?"

"Well like Oscar Wilde said, it's not as bad as not being talked about."

"Such a nut. Local man?"

"Hardly," I says. "What do they say about me?"

"That you've changed. That you've become a snob and a caution. That you've kicked up your heels and lit over the hill like a colt in flytime."

"It's because I have that Geneva's back in with the quality."

"I doubt that was your aim, but we'll grant it as a byproduct. Yes we're all glad for her, but still sad for you, Frank. You ain't let up now the aim's realized. I hear you entered your Lizzie in the car show at the Country Club."

"What's wrong with that?"

"They're not our sort, Frank, the gazebos who go in for that," said Mrs. Punck, using a term that rolled us back in time to about the year the Lizzie come out, 1926. "You'll never more than half belong in that world, while losing your footing in the one you do. And that leads to the greatest heartache a person can have — not belonging. Geneva'll belong, in the long run, I suppose, but leave it for her, Frank. Now that you've got her on the road, come back yourself. Come home to us. This trying to rise above our station." I could imagine her sad headshake. "You remind me of a man with his feet on two cakes of ice to once, pulling farther and farther apart, till at last he splits down the middle like a wishbone and falls in the water and drowns."

"Block that metaphor!"

"What?"

"Nothing. Skip it."

Personal as the discussion had been so far, it now become even more so. It become intimate. I could sense Mrs. Punch herself turn away as she sent it along in that direction, so that we were probably now standing back to back as she said: "I think that when all is said and done, your hankering is mainly that of a man without a woman."

"The world is full of women and of hankering. They rouse more of it than they could possibly satisfy, and that's the godawful and everlasting Nature's truth of it. But I guess we're meant to hanker. Without it there wouldn't be no art or poetry or music. No nothing. I sometimes think it's all one great mating cry, mostly out of season."

"You know what, Frank? It's when you lapse into your real self, your old-fashioned self, talking the way *we* talk, giving that self a chance, that you make sense. That you say noteworthy little things. When you put on airs and try to talk like *them* is when you say things nobody will remember tomorrow, or even wants to listen to today."

"Let's not be chintzy, darling."

"You just dropped ten feet in talk level, Frank Spofford." I could hear her tug her pretty dress to rights and give the sniff that accompanied pithy summings up.

There was a short silence. Then she pushed the conversation forward, with the critical turn I had been steeling myself for.

"I'm not blaming you for the other night. For what happened in the bedroom. It was as much my fault as yours. Or say it was nobody's fault — it just happened. My point is that it proved the hankering in both parties."

"And mine is that those two parties lack what I said, to make what one of them calls a 'go' of it."

I spoke with such finality, turning around as I did so, that Mrs. Punch reached for the broom which she had propped against the counter and resumed sweeping the floor, this time more briskly. She had no intention of relinquishing the subject however. After a few minutes she paused again and, leaning a forearm on the broomstick while holding it with the other hand, said, "Do you know what I'd like, that I think might be helpful? I'd like to hear you talk to some of these people. That you claim you've got this rappaport with. I'd just like very, very much to get an earful of that brittle talk once. Just to know what I'm up against."

"You've heard me talk it."

"To us, but not to them."

"You heard me with McGland and Mopworth the other night. That ought to give you a rough idea what you're up against."

"You didn't have much of a chance to get a word in, besides I want to hear you talk it with a *woman*. This other language you keep harping on. Then I might pick up some pointers, and know more what you're looking for in a mate."

"I doubt whether it would do any good. It's too late."

"It wasn't for you. *You* learned. And I do appreciate some aspects of what you've become — I don't want to be misunderstood on that point. Your enlarged vocabulary as such, the way you dress. That dogtooth jacket is very becoming."

"*Hounds*tooth! You see? I need someone who speaks the English language with a little precision. It's all I ask, but I do ask that."

We had been discussing matters in this vein for several minutes when an open blue Jaguar swept into the driveway and came to a stop. It was Mrs. Beauseigneur herself behind the wheel.

"There's one of them now!" Mrs. Punck spoke rapidly, suddenly quite agitated. "Now look, why don't I hide in here somewhere and listen? Right here under the counter would be perfect. I could hear everything."

"Oh, I don't think so."

"Why not? There's plenty room, and I'll be quiet as a mouse. Besides you owe it to me. To both of us. To all of us. We've been going through a lot with you, Frank, and —"

"Oh well, all right," I said at last, figuring what could I lose. I shoved Mrs. Punck hurriedly under the counter as Mrs. Beau sprang out of the car and came toward the salesroom door. I should say that there had been a slight thaw in the cold war with the suburbanites in the past few days, thanks to the turn matters had taken. Mare had agreed to accept a limited number of them to do business with, and these were added to another, considerably smaller, quota on which I had insisted as part of my terms for taking her mother in the house to live with us, once I had pulled myself together after recovering from the humiliation of getting caught stealing my own chickens and drawn myself up to my full height on all that matter. These were a handful of close friends and employers, people who had a drag with me. Mrs. Beau was definitely one. Hence her blithely coming in here expecting to be waited on no matter who was on duty. Still she was glad it was me, I could tell from her expression, when I had straightened up again after stowing Mrs. Punck under the counter. *Well* under, I saw to that. I shoved her as far back as I could into a corner against the wall, where she settled herself as comfortably as she could on all fours. I may have handled her a bit roughly as the haste and other circumstances required, because she stuck her head out one last time and said, "You usen't to be so uppity when —"

"Under! Under and quiet."

Mrs. Beau was bright as a poppy in a red silk blouse and beige slacks, and as usual give her charming impression of one shattered by reality as she poked strands of hair under her headscarf and fought the door. "Disintegrating," she laughed. "Well, Frank, I see you're at the old stand again."

"For my sins. The whole famn damily's out. You look more than usually charming today."

"Thank you." Mrs. Beau saw the book open on the counter and swung it around to read the title. "*Vanity Fair.* How are you liking it?"

"All right. I thought it sort of drug in the middle, like the Old Testament."

We chatted a few minutes more in the vein that the unseen listener wanted to hear. Then Mrs. Beau looked at me and said: "Frank, I hear you talked to the Golden Age Club on Gowan McGland the other day."

I threw up my hands, regretting Mrs. Punck couldn't see, because the gestures and mannerisms are all part of how this sort of thing is done. "Bad news travels fast. How do they say I was? Show me no mercy."

"They say you were fine. You read some of his current things? Which is more than I have. That'll learn me to give *you* magazines. Do you like him?"

"Very much. Some of the lines take a little doing — sort of Ambiguitysville — but then that's par for the course. In fairness to myself I did try to get Gowan on the blower first — their speaker got sick you know — but I couldn't. Oh you mean how do I like Gowan personally? Very much. I mean he wears well."

"Where did you meet him?" she asked me, curious.

"At the Springers. He's staying there of course."

"Yes I know. I haven't met him but I hope to Saturday."

"Ah," I said, "you're going to the big do for him."

"Yes. Will you be on deck?"

"Now, Mrs. Beau," I said, "*some* of us have to stay home so the rest of you can be exclusive."

She laughed and said, "Frank, you're impossible. Look, I've been meaning to thank you for helping Bobsy Springer out with her roses. I heard you went. It was sweet of you. I didn't get a chance to tell you at the Bronsons party. You didn't seem very happy there that night."

"Well I'll tell you. I have no objections to serving American wines. But those bottles with the caps on instead of corks, that you screw off? I mean handling the account is no excuse."

"Now Frank, you're getting to be a terrible snob. But leave us not talk about it. They don't care about wines. But the food there is always superb. You must have tucked in your share of stew."

"Better than you did. Don't tell me you're dieting again. Look, here's my rule about that. A woman doesn't have to watch her figure as long as the men still do. That's Spofford's Law. We don't want the ladies walking around like scarecrows you know."

"Well you're very sweet. But the fact is I'm getting in shape for all that food on the *Flandre*. We're sailing for Europe the last of September. Did you know?"

"No, I didn't know. That's wonderful. And going sort of out

of season. That's playing smart. How long will you be gone?"

"Well Lester's taking a month, which will give us a good three weeks, because we're flying back. Time to take in the whole Continent."

"In one swell foop." I climbed up on top of the counter and sat on it with my back to the wall and hugging my knees. "Tell me, you going to tuck in Spain?"

"I think so."

"Because otherwise Mrs. Wilcox will ploy you out of town."

"We may even take in Athens. That'll larn her."

"But get her to tell you about the cathedral in Zamora with the obscene carvings on the choir seats, if she already hasn't. Terribly amusing to hear her go on about it. Anyhow, you're smart to go out of season."

"We've no chers, actually. Lester has to take his vacation then. Look, I hope we can bank on you to keep an eye on the house while we're away?"

"Don't give it a thought."

Mrs. Punch had kept very quiet up to now. But here her cramped position, or probably the strain on her sacroiliac, must have had gotten so that she had to move. So she shifted slightly, and in so doing made a little rustling sound. It was quite audible in a lull in the conversation. "What was that?" said Mrs. Beau.

"What?"

"A noise. Under there."

"Oh, mice probably. But don't mind them. Well what can I do you for today? We've got practically everything on hand."

"Just a dozen eggs today, Frank, thanks. I thought I'd fix an omelette tonight. More training for the trip."

When she had bought her eggs and gone I said, "All right," and Mrs. Punch crawled out from under the counter.

"Whew! . . . So that's the way it goes."

I shrugged. "I don't know whether you got anything out of it or not," I said. "But there it is."

"I don't get what's so fancy about it half the time. She said 'larn her.' Even I with my little education know better than that. And 'leave us not talk about it,' and 'chers' and I don't know what all."

I stamped my foot, beside myself. "*Because she knows enough not to. She's doing it on another level. God!*" I was being worn thin by all this. It all seemed so futile. We had lost more ground, if anything.

I noticed at this point that Mrs. Punck was not getting up but was remaining on all fours on the floor. She had crawled out to the middle of the room but that was all. "Why don't you get up?" I said. "She's gone."

"I can't."

Propping herself carefully on one forepaw, Mrs. Punck gingerly raised herself a little and felt her back with the other hand. Instantly a grimace of pain crossed her face and she dropped back to her former position. I became apprehensive, remembering her sacroiliac had periodically given her trouble and once caused her to be hospitalized. Slowly, carefully, she tried again to straighten, with no more luck. The effort ended in another twinge.

"Frank," she said, "I think it's out again."

"Oh, Lord."

I got down on the linoleum beside her and tried to help her up, but my ministrations only made it worse. "It's no use," she said. "It has to be done exactly right, by someone who knows. You'd better call the doctor."

"Right." I rose and started at a gallop for the kitchen telephone, automatically intending to call Dr. Kershaw, our family physician. In the doorway I turned to ask whether it was hers too. "Yes but come to think of it he's been on vacation," she said. "I'm not sure whether he's back yet. They'll tell you at the office or the answering service who's covering for him if he isn't. Hurry!"

I hoped the fellow covering for him wouldn't be Northrup. Doctors and cops shouldn't be younger than you are — it gives you that uneasy feeling. This kid looked so young I figured he might be working his way through medical school by practising — an impression the advice itself didn't do much to offset. From the kitchen phone I could look through the open door and watch Mrs. Punck shift experimentally around on the linoleum, there on all fours, trying to ease her discomfort by slight changes

1 6 3

in position. Without much success. But my conversation on the phone soon gave me something else to think about. There was a kind of peculiar development, though one I was in a way prepared for by a reference Mrs. Punck had made a while before, when all the confusion and misunderstanding had been at its height between us. Dr. Kershaw *was* still away, and the man covering him was this Dr. Rappaport she had mentioned.

"Well that's an odd coincidence," I said, when I came back to report to her, somewhat sobered.

"It's a sign," she said, watching me from the floor like a reproachful animal.

I had reached the doctor's office direct, and since he was just finishing up with a patient and had no others waiting for him in the reception room he arrived in less than fifteen minutes, an interval I spent trying to comfort and soothe Mrs. Punck and feed her brandy, from more or less the same quadruped position as hers. Not neglecting to take a much needed nip from the bottle myself. The doctor didn't drive but came crosslots from his house in Punch Bowl Hollow, where he had his office, scrambling over the stone wall with his black bag, so we weren't alerted by the sound of any car turning in and were unprepared for the sight of the sharp bearded face at the window of the door and then coming in. I had told him to go straight to the salesroom, not fancying Mrs. Punck crawling up the stairs into the house like a dog. He was a short dark man in a tight seersucker suit and a big flowered tie which hung out of it in a disheveled way. He was breathing heavily. He had burning brown eyes, with which he took in the sight of Mrs. Punck only a second before getting down on his knees beside her.

He was both gentle and amazingly skilful, manipulating Mrs. Punck's back with a competence that suggested some shady background in osteopathy rather than a standard medical one to me. Inside of five minutes he had her straightened up on her knees, in two more on her feet. He walked her around the room like an animal trainer walking some afflicted horse, and she looked at him with a kind of dumb, grateful trust. All the while

he murmured words of assurance to her in a tender, almost cooing voice.

Things weren't as good as they seemed at first blush though;
the least wrong move brought on a fresh wrench, and Dr. Rappaport didn't seem satisfied with what his probing finger felt.
"We'd best take you to the hospital for an X-Ray. Then we'll
know what's what," he said. He looked at me with his sort of
gentle glare. "Can you drive us?"

"I'm minding the salesroom now. Can't you take her in
your car?"

"I have no car," he said. "I don't drive."

"How do you get to your calls?"

"Oh, people generally give me a lift along the road, and one
thing and another. And I like to walk when it's possible. I mean
if you don't wish to close up the store for our Mrs. Punck . . ."

"Of course I will."

I put a Back in An Hour sign on the door and locked it. I
knew Mare and George would be back before then. We all
squeezed into the Ford, Mrs. Punck between us. Dr. Rappaport,
who took up very little room, patted her arm when we went
over bumps, and when not murmuring the dove-like words of
encouragement was asking me to drive more carefully if at all
possible. I was turning over in my own mind something else
that continued to eat me with curiosity.

"You mean you hitchhike to your patients?" I said.

"That is correct. I have not driven since 1954, when I lost
my wife in an automobile accident. We lived in New Haven
then. I've come to Woodsmoke to retire. I take very few calls,
and fill in for other doctors now and then. People are very
kind. They'll always pick up a doctor thumbing a ride. Sometimes my patients themselves come to fetch me, if it's urgent."

He stayed to read the X-rays, by which time he already had
Mrs. Punck in bed, being prepared for traction. The plates only
confirmed what he already suspected from what she'd told him
of her history and his own preliminary diagnosis — that she had
both the nerve pinch that usually constitutes your sacroiliac, *and*
a disc out. She lay under sedation, happily tucked in the sheets
with the good doctor sitting in the chair beside her. Talk about

your bedside manner! He was the epitomy of it. He had nothing else to do he said, and would be glad to stay till he was sure she was comfortable. He said that doctors were beginning to eliminate traction, relying simply on a hard bedboard arrangement for a short period of complete rest, but he still held with the traction system as contributing something to the treatment. Of which the main thing was complete rest so the spinal muscles and nerves concerned could relax. Most such spasms came from tension he told us. He asked Mrs. Punck whether she had been going through a period of strain lately, and she said "Yes, I guess you could call it that," giving me a look. But she did it with eyes already growing heavy from the sedative. Dr. Rappaport picked up a magazine when she dropped off, and began to read.

"You going to stick around?" I says.

"That is correct. I want to make sure she's O.K. You run along if you'd like. You probably have things to do."

I beat it home to report to Mare and George, who were pacing the floor in the stew that could well be imagined. I gave them as coherent an account as I could of what had happened in their absence. Then after a hasty supper I drove Mare to the hospital.

We were quiet the first part of the trip. I knew what was on her mind. She had been thinking over something in my story that I had tried to skim, but that I knew would have to be dealt with in detail sooner or later. Now she wanted to know more about that.

"You say my mother was under the counter," she said. "What exactly was she doing there?"

"It's kind of hard to explain," I said. "It was where she wanted to be. You see, she was hiding there so she could listen to me and Mrs. Beauseigneur talk. It was her idea, Mare, not mine. I swear it."

"To listen to you talk funny?"

"That is correct. She wanted to get some pointers." I was beginning to wish I had skipped that whole can of peas and let Mrs. Punck open it if she wanted later, because it only revived Mare's confusion and along with it her hostility. I was now completely on the defensive again if not on the run, after the slight progress I had made getting back into everybody's graces. "Was it my fault? Was it?" She didn't answer.

When we walked into the hospital room Dr. Rappaport was still there, or rather there again after a bite of supper downstairs in the hospital cafeteria. He was smoking a pipe in the easy chair beside the bed, whereon Mrs. Punck now slumbered dreamily among an assortment of weights and pulleys. "We'll have her out in a week or two," he assured Mare, who of course he sprang out of his chair to give it to. "But I think a bit of traction is indicated. These backs are very tricky. Half of us have cricks coming and going and things popping in and out it seems. Look, I wonder if I might trouble you for a lift. I'll just wait down in the lobby while you have your visit. Nice to meet you, Mrs. Spofford." He tiptoed out, Mrs. Punck being very deep in what she herself would of called sleepsin-bye.

Rappaport was generally there whenever I visited Mrs. Punck, which was often out of curiosity as much as conscientiousness. "He's most nice," she told me once when we were alone together. She directed my gaze toward a basket of flowers enormously dwarfing my own dozen carnations. "He's the gentlest man I ever met." She added, smoothing the bedclothes on either side away from her, "And one of the few Christians."

Once I seen Rappaport draw a rose from a vase with deadly suavity and hold it down for her to smell, his cheeks crinkling as he smiled and his teeth, brilliant for a man in his sixties, glittering like a knife. Or he would compliment her on her bed jacket. Or he would stand with an arm outstretched along the head of the bed, the other in a pocket of his trousers where he would gather up all his loose change and let it slide in a cataract off his palm while he spoke of the years in New Haven, where he had lost his wife in that traffic mishap. When Dr. Kershaw got back from his vacation we told Mrs. Punck about it, assuming she would want him to take over. But no. She wanted to keep Dr. Rappaport. There was no mistaking developments. I went home one night to lay it on the line to Mare.

"Your mother is emotionally involved with a Jew," I says.

"Jew A is not Jew B," she says, turning the pages of a newspaper spread out as usual on the kitchen table. "That what it says in them magazines you been reading? That what you been preaching to us around here?"

"That isn't the side of it I mean. I mean the religious. Your mother's religious."

"But he ain't, so there's no conflict there. He wouldn't be trying to drag her to the temple while she tried to drag him to church. He even says he wouldn't mind going to church with her once in a while. He's a wonderful man without no standards getting in the way. He never misses Handel's *Messiah* at Christmas time. They've gone into all that, so they must be serious." Here Mare's calm front suddenly cracked. She brought both fists down on the table and rose shouting, "They're serious do you hear! They're talking about getting married! Married do you hear! And all because of you! It's all your fault. You're to blame for the whole thing, for everything that's come over us."

"Now wait a minute, darling," I said, trying to recover the old manner, that is the new one. "I mean if you're going to stand there shrieking like Tosca." I tried to say it in the drawl but it come out in a dry falsetto, as I found myself backing away. "Why is it my fault?" Of course it was like asking a question in a catechism to which there were fixed answers. She lost no time in opening up *that* can of peas again.

"Because it all started with your gallivanting around. We were eternally gratefully to you for a few days there — all too few. Now we're back where we were, thanks to you. Everything that happened is a direct result of your shenanigans. Why shouldn't she get married, to a member of her faith? She's got vital years left, so have you. Why couldn't you get fixed up? That would of solved everything. But no, you had to branch out in new ways. You had to have fresh feathers. If you hadn't started that it wouldn't be ending this way now. Not that the end is in sight, the way it seems."

"What do you mean, Mare?" I asked in the falsetto, further unnerved by something in her manner.

"Geneva. All this seems to've taken your mind off the big party and what happened there, I see, but do you know what did happen there? Or since then? Do you know who she's taken up with? Because I don't know from one day to the next where she is or who she's with or what she's up to, now she's become a social butterfly. Things are worse than they ever were. There's the doorbell now again. Why don't you go see who's picking her up this time? Because I don't dare look."

The above rough sketching in of the Rappaport-Punck thing gets us a little ahead of our story, of course. Now I must go back and take up the main thread of that again where it was left off.

sixteen

SINCE MY PROMISE to Mare had barred me from the Springers in any guise, menial or otherwise, I jumped at the chance to sit for the Hackneys, who were going socially, and whose acreage stood back to back with the Springers. The Hackney children — 3 girls of assorted ages but so similar in size and appearance that they seemed a litter to which Mrs. Hackney had given birth at once — had not been 10 minutes asleep before your correspondent stole across the darkening slope of lawn through a woodlot where the property ended and that of the Springers began. Strains of music floating faintly through the evening air grew louder as I approached. The instrumentalists were a trio of sinister looking men wearing gold earrings and head scarfs. Their getup helped identify as Gypsy the melodies they produced. They stood with their backs to a grove of spruce in which I hid myself to watch. They were a fiddler, an accordionist and a cellist. The last-named spun his instrument by the neck once during an especially catchy passage, to presumably inject an American touch into the Transylvanian folk rhythms.

The party was in full swing. Several couples were dancing on the pavement around the pool, one or two on the grass around that. A woman kicked off her shoes and waltzed in stocking feet to fixed smiles of appreciation from the onlookers. A few who had acted on the invitation to bring bathing suits were in the pool. One of these was a fat man who stood waist-deep in the water holding a martini, not so much it seemed because he enjoyed doing this as to give formal expression to the principle of extreme Fun. Every one on dry land had a drink of some sort or size. I see Haxby the chunky dentist from Greenwich with whose wife McGland was trying to make time, according to the conversation I had accidentally overheard, holding a Sazarac in one hand as though it was McGland's neck. I knew it was a Sazarac from his preference at the Beauseigneurs' party, where he had showed me how to mix one. Most of the guests sat at tables over which were strung scores of Japanese lanterns, like at the Beauseigneurs, their festive serieses intermittently varied by tongues of sulphurous flame burning furiously on standards as deterrents to mosquitoes. Haxby's normally flushed face and bullneck were caught in a hellish light cast by one of them, giving him the look of a demon in Hades. It crossed my mind that I would hate to be the butt of his vengeance — if that was in store for the poet. He wore a white linen coat, with a Madras bowtie and a bustin'-laughin' cummerbund of the same material. Otherwise it was a divine evening, with a full moon beginning to clear the treetops.

I altered my station among the evergreens to case the crowd for more familiar faces — with a last look at the fat guy still allegorically representing Gaity, who seemed rather sad, standing sawed in half there holding the martini in this tablow nobody paid no attention to. The first one my eye lit on was Bobsy Springer. No anxious hostess given to pretty little sorties to keep things moving she; she sat at a table chatting and smoking like a guest herself. She was in a sheer black dress, leaning back with her legs crossed. But from time to time she did dart glances about — on the lookout for the same people as me? I think we both spotted McGland at the same time. He was strolling out the house with a pretty, somewhat stooped blonde woman in a green dress — Lucille Haxby, the sister-in-law Mrs. Springer had such a cow over. Though he strained the buttons of his white coat — or one of C.B.S.'s coats — like a business man in early middle age, his face looked younger than ever. It wore its boyish, up-to-no-good smile as he said something to the woman, or more likely asked her something, because she nodded once and walked away as though some kind of agreement had been reached. There is no mistaking that kind of exchange. The movie *The Fallen Idol* opens with Ralph Richardson and the woman he is having an affair with engaging in that kind of whispered conversation, of whose nature we are sure though the camera is behind them and a mile off. I shot a look at Haxby and then Mrs. Springer. Their expressions left no doubt we were all thinking the same thing.

We all now followed McGland's passage through the crowd to a small group of young people on the opposite bank of the pool. There were five or six of them, and my heart jumped at the sight of Geneva. A shift in the ranks to make room for McGland suddenly brought her into view. She was a dream in a cloud of a white dress that set off her sun-ripened arms and shoulders, as well as her face with the big incandescent eyes that gave it that kind of goofy beauty. Now occurred one of them moments when a random scene conveys something to an onlooker unbeknownst to those taking part in it; when he seems in some queer, almost mystical, way to stand outside time and reality, like God himself — something piercing and special.

McGland trained on Geneva his famous carnivorous stare while she regarded Tad Springer, who was on her left, and who was in turn talking to a girl on his left. Now get this. It was obvious Tad was speaking about Geneva, because after the remark he jerked his head toward her and she lowered her gaze. Then she decided to laugh and punched him on the arm for what must have been some kind of crack about her. Tad put his arm around her and gave her a squeeze. I looked quickly back to Mrs. Springer. She was on her feet, watching the scene like a hawk like me.

What drove me crazy was that I couldn't hear a word that was being said, but must take in the whole complex and spreading tissue of this thing by eye. The entire party including the damn pool stood between me and those I was most anxious to overhear — who most deserved the benefit of my eavesdropping too. Near the young people a large forsythia, which I had trimmed, offered itself as a handy cover from which to listen, but as I skirted the house in a wide arc designed to fetch me up just the far side of it, there was a pause in the music in which I could hear the tinkle of a distant telephone.

With a shock I remembered the Hackneys habit of checking in once or twice in the course of an evening to see how the children were, and veered off to their house as fast as my legs could carry me. Which wasn't very fast, as it was all uphill this time. As I stumbled up the path I counted the rings, growing louder and more frightening with each peal: four, five, six — God knew how many before I started keeping track. Panic quickened my hammering pulse. By the time I gained the back terrace I thought my head would explode. I tore through the screen door into the kitchen where the nearest extension was, but even as I grasped it, still ringing, I caught myself. Rather than betray that I hadn't been at my post by answering it, why not wait until it stopped and then resumed, on the ground that Mrs. Hackney would hang up and try again on the theory that she had dialed the wrong number. Quick thinking, whether good or bad. It was nerve-racking listening to it shrill on and on. But in a minute it did stop, leaving a silence that was equally shattering. It started up again instantly.

I gave it two rings and then said, "Good evening. Hackney residence."

"Mr. Spofford?" said an anxious Mrs. Hackney.

"Oh hello Mrs. Hackney. Everything's okie doke." I put my hand over the mouthpiece between speeches to conceal my breathing.

"Have you been in the house all the time?"

"Of course. Why?"

"I just called and nobody answered. I must have dialed the wrong number."

"That's probably what happened. Everything's shipshape here. All asleep. Have a good time."

After looking in on the children to make sure my story was true, I sat on the terrace with a beer from the icebox. "I've got youngsters of my own to worry about, you know," I said aloud to unseen witnesses, or accusers, or whatever. The music floated faintly on through the deepening night, and in its silences could be heard the drift of wealthy laughter. I dozed off and awoke and dozed off. After midnight there were audible splashes of water alternating with ripples of applause. The young people would be diving in the pool. Had our Geneva taken her swimming suit? She cut a pretty good figure on a springboard. I had a fancy of young bodies sailing forever in a summer dream through moonlit air, succeeding one another in an eternal, etherial circle, through space then water then back around through space again, to repeat itself in a never ending wheel, watched by aging faces wearing sad smiles, and by God Almighty.

At two A.M. the dark shapes of the Hackneys were seen toiling up the path, Mr. a little unsteady, Mrs. supporting him from time to time as they both laughed a little. They had stayed till the last dog was shot, he assured me in rather slurred tones as he fumbled for his wallet. It seemed to me I could still hear a few dogs being shot. "Marvelish evening," he muttered happily swaying on rubber legs. "That poet didn't read goddam thing." That was his recipe for success! I watched him shuffle through lettuce in his wallet looking for the right denominations — I could have rolled him for the whole wad and he'd never known it. As I pocketed my pay and left, I debated the advisability of sneaking down for another look; but though Hackney was too boiled to put two and two together, Mrs. Hackney would have noticed my not leaving promptly in the Lizzie, so I climbed into that, started her up and headed reluctantly for home.

I couldn't sleep. I tossed about in bed, waiting for the sound of Geneva's return. Toward three o'clock I heard a car in the driveway below. McGland had called for her in a cab, but it was no cab that throbbed for 10–15 minutes under my window. It was an open Cadillac convertible. Its engine had such a quiet purr that I could hear Geneva say, "Well just a quick one," as she walked down the porch steps and got back in and drove off to town with Tad Springer, their young hair blowing.

It was then that I snapped my teeth together, remembering something.

What was Tad Springer going to Dr. Wolmar for? Damn! I thought as I twisted in my nightshirt again, chicken on a spit, why had I gone soft and put the dossier away before finishing it that night I sat for the Wolmars? Going to a analyst in this part the country didn't necessarily mean anything, but it might. The trouble could be trivial or it could be serious, some variation of the hereditary blight that in his mother's case took the form of round heels, in the father's drink. So might our Geneva be taking up again with Tad after it developed that the *Springers* were bad stock, not the Spoffords, for God's sweet sake? Go to sleep I told myself, think about it tomorrow in the cold light of day. Mark Twain says we're all a little insane at night. O.K. but what did Geneva mean by just a quick one? Just a quick what? Not hamburger for God's sake, or milkshake. Hell, we'd gloated over the triumphal return as one that would open *other* doors to Geneva, not get her in solid again with a family that, it turned out now, hadn't been worth regretting the loss of. That the way it was all going to backfire? Go to sleep. The chicken revolved on the spit.

I could hardly share with the rest of my family the dilemma on which I was now what-do-you-call-it. Impaled. And impaled the more during the next week when Tad took her out again. Of course McGland called too, as did one or two other boys in the local set, boys she mightn't seen since high school and who now had a close look at what she was blossoming into. Even Mopworth the English jessie came to pick her up in his Volkswagen. That was the evening Mare sent me to answer the door, when she was in too much of a stew over her mother and Dr. Rappaport to take any more. Because it never rains but it pours — we had the two crises building up together. Still Tad seemed the favorite, and I cursed again the ill-timed compassion that had made me put the casebook away because another little boy had softened my heart. Just one more what? Was the drink that afflicted his father getting its hooks into the kid already, and the challenge posed that of a "troubled" young man getting his emotional hooks into a young girl whose own trouble might be an insecurity that left her wide open for someone who needed her, a sucker for the maternal role? Go to sleep. You're an old man blown into a corner like a dry leave. You're just mulch now for the next generation. The sap runs in other roots now. Go to sleep.

I decided I owed it to all of us to go see Dr. Wolmar and ask if he could offer an enlightening word, to whatever extent professional ethics allowed of course. But when I telephoned I was told by the answering service that the Wolmars were away on vacation and would not be back for two weeks. Which was when I got the idea of making my way into the house and having a look for myself.

After all this was only an extension of my making my way from the house into the basement while sitting for them, which I had already done, and added nothing to that act as far as irregularity was concerned. I would not be stealing anything, only availing myself of information to which I was morally entitled, and that not for myself anyway. I cooked up this plan of action when mentally distracted by a distinct warming up in the Rappaport-Punck mess. Mrs. Punck was home again, and still being called on by Dr. Rappaport when there was no longer any medical need. He would sit in the parlor and relate the latest wonders of science or analyze for our benefit the finely shaded distinctions of organized Jewry, of which he was an objective observer, always at some point lighting a Havana cigar, often a defective one from a box he said had proved on opening to be worm-eaten but not therefore harmed in quality, putting his fingers on the holes so it would draw as on the stops of a flute, so that we would watch fascinated as he puffed, ½ expecting melodies to issue from it, while Rappaport himself would from time to time look at me as though he might be going to offer me two bits to disappear, like some kid brother. How did all this get started? There must be some rational explanation for it. The entire trend of things was getting on my nerves, undermining my judgement.

I did have second thoughts about breaking into Wolmar's in the cold light of breakfast. But that night Tad appeared in a condition open to suspicion (what did he do, build himself up during the day in order to dissipate at night?) and my gumption was revived again by something I seen going by the r.r. station. It was one them *Reader's Digest* billboards which advertise the current issue of the magazine by a summary of one of its articles? The ad read: "How often have you missed out on an excellent opportunity because you failed to act on some 'inner flash' before it cooled off? Read why 'thinking it through' may be the wrong thing to do . . . and how you can easily develop the do-it-now technique of successful executives."

Spofford went home and put together a kit of burglary tools: a flashlight, hammer, chisel etc., before he should lose the spontaneity of successful executives. It was dark when I approached the Wolmars house in its dead-end lane of Punch Bowl Hollow, on foot, and with these implements distributed in discreet bulges about my person, rather than the single more noticeable kit which I had at 1st assembled and then discarded. Burning somewhere in the house was of course that single bulb that so pathetically tips off prospective thieves theres nobody home. Nobody home is right when you leave that one on! I entered the basement office through the window at the rear with little more trouble than I had descended into it the time before from the parlor. I just rapped out a pane of glass, which tinkled merrily to the floor, reached a hand in, unlatched the window, slid it up and climbed in over the sill.

The gray-green metal desk in a deep lower drawer of which the good doctor kept his notebooks was locked. Setting the flashlight on a drawn-up chair so that its beam was trained on that side of the desk, I inserted the chisel in the crack above the drawer, where the locking bar was, and began to hammer.

This mechanism proved more sturdy than expected. I banged away at the chisel for several minutes, then changed to a stout screw driver I had added to my tools at the last minute, and which I could pry farther into the slit. Suddenly I remembered something that made me slap my brow. Desks are often locked up completely when the top center drawer is merely shut tight. I slid that one open a little and found that it released all the rest too. I was pulling the drawer I wanted open when I sensed a unexplained increase in the amount of illumination I was working at. Turning I saw a beam of light coming in the window, apparently from a flashlight stronger than my own. Unable to see what was behind it, I picked up my own and trained it back. In the light of these mingled beams I could dimly discern the figure of a policeman. It was the fair young sergeant named Lawson, who had accosted me at the Beauseigneurs party, who had booked McGland and me the night of the fracas at Indelicato's, and who had probably heard about my speech at the Golden Age Club. Because he said rather pleasantly after flicking on a wall switch, "You certainly get around, don't you Pop? What are you doing now?"

"I don't see that that's any of your business," I says. "You get around yourself pretty well. What brings you here?"

"Spot checking empty houses. Always remember to give us your name when you go out of town. Its a service your entitled to as a citizen."

As he went on in this tone he examined the desk I had been jimmying. Nearby was a file of which one section was a safe, which obviously hadn't been tampered with. He shook his head, whether despairing of his ability to grasp the motivation here or in simple wonder at the range and variety of one man's activities. "What's the *matter* with you?" he asked, but there was a touch of aw in his voice. "Well come on. Let's go down and book you on a charge of breaking and entering. I'll take those tools."

Lawson was alone on his round of spot checks. On the way to the station our headlights picked out the figure of an elderly man in a neat summer suit on the road, carrying a black bag and thumbing a ride. It was Dr. Rappaport out on calls. I doubted whether Rappaport recognized me as we went by in the patrol car, but we met soon enough that night. When the family finally came down to headquarters to bail me out, following a short hearing in which bond was set at $500, he was with them. In fact he took charge. Geneva being out with the family Buick when the call came in from headquarters, Rappaport, who was setting a spell with Mrs. Punck, summoned a cab and inside 15 minutes had them all at the station, where he very solicitously settled Mare and Mrs. Punck on a bench and went over to a desk with George to sign the necessary papers. He was no less sympathetic to me, who he perfectly believed when I finally decided the best way was to come clean and let them in on the whole story. This in another cab heading for home, around

177

midnight. I sat on a jump seat, filling them in on the essentials. I couldn't quite figure Rappaport. He was either "being reasonable" to impress Mrs. Punck with his tolerance and charity toward the only possible rival in view for her interest, or he really meant it when he said *my* course of action seemed to him a reasonable one under the circumstances in which everything had gotten so entangled. He was one of those composed men who don't seem amazed by anything in the way of human life and conduct.

My own family were not so easy on me. They lost no time in informing me what they had just that day learned on their own: that it *wasn't* Tad Springer who must be worried about after all, but McGland. Geneva was apparently seeing him secretly while the others turned up openly. Four days after the "farewell" party (one of many that were being constantly given for McGland and that didn't take) he was still in the Springers guest cottage, reputedly working at white heat on some new poems, but meeting Geneva on the sly. She doing the driving because he didn't have a car of course. God alone knew where they were tonight in the family Buick.

Mrs. Punck threw in the bombshell. "Did you know that your Mr. Gland was married, Frank Spofford?" she said. "That he has a wife tucked away in London or somewhere, your fine-feathered friend?"

"How do you know?"

"The notes on contributors in those magazines you bring home. I can't read the poems, most cases, but those back sections have some interesting items in them. Well here we are home with no Buick still in the garage. Well so we have a girl mixed up with a married man. How modern!"

As we piled into the house, Mare went on to Rappaport with her gibble gabble about geriatrics, still thinking this was a *complaint* of senior citizens instead of a method of extending their productive years and giving them a new lease on life. She seemed to have the idea it referred to the mental instability, or "going off on a tangent", that sometimes strikes those of riper years. Not understanding this, Rappaport didn't answer her at all about what "could be done about it," but went on instead about the great future for it.

I headed for the icebox and got beers for all the men. "I'll talk to McGland," I told them. "I'll go over first thing in the morning and have it out with him."

"No you won't," said Mare. "You got us into this trouble. We'll let one of the rest of us see what they can do about getting us out of it. Someone else will take over now, and try to do the unravelling, Pa Spofford. We'll decide tomorrow who. We're all too tired tonight."

They settled on Mrs. Punch. This because she was the most diplomatic, the most level-headed and even-tempered, the least likely to antagonize McGland by either harsh words or making a scene. The only possible exception where that list of qualifications was concerned was Dr. Rappaport, but he was not yet an official member of the family — though he obviously soon would be — and would not carry the weight of a blood kin. Also, she liked poetry, and quickly and without hesitation selected some verses to read to McGland that covered the situation, from the anthology of Poems for All Occasions that she owned. It had always been one of her treasures, and had seen her through many a trying situation.

She spent much of the next afternoon in Geneva's room with her. The girl refused flatly to discuss the crisis with any of us, and whether she opened up to Mrs. Punch was a moot point. I still don't know, and probably never will. Because Mrs. Punch herself clammed up. She declined to reveal the gist of their conversation on the grounds that that would be a betrayal of the girl's confidence, and if that was lost the talks would break down, but assuring us with a smile that some progress had been made in them. Then she dressed to make her call on McGland, after telephoning to forewarn him of her arrival. She came downstairs in a bright cotton print with a striped parasol. She also had with her the anthology that had been in her family for years. She was sweating bullets.

"How do I look?" she asked, striking an attitude with the parasol.

"Most charming, my dear," said Rappaport, beaming at her.

To do this, he had to turn from the mantel, where he had been again contemplating an old heirloom of ours that he admired. It was an enormous clock, the face of which was completely encircled in a wood carving of two male elks, both near exhaustion, fighting with interlocked horns over a mate.

"I'll drive you over," I says.

"No!" came a chorus.

Mrs. Punck said: "I'd rather walk anyway. It's not far, and it will give me time to collect my thoughts and rehearse again what I've prepared to say to our Mr. Gland."

We all trooped out to the front porch to see her off. She went down the road with the late sun slanting against her parasol, turning it into a sort of halo, behind which she was herself invisible except for her swaying skirts and buckled shoes, and the anthology clutched in one hand, that she was evidently going to read to McGland out of! And I thought as I watched her go *This is the end of my story. This concludes my part in this. It may go on, it probably will go on, but with other principals. I slip into the shadows, there to remain a minor character in action I have presipitated. Others will come after me, in this unending rigamarole which is Life anyway, but I remain alone and to one side in — where? No place. For now I am displaced indeed, belonging neither to that world I stole briefly out of to explore another, nor in that other I slipped out to explore. A foot in each. Even Mrs. Punck is probably lost to me, in case I might decide to reach out and take her after all, a companion to spend the cool of the evening with, suddenly desirable now that she may no longer be available. The voyage is over, but it might of been pleasant to bob at anchor on the tide for a little yet, with the likes of . . . Oh well. Neither I suppose will I try to get any more of this down on paper, since from here on it looks to be somebody else's story. Well good luck to them. More power to them. In a way it's a relief on both counts. Never again will I be found in the throws of composition or romance. Which has something to be said for it. Well so be it . . .*

There went Mrs. Punck in the last of the evening light, twirling her silk parasol on her shoulder now and again, a new Mrs. Punck, setting forth on a new life.

McGLAND

seventeen

McGLAND WAS AWAKENED by the persistent ringing of bells, which they had been told aboard ship was a signal to rush to the lifeboats, wearing preservers. When this mental confusion cleared and he realized he was in bed, his next conviction was that he was being roused by the alarm clock supplied by his hosts, which it might have occurred to him to set as he sank into the swaying bed the night before. The memory of the bed's behaving like a lifeboat on disturbed water had no doubt survived whatever number of hours he had slept, and determined the nautical turn of his dream. When smothering the clock and all its latches and levers did no good, he understood it was the phone ringing, and groped successfully for that.

"Hello."

Speaking the word dealt his head a jolt, reviving again the mystery of hangover: why the same number of drinks could mean purgatory one morning and a head clear as a bell another. Someone had been striking matches on the roof of his mouth.

"Hello, Mr. Gland. You were no doubt looking at the sunset?"

"Look at whuh?"

"The sunset."

He wallowed over on his back, carrying the telephone with him, entangling himself in the cord. "Whassama wi'?"

"The matter with what?"

"Susset."

"Why, nothing. It's simply beautiful. Such an inspiration. I thought since you didn't immediately answer you were probably outside, writing an ode to it."

Something in the sheer novelty of the idea that poets any longer looked at sunsets, much less consciously seated themselves on stumps to celebrate their effects, stung McGland into new life. "Who is this?"

"Mrs. Punck."

"Who?"

"Mrs. Punck. You remember. What is the matter, Mr. Gland?"

He was mumbling incoherently. "Sun come up?"

"Why, no, it's not coming up. It's going down!"

"Third and las' time?" His head lolling to one side, his tongue hanging out of that, he feared he might be going to be ill among the bedclothes.

"What in the world is the matter with you? Don't you feel well?"

"Uh *uh!* Fee' awf'."

"There is something that's been going around." McGland lay there watching the room do more or less that, absolutely unable to speak for a few moments; he had a slaughtering katzenjammer just above his eyes. "Very frequently they say our water here affects visitors. Digestively. Do you find it so?"

"Oh, yeah," he breathed without any movement of his parted lips. He lay panting quietly, like a dog resting after exertion, any words merely slight changes in the nature and pace of his respiration.

"I can't think just now whether you still have well water out there or whether city water has gone that far. Do you know what the Springers have? Well or city?"

McGland had moved the phone away from his ear in order to relieve the vibration set up in his head by the incoming queries. For a moment he had the thought that a solicitation for some kind of hydraulic installation was being made, and grasping at it said, "You'll have to call them. I'll hang up and you ring the main house again."

"No, no, I don't want the Springers. I want you. This is Mrs. Punck, Geneva's grandmother. Remember now? I'd like to call on you if I may, and pay my respects."

That was the second stunner — that anyone any longer "paid

respects." It was scarcely less quaint than that the function of the artist was the commemoration of beauty, and in some ways perhaps even more extraordinary. The whole conversation was like a lace valentine. McGland was. so touched that now he feared he would indeed be ill, so he said, "Tomorrow," and hung up and pulled the covers over his head. Or tried to. For in his eagerness the order became reversed, so that he still had the phone in one hand after the other had drawn the bedclothes well up around his ears, and it was through enmeshing thicknesses of linen that he heard Mrs. Punck going on in a now urgent manner. He said, "Iss a lah de betta marda morda."

"We'll leave it that way then."

Now he did manage to deposit the phone in its cradle and draw the remaining arm back into his cocoon. He buried his head.

Danger lulled McGland where it might rouse others. He was a hibernator, able to flee the inclemencies of human and other realities into a warm cavern of detachment and withdrawal, a kind of stupor like a thickening hide. After a terrible scene, such as a clash with a woman or a husband, or with a literary adversary, he might sleep for two or three days running: the happy survival of infancy when shock can send us into peaceful slumber. So men sometimes behave on the battlefield. He was in any case soon dead to the world again.

McGland was one of those people who combine tremendous ambition with overpowering sloth. As a child he had always thought what he would like to be, rather than what he would like to do. A typical daydream then had been that of a symphonic conductor bowing to thunderous applause, rather than sawing the air in the exertions normally preceding its dessert. There was the lock of hair falling over one eye, the crumpled shirtfront and the tailcoat drenched with sweat, rarely the labors productive of this dramatic pleasure, much less the hours of grueling rehearsal behind those. This combination of drive and lethargy can be hard on people whose makeup includes them in equal ratio. Talent possesses them in juxtaposition oftener than is perhaps generally known.

While McGland had never availed himself of psychiatry, he was familiar with its precepts and knew that memory is not just a chance repository but a selective principle offering clues to one's basic wishes. He seemed by this criterion to want unearned fruits — the Paradisal myth itself — for his own earliest recollections were not of anything occurring but only of himself imagining their occurring: thus he vividly remembered fancying himself showered with future fame. He had read most of the literature on the psychopathology of sloth, including an analysis of Doctor Johnson, without being convinced that anybody really knew very much about it. But its victims know it to be a curse and a cross. "I *wish* I'd get up. I *wish* I'd go there or do that. Oh, how I want to want to!" Oh, the first discovery that one is to be henceforth the tormented fulcrum of apathy and aspiration.

He had been one of eight children. Since his father, an impoverished weaver in the north of Scotland, was half Welsh, and his mother also — her other half being Irish — there was "more Welsh rain in me than Scotch mist," as he was later to tell an interviewing journalist. Yet this dominant strain was not represented in his final published name. It had been as a concession to the maternal Irish that he was christened Gowan, with the Welsh proclaimed in his middle name, Glamorgan; vainly, since it was dropped for all practical purposes as making the whole far too euphonious, even for a poet. McGland later regretted not having come on the literary scene as Glamorgan McGland, for at the time he did, there was far more *éclat* attached to being Welsh than Scotch, or Irish. Still, he was often thought of as a Welshman, rather than a Scotsman.

His father said that having that many children was like running an orphanage, which the children for their part often felt they'd as soon have inhabited, there on the blasted coast "between the snarling river and the mumbling sea," as the young Gowan was to write in one of his earliest published poems. His parents fought and bred in about equal measure. "You're a mean, swilling spendthrift." "And you're the little Bitch of Sunset Lane. Ask anybody." After an hour or more of this they would be found together in the inglenook nibbling one another and murmuring endearments by the fire. Gowan could never without amusement hear of the "feelings of insecurity" said to result from domestic discord; in that congested cottage alarm was oftener inspired by the sight of their parents hitting it off.

The feeling for words comes at an early age — or rather it is lost in most cases at an early age, leaving the rest poets. The boy Gowan could remember his interest on learning that the skin eruption covering his face and creeping into his scalp was called impetigo. Surely that was no disease, but the name of a river in American Indian country, something you found love on the banks of? "The Impetigo winds lazily through valley lands, dwindling to a trickle in the fall but overflowing its banks in the spring when the tributary streams, swollen by melting mountain snows . . ." Cowboy and Indian adventures were his favorite reading then, also the fare for which he most eagerly put down his sixpence at the local movie window, and it seemed to him that "the Impetigo Indians" rang true also as the tribe for which the river was named, savage redskins roaming the Michigan or Minnesota wildwoods two hundred years ago, which he would one day visit . . .

One of the calamities of his boyhood was a fight in which he lost two front teeth, for he had a sad heritage of teeth and could ill spare them. He had since then lost several more through natural causes, till at last his smile was a bright octave of counterfeits about which he was more self-conscious than he had been over their poor forebears. They were affixed to the five left in his upper jaw, one more, a dentist had told him, than the absolute minimum on which in his case a bridge could be suspended. If he lost two more, that is . . . But his mind recoiled in horror from that thought. Teeth were by now an obsession with him, a mania. He dreamed about them, he awoke from nightmares about them, grinding them in the very fear of straining them unduly. Toothlessness would be for McGland the moment of truth. Toothlessness was for McGland chief among the range of cosmic insults heaped upon man, final proof of his total and tragic ludicrousness. He had lost his perspective on that subject. His terror, coiling unsuspected in the core of him, made him a critic of every smile he met. He could spot capped teeth at ten feet, a bridge at twenty. The notation of a full denture was not cruelty, or even pity, but clairvoyant anguish, a premonition of that certain day when only three sound ones remained to him and the dentist, leaning against the wall with folded arms and a kind expression, must tell him that they too — No! That would be the sign that all endurable life had, for McGland, ceased on this earth. That humiliation he would spurn. In the long, strategic retreat called human life, he saw himself as backing toward his grave tooth by tooth and poem by poem, and he would go to his own voluntarily, with a few of each still left in his head.

This premonition of his end was also part of his heritage. At sixty his father had drilled his sclerotic old brain with a bullet from a pistol gotten God knew where. His mother stuck it out to the end. But McGland, armed now with the adolescent's informed gloom, saw in her courage only further proof that in the end the universe spits on us; that, worse than Nothing, might very well be a malevolent intelligence to whom all our humiliations offer an eternally unfolding comedy. Why not? Because consider. She had cataracts, which they hopefully let ripen, to find on removing them that in the meantime she had contracted glaucoma and gone blind anyway. Both breasts were successfully removed. When she was too old to walk she crawled, singing hymns to nourish her tried belief: "There is a fountain filled with blood drawn from Immanuel's veins." That she "never lost her faith" was for McGland the final twist of the whole bad joke, for brooding by the waterside now he thought about the writers he was reading, chiefly then Hemingway, who had insisted that the horses running around the bullfight arena with their entrails hanging out were not tragic at all, but funny. Perhaps there was a power higher than us, as we are higher than a horse, to whom the sight of a blind and mutilated old woman crawling on all fours through a mortgaged house thinking she is going to heaven is irresistibly funny. Such was at the time the state of his thinking. Maggie McGland had had him late in life, so he saw his mother's old age while still relatively young—and she had been old at sixty.

McGland was already then being groomed for a central role in this comedy, if such it be. The first of his permanent afflictions (after that of having inherited a mouthful of chalk) was what are known as "cluster headaches."

These variations of classic migraine, so called because they occur in clusters, or closely bunched sequences, are hard to describe to anyone who has never had them, and impossible for medicine to explain. They are accompanied by visual manifestations. The victim becomes temporarily blinded in one eye, not Stygianly blind, but with all sorts of fiery lights and coruscations appearing on the affected side, usually in waving, slowly changing patterns, like those in a kaleidoscope. The attack lasts for anywhere from a few minutes to half an hour or more, and inspires in the victim the urge to pace (in distinction from orthodox migraine, which makes him lie down). Walking the floor many a time, McGland analyzed this as the impulse to outflank the pyrotechnics, as one does a car on the road, and so leave them behind. One knows this to be absurd but, even so, is unable to sit still. The frustration recedes only when the attack does and one's vision clears, as in the end it always does, to be succeeded in due course by another. Cluster headaches are, along with toothlessness, gout, hay fever, asthma, impetigo and arthritis, among the more innately hilarious (to other people) ordeals which fate has dished up for human edification.

McGland's arthritis was cervical. There were times when he could scarcely turn his head, such was the inflammation at the back of his neck. The pain was neither extreme nor progressive, but always bad when he first awoke in the morning, or whenever it was that he awoke. He began each day by sitting up in bed moving his head from side to side, to work the joint loose, like a rusty hinge. This visitation was to McGland another prophetic whiff of death, for in spite of the doctor's assurances to the contrary he saw the inflammation spreading from joint to joint, till he was locked immobile and helpless on his back. The doctor recommended a traction. This was a wide orthopedic collar on which McGland's head reposed like that of John the Baptist on a platter, and which was equipped with straps to the other ends of which were affixed hooks, like grappling hooks, by means of which the patient suspended himself partially from any convenient ledge, such as the lintel of a door. "It amounts to hanging yourself a few times a day," the doctor said, being a great believer in humor as a balance to life's trials and a means to perspective.

"What if there's no molding over the doorway for the hooks to catch on to?"

"Throw the straps over a tree limb, a rafter in the attic, anything so long as it will support you enough *so your head pulls away from your neck*, and eases the inflammation in the joint. Here, look, I'll demonstrate the principle of traction," the doctor said, coming briskly round his desk. "Come here."

The doctor held his arm out at his side in the shape of a noose for McGland to slip his head into and then, tightening it, began to pull and haul McGland about the consultation room like a wrestler with his opponent in a headlock. "Don't come along with me, man, resist. So your neck bones come *away*. There, hear that?" McGland gave a grunt of assent at the grinding sound which indicated that the vertebrae were indeed parting, in the manner desired. "There, that feel better?" the doctor said, releasing him.

McGland staggered drunkenly around the room when let go of, bumping into the healer with a hand extended as he groped his way past the desk — for one of the cluster headaches had got started. It was a little like the time he'd had his teeth worked on while he had something in his eye. "That feel better?" the doctor persisted in knowing. McGland nodded.

When the orthopedic collar, ordered from Edinburgh, finally arrived, McGland found himself quite eager to try it out. He experienced a fascination with it that had nothing to do with its curative intent. He would fancy that he *was* hanging himself. The romantic in him took over every time he slung those leather straps over the attic rafter from which he conducted his home exercises — or rather the ropes to which he tied the straps, for they weren't in themselves long enough to reach. The whole arrangement was rather like a swing suspended from a tree, except that he hung from it instead of sat in it. Soon merely imagining that he was hanging himself was not enough.

He began to experiment with ticklish approximations to the act.

The instructions he had been given were as follows. He was to stand with his head in the halter for about five minutes at a time, his feet planted firmly on the floor and bending his knees just enough to exert, at the neck joint, the pressure required to work it loose a little. That was all. Soon, however, he took to lifting one heel off the floor, then both. Then one foot altogether, so that he was balanced precariously on a single toe. Then he lifted that off the floor too, and for a split second hung by his neck in midair — tasting for that fragment of time the rapture of self-destruction. There was something more to this than play-acting. Thoughts about hanging, shooting, stabbing or poisoning himself had helped him while away the hours of many a sleepless night (as Nietzsche advises) but there were in them odd quivers of premonition, the sense that he was not merely acting, but rehearsing.

But there were the miles to go before one slept, and his first job was on a weekly newspaper in a nearby town of some size. Fifteen thousand as compared with the fifteen hundred in his native village. His duties were simple: to write the entire contents of the paper. This meant noting the births, deaths and social events of the community, and when they did not fill up the space, combing the countryside for old men who could remember forty below and who attributed their long lives to plenty of red meat and whiskey, as they were quite willing to say when bought a drink in the course of an interview on their birthday. It was on these rounds that McGland's flesh first proclaimed its aversion to work on a scale that only total collapse would bring out into the open and into adequate focus. Every muscle and bone in his body protested the exertions to which it was put. Every limb had, like a rebellious mule, to be flogged to its toils while it cried out against the inhumanity of regular employment. Until McGland could scarcely drag one foot after the other. A flight of stairs was like a mountain to be climbed. Chronic fatigue enveloped his limbs like lead. He fell asleep over his typewriter. Nightmares of what the day would bring, and then at last complete insomnia, made a mockery of his lying down. Until at last one morning he could not get up. *He simply and absolutely could not get up.* The doctor (plying rounds into which terms like neurasthenia had not yet crept) called it nervous exhaustion, and prescribed a tonic and a few weeks' vacation.

They did McGland a world of good. He ate well. He slept soundly. Deliverance from the specter of having to arise enabled him to spring out of bed with a will. His spirits rose as well, so that he could even begin to think again about suicide (that feat which contrary to assumption cannot always be performed in total depression but requires a certain emotional energy, even a kind of excitement). He wrote a little poetry. One of the poems sold instantly to a London literary journal:

That sempiternal slut, the Sea,
Spits and hisses in my father's sleep,
Sprawls, crawls, sucks her soft sad sand gums, moans
At the full moon caught among the rocks
Like a lozenge in her broken teeth, mumbles,
Fumbles at the lock, the salt sill
Where my father snores into the tide all night,
Blowing the little fishes back to Blatherskite.
And I, a dull and muddy-mettled Pascal,
Think how all her white limbs and his red hunger came to this:
A night hag riding the Atlantic deep
While he dreams of brooms in his disreputable sleep.

But in my boy's case a mere, dear green year ago,
The moon like a struck gong awoke me, fetched me trembling
To the window, where I stood, white as my unlit candle held
Straight as that the poor shorn novitiates kiss
When, taking Jesus, they forsake all this.
And there she stood, her white feet in the sand,
The shepherdess of sheep, equestrienne of the plunging steeds,
For whom I heaved my Thracian sigh,
The sempiternal queen, the Sea!

The editor of the paper had agreed to keep his job open for a fortnight. When it was up, and the morning dawned on which McGland must return to work, the same feeling of exhaustion palsied his members. He could scarcely drag himself out of bed again, much less out of the house, but drag himself he did, across town and up the stairs to his office.

Hauling himself about his rounds once more, he kept an eye peeled for more congenial modes of employment as much as for items of news interest. Once on the main street, in the heat of the day, he staggered to a stop before the window of a showroom where motor cars were sold. Everything beyond the plate glass — the floor on which the handsome new models were displayed, the duties of the salesmen, who seemed to do little more than occasionally lift the bonnet of an engine for a customer, when they were not lounging about smoking cigarettes — looked so pleasant by comparison with his own drab and unabating chores that he went inside, intending to ask for the manager and see about such a job.

A salesman advanced, smiling hopefully and with a pantomime of soaping his hands. He told McGland the manager was out, and added, "May I show you something?" He gestured toward a nearby sedan, of which the back door stood invitingly open. The sight of the roomy seat with its deep upholstery was so tempting that McGland, now more dead than alive, nodded without a word and climbed in. He sank with a grateful sigh onto the cushions.

The salesman began a recital of the product's merits, his head thrust partway into the tonneau. He stressed its durability, economy, and luxurious riding qualities. McGland sat in a trance of comfort, staring out the open door, hearing nothing the man said, seeing nothing but his eyes, like a patient in hypnosis. The deception added a note of guilt to his sensation which completed its resemblance to a carnal pleasure. "Would you like to go for a ride in her?" the man said, on completing his spiel. McGland gave another glazed nod, and was presently being chauffeured around the city and into the outlying countryside in a kind of demoralized vegetable bliss.

He had no idea even of the make of the car, and did not trouble to ask. He rocked deliciously along on the back seat in a purring half-consciousness, watching the outskirts of the city slip past, then cottages giving way to a subdivision and this at last to open farmland. Several men naked to the waist were digging a trench for a water main. He marveled vaguely at their exertions, five minutes of which would have killed him.

When the ride was over and a card bearing the salesman's name together with some illustrated folders had been pressed into his hand, he thanked the man and went immediately to a place where there was an agency for another car, and did the same thing. A note of secrecy and shame, such as he might feel were his destination an opium den or other house of iniquity, added progressively to the sensation which he sought and to which he now abandoned himself. The second agency visited, he slipped through the streets to still a third, feeling as though he had invented a new vice, one whose possibilities he was eager to explore. No doubt an ingredient in his delinquency lay in a certain pleasure he took in making other people waste *their* time as he was wasting his. That much was to be assumed. But it was only a small part of it. Uppermost was a curious but definite physical gratification, bordering, at times, on the voluptuous. When the automobile showrooms in that general vicinity had been exhausted, McGland had people demonstrate motor boats, gramophones, household furniture — anything to approximate the kind of sensual passivity that lay at the heart of this novel indulgence. He lolled in scudding speedboats or in overstuffed chairs and even on beds, or rocked gently in hammocks on display in garden centers, while the sales talks droned pleasantly on like insects on a summer afternoon. One saleswoman demonstrating a lounge chair equipped with a vibrating mechanism which administered a massage to one's reclining limbs, a highly sybaritic contraption imported from America, could hardly get him out of it again, so profound was the stupor into which he had been lulled. His path was not so vague in distant spheres, however, that he was oblivious to her bosom as she bent over him, manipulating the buttons on the arm of the chair on which he lay supine. It required an effort to keep his hands folded on his stomach. This was in Glasgow, where he now pursued his perversion on secret sorties. He had of course lost his job, and three more as well by now, but it was from the fragmentary spasms of income as well as the severance pays provided by these brief spells of employment that he financed his addiction, practiced now on the widening scales afforded by the large metropolises. In London he had a real estate broker drive him for days on end from house to house he had no intention of buying. In a travel agency, a girl with a full red mouth and large hips sketched out a detailed itinerary for a trip through the Rhine Valley. The low warble of her voice, the rustle of the ever unfolded "literature," the scent of her perfume and even the scratch of her pencil, all blent into the erotic haze in which he sat close beside her at her desk, as he dreamed of traversing with her the vineyards among which she recommended he bicycle in the spring.

It was his poetry that saved him, in a rather roundabout way.

McGland had always been given to reciting Shakespeare and Yeats by the seaside in his native village. Now he took to shouting lines of his own into the wind and tide. It was a way of testing them. After the revisions, there were the rewards of declaiming the finished product. It was while doing this that he was struck by the resonance of his voice and the purity of his diction. He began to wonder if radio acting mightn't offer the pleasant and easy livelihood for which he was still on the lookout. He was unsuccessful in his first attempts, but did land a job as an announcer on a station in Liverpool. That gave him an inside track there, and he wrote a few plays, which he produced and acted in himself. He had a natural dramatic instinct with a line, and could do amazing tricks with his voice. A London producer heard him play an eccentric Scotch landowner and immediately asked him to audition for a Shakespearean series he was planning to do on the B.B.C. in the fall. The audition was a success, and McGland moved to London with a contract in his pocket. By the time the series was over he was established as a free lance radio actor.

He walked into a London studio one day for rehearsal to see a tall, slender young woman with skin as clear as honey pacing the floor reading a script aloud to herself. She wore a tweed coat loose over her shoulders. Her pale gold hair was long and straight, and from time to time she would toss her head to fling it out of one eye. This movement would dislodge the coat, which she would have to grasp and settle on her shoulders again. She was a girl of English and French extraction named Edith Chipps. Together they were to play a scene of which the climax was a chase through the woods, in which Miss Chipps was required to pant for several minutes before the microphone. This is almost impossible to do without becoming dizzy, and she blacked out. McGland caught her as she dropped, both their scripts falling in disorder to the floor, so that he had to improvise the end from what he remembered of the lines from rehearsal while another woman, rushing from the control room with a fresh script, read Miss Chipps's for her. Miss Chipps came to on a couch, fluttering her pale blue eyes open to the sight of McGland bending over her, chafing her wrists in the manner in which he had seen it done in films. He took her down for some coffee, over which he made no secret of his contempt for the "piece of rubbish" for which she had performed so nobly.

"Thank you," was her answer, "I wrote it."

McGland gave the contrite-boy smile by now characteristic of him, but he needn't have worried. She relished his disadvantage. Miss Chipps liked being wronged, for the pleasure of watching him wriggle across the palm of her hand as it were, to some sort of amends. She delayed revealing that her father had been a street sweeper until McGland made some idle reference to that employment. "At least it's better than sweeping streets," he said of radio acting. "It's what my father was," she said, and watched him squirm. She had a knack, if not a genius, for manipulating the precise moment when the maximum in moral reimbursements could be exacted.

"I didn't mean — I'm sorry, Miss Chipps," he faltered.

"It's all right. Call me Edith," she said, her thin lips wreathed in a smile, and flung her hair out of her eye.

McGland had lost three more teeth and his own smile was brightening by the month. He had sold his fifth group of poems and had begun to cause a stir in literary circles as a new voice heralding the return to rhetoric after a quarter-century of understatement. Critics were quick to assure him, however, that rhetorical though his poetry might be, it was still irreproachably antipoetic. It was undisfigured by charm, free of any taint of conscious Beauty. No charge could be brought against it on that score. Edith had meanwhile launched a radio serial called "The Tuttle Family," on the double income from which — she as author, McGland as principal — they felt they could marry. He had become thoroughly infatuated with her. She had looks, vibrancy, spirit. She could cook though having no taste for that chore as a daily grind; so that when they were not dining on some succulent dish they were foraging in tins. She was, if not affectionate, at least amorous. Or, if not amorous, certainly erotic. She put her hair to pleasant and often astonishing uses. She would hang it down over McGland and swing it from side to side, delicately brushing his skin with its golden tips. It was only one in her range of rather exotic caresses, for she was a woman who made up in passion what she may have lacked in emotion, in heat what she may have lacked in warmth. "She's cold but, damn it, she's hot," thought McGland, who brought to their union, of course, contradictory currents of his own.

Passive types burst into reactions as unexpected as those lapses into docility with which volcanic temperaments surprise us, in keeping with that divine law of polarity on which all the universe and everything within it seem to run. Thus nothing is more characteristic than behaving "out of character." We are best educated to understand this by marriage, that arena for the display of private contradictions. Women accept the fact more naturally than men, the evidence being in the very "fickleness" of their judgments. We accuse them of being friends with somebody one day and wanting nothing more to do with him the next, when the truth is that the friend will deserve favor on the one day and its reverse on the next. Their "inconsistency" is only a reflection of reality's. They blow hot and cold as do the winds of heaven itself.

No one went on more abrupt holidays from his official nature than McGland. Lazy as hell, he plunged into bursts of work it was as hard for him to stop as it had been to get started (the law of inertia being the tendency not only of stationary objects to remain stationary, but of moving ones to remain in motion). If their marriage was not destined to be peaceful, at least it was eventful. Their temperamental flareups locked them in fights as passionate as their mating. These even involved physical violence, which in turn sometimes verged on mortal combat. They not only threw things at one another, they rolled on the floor like two brawlers in a bar, clawing and kicking at one another. In addition to a small flat in Chelsea, they rented a cottage on the Welsh coast, where they would go for week ends and holidays. Once, crossing to Dublin on the ferry from Holyhead as they frequently did, they tried to throw one another overboard into the Irish Sea. They came to their senses at last, panting at the ship's rail, surprised that they had so much feeling for one another.

Often after such scenes McGland would return to the practice of his vice. He would steal away secretly to some hitherto unexploited corner of London and have something demonstrated to him. Then while rolling through the streets in the back of a Daimler he would review with dull, spent amazement the extremes of which man is capable, and the irony of their flowing, at their worst, from his most ennobling bond. Yet at the same time the pursuit of his vice helped him forget, for a little, the indignities to which one is subject, such as very nearly pitching one's wife overboard as an alternative to being pitched overboard, and in the vegetable bliss which was its object sad cares would flee away, all emotional fret for a time be purged and soothed from his spirit.

"She ride beautifully, governor?"

McGland nodded behind the glass. The ride over, he took the man's card and folder and headed for a sporting goods store, where he was soon curled up in the placental warmth of a sleeping bag, deep in the seclusion of a display tent. It was while drifting through these Lethean depravities that he received one of the shocks of his life.

He was slumped in a chair in a television store watching the program flashed successively on a screen by a plump, motherly saleswoman turning the dial for him when, through the customary glaze of abstraction, he heard something that made him slide erect. "Yes," an announcer was saying, "the Tuttles are going on the telly! Monday week, that popular wireless family will start coming to you over this —"

"Turn that back on!" The woman had changed channels and now switched back. McGland's worst suspicions were confirmed. The serial in which he had made such a pleasant living for a year was leaving the wireless for television. Why had Edith not told him? Why had no one mentioned it to him at the broadcasting studio? There could be only one reason. He was to be dropped as the leading man when the change of medium occurred because he was not good-looking enough. He could play the part of a handsome young romantic so long as he was heard and not seen, but the illusion would not survive photography. They had not even bothered to test him. McGland rose and stumbled out of the store, crushed.

Now began one of those bouts of drinking which, together with the wenching with which they were often accompanied, were destined to add the tarnish of notoriety to his fame, making him a "legend in his lifetime." Braced with the first few straight whiskies, he put in a call to Edith, who was working at the seashore. Her voice rang like a handful of false coins.

"Gowan, I thought you knew about it. I thought you assumed it all along, as we did. You've got to make the switch these days, you simply do. It's where the real money is, for one thing." Sensing his black mood at the other end, she raced on to get in as much as possible before the receiver was banged down. "Don't you see, Gowan, it'll be twice as much income — more with me stepping in to Harriet — didn't you know that either? So now you won't have to do anything at all. You'll be completely free to write. It's what you want, isn't it? I mean my God I took *that* for granted — Gowan!"

The binge lasted for three days. In the course of it, to make his hell complete, he laid eyes on the chap who was to replace him. It was at a party into which he wandered on the third night, where most of the guests were the wireless and telly crowd with whom the McGlands had naturally fallen in of late. The new Hilary Tuttle was a tall, lean stunner named Alvin Mopworth, with wavy black hair and a smile that cut McGland like a knife. In a spasm of rage and despair he remembered he would be toothless by forty. There was only and always one cure for this now: reach out for any woman his widening vogue made available to him and clasp her like a poultice to his abscessed heart. It was what his henceforth Gargantuan philandering amounted to — slaking in as many arms as possible the thirst for reassurance in the race with Time.

He had seen the girl in the blue wool dress note his arrival at the party, which was in a flat near Piccadilly, and when she said, "Aren't you Gowan McGland?" he knew only too well what she meant. She meant, "My God, are *you* Gowan McGland?" For she was familiar with the Henry Hulan charcoal drawing of him that had been widely reproduced, and was undergoing the sensation common to those who were, and were now confronted with the original of that idealization: the shock of finding the man rather a caricature of the likeness. "Guilty," he said, taking in her not very shapely but probably cozy body. She was a foot too short and round as a cheese, but he was no prize either he reminded himself as he sensed her appraising the thickening features and damp tangle of hair against the faun's head Hulan had popularized. Where had Hulan found that comely daemon? A glimpse into the subject's heart of hearts had uncovered that lurking self-image for the artist, no doubt. McGland felt himself the victim of a wily prank, if not a stroke of suavely ironic cruelty. "Thank God I can write better than he can draw," McGland thought as he permitted himself to be towed possessively toward an unoccupied sofa.

After the first compliments about his latest group, as well as some elucidations by the girl of meanings in them McGland had not suspected, they fell silent, watching the growing jam of guests. He knew that now he would sober up. He did not formally meet Mopworth that night — Mopworth was pointed out to him by a fellow actor. After that he could hardly keep his eyes off him. The couple giving the party were indifferent hosts, preferring to enjoy themselves like guests while Mopworth, a close friend who was at present staying with them, darted about, filling highball glasses and passing refreshments round, emptying ashtrays and lighting women's cigarettes. "Mother's little helper," McGland muttered. Mopworth was the picture of grace, sidling round furniture and popping through clefts in the crowd with a fluidity and precision that made his actions seem like pantomime in a ballet. His grooming oppressed McGland, whose own jacket and shirt were flecked with stains of food and drink which, however, he was inspired by the other's example to scratch at with his thumbnail from time to time. Mopworth wore a double-breasted blue pinstripe suit, neatly creased, a white shirt and red foulard tie. He seemed to avoid McGland. When momentarily free of his volunteer chores, he would wedge himself back between two girls with whom he kept up a run of broken shop talk, turning his head regularly from the one to the other, like a spectator at a tennis match, and smiling frequently.

"He makes a charming hostess," McGland's girl said.

"Why do you say that?" McGland did not differ with this slur, he wanted to hear it developed. It cheered him to think that he had been replaced as leading man not by the real article but by a photogenic counterfeit, while he, McGland, was the genuine coin, a little chipped and worn to be sure, but ringing true in the marketplace of sexual negotiations. "Why are you so sure of that?"

"Well, the ladies' man stuff, for one thing," she said, munching a pretzel with her free hand, for McGland had a firm grip on the other. They both leaned well over toward her side, like two figures rounding a turn at breakneck speed in a fast vehicle. "Nobody but a jessie would work that hard at playing the gander."

"To cover up. I see what you mean. Has he made a pass at you?"

"Well and I mean the Mother's Little Helper bit. That. Don't you think he's got that look?"

McGland nodded, watching. "Malady of our time. Infectious mammanucleosis."

They watched Mopworth at his pavane of hospitality, bobbing, bowing, marching left and right, always picking up his feet. McGland's question to the girl remained unanswered, but the object of the discussion smiled at enough other girls, God knew, and looked down enough dress fronts to hang a hundred men in an age imbued with the principle that everything is the opposite of what it seems. "He avoids me," McGland said.

"He can hardly expect you to like him under the circs," the girl said. "Forget it, Gowan. He can't write poetry."

"I hear he's had some light verse in *Punch*," McGland said, worriedly.

"That's not poetry. Yours is poetry. You're a new voice, so be still." She turned on him eyes as dark as his own, under tarbrush brows. They left for his flat shortly after midnight.

"I like particularly the one that goes, 'The Lord my God has widgeons in his hair,'" she said as she peeled a stocking from a fat thigh. McGland nodded from the pillow. The sensation was beginning to come over him that he experienced when having something demonstrated to him that he had no intention of buying. One was not merely wicked, debauched and depraved — one was naughty. Released from their supports her breasts dropped like hanged men. The rest of her sprang free of its elastic prison, and she was in beside him, warm and cold both, and thrillingly clammy.

"Recite some poetry to me," she murmured in his arms when they were at rest.

"*Post coitum omne animal triste est,*" he said.

"I mean something of your own. The one that goes, 'I deem these rather smashable guts.' I like that one too."

An idea for a bit of light verse was coming to him. It became a quatrain it should be a cinch to sell to *Punch*:

> *After the stout and the Stilton*
> *Is it the old or the newfangled line?*
> *Did he win her by reading her Milton*
> *Or I lose her by reading her mine?*

Three quid at least, he thought, squeezing her fat billows gratefully. He recited her something anyway, first the one she had requested, then one from a new group on which he was at work.

"I love you," she said, when he had finished.

"I love you too." Mopworth had tended rather to swirl his beer about in his glass, had he not, as though it were some fine old brandy, gazing into it while he gave the girls some talk probably as far from good conversation as the beer was from brandy. "I feel as though I've known you all my life," the girl murmured, and he buried his face deeper in her breasts, hiding from her. "I'll tell you something, Gowan. I'm a virgin. I mean I was until tonight."

This was something McGland might have found easier to believe had he not in the ensuing week had occasion to visit his physician. He felt no bitterness toward the girl, only a fresh installment of a chronic outrage at human trials on both their behalfs. Indeed, any sense of injury was quickly superseded by the fear of having in turn given it — for he had patched it up with Edith and they were living together again. His gloom had vanished when a publisher sought him out with an enthusiastic offer to publish a book of his poems in the fall, with a handsome advance which made him feel a person in his own right once again.

Now he was back at the bottle, walking the seaside in numb, dumb fear. He watched Edith for any signs in her expression. Medications had him swiftly again in the clear, but what of her? It was like living with a time bomb, set for an interval of which he was not certain. She typed at her scripts all day and settled down with a mystery and a highball in the evenings. She washed her hair every other night, reading while she blew it dry with an electric dryer. Sometimes she ate an apple.

McGland looked ghastly. He fascinated himself in the bathroom glass, dwelling on his hollow cheeks and red-rimmed eyes. With his removable bridgework out he looked like a jack-o'-lantern; he smiled to prove it, recovering to himself thereby the sense of outrage. What did Edith have to complain about, even if this did befall her? She was beautiful. Her teeth were like a flock of sheep which go up from the washing, whereof every one beareth twins, and none is barren among them. She was successful. She had everything . . .

At last his worried glances were rewarded by the change in

her manner which he feared. She seemed to be appraising him speculatively. Once he caught her watching him in a mirror while she stood drying her hair. He knew the jig was up when she disappeared the next afternoon with no explanation except that she had "an appointment in town." The secret was out. There was nothing to do but confess it.

Yet his tongue could not be pried into speech. The words stuck in his throat. The old inertia jammed his emotions and paralyzed his brain. Broaching the subject was like shouldering a weight he could not possibly be expected to lift, it was like taking on a year's work. She would not speak to him.

Toward evening, on her return, she went for a walk by the sea. He watched her from the cottage doorway, far below, her head bound in a scarf and her hands plunged into the pockets of her red wool coat. Occasionally she picked up a stone and flung it into the water.

When she had become a faint dot against the ocean, he suddenly saw her as an abstract, or symbolic, human cipher, carrying their misfortune along with her till it too faded to a mere speck. It gave him perspective. How petty the human fret when absorbed into the all-healing seascape! How trivial their troubles when viewed against the eternal play of wind and cloud!

He ran down the twisting path and raced along the beach after her before this perspective vanished, leaving behind in the cottage doorway a second self to hold the picture in focus while he got the hullabaloo over with. He pretended it was himself still back there in the doorway, watching both of them with an all-resolving humor and affection. It would be all over in a minute.

"Have you noticed anything lately?" he gasped without preliminary, overtaking her.

"That's what I was going to ask you."

"Then you know what I'm talking about?"

"Yes. Oh my God, Gowan!" She had quickened her step, and now they hurried laboriously through the sand side by side, as though they were running a race. He began to plead.

"It could happen to anybody. It happens in the best . . . I

mean you pick somebody up when you're in absolute . . ." His voice stumbled on like their feet, his breathing audible above the furious scuffing. He stopped her in her tracks by catching her arm and spinning her around. They were at last face to face. "Things can be the same again," he said, and sank to his knees, encircling her waist with both arms. "We'll go to Dublin. The way we used to. Or for a holiday to Paris . . ."

She stood like a statue gazing out to sea. Her body was rigid as stone in his embrace, though presently he felt her hand drop gently to his head. "Oh, Gowan. Then you forgive me?"

He held his cheek firmly against the rough cloth of her coat for some time. Then, either because she had repeated her words or because they had finally penetrated his mind through the delirious beating of the surf, he slowly leaned his head back and looked up at her. "Whuh?"

"I won't spare myself. You sometimes just stumble into those things, yes. A rather nice poor bloke I got to talking to at the pub. Well there you were in London, off for good you gave me to believe. What did you expect me to do? I don't mind what he wished on me, except for passing it on to you. I mean I'm not offering any *moral* excuses, because after all the whole thing wouldn't have happened if you hadn't run off to London. Still you're taking it rather sweetly . . ."

His mind was still a lap behind his hearing, and that still another behind her words, but the substance of what she was saying did finally pierce his comprehension, as though the information were being violently whipped into his head by the wind. "You mean you had an affair while I was gone?"

"Oh, you could hardly call it that!"

"Who was it?"

"Oh, don't ask me that. Please!"

"All right. Then I won't." He got to his feet and led her toward a rock. He was going to be big about it. He spread a handkerchief on its flat top and hoisted her up onto it. She seated, he standing, they looked out at the churning water for some time.

"When did you first notice?" Edith asked.

"We're not going into all that," McGland said, generously.

"We're going to forget all about that whole interval of time. I will not have you torture yourself any more. It never happened. It never was. We'll start fresh."

"My Gowie." She took his hand in both of hers. The wind caught strand of her hair and lashed him across the mouth. "So kind and understanding. Then you do forgive me?"

"It's nothing to do with forgive. It was all my fault. Running off in a flap and leaving you alone here. What did I expect? That you'd sit home and twiddle your thumbs?" He looked out to sea, ecstatic, and savoring his ecstasy. "Now the episode's closed. *It will never be mentioned again.*"

"Except for one little bit of unfinished business," she said rather grimly. She looked toward town. "A word with my gay Lothario."

He might have known his luck would be no more than five minutes in a fool's paradise. "No," he bleated. "Skip that. What good would it do?"

"Don't ask me not to tell him what I think of him." She spoke through her teeth, and he knew that she meant it. "Don't ask me that. He's supposed to be a pillar in the town. If I told you his name you'd know it."

"Maybe he's not the culprit."

"What do you mean?"

McGland sighed and gave his freedom back, like a wallet one has found whose contents are to be fingered only for a moment before yielded up, with the hope, at best, of some tiny reward — a quid, say, of the fortune it contains. But there was no sense in taking the risk — questions and accusations would smoke him out in the end.

"Me," he said. "You asked me when I first noticed it. It was while I was still in London. I committed a little indiscretion there. As you say, not even an affair, just two people thrown together for a night. But now it's all over and done — I mean it *could* just as well have been the way you thought — And now we'll wipe the slate clean like two intelligent —"

He did not finish. They were running down the beach again, this time Edith in pursuit, stumbling a step behind him as she pummeled his back with both fists shouting: "You heel! You conniving little — You'd have let me go on thinking it, wouldn't you? All our lives you'd have had that to hold over me. You the noble, forgiving one, me the — Oh, you louse, you bounder!"

"But don't you see? I couldn't let you go to him and make a fool of yourself. That I couldn't do, I thought too much of you. Don't I get any credit for that?" he asked with his arms over his head, on which the blows were now raining. "I could have said nothing and you'd never have been the wiser. He'd have denied it but you'd have expected that — you'd never believe him. I need never have spoken up. But I did. Wasn't that a fine thing to — ?"

"You rat! You slinking unscrupulous two-timing whoring slinky slime. You make me sick, do you hear? Get out of my house and off this beach and don't ever let me see you again. I never want to see you again. Is that clear?"

"What will you do?"

"Try to get back to some sense of being myself again. So pack your things and get out of my house. In an hour. I'll wait down here till you're gone. Because I don't ever want to see you again."

McGland's first book, *John-a-Dreams*, appeared in the spring. There was no telling how far the poems would have gone on their own. Certainly they would have made their way. But they were given a tremendous push by his readings on the wireless, and the recorded album which speedily followed. It sold at a hundred times the rate of the book. McGland took to the lecture platform for public readings, to which people flocked. The album only made his hearers the more anxious to see him in person. An invitation to tour the States followed in due course, and was instantly accepted.

McGland sailed in the late summer of the next year, on the *Queen Mary*. On board ship he met a New York woman, a widow of early middle age returning from a spell among the Continental watering places, who planned a dinner party for him straight away, and who spoke at length of the other hostesses to whom she would introduce him or whom he would meet.

Thus life in America began, still a thousand miles out at sea.

eighteen

McGLAND LAY with his head propped on a wadded pillow, staring across the foot of the bed while Mrs. Punck read to him from the collection of verses which she had entered clutching in one hand. There was no mattress on the bed. It had been hauled out for an airing in the bright sunshine by the maid, but McGland felt so poor he had stretched out on the bare boxspring after seeing whom he had admitted. He could not remember having arranged, the day before, to let the woman called Mrs. Punck come pay her respects. She wore a peppermint stripe summer cotton which gave her height but also doubled her bulk, and she sat close beside the bed in a cane chair which creaked under her gestures and even from her breathing, for she read with expression. He was evidently to be spared nothing. Her parasol lay on a nearby table together with the white elbow-length gloves she had peeled from her forearms at the outset.

McGland figured out the kind of poetry this was. It was not poetry at all but "poems": intact packets of sentiment rich in words like "yesteryear" and "heartfelt," of which the authors were dim contemporaries of Tennyson and Tom Moore, not even known in their lifetimes. But there was some other category which nagged his mind and which he finally put his finger on. These were the verses of which the first lines were supplied by readers always writing in to the book supplement of the Sunday *Times*, in letters asking whether anyone could supply the remainder. The requests always reminded him of the joke about the tramp who handed a housewife a button and said, "Lady, could you sew a shirt on this?" He had occasionally glanced, in vain, for opening lines of poems by himself.

Mrs. Punck read:

> *Never wedding, ever wooing,*
> *Still a lovelorn heart pursuing,*
> *Read you not the wrong you're doing*
>   *In my cheek's pale hue?*
> *All my life with sorrow strewing,*
>   *Wed, or cease to woo.*

She paused, and though McGland kept his eyes fixed ahead
he knew she had not completely closed the book, but kept her
finger in it for a marker, and would go on. Instinct told him
that the anthology was subdivided into categories having to do
with the large, monolithic verities of human experience — Love,
Grief, Nature, etc. — and that this selection was carefully made
from a section probably entitled Heartbreak, in keeping with
the admonitory purpose of the call, now apparent.

"Isn't that beautiful?" she said. "Would you like to hear
some more of it?"

McGland nodded, out of a boredom so bottomless it was a
kind of peace, akin to the nirvanas which were the object of
the "demonstrations." In a sense, he was having Poesy demonstrated to him, for his sins, and by a Poetry Lover, that race
against whom he and his kind had most sinned. All this, together with the inability to say no to anybody at all assertive,
and the old pursuit of passivity, accounted for the docility with
which he listened to Mrs. Punck read out what he "had coming
to him."

> *Rivals banished, bosoms plighted,*
> *Still our days are disunited;*
> *Now the lamp of hope is lighted,*
>   *Now half quenched appears,*
> *Damp and wavering and benighted*
>   *Midst my sighs and tears.*

He knew there was even more; that she had only stopped for
breath. A breeze stirred the draperies at the open window,
admitting a shaft of late sunlight that cut his aching eyeballs

like a knife, and he flung an arm across his forehead. The voice resumed:

> Charms you call your dearest blessing,
> Lips that thrill at your caressing,
> Eyes a mutual soul confessing,
>   Soon you'll make them grow
> Dim, and worthless your possessing,
>   Not with age, but woe!

With a report like a gunshot Mrs. Punck closed the book. "I believe you know what I am driving at, Mr. Gland?" He nodded. "And to think that on top of all these other charges, you *are* wed. Oh, oh, oh. So will you give her up?" Again his head bobbed in dull acquiescence as he settled his arm across his eyes. A splitting headache, momentarily abated, threatened to resume.

"Who wrote that poem?" he asked, curious.

"Well, I'm rather surprised to hear you ask that, a poet yourself. You've heard of Thomas Campbell?"

This time he shook his head, as though in admitting to this ignorance he was confessing to something "naughty," like a schoolboy to the neglect of his lessons; recognizing at the same time this factor in the complex feelings involved in the stolen pleasures of the demonstrations. Something in him relished and required the sensations of miscreancy and shame. It was all a curious business, to the roots of which he would have liked to get were it not for fear of finding elements even more disconcerting than those apparent to casual introspection.

"Then we shall never see you again?" said Mrs. Punck, rising and twitching the skirt of her dress to rights.

"That's correct."

He had never been as happy to see anyone's back. After she had gone he lay on his own in an ecstasy of relief, savoring the peace of the room; even, almost, the aches and pains to which he was once more free to give his full attention. He planned the next hour, the last hour of the afternoon and the first of evening, an evening of solitude or of resumed prospects, cooled perhaps, as the day had been, by intermittent showers. First he would hang himself. Then he would have a little something to eat. Then —

The closed door opened again and Mrs. Punck's head reappeared. A round paw beckoned him. "Come outside. I want to show you something."

"Can't."

"But it's a rainbow."

Somehow (as writers of rotten fiction said) he dragged himself through the door which Mrs. Punck held open for him. Going to look at something in nature was a kind of amends he "owed people" — especially people like her — a sort of expiation for all the sins of the antipoetic committed by two generations of poets from Eliot through Auden and to him — indeed, from Baudelaire on. While he represented all these, Mrs. Punck was surrogate for the offended and bewildered millions of Poetry Lovers in whose face their desecrations flew, whose comfortably recognized "sentiments" of Beauty and Hope and Evening they had hacked to ribbons with the meat-ax of the Absurd. Yes, it was the least he could do, this token, if rather hypocritical, obeisance to Beauty, this after all rather arduous pilgrimage to the out of doors. All the more "least he could do" for being, in plain physical fact, absolutely the most he could manage.

"It's raining over *there*, the sun's setting over *there*, and so *there* . . ."

McGland blinked into the cruel light. Presently he made out an overarching radiance that was undoubtedly the rainbow. He was surprised; he had almost thought them obsolete. He nodded slowly in contemplation, but he found that the sudden stir had begun to make his stomach queasy.

"My heart leaps up when I behold —" Mrs. Punck began.

McGland turned and plunged through the door, realizing as he entered the house that he should instead have run around behind it, to be sick. He bolted for the bathroom, where he sat on a wicker laundry hamper for some time, retching inconclusively. The nausea subsided without incident, and it came to him that he had eaten nothing for a whole day.

He stole toward the open front door and peered cautiously round it into the yard. The woman was apparently gone now, and he closed it gratefully again. He remembered the cry with which he had run back into the house on being threatened with the Wordsworth in its entirety. There were limits to what flesh and blood could stand. His headache had subsided a little, now, and his neck, possibly from recent exertions, seemed to have eased too. He need not hang himself just yet. For the moment he concerned himself with sorting out the sensations of nausea from those of hunger, and in the end decided he was starved.

He wandered into the kitchen to forage in its now familiar quarters. He polished off a lunch the maid had left some time before. In the refrigerator he found a sardine can with one sardine left in it, which he fished with difficulty from its slippery corner, like something that had to be caught twice. A further search of the refrigerator's lower shelves yielded a hard-boiled egg and a remaining slice of homemade apple pie, both of which he ate with his hands, standing up and washing them down with a bottle of beer. He drifted back into the main front room, which served as a combination sitting and bedroom. His bathrobe hung open. He wore, for house slippers, a pair of old rubbers, no doubt C.B.S.'s.

Looking out the window at the roses he thought of Spofford. Would the man come back to work in the garden now, or was there bad blood for once and all between him and the Springers? Thanks to McGland. A mania for stratification seemed to have seized this democracy, and a thousand anthropologists were busy sorting out classes by means of such physical criteria as automobile makes, window sizes and shirt collars. Americans studied their own everyday artifacts as though they were those of a civilization long vanished — an odd preoccupation for a young and robust country. How much sense did it all make? You might tag Bobsy Springer but how about Spofford? Where did he belong? Nowhere, thank God — in which lay the defeat of the pigeonholers and the hope of man. Trying to put him into one or another of the official divisions was like trying to maneuver and diddle one of those pellets into the hole of a puzzle: you no more than get it in than it rolls out again while you try to do the same with another. He was ignorant and knowing, hick and hep, sociable and solitary, a wit and a pest. Classifiable only as American; that is to say, fairly distinguishable from the British, Welsh and Scotch versions of rusticity. Otherwise he eluded category. He was a misfit who belonged exactly where he was — maybe. (But where the hell was he? At that precise moment, that is.)

As McGland pondered these things he took occasional moody sucks on the bottle of beer he had carried with him, alternated with chocolate creams he popped into his mouth from an open box on the table. He could see the mattress in the yard. It had gotten a proper soaking after the sunning for which it had been dragged out; now it was drying again. If it was not hauled in it would no doubt get wet in turn from the dew. A line for a poem began to form in his head. "The last curmudgeon in the village snow." No. "The last codger pruning roses here." No. Hell, hadn't Yeats done something about curmudgeons or codgers? How did his line go? "Where are all those golden codgers now?" Something like that. He must look it up.

"Does Bobsy want me to pack up and leave?" he asked aloud, of no one. He turned from the window, mumbling the words, just as he did the flustered apologies that must inevitably follow nine out of ten passes at girls. He had once overheard two girls at a party in Philadelphia discussing the look on his face then. "He's so *sheepish*." They had been primping in a bedroom into which he had glanced through an open door, combing their young hair and drawing their stockings up. The memory brought a pang of despair, for he had tried on separate occasions to kiss them both. Recalling their conversation now filled him with such chagrin that his expression must be precisely that about which they had commented — so he rushed into the bathroom to get a look at it.

His face in the glass went ashen at the sight of itself. Bloodshot eyes, a stubbled chin and cheeks hollowed by fatigue made him look sixty. He had again the sensation, divinable in those seeing him for the first time, that he was a caricature of his likenesses. Cruelly he completed the lampoon by removing his bridgework and displaying the five scattered teeth that composed his jack-o'-lantern grin. Wagging a finger at himself he said, "You'll look like that some day." It was to warn himself to gather rosebuds while he might, to hurry, hurry, to let no woman's reproof or no man's derision, or the memory of such reproof or such derision, sway him from the course justified by the batting average firmly fixed in his mind; *one out of ten*. The single overture that paid off was surely worth the nine humiliating slaps across the cheek.

Of course not all of them slapped your cheek. Crueler far was the method of turning their own as you made for their lips, sliding that target with gentle irony into place. Worst of all was to be shown respect. "Mr. McGland," they would say. Ah, the young dreams that had put him in his place by showing him respect. "Sir . . ." Ah, that stung.

It all stung, stung and entranced, tormented and enthralled. He had been shot twice through the country and back by avaricious lecture agents, and every campus was an infernal Eden, a paradisal hell, of girls. Rich girls flaunting both their expensive flesh and the wherewithal to buy and keep it; poor girls cradling their books on their arms as they one day would their infants. Girls, girls, girls . . .

Geneva was like none of them, somehow. She neither kissed him nor slipped her cheek into place, neither thrust him away nor called him sir. She eluded category, like her old grandfather himself. That was due to a peculiar ambivalence, a seeming resolve neither to accept nor repulse him. She had let him kiss her, without quite responding herself. She called him Mr. McGland but let him kiss her. She was a puzzle, a curious blend of emotion and restraint, warmth and withdrawal, open and shut, yes and no. She reminded him a little of Edith in the way she liked to get you at a disadvantage, but with a crucial difference — not to relish your discomfiture but to correct her own. You could feel that warm current running under ice, seeking out the wretch in a man. So he had learned to offer himself up in many forlorn guises. He played in turn the Poor Devil and the Lonely Lion and the Unhappy

Boy, with what sweet tentative results! When he found himself losing his restraint at table, he would quickly recover his Falstaff-at-Elsinore pose, poking food into his mouth and abstractly swilling ale as though they were but anodynes to tortured Thought. Sometimes he played his trump card. He Doubted Himself, and then . . . But though these devices had gained him her breast, never yet her breasts. What stratagem could unveil that treasure? Neither prudish nor conventional, she still reserved herself for some — what? Some ultimate opportunity to succor one as "insecure" as she herself? Did it make sense to be talking here in the American jargon about "needing to be needed?" McGland quickly tired of this line of thought. It was a hell of a way to conduct human relations, yet apparently the way they were now conducted here Stateside. So in what spiritual tatters must he come in order to be fully solaced? Visualizing again those breasts, he closed his eyes and murmured, "Death by suffocation."

He wondered whether Geneva knew he was called "The Welsh Rabbit" over here. It was a nickname in which he took no pride though aware of its accuracy, perhaps far more than the wags who had bestowed it: he possessed the two chief characteristics of the creature in question, virility and cowardice. Make love and run were about all he could do. Except write poetry of course.

McGland went to brush his teeth. He scoured each survivor lovingly, and rinsed his mouth out with beer. Next he shaved, using two razors to harvest the cactus on his chin. After splashing cold water on his face he dried it briskly with a clean towel and put after-shave lotion on it. Then he powdered his jowls with some talcum also obligingly supplied by the management and bent to scrutinize the result more closely in the glass. Apart from some faintly oozing nicks and scratches he looked a lot better. He certainly felt a lot better. He remembered a few lines he had been carrying in his head for several days now, and went to the writing desk to jot them down, stopping to scoop up the last of the chocolate creams on the way. He sat down and scribbled rapidly on a clean sheet of foolscap:

The world is riddled with betrayal
And checkered with the heart's alarms;
So put away those lamentations
And hurry to my faithless arms.

These lines were in the nature of some experiments he had wanted to try in rather stricter verse forms than he had generally worked in. Perhaps a series of more conventional love lyrics would result. He tried to carry this one forward, but after a few false starts dropped the pencil. His eye had been caught by a small rectangular box, of some transparent plastic and about twice the size of a matchbox. On its lid was printed in blue letters the name Kwik-Kleen. It had been supplied by his hosts along with the paper, pencils and typewriter itself. Inside was a fresh block of some putty-like substance, also blue, accompanied by a slip of paper which explained that the contents were a new and handy kind of typewriter cleaner. One merely pressed it on the keys and it would come away with all the ink and grime from the type face adhering to its surface. The ball of Kwik-Kleen could be used indefinitely as the dirt was simply kneaded into it. "No more fussing with messy and combustible liquid cleaners. No more brushes and rags. Just press Kwik-Kleen on the keys and presto — the dirt becomes *engraved* into it."

McGland never used the typewriter except to press his neckties with. He would screw them into the carriage to the place where they were wrinkled from frequent knotting (he only had two) and leave them under the roller overnight. He began to work the fresh bar of stuff in his two hands. It induced a curiously pleasurable sensation which recalled the passage in *Moby-Dick* where the crewmen dig their fingers into the lumps of coagulated whale sperm. Kneading it generates a sort of mooning sentimentalism among them. After worrying the Kwik-Kleen about in this fashion for a bit, McGland was struck with an idea. If the stuff would clean typewriter keys, why not teeth? It might be handy to carry about and use between brushings, as an extra precaution. He put the wad into his mouth and bit down. Any leftover food particles must now be adhering to it, as the grit from the keys. He chewed the wad over, making sure he missed no area in his mouth. It did not taste bad. Perhaps he should make a habit of keeping a quid of it on his person for purposes of dental hygiene.

The door opened and the maid came in.

"Oh, you're still eating."

"No, come on in," McGland said, covertly disgorging the ball.

"I've come for the tray."

"Take it, Milly. I'm through. That's excellent chicken by the way, even cold."

"It was hot when I brought it."

"I know, I know," he said, sympathetically. She gave him a wide berth as she moved about collecting dishes and stacking them on the tray. She was a bright, brisk, red-haired girl in her late twenties, with a look of expectant suspicion in her green eyes. "Sit down and have some hot coffee. I'll heat it for you on the plate," McGland offered.

"Why don't you haul the mattress in? Couldn't you see it was raining?"

"Yes but then it was too late. So I left it to dry again. And so on."

"It's dry enough now. Come help me with it, will you please?" she said, darting past him out the door.

Together they lugged it into the cottage and dropped it onto the bed. McGland sat down on it a moment to get his wind. The maid tidied her hair and blouse. They were both breathing heavily. McGland reached out to draw her closer. She stepped back with a glare that changed to a deploring laugh. "You ought to be ashamed of yourself."

"Oh, I am, I am. Now don't you have more respect for me? You see, I'm not such a monster after all, am I? Come on, give us a kiss," he said in his cockney sailor-home-on-leave voice.

"If you want that bed made you'll have to get up," she said, drawing an armful of clean sheets from a drawer. He helped her make the bed, tucking in one side while she did the other. She fluttered the sheets out skillfully, watching them drift to rest with a taut expression about her mouth and sharp, concentrated eyes. "I'd sure like to climb between these with you," McGland said, thrusting an end in. *One out of ten.*

"Why do you act like an animal? Like a beast of the field."

"Because a man's days go up in smoke, while the likes of you go around smelling like the fields of heaven. Come on, have the decency to satisfy what you provoke."

She paused and took in his sad hulk, bent over his ridiculous task, tidying up what he longed only to dishevel with her. Her eyes softened, as had her manner toward him over these weeks. "You're famous, aren't you?"

"Why, I —"

The door creaked open and Bobsy Springer wandered into the room. She was smoking a cigarette in a long holder and wore tight striped slacks and a blue silk shirt, with a Liberty silk scarf fluffed at her throat. The maid finished making the bed, deftly and alone, with McGland taking his place beside Bobsy Springer as spectator. She snatched up the tray in one hand and a bundle of soiled linen with the other and scuttled away.

Bobsy circled the room for some minutes, smoking. She twisted the cigarette out of the holder at last and dropped it into an ashtray. Her face indicated that words of some kind were not to be avoided.

"You're being quite unfair to me, Gowan," she said at last. "People are talking about us."

"Because we're not sleeping together now? Is that what has set tongues to wagging? What an odd community this is. I didn't call it off, Bobsy?"

"Did you expect me to share you with a twenty-year-old schoolgirl?"

"I haven't slept with her."

"That's not the point. You're chasing her like a schoolboy yourself. And then cutting my own son out — really, *really*, Gowan!"

"I thought you disapproved of the match."

"That has nothing to do with it and you know it!" she said, suddenly flashing anger. "Really, Gowan, you're impossible."

She stood grasping a rail of the foot of the bed, on which

McGland again sat, leaning over on one elbow, his legs crossed. He stared unhappily down at the counterpane. When he glanced up at her it was to find her staring down at the rubbers on his sockless feet. "You want me to leave, don't you?"

"You *are* compromising me." McGland noticed the subtle knotting of the scarf, designed to conceal the lines at the soft throat. He saw that, for all the violence of her manner, she stood with her "good side" carefully turned to him. Of course everybody did that, men and women, choosing seats at parties and in public conveyances so as to present themselves to advantage. He would have wagered that, if a study were made, suicides would invariably be found to have shot themselves in the bad side of the head, pouring into that all the hate and rage finally turned on the self. The "proud tilt" of her chin was also touching.

"I'm not going to see Geneva again," he said. "I'm not going to call her."

She looked at him quickly. "Are you telling the truth?"

"Mrs. Wiggs of the Cabbage Patch was just here — her grandmother — and if I wouldn't give her up for her — God, what a phrase! — I would for her grandfather. They don't know how ridiculous they all are in thinking *that* girl can't take care of herself, but then. Anyhow that's that. Now do you want me to leave?"

"Of course I don't 'want' you to leave. But I'm a little curious why you stay — now . . . Why do you, in this part of the country?"

"I've got that damned reading in New Haven the fourteenth, and until then of course you know I'm broke."

"Oh, don't talk about that. It's too silly. Forget it. Anyhow, there's the Haxbys' party Saturday. I think you promised Lucille you'd read a few things for them. But now for God's sake, Gowan, let me warn you again — *keep away from Lucille.* I know you think I'm being dull about Jack, but it's the truth. You'll regret it." She sighed and gave her scarf a touch. "Now I've got to get back to the house. Clean up and come over for a drink later if you'd like. C.B.S. will be home in a foul humor.

He just called. They're trying to launch a mentholated cigar for a tobacco client, and it's going very poorly."

After Bobsy Springer had gone, McGland lay for a few minutes on the bed and gave himself over to some thoughts about the Haxbys. Haxby fascinated him as much as a dentist as he did as a rival. Confirmations of his eminence had come to McGland from all sides. "He's one of the half-dozen top men in the country, no doubt about it," someone had assured him. Dr. Haxby was evidently responsible for many of the smiles flashed at one from stage and screen, having capped the teeth of their possessors. Hollywood actors flew to him regularly, it was said. How much better off he, McGland, might be now had he had Haxby instead of that awful tinker in Aberdeen, and the one in Edinburgh who had been scarcely better. As for the dolt in his home town! No wonder he'd had no practice, outside the McGland family. Once the boy Gowan had mounted the stairs to his office to find him sitting in it eating pecans, using his instruments for nut picks. He had been a great believer in pulling teeth to save other teeth, as you chopped down one tree to give another a chance.

McGland sent his tongue now on a cautious tour of his mouth. There were scorpions lurking in his gums, ready to do him in; he had imagined a new one flicking its tail there, an occasional twinge at the root of an absolutely indispensable molar. Or was he merely imagining it, fearing the resumption of yet another round of anguish and humiliation? He shifted his attention to other parts of his body where other symptoms competed for his attention. Pains twitched in his middle like goldfish in a bowl. McGland played mental tricks with these, trying to outwit himself into some semblance of peace of mind. Just as he had once exaggerated insignificant symptoms he now ignored clamorous ones, banking on the fact that he was a hypochondriac. How long, O Lord, how long . . . ?

Time now to hang himself, he thought, rising. Hang himself and then a good soak in the tub and so to the Springers'. He squeezed the back of his neck with his hand, to ease it, working the muscles there by swinging his head around in a circle. The orthopedic harness he dug out of the drawer here was by now nearly all rope. This was necessitated by the height of the beam, an original timber left over from the barn out of which the cottage had been made, over which he slung it, catching the end and fastening it to the leather straps, which converged a few feet from the collar to which they were in turn attached. The beam, which ran the length of the room, was twenty feet from the floor, and with only thirty-odd feet of rope McGland had to stand on a chair to get any traction. He placed a straightback in the center of the room and, dragging his coils of equipment, climbed up onto it.

He threw one end of the rope over the rafter, caught it, and began to knot it to the leather straps, or rather the hooks in which these ended, making for a single suspension rather than the double dependence from a door lintel for which the apparatus was originally designed. There were no inside doorways here on which the grappling hooks could conveniently catch hold. As he went forward with these preparations, he thought he heard a footstep, or rustling, outside. He paused, listening, heard nothing, and resumed. He tested the knot to make sure it was secure. He was about to slip his neck into the nooselike collar when the door flew open and someone rushed into the room calling, "Gowan, don't!"

It was Geneva. She ran to the chair, knocking it out from under him with a force that sent him sprawling to the floor. She flung the overturned chair out of the way and dropped down beside him. "Gowan, how could you do a thing like that? Oh, how awful. Oh, Gowan." She crushed his body to hers, uttering murmurs and exclamations by turn. "Why would you want to do a thing like that?" she said, rocking him.

"Nobody wants to."

He had recovered from the initial shock of what had been, after all, a mutual surprise, and, settled in her arms, he tried to wriggle and kick free of the coils of rope in which they were both entangled, without disturbing their positions unnecessarily. These were such that McGland lay in a half-reclining posture with his head on her breast. He could hear her heart beat.

The rain of endearments continued, in passionate whispers stilling at last to a hush as she rocked him, stroking his hair and kissing his cheek. At length he moved his free hand, tentatively upward along her arm and then to the top of her blouse. Among its buttons his hand encountered hers, but not in resistance and not for long. It fell away and with a last sigh she let his fingers go to work, willing at last to offer that harbor and that haven for which he had so sorely yearned, and which under the circumstances no woman worthy of the name could, in all conscience, deny a man.

nineteen

THE HAXBYS' PARTY had started off with a bang, but now most of the men were slightly ill from the mentholated cigars C.B.S. had passed out after dinner on behalf of the sponsors of his television show, who were "pushing" the experiment in some Eastern regional test marketing. "Maybe they're putting a little too much menthol in them," said Jack Haxby, scowling at his. "Well you see, that's the sort of thing we're trying to find out," C.B.S. said. Haxby was now irritated with himself for having let his brother-in-law make guinea pigs of his guests. He ran a palm across his short thick gray hair, which in color and pile matched the carpeting under his feet, as though the entire house had been decorated around him. He wore a plaid Madras jacket with black silk lapels. A solid, barrel-chested muscularity, together with a dented nose, made him resemble a handsome prizefighter.

He was anxious to talk about the pet project with which he currently relieved the strain of a distinguished dentistry practice, as well as gave his life some measure of cultural substance — speed reading. He was an advisory vice-president of the local branch workshop of the American Reading Clinic, and was impatient to explain its merits to three business executives who were present, conceivable prospects for the six months' evening course. Accelerated reading had proved a boon to so many businessmen who despaired of ever getting through the reports accumulating in their briefcases. However, the after-dinner moment Haxby had chosen for introducing the subject proved inauspicious: two of the executives — Hugh Shotwell of United Rubber and Jumbo Harper of Harper Matchbooks — were quite green from the effects of the mentholated cigars, while the third, Art Meighan, proprietor of a chain of shoe stores, was clearly bucking to get to the billiard table.

As he sat waiting for his guests to recover, Haxby pondered again this whole business of recreation. It honestly seemed to him that middle-aged men became worse wrought up over their hobbies than they did about the jobs from which the hobbies were intended to offer escapes. Here he was, itching to hold forth on the nation's reading lag and tensing up perceptibly because he was balked by a lousy cigar somebody else had probably dreamed up to amuse *him*self with. "I'm never this on edge when I have a tricky tooth to save," he mused. He was candid about all that with himself.

His eye moved to McGland, who had quite brazenly strolled away from the half of the L-shaped living room to which Haxby had herded the men for a spot of brandy and good talk, and was peering round the elbow in the wall to the half where the ladies were chattering away over their crème de menthes. McGland had declined one of C.B.S.'s cigars and so felt fine. Haxby bridled. Background "mood music" issued unobtrusively from stereophonic speakers set in two corners of the ceiling at the elbow, but their gentle strains seemed to do very little to soothe Haxby: his mood was growing fouler by the minute. If that blackguard so much as rolled those eyes at Lucille one more time he would knock his block off. How could a man no more prepossessing than that have his pick of women anyway? Yet there they were, vying with one another to show him off, to have him read, even for the privilege of doing his laundry, which God knew they must pitch into the Laundromats with eyes averted; to be included, in some small way, in the growing McGland legend. He was a legend, was he not? The Welsh Rabbit didn't they call him? He was a poet having a vogue (as he, Jack Haxby, was having a vogue as the dentist to go to). That part was all right. He had no objections to that. But it riled him to see refined women, like his wife, take a shine to a satyr in a tweed coat that had obviously never been pressed and socks that, literally, were not mates. One was a red and white check while the other was plain red with gray clocks. Haxby had noticed that. He remembered a joke a comedian had had twenty-five years ago. "I've got another pair just like it home."

C.B.S. was as irritating in this matter as in that of the cigars; no help at all. How could he be expected to notice someone was chasing his sister if he didn't realize one was after his wife? Moving McGland in under his nose to the guest house was a stratagem that had apparently worked. Well, no one would throw dust in his, Haxby's, eyes. The word "cuckold" flashed into his mind, causing his fists to bunch. How appropriately silly was the very sound of it, how utterly indicative that a husband sexually wronged was not seen in the eyes of the world as wronged at all, but only a fool. It would not happen to him.

Haxby stirred from these bitter ruminations to find that a heavy silence had settled on his male guests. Sitting around the circular coffee table in their own Madras or linen jackets, they looked like metropolitan clubmen who have just heard of the election of a liberal Democrat. Someone simply had to say something, though the time was not ripe for the subject of speed reading.

"Has anyone here not heard the one about the Scotchman who kept getting off the train to buy his ticket from stop to stop?" Haxby asked with a determined joviality.

At that moment Jumbo Harper coughed, propelling halfway across the room a digestive mint on which he had been surreptitiously sucking. They all watched with interest the lozenge roll along the edge of the carpeting to the hearthstone and come to a stop, remaining upright. This lent to their silence a quality of awe, as at a feat of skill which Jumbo had executed intentionally. "That was a fine dinner," someone said. Haxby clenched and unclenched his fists.

"He had heart trouble," he said.

"Who?"

"The Scotchman." Haxby twisted round in his chair to make sure McGland, who was of course part Scotch, was still out of earshot. "That was why he bought a ticket from stop to stop instead of all the way through to his destination, you see. He wasn't going to take a chance on possibly wasting money. Who would like some more brandy?"

McGland returned, holding his snifter responsively aloft. He had heard that. Strolling, he chewed an appetizer scavenged from a plate left behind by the maid: a cheese straw like a cigar in his mouth. During cocktails Haxby had seen him tossing after-dinner mints into his mouth. He was worse than the bad poet of three years ago, who had put exclamation marks at the beginnings of lines. A rather nice chap, personally. It was always like that. The good ones were always worse than the bad ones. But they shared this antipathy to jokes such as the one McGland was amiably aborting. Haxby recalled that all intellectuals were said to dislike "funny stories" — that practicing humorists particularly detested them. Resentfully, he filled McGland's inhaler nearly to the brim. McGland grinned, hoping no offense was intended.

"McGland, do they have speed reading in England yet?"

"What reading?"

"Speed. Accelerated reading."

"Oh, those clinics where they teach you to read *War and Peace* in one night or some such rot? No. Tell me about them."

Haxby turned to set the brandy bottle on the table. As he did so, one or two guests tried to catch McGland's eye and shush him with warning expressions, quickly recovering an air of nonchalance when Haxby again looked up.

"I'll be glad to," Haxby said. "The fact of the matter is that we still all read more or less at a child's pace. The way we did when we first learned. Our eye doesn't pause over every word, to be sure, but it does on every third or fourth — which is where most of us stay. At about twenty per cent efficiency. A page every two minutes, say. Well, proper training can up that to a minute a page, then two pages a minute, then five. Till, yes, we can read a whole book in an evening."

"What for?" McGland had moved to the only chair available at the circular coffee table, but instead of occupying it he paused to admire it. It was an early American bowback Windsor, whose spindles he fingered appreciatively, and which he tipped forward to inspect the workmanship on its underside.

"What for?" Haxby looked round the table, inviting the others to share his amusement. "Ask Shotwell here, or Harper. Or Meighan. Or even C.B.S. How many miles of business reports have you boys got piled up on your desk and in your briefcases? Eh, Hugh? Jumbo?"

"Plenty," Jumbo Harper answered. He was a sandy-haired man of a size implied by his nickname. A look of two-fisted practicality was sufficiently modified by a creamy, well-fed humanitarianism for him to resemble those businessmen seen in charity posters leaning across their desks and saying, "It *pays* to hire the handicapped."

"And Hugh? Ever wish you had six pairs of eyes?"

"Sure do," said Shotwell, smiling. He gazed down at his ankle, which was crossed on one knee, his hand resting on the black silk of his sock. "Of course as far as office reports are concerned, I've gotten so that I can delegate —"

"Ah, there you are!" Haxby was leaning forward in his chair as though he might be about to spring out of it and resort to physical violence, addressing himself to McGland, who, however, continued to admire the chair. He seemed unaware that the spirit of controversy engendered in the room had been touched off by himself. "He has to delegate his reading, hear that? But he needn't if he corrected his reading *rate*. Six months at one of our workshops and he'll be able to get through everything he has to in an hour a day. That answer your question, McGland?"

McGland now at last sat down in the chair, to sense for the first time the atmosphere of dispute. One look at Haxby made that clear. Haxby's hands clutched his knees and his face was flushed. Noting this, McGland said as genially as he could, "I don't care how long it takes Mr. Shotwell to get through the contents of his briefcase. I want him to read *Tender Is the Night* as slowly as possible."

Haxby sat back, unable for the moment to digest this fact.

Shotwell laughed and murmured something ambiguous to the effect that he would do as McGland wished, as soon as he found the time. Haxby ignored this, pursuing the argument in a manner indicating that he would not be deflected by frivolities.

"You mean you yourself haven't got books piled up that you can't seem to get around to?" he asked McGland, quoting from a promotion folder he was preparing for the Clinic.

"No."

"You mean you don't wish there were forty-eight hours in a day, so you could catch up on your reading?"

McGland shook his head. "No, I don't seem to —"

"You mean you've read everything. All the classics that man in his centuries of —"

"Hell, no. What do I want to read all the classics for? Man is groaning under a terrible hoax about the classics. Screw the classics."

Haxby glared uncomprehendingly. "Swinburne," he said wildly.

"Can't read him."

"Why not?"

"His poetry always reminds me of the work of some young punk who has just read Swinburne."

Haxby, who had in the heat of debate recovered his crouching position, now flopped back in his chair. He was frankly baffled by the turn the argument had taken. The sides seemed to have got switched around, somehow, from the way they should be, each taking the part the other would normally have been expected to espouse.

"But you just said you wanted Hugh Shotwell here to read *Tender Is the Night*."

"That is correct. I do not object to *all* literature."

Haxby reached for the brandy and poured himself a fresh drink, nearly as much as he had ironically sloshed into McGland's snifter. He looked more than ever like a boxer, perhaps because of the slight shake of his head he gave, like one rousing himself from a daze preparatory to getting up from the canvas.

"Now that novel of F. Scott Fitzgerald's," he said pedagogically, after a generous gulp from his glass, "would presumably be the first in a list of books Mr. McGland would want Hugh — or anybody else — to read. Right? Right." Here his intention to lecture the group at large broke down under the need to address McGland individually again. "What would be some others? Give us a list of, say, a dozen musts. Go ahead."

McGland obligingly murmured a few titles, most of which Haxby had never heard of.

"Good. Now we're getting somewhere. Now that stack on the old bedside table" — he pointed dramatically to his left — "is really growing! Still it's only a start. You could make it a hundred easily. And we'd all want to read all of them, believe me. But there isn't time. For each one you get around to, two more have joined the pile. So it will continue to be *unless we accelerate our reading rate.* 'How do I do that?' I hear you asking," he went on in the silence that followed. "Why, by unlearning the old-fashioned method. We all of us tend to subvocalize. That is, we *pronounce* the words to ourselves in our mind, whether we actually move our lips or not."

McGland turned around, hoping that a stir at the other end of the room meant the ladies were coming to join them, in despair of being joined. This turned out to be the case. The women rounded the turn in easy formation, chatting and laughing. The men rose to face them, conscious of their postures. Standing in a semicircle, stomachs in, shoulders back, they resembled a glee club waiting, if not for a sign from their leader to burst into song, at least for permission to disband. Haxby however had no intention of relinquishing the floor purchased at such pains, now that his audience had doubled.

"Many of us feel that this subvocalization is not essential to the reading process *qua* reading. There is a school of us who are firmly convinced that the written word can be taken in *in a purely optical manner and converted by the brain into comprehension without subvocalization.* It is by training people to use only their eyes — to bypass the ear — that we work the miracles we do at the workshop in speeding up people's reading. Ah, Jumbo —"

"Holding forth, darling?" Lucille Haxby asked. She paused in a manner that brought the company of women to a halt behind her, like a scouting party in doubtful territory.

"Loomis, for instance, of Allied Fertilizer, came to us in a state and said he simply could not get his work done because of the reports piling up on his desk. He was actually desperate. His stomach was acting up, he was in a state. Six months at the workshop and he can read all he has to for the day in an hour with *no loss of comprehension*. Reads by eye, you see, he doesn't waste time with the ear. He simply photographs the words off the printed page. You were speaking facetiously about reading a book in an evening, McGland. Well, that is exactly the case. Our star pupil, a graduate of the University of Vermont, read *Doctor Zhivago* in fifty-five minutes. He was clocked by a neutral committee."

"He read it the way your fertilizer man now reads reports on business figures. He did not read the book as a book," McGland said.

"He could give a complete and accurate account of its entire contents. The same committee tested him."

"But only as a body of information on the so-called action of the novel — on what happened next and what became of the characters, and so on. I repeat, he did not read the book."

"Maybe we don't mean the same thing by 'reading a book.' "

"I suppose not."

"Just what do you mean by the term?"

"What it says — reading a book. As an aesthetic experience, to be had on the writer's own terms. Because prose is *meant* to be heard and not just seen, good prose anyway. Heard on the inner ear. Bypass subvocalization, as you call it, and you do permanent violence to something essential to reading. Fitzgerald has a tempo, Hemingway has a tempo, so does Boris Pasternak. Speed these up and you defame them just as you would defame Brahms if you sped up to *allegro vivace* a movement he had clearly marked *andante*, just for the sake of getting through the damned symphony faster."

"Hear, hear!" a mousy little woman in the background said — Mrs. Shotwell. Which caused Haxby to flush a shade deeper than he already was in an exchange which, everyone now nervously saw, had reached a pitch ominously higher than that of lively after-dinner conversation. Haxby said: "That is quite all right, in theory at least, and for people who have nothing more to do than read novels in their own sweet time, not to say merely reread those they already have. But for those who are busy doing the work of the world — presidents not just of corporations, but of countries — it gets to be quite another story. How much do you think Kennedy would get read of the apparently mountains he is able to get down in a day, if he dawdled through everything savoring the author's style and tuning in to his tempo? Because he happens to be one of our finest examples of speed reading, I have on good authority. It must be simply phenomenal. He gulps down a page at a time."

"I don't think he reads Robert Frost that way."

"Well now that you mention poetry I'll tell you something. I finally got around to reading your book the other night. *John-a-Dreams* was a treat I had been postponing for myself till I had time, and which I advise my other guests not to deprive themselves of if they haven't yet had the pleasure," Haxby went on, a smile of hideous benevolence twisting his lips. "I read it in twenty minutes. And I say I got everything in it. I can quote you from it."

"In that case, this is what you did."

McGland's reference to Brahms had not been academic. It was the Brahms violin concerto that had been softly going on the phonograph in the corner. The record was finished but still revolving on the turntable. McGland now turned on his heel and marched over to it. Snapping the speed adjustment lever from thirty-three and a half, where it was, to seventy-eight, he set the tone arm down at random on the record, at the same time twisting the volume knob up. A rapid insane squeaking and gibbering filled the room. Haxby himself now darted forward, his face crimson.

"Do you want to wreck the machine then, man! That speed takes a different needle!"

They all watched in horror as he lifted the tone arm off and set it carefully to rest. Unintelligible deploring murmurs from the frozen company filled the air. The mousy woman who had at first said "Hear, hear!," recognizing that she had probably in so doing stoked a controversy into a crisis, mumbled something about there being no doubt "something to be said for both sides." Lucille, a slender, wistfully pretty woman near forty, nodded agreement. "Of *course* there are two kinds of reading — for mere information and for aesthetic pleasure. We all skim some things and linger over others. Just sort of soak ourselves in the author's prose? Or poetry. So the whole argument is rather silly, *but* I must say it does a woman good to see two men feel strongly enough about something to fight about it. That's a relief in an age of conformity and pussyfooting. Cleans out the liver, eh, boys?"

Here the mousy woman repeated "Hear, hear!" with her original zest, provoking thereby a round of assents and even some applause. Lucille drew the two men together, looping her arms through theirs, and made them shake hands. McGland grinned, apologizing for having been so contentious — and noting privately, again, the savagery with which passive types like himself could occasionally fight once roused.

Haxby's emotions were more complex. He had permitted himself to be made a fool of on his home ground, with his pet subject, and before precisely the men he wanted most to impress; not to mention before his wife in connection with a potential cuckolder. He scarcely knew whom he hated the more for this, himself or McGland. But it was essential to his ego to mask his chagrin. That, more than the social amenities, required that he appear quite unriled by the fracas. Therefore at the height of the evening's gaiety, when they were all dancing in the recreation room, he loudly invited McGland to dinner the following week to meet the traveling secretary of the American Reading Clinic. He did this in a pause between records, when they all stood waiting with their partners, McGland with his arm around Lucille.

"I might add that she's a very charming young woman in her twenties," he said. McGland called back the length of the room some word of pleasure at the prospect of joining them. "You must promise to read the Clinic's brochure beforehand though. Will you do that?" Haxby said, waiting for the music with Bobsy Springer. "If I can find a minute," McGland said, and they all laughed as a fresh chorus was struck up and the dance resumed.

The ladies had never looked more beautiful, the men were quite convalesced from their mentholated cigars, and the party swept on toward its carefree midnight. Lucille acceded to McGland's plea not to ask him to read. Everyone was having fun, alternating dances with turns at the billiard table at the other end of the room.

Haxby alone was wretched. He had decided it was himself he hated most. When McGland left with the Springers, he shouted down the stairs a reminder of their dinner date the following week. He would phone him later about the time and place.

twenty

THEY WERE HALFWAY to their table in the Burgundy before McGland realized that he still had his gum in his mouth. They moved over the deep carpeting in a file led by the captain, Edouard, followed by Miss Iverson, the Reading Clinic girl, then Lucille, with McGland appreciatively trailing her, and Haxby bringing up the rear.

Haxby had entered with the happy assurance of one who can crown twenty years of hard status search with the certainty of being able to shepherd his parties into the best restaurants and of being treated in them like a familiar and favored guest. He wanted particularly to show Miss Iverson that the Clinic was lucky to have him on the Board for more reasons than one. His expression had changed to one of surprise when Edouard, after no more than a curt nod, had ushered them past the choice front tables where those who mattered could see and be seen, and where he had had every confidence of being seated, then to one of outright consternation as they were marched into the back room straight to the worst table in the house — that next to the swinging door to the kitchen. Haxby himself was given the chair the back of whose occupant's head was most likely to be endangered by the constant flapping open and shut, and by trays of food precariously tilted. Beyond this humiliation lay only the upstairs room to which were banished strangers and pariahs, and known among the elite as Siberia.

"There must be some —" he began, but Edouard was gone.

For a speed reader, Haxby took some time over the menu. He was both hiding behind it while he licked his wounds and, by informedly editorializing to Miss Iverson on the specialties of the house, trying to offset in some degree his demotion — which puzzled everyone but McGland. McGland had been with the Haxbys the last time they had dined here when Haxby, then host to a gay party of six at a front table, had left a ten-dollar bill as a tip. To McGland, then in dire financial straits, that note had looked like the world. Sumptuous as the meal he had just eaten had been, he was the one man in that restaurant about whom it could honestly have been said that he didn't know where his next was coming from. Contriving to be the last to leave the table, he had furtively pocketed the tenner, substituting for it seventy-five cents — absolutely his last moneys. So Haxby was now, as far as the general staff were concerned, not merely persona non grata. He was a cheapskate and a piker who deserved to be frozen out — provisionally put here in limbo preparatory to being banished to Siberia if he did not do something to redeem himself tonight.

It was while they were all ensconced behind the voluminous menus that McGland succeeded in disposing of his gum. He slid it unobtrusively out on the tip of his tongue and pasted it securely to the underside of the chair. He set his menu aside when the Old-Fashioneds came, telling Haxby to order for him. McGland never cared what he ate: he was far too fond of food.

Sipping his drink, he watched Miss Iverson's menu come down and reveal her face and broad expanse of shoulders. This was his first chance to appraise her closely, as she had come to the Burgundy separately in her own car. He saw that she was your "fresh" type: rosy cheeks suggestive of healthy walks in the woods or even a history of scoutmastering, straight chestnut hair drawn into a plump wad behind, the scrubbed look and clear gaze suited to one committed to projects of social worth. She turned to Haxby to ask what *escargots* were. "Snails," he said, "but they're only so-so here. Have the *pâté*. I wish you all would. I've got my eye on a Pouilly Fuissé '59 to start off with. We can have a bottle of red later. Think you can drink your share, McGland?"

"I'll try."

McGland had by now firmly labeled Miss Iverson. He sorted women into two types. They either did or did not have "a floral quality." Lucille had it, Miss Iverson did not. She was fruit, or possibly gem, rather than flower. It was no fatal deficiency in McGland's eyes, who liked women as indiscriminately as he did food. While he had been watching Miss Iverson, Lucille had been watching him.

"Read the brochure yet, Gowan?" she asked. "As you promised?" She assumed a posture enabling her bosom to overshadow Miss Iverson's though Miss Iverson's was twice as big. The latter wore a blue serge dress with a Peter Pan collar, Lucille a silk frock of apple green with a shirred front that delicately cupped, as well as half revealed, her pretty little breasts. They were what bad poets called "doves cooing in quiet porticoes," and the like, lines of the sort McGland could not possibly write though he often found himself under pressure of circumstances having to quote them. "The Reading Clinic brochure."

"Haven't had a chance."

"Too swamped with other stuff. You see — Jack is right."

"No doubt about it. And the brochure is the last thing I'd skim."

McGland had resolved on an attitude of friendly deference toward Haxby and his hobby. Haxby was a bore, but he was a dangerous one, plus being his host, and the least McGland could give in return for all this good food and drink were those lighthearted quips with which he was known to sing for his supper. Haxby, too, seemed determined to bury the hatchet. He grinned across the table and said to Miss Iverson, "Gowan here says they haven't even heard of speed reading abroad. At least that he knows of."

Miss Iverson clucked her tongue with a deploring pout. "They haven't?"

"No," said McGland. "I figure we in the British Isles are from fifteen to twenty years behind the cultural decline going on everywhere else in the world."

Miss Iverson threw her head back and laughed, and Lucille laughed too, but Haxby's fists clenched and unclenched at his sides. "Ah, here comes our Fouilly Poussé," said Lucille, who could never keep the vineyards of France straight and often got their names twisted around as well. At the same time she reached under the table and gave McGland a warning poke in the knee. McGland, misunderstanding the movement, took her hand and squeezed it responsively in his. Miss Iverson said, "Have you traveled much in Europe?" and McGland answered, "No, I believe in the motto See America First."

It was only the reception accorded his dissertation on white wine that at all repaired Haxby's mood. McGland was perfectly willing to let him shine in that department (being, to complete the parallels, also too fond of liquor to give a damn what he drank) and it gave him personal relief to see Haxby attentive to Miss Iverson; it meant the relaxation of Haxby's watch, lately quite sharp, on Lucille. McGland had more or less decided to press on to its conclusion his campaign for Lucille's favor — to make the pitch as they said in the States. Something happened midway the dinner that made him resolve to mince no words and lose no time.

As they were lifting their first glass of the red wine, to go with the duck Bigarade they had all ordered, he felt a sudden sharp twinge in his upper jaw. While the rest were bent over their food, he covertly thrust a forefinger in to where, more precious than rubies, were the only adjoining pair of teeth left in his head, a right bicuspid and its neighboring molar. He went sick as the twinge was repeated.

He choked his duck down somehow. When during coffee the ladies absented themselves together, he found himself alone with Haxby. Haxby took on the symbolic monstrosity of all dentists, for McGland the very heralds and legates of the Grim Reaper, for time had only deepened his certainty that he could not emotionally survive that last emasculation which it was written one of their number would perform. *I shall bite into every apple I can while I still have teeth.* The hunger for reassurance made him waste no time in making those inquiries which might, of course, expose him to the worst.

"I was reading in the paper the other day about some of your latest triumphs," he said, wiping his palms on the sides of his trousers. "An abscessed tooth is no longer a goner. That right?" He turned his dog's eyes upward.

"Not necessarily." Haxby smiled as he noted the beads of perspiration on McGland's brow. As "the" dentist for actors and actresses to go to, he had had too many quivering egos in his chair not to recognize the mortal fear of defacement behind the nonchalant expressions and the brave smiles. He had long ago analyzed McGland's smile. He knew its every constituent as well as if he had looked directly into his mouth. "Why? Concerned about something?"

"Twitch or two on one side."

"Come to the office in the morning and we'll have a look. We can squeeze you in."

"That's very kind of you. I know your reputation, and I mean at the moment . . ."

"Nonsense. We get enough from those who can pay to write one off to international relations once in a while. And I know how it is. When I was your age I was only making ten thousand a year."

"It's a condition to which I aspire."

A sense of shame, unreasonable but persistent, made McGland apologize in advance for what Haxby would find, explaining that those ravages were as much the fault of bad dentists as poor heritage. He told the story of the rural Scotsman whom he had found using his instruments for nut picks as he sat cracking pecans in his office. This caused Haxby to put his head back in one of his rare straightforward guffaws. He certainly had a hearty headful of teeth himself, though one had the sneaking suspicion that if he were flung to the ground and forcibly held while a count was made he would be found to possess more than the conventional thirty-two. Both men were laughing rather hysterically when the ladies returned.

McGland willed his hand not to reach out and palm the tenner which Haxby again left. Since Haxby was the last to go, herding the rest before him, self-control was not of the essence as they rose to leave. But as they approached the foyer, McGland walking again behind Lucille, he felt another shooting pang in his jaw, which routed his scruples. He turned around murmuring, "Left my cigars." He pocketed the note with no trouble while leaning over to pick up the empty Between the Acts tin where he had left it. While Haxby was shimmering under the grateful smiles of the two hatcheck girls, he was again roundly cursed by Edouard and the waiters in tones leaving no doubt that Siberia was for him if he ever showed his face around here again. McGland was at least secure in the knowledge that he now had enough to take Lucille to lunch, if he could wangle the chance.

Back at the Haxbys' house they had brandy and cordials and settled down to watch an old Marx Brothers movie in the television room. The first moment he found himself alone with Lucille, McGland said, "How about lunch the day after tomorrow? Will you come to Woodsmoke and stay the afternoon? Oh, please?"

"Why so urgent?"

"Time's wingèd chariot." They were standing at the base of a winding staircase up which Haxby had momentarily gone for something while Miss Iverson was making a telephone call in another room. He seized her shoulders and kissed her. "You're so beautiful," he whispered huskily. "Please come."

"But the guest house?"

"I've left there. I'm back at my motel. That Dew Drop place."

"Bobsy?"

"That's over. Why do you think I've moved out?"

"I should have guessed because it *wasn't* over."

"But it is. Please, please. Meet me at the restaurant they have there, the Period Room they call it, at twelve, and I'll love you for the rest of my life. I do adore you."

"Well, more like one o'clock." After seeing to it that he had scrubbed the lipstick from his mouth, she hurried away to tune the television set.

Miss Iverson bustled back into the other end of the room just as Haxby came back down the stairs, carrying an unopened bottle of brandy. McGland had noticed his shadow moving along the wall above, some seconds before Haxby himself came into view, after what McGland had been sure was a safe interval. What he had not been aware of, in his desperation, was that Lucille and he also cast a shadow across the foot of the stairs, from the television room, which one pausing on the steps above would have had no trouble interpreting even if he had not heard the hurried whispers which accompanied it.

Throughout the evening there had been discussion of accelerated reading, with Miss Iverson carrying the ball. She also spoke of remedial reading, quoting some rather grave statistics about the percentage of children with problems in that department, and what the Clinic hoped to do about that. McGland did not argue, contenting himself with asking questions. Now as Miss Iverson returned from her phone call, which had been to a local school superintendent with whom she had an engagement the next day, she made a last point or two about reading problems among college students, and then the evangelical aspects of the evening were forgotten as they settled down to watch the movie.

They broke up about midnight. Miss Iverson insisted on driving McGland home in her Chevrolet coupé. "Little last minute proselytizing," she said from behind the wheel to Haxby, who stood on the curb with Lucille to see them off. "Work on him long enough and we may get his name on the Sponsoring Committee."

"Do that," Haxby said. To McGland he said, stooping a little and talking past Miss Iverson, "By the way, will I see you in my office tomorrow?"

"If it's all right. It's very nice of you. I'll call first and make sure about the best time."

"I'll be ready for you."

McGland sat in the chair watching Haxby hold the X-ray up to the light from the window. His hands clutched his knees and perspiration trickled from his armpits down the sides of his chest. His heart thumped. His mind froze in the familiar numb apprehension with which he awaited these verdicts.

"They both seem O.K.," Haxby said at last. "No abscesses, or even cavities."

"Good. Then it's probably just neuralgia."

"Not exactly. What's happened is that the bicuspid — that's the forward one — has shifted position. Or I should say become tilted. Here, look."

He moved the negative in midair so that McGland could see it against the light, and indicated something with his little finger. "The root has worked itself forward, away from the molar, while the tooth proper has come back *toward* the molar. The result is this triangular pocket in which some infection has developed, causing the tenderness and pain you've been feeling. It's probably a low-grade infection and we might get rid of it now with a shot of penicillin. That's no problem. But the thing is, it's certain to come back. It's a perfect breeding ground for food particles and so on gathering there in the gum. The danger is that in time — maybe a year, maybe next week — it'll infect the molar. And we don't want that, do we? That way you might lose them both — which would be the end of any possible bridgework. There's only one safe thing to do."

"What's that?" McGland asked in a dry voice.

"Give up the bicuspid. It's much the less valuable — in fact it's no use to you at all. You've got a bridge clip on it but it's not offering any real support. It's your molar that supplies your support on that side, and when that goes —" Haxby smiled understandingly. "When that goes you lose them all, because you won't have enough anchors left, or rather the three left aren't distributed properly for a case. All that stands between you and a set of false teeth is that molar. I'll be glad to pull the bicuspid now . . . McGland? . . . Miss Thompson! The smelling salts, please."

McGland had slumped so far down in the chair that he was almost out of it. His feet were on the floor straddling the footrest and his nose just grazed the underside of the instrument tray as he slithered past it. Haxby swung the tray aside, and between them he and Miss Thompson, the nurse, hauled McGland into a more or less upright position on the chair. His head dropped forward, but straightened up after the nurse had stroked the bottle of restorative across his nostrils. It was a phial of spirits of ammonia, which they continued to call smelling salts in the office. Finally his eyes blinked open.

"Miss Thompson, get the brandy from the cabinet and pour Mr. McGland a drink."

McGland had a slug from a paper cup, then another, and presently had more or less pulled himself together. "All right, let's get it over with," he said. "One more strategic retreat."

"That's the spirit!" Haxby said.

In ten minutes the Novocain had taken hold, in another five the tooth was out. In ten more McGland was downstairs in the street, hurrying into the nearest bar. He downed Scotches so fast that inside of another hour he was drunk — which was what he had deliberately set out to become. He walked the seven or eight blocks between Haxby's Park Avenue office and Grand Central station. The next train to Woodsmoke was the five o'clock. Thank God it had a bar car.

As he sat slouched in his seat, sipping a beer through the side of his mouth away from the still faintly oozing socket, he noticed across the aisle from him, crisply young and fresh among the middle-aged commuters, a girl in a blue linen suit, watching him. "Pretty girls don't commute," they said around here, but that wasn't strictly true, was it? Something told him she was an office girl, sitting in the bar because all the other coaches were full. She was drinking a Coke; or rather, not drinking it. She took him in over the top of a magazine she wasn't reading — being only one of several who had noted his condition. Some exchanged glances and those smug headshakes with which people deplore public spectacles. A spasm of anger stirred his murky misery, seizing him with the desire to outrage. He drew out a pocket comb, dipped it into his beer, and began to comb his hair. Most of the onlookers remained under his spell, but when he had finished grooming himself he saw that the girl's eyes were lowered again to her magazine. She was blushing and smiling both.

The door opened and a conductor called for tickets. When he reached McGland, he stood there waiting while McGland fumbled in his pockets for the return half of the two-way ticket he had bought that morning at the other end. The search proving fruitless, McGland mumbled apologetically and took out his wallet. He knew there would be nothing in it. The tenner from the Burgundy dinner was hidden in a drawer in his motel room; that was absolutely earmarked for his lunch with Lucille tomorrow; nothing could have made him take that along and risk blowing it in town. Having pocketed the wallet, after obliging the conductor with a view of its empty interior, McGland began to fish in his pants pockets for loose coins. The conductor was twirling his ticket punch impatiently on a forefinger. At that point the girl rose, stepped across the aisle and told the conductor that he might punch McGland's fare from her ticket.

"Sorry, this is a forty-ride, ma'am, and can't be used by anyone else. You see it's marked Female here. Can't be used by a man."

"Then I'll pay his fare," she said with sudden temper, "when you get around to my seat."

The conductor shrugged and resumed his journey down the line. McGland began to thank her, but she cut him off with a vehement shake of her head. Leaning down, she said in a gentle whisper, "I heard you read at Wellesley three years ago, Mr. McGland, and I figure it's the least I can do."

She turned and walked back to her seat, picked up her magazine, crossed her legs and resumed reading. McGland rose after a few minutes and groped his way to the washroom. He stood there gripping the metal bar that ran across the opaque window, swaying, as the train pounded into Connecticut and the tears streamed down his cheeks.

twenty-one

A FEW WEEKS LATER, enriched by a royalty check for several hundred dollars that had caught up with him, McGland sat at the desk in his motel room and wrote out the fourth draft of a poem:

Come let us spread a picnic on the precipice,
Eat, drink, be merry with our backs to the abyss,
Till in that dusk where bats cannot be told from swallows,
Gifts from threats, we'll banish solemn songs like this.
This is our hopeless heaven, these flowers our eyes have watered,
Wine drawn from our veins, tunes piped from hollowed bones,
And gaiety pouring from every wound.

He had deleted from the previous version the lines, "The world's too mad for anything but mirth," and "We know at last the quintessential hoax," which struck him now as dreadful. How could he have written them? He remembered something he had told a New York journalist in an interview about his "working habits," a dull subject about which people remained curiously interested in the case of writers and artists. "Sometimes I write drunk and revise sober," he had said, "and sometimes I write sober and revise drunk. But you have to have both elements in creation — the Apollonian and the Dionysian, or spontaneity and restraint, emotion and discipline." Perhaps he had written those lines drunk. Well, he was sober now, and not going to stay that way long, so he'd better get the poem fixed while he was. Maybe the whole thing was no good — high-grade Pagliacci it was beginning to sound like on cold reconsideration.

The pain in his jaw had not abated, despite the removal of the bicuspid. The original soreness persisted, clearly distinguishable from the dull ache of the socket, now largely healed. Could it be the molar after all? Oh, dear God, no.

He delayed inspecting it by prolonging the ritual of assembling another drink. He carried his glass to the bureau on which sat the plastic bowl of ice supplied by the management. He dropped three cubes into the glass, in the name of the Father, the Son and the Holy Ghost, then twisted the cap from a fresh bottle and poured a generous stream of whiskey over them. "This is my body which is broken for some reason apparently none of my cotton-pickin' chicken-pluckin' goddam business," he said. For the rest, he stood at the window looking out at the traffic on the Post Road, for all the world like any man casually having a drink. Suddenly he set his glass down on the window sill and rushed into the bathroom. He lifted his lip as far back as he could and looked into the lighted mirror. The molar was abscessed.

He emptied his glass sunk in a chair. He instantly poured another, swallowing that till the raw blaze in his stomach overshadowed the throbbing in his mouth. He opened the phone book and found the name of a local dentist whom he had heard praised at house parties here. He tried to force from his mind the mad suspicion that was forming there. Would a dentist draw the wrong tooth deliberately — or at least unnecessarily — knowing all along that the one next it was doomed to follow? He remembered a story he had once read about a sadistic doctor who had amputated a man's leg unnecessarily. In no case could he go into New York and face Haxby again.

"Dr. Ormsby is busy this afternoon," the receptionist told him when he phoned.

"I've got to see him."

"Emergency?"

"Yes."

"What seems to be the trouble?"

"Toothache."

"Just a moment. I'll see."

He could hear the phone being put down and then footsteps, followed by a consultation in the background in which a man's voice could be faintly discerned. Then the return march and the clatter as the phone was picked up again.

"Can you be here at five? Dr. Ormsby will stay down to see you if you think it's that urgent."

He was quite drunk when he climbed the flight of stairs to the office, but his mind retained the stark clarity of panic. "Did Haxby see or hear us on the stairs?" it kept asking, and, as he settled back in the chair, "Is this the last humiliation cunningly planned by what may be then quite accurately termed insane jealousy?" Well, so Bobsy had tried to warn him.

Dr. Ormsby was in any case a short, cherubic sort with pink cheeks and merry blue eyes. "What seems to be the trouble?" he asked amiably as he washed his hands at a basin behind the chair. McGland sketched in a brief history of the problem. "Well, let's have a look."

A glance sufficed to confirm the belief that the molar was abscessed.

"That's not necessarily a death sentence for a tooth nowadays, is it?" McGland said, looking up with his whipped dog look again.

"Oh, no. No, certainly not. But I'm afraid that's not the whole story here." He drew up a stool in order to sit closer to McGland, and even have a cigarette with him. He was clearly a kind man. In a distant room could be heard the sound of young girl employees getting ready to go home.

"This tooth as such we might save. We can go in there with antibiotics, and if that doesn't work, drain the abscess surgically. We might draw out all the pulp and still have a shell which, cracked as it is from top to bottom — you must know the enamel's split — might still hold together for a while. But there's something more serious than all that. Your gum damage around it. Periodontal disease has left a lot of gum breakdown that's about to cost you the tooth even if by some miracle all the other factors work in our favor. Didn't your dentist explain all this when he pulled the bicuspid?"

McGland shook his head, rolling it on the rest without looking at the doctor.

"And did he have to pull it? That's what puzzles me, a little. He must have known that pulling it was as good as rendering you toothless, because now of course you'll be stripped clean on that side and we can't hang a bridge on what's left. I'm sorry.

But you'll have to have them all — Miss O'Connell! Are you still there?"

She was, but left mercifully soon after McGland came to on a couch in the consultation room. Dr. Ormsby offered him no liquor even if he had any about, well aware from McGland's condition that that would have been a matter of coals to Newcastle. He smoked another cigarette and walked the floor as he talked.

"I make it a rule never to run down predecessors," he said, "but it's a foolish economy not to get the best. Often I find people go to dentists because they're friends. Is this man a friend of yours?"

"Not exactly, though we see one another socially."

"Ah, yes. I won't ask his name — I'm not interested in that — but you do see the importance of having someone who knows what he's doing."

"I think he knew what he was doing."

McGland picked his way down the stairs "as if in a dream," a phrase by which we seek to suggest something of the sensation of a man moving in an environment with which he is not in organic touch. The very familiarity of the streets and buildings among which he wandered deepened this sensation, for he could only view the world now as an exile from it. The store fronts, the houses, the sunlight and the girls walking in it, these no longer had anything to do with him. He was not a total stranger to this alienation — not total. He had for all the years of his sexual manhood carried it mystically in his blood, the destination toward which he knew he moved.

He had been prepared for this Truth by perpetual fears of it, by recurrent glimpses of it, as of a veiled face, seen dimly and imperfectly, now with the last veil removed. "I have seen that face before." It had been foreshadowed in moments clairvoyant of this moment. And in those fleeting divinations he had sensed that final despair in which alone lay his hope of a dreamless sleep.

He wandered from bar to bar, till afternoon wore on into evening and the lights began to go on, and even out. He wondered that nobody seemed to notice anything unusual about him, apart from the fact that he was drinking rather heavily, which made one bartender refuse to serve him. Surely there must be something special about him tonight, that might indicate to one human spirit another in extremity. He thought this while entering a tavern he had been in an hour earlier. Surely there must, to anyone who really looks at a man, be clearly evident in his aspect some hint that here was one living his last day on earth. As he walked in, two men on barstools momentarily shifted their gaze from a television set to him with no change in their expression. They gave the impression of meeting reality with the same drugged abstraction granted the scene on the screen, so that nothing would have surprised — or, really, entertained — them. So that if McGland were to stagger in like a character in a crime story (which after all he was) exclaiming that he had been shot or stabbed, and opening his coat to reveal wounds so inflicted before collapsing to the floor, they would have followed his movements with the same glazed indifference accorded the violences and grotesqueries to which this nightly substitute for conversation and dispute had habituated them. It was to a commercial showing a woman spraying her flesh while she smiled with secret confidence in her own palatability (the Mona Lisa of the advertisements) that they turned back as McGland advanced toward the bar. He left again without finishing his drink.

The idea of Yeats in his old age had got firmly rooted in his mind. There were the mackerel-crowded seas, the young in one another's arms, and Yeats left with his "worm" and his rage. McGland had a friend with a painful story of the poet in his last days, trying to read publicly with (as McGland recalled it) the same impediment to diction as that to which he had just been doomed. McGland held on to that picture.

He went back to the motel and checked the phial of seconal he had there. A dozen of the red capsules remained: surely enough. He moved in a kind of leisure now, a crystal certainty of what he was doing, looking into drawers and into the pockets of his clothes for letters, papers, other things he would not for obvious reasons or obscure ones want to leave behind, tearing them up or otherwise disposing of them. The new poem was rent in twain from top to bottom, but the two pieces were left in a desk drawer. He set fire, for some reason, to a shirt and a pair of torn socks, sitting in a chair with a drink watching them burn to ashes in the metal wastebasket. All this while he reviewed what he knew personally of the long outrage of human existence, to justify and confirm his departure by arguments more universal than his own no doubt petty grievances.

There were his father and mother, each in the end a monolith of misfortune. There was his grandmother. Involutional melancholia has its highest instance among the women in rural Scotland. No one knows why. It's just one of those facts. One of his earliest memories was of his grandmother dying in a mental hospital. His grandfather had been more exquisitely spat upon. He was burned to death in the church for which he had always made financial sacrifices, while briefly napping in the furnace room where he donated his services as janitor when the congregation couldn't pay him. McGland tallied up each life story like a number in a column at the bottom of which would be the figure he wished before departure to confirm: zero. Nothing he could throw in of his own life greatly disturbed that limpid answer. Finally there was the piece of human cruelty of which he had himself just become the victim. It was in this very room that he had possessed the woman over whom the emasculation had been committed. Did that make any difference?

He sat back in his chair to finish the drink. There was one more memory that wanted rehearsing. It was probably the most vivid of his childhood days in that seagirt village.

Mrs. McLaughlin, ninety years old, had lost everything and everybody, through the simple principle of survival. Not only her children lay in the churchyard next to the white cottage in which she lived, but her two grandchildren too — one drowned, the other taken by sickness. She lived out her own old age with both legs crippled. Yet each day when the weather was fine she went out in her wheelchair to her garden patch, where she would pitch herself forward out of the chair and on her hands and knees crawl between the rows of vegetables, weeding and tending them. That done, she would crawl on through the open gate leading to the cemetery and do the same thing in the family plot, ending with the last grave, her own, awaiting her there. Why did she go on day after day, year after year, to eke out the tail end of an existence that had no longer any substance or meaning? Because she represented human worth at its highest: virtue in a void. That final courage which consists in knowing courage to be useless.

Did he, McGland, have it? Why should he want it? What would he do with it?

He finished the drink and lit a cigarillo. Drawing on that, he walked down the Post Road to a drugstore, where he bought a quart of strawberry ice cream. He wondered, as he carried it back to the motel in one of those insulated paper bags, whether he had a bowl in his room. Yes, of course — the plastic bowl in which the management sent over ice. There was even a spoon in it.

When he got to the room, he took off his coat and hung it in the closet. There were two ice cubes melting in water in the bottom of the bowl. He emptied them into the bathroom sink. Standing at the dresser, he got out the ice cream and began to spoon it into the bowl — the entire quart. He emptied the phial of seconal capsules over it, one by one, mixing them well into the ice cream. He stirred it for several minutes. Then he carried the bowl to the armchair beside the window, sat down, and began slowly to eat.

twenty-two

THE TELEPHONE SCREAMED on in McGland's ear. It was like the ship's alarm again, only this time ringing as though under water. The vessel along whose decks it sounded was a derelict that had sunk to the bottom, and was being explored for possible salvage. There had been, in his dream, something about their trying to drown McGland by throwing him overboard, and the ironic sense of doing this from a ship itself fathoms deep on the floor of the sea. At the services for him, there had sounded, like a blast from a trumpet, McGland's favorite line of poetry, not poetry at all actually, but a sentence from Sir Thomas Browne's *Religio Medici:* "And thus was I dead before I was alive; though my grave be England, my dying place was Paradise; and Eve miscarried of me, before she conceived of Cain."

The fact that this was the telephone at last penetrated the fogged, clogged corners of his brain, enough to send his hand out across the pillow toward the night table where it shrilled away.

"Mr. Gland? This is Mrs. Punck again. How are you? I hope you haven't retired?"

He emitted a gurgling sound, apparently interpreted as a negative reply on the other end.

"I'm calling for a couple of reasons. I learned where you're staying from the Springers' maid. I happen to know the proprietor of that motel, and now if everything isn't perfectly satisfactory you let me know, do you hear?"

"Do dah."

"Secondly, Mr. Gland, I want to thank you for keeping your promise not to see our girl, as you seem to. At least you have as far as we know. It is true, isn't it?"

There was a pause. The woman was apparently fishing for information, of which she was in doubt rather than certain. But it was not forthcoming. She went on:

"I appreciate that. We all do — as she will too, in time to come. But another thing I want to call to your attention while I have you on the phone. I just stepped outside and saw what a beautiful evening it is. But perhaps you've noticed it?"

McGland felt as though, while he slept, cunning hands had removed and unraveled his entrails and wound them around his neck. A faint, strangled sound escaped him now.

"It's a real inspiration. There is a quarter moon — a dry moon we used to call it because it's tilted so that if you poured water into it the water would run out? — swimming in fleecy clouds — sheep clouds — in a sky of the purest blue you've ever seen. No artist could paint that scene, but I know a poet wouldn't want to miss the sight. The stars are bright too, because the moon is only a quarter. You have no doubt read Longfellow?"

The cunning artificers who had rearranged his constituent vitals had left his stomach in place. A wave of nausea now made him clap a hand over his mouth and sit up involuntarily. The furniture rolled like that on a ship in a storm — indeed, like objects propelled about the air in a whirlwind. Through the dense fogs of confusion, which included the uncertainty as to who he was, he had the memory of some outrage committed against him before, perhaps in another life, or in a remote, recollected dream of which this was the reality. Then he remembered: having poetry recited to him by this same voice.

" 'The stars, the forget-me-nots of the angels, blossom one by one in the infinite meadows of heaven.' "

He shot out of bed and bolted for the door, letting the phone drop behind him. He thought he was headed for the bathroom but in his confusion he made straight through the main door to the porch, where he hung over the wrought-iron railing, heaving into a small cluster of rhododendron bushes below.

It was indeed a beautiful night. The air was warm, but cool compared with that in the room, as well as damp, and so felt refreshing to his flushed cheeks. The Longfellow proved as thorough an emetic as could have been wished in the circumstances, and though his head continued to throb, he felt his insides clearing. Realizing where he was, he noted that fortunately he hadn't gotten into his pajamas but was fully clothed except for shoes and coat. Something else invaded the wild assortment of impressions.

There were footsteps running rapidly up the short flight of stone stairs leading from the concrete walk below, then a hand laid sympathetically on his back. "Bit of the old heave-ho? The traditional upchuck?" It was Mopworth, inhumanly spruce in his seersucker suit, tab-collared shirt and figured foulard tie. He spoke in the supportive, encouraging measures of a midwife. "There we come. Another good one and we're home. Last of the old whoppers, eh? That ought to make us feel better." Still patting McGland's back, he glanced through the open doorway and saw an empty whiskey bottle lying on its side on the dresser. "Bit overmuch of the well-known grape?"

McGland nodded, wiping his mouth with his tie. Mopworth

turned him solicitously around, steered him through the door and toward the bed, onto which McGland flopped on his back. Mopworth pulled his feet up and settled them on the counterpane, which was folded back. He took charge, knowing exactly what to do and doing so with brisk efficiency, and without consulting McGland. Seeing that the ice bucket was empty, he rinsed it out and popped down the porch to the kitchen for some more cubes. He was back in a minute, without having consulted the management.

"Do you have an icebag?" Instinct had already sent him to the drawer to which McGland pointed. He unscrewed the cap and dropped several ice cubes into it. "Fancy me trying to pick up your trail all over town and finding you right here at the Dew Drop, three rooms down from my own!" he said, settling the icebag on McGland's head and then McGland's hand on the icebag. "We won't even talk about resuming the brain picking till this hangover's well forgotten, of course, but you'll be glad to hear *Esquire* seems keen for an article or two on you. A few chapters run in magazines will help pay for the book while I'm writing it, because needless to say I haven't got a very princely advance."

McGland revolved the possibility of Mopworth's making more money writing about him than he did himself on this poetry. And of course there would be Mopworth mopping up indeed, lecturing round the country after he was gone — if he could ever get to that point with all these interruptions.

"Why didn't you stay in television?" McGland asked, closing his eyes because Mopworth seemed to be circling in and out of view as well as bobbing up and down, like a rider on a carousel. Another thing was that, true to habit, Mopworth was throwing peanuts into the air and catching them in his mouth with shattering skill. He always seemed to carry a supply in his coat pocket.

"Oh, acting doesn't satisfy a chap. You know that." He sat on the bed. "I've always wanted to be a writer. I'm not, those few bits of light verse notwithstanding. But writing about chaps who *are* sort of gets me in the side door. But throttle down, Gowan, you look as though you've just been born again. We'll go on with the interviews when you're feeling more yourself."

"I am myself. What else do you want to know?" The idea of tidying up the "legend in his own lifetime" that he had become, of gathering in the loose ends — or perhaps even adding a few more — struck him as a good one now. Mopworth forsook the bed for the armchair beside it. He drew the spiral-bound notebook from his pocket and opened it over his knee. He poised a sharp pencil over it and watched McGland, who lay still as a figure on a catafalque, except for the icebag which he occasionally raised a hand to shift.

"Of course in a weakened condition a bloke's defenses are down, and he's apt to dish out more intimate stuff than he might otherwise. I've always wanted to know something about your philosophy of life, Gowan, so if you want to pull out the old hairpins now's the time." A brief pause followed, in which McGland uttered nothing but a faint, strangled murmur, indicating nothing much but a sense of disgusted impatience with the subject. He said finally, as though in a last, reluctant concession to precision, "Nobody ever will figure it out. The combination is locked up inside the safe."

"'Man —?" Mopworth cued him, writing hastily, "Comb. locked safe. Man?"

"Stinks. Introspection must have taught you that."

Mopworth paused in his scribbling, and said: "Do you believe in God?"

McGland moaned faintly, and then began to mumble what sounded like, "No Christian."

"You're no Christian," Mopworth said, writing again.

"No, no. He isn't. God. He's no Christian."

"I say, Gowan, now that's a bit close to the verge. I mean on second thoughts you may want to take some of this back, and I'll read it over to you in the cold light of day, mind you, but I'll put it all down for the well-known nonce. God . . . no . . . Christian. Care to develop that?" he asked, giggling nervously.

McGland turned on his side with another groan and began to mutter a series of couplets he had never been able to do much with:

He makes a world in which one thing eats another,
Then sends his only begotten son to be our brother.
Wish he'd make up his mind instead of leaving us in the lurch.
I doubt he says his prayers, or ever goes to church."

"I say, Gowan, this *is* playing a bit close to the Pit, but, again, I'll give you a gander at it in the well-known dawn. Sort of thing we repent on our deathbed and all that, but for now . . . Let's see . . ."

McGland noted again the detail with which Mopworth continued to talk and act like Hilary Tuttle, the character in which he'd succeeded McGland in the television serial. He, McGland, had originated Hilary, a Silly Ass type of Englishman, for the wireless, purely through voice. But when Mopworth assumed the role on the telly he'd had to do him *to the life,* had to be *seen* popping in and out of doors with a bowler and a furled umbrella with which he hailed buses and inadvertently poked girls once he'd boarded them, etc. The thing was, Mopworth *continued* to be Hilary (or at least the Silly Ass Englishman) to the life, nearly a year after chucking the role to take a whack at (oh, my God) writing. Or was this natural with him? Had he always talked and acted this way? Was he the Silly Ass Englishman by birthright? They'd exchanged no words that night at the London party where he'd first seen him, at the time of the takeover, and he'd not heard him speak before that, so McGland had no way of knowing. Perhaps he would never know.

Mopworth continued to laugh appreciatively at the shockers, at the same time egging the other on. "Care to dish up any more blasphemies? Do you good, get things off your chest. What about religion for other people? Of which art may be a substitute for . . . other people."

McGland moaned again, this time a muffled bleat into the pillow. He wished the jessie would go. What was all this folderol but the idiotic wish to be remembered for a few minutes after one was gone? At that point he heard the other get to his feet and say, "Well! Come in!"

McGland rolled onto his back again. In the doorway, which had been left open to the warm night, stood Geneva Spofford.

253

She was dressed in a navy blue skirt and white silk blouse with a broad V-neck. Her gold hair hung to her shoulders, neatly brushed, lustrous in the porch light behind her. She smiled tautly, clutching a black patent leather bag in two hands. She looked like a caseworker about to visit a scene of unutterable squalor which would nevertheless be valuable as part of a sociological survey she was helping conduct.

"What's the matter with Gowan?"

"Bit under the weather. Bit of a katzenjammer."

Mopworth did the honors, waving her to the chair and striking a match for a cigarette which she promptly took out. He retrieved the icebag, which had fallen to the floor, and helped settle McGland with it in what was more of a sitting position than he'd been in up to now. He asked McGland whether he might get him anything, like black coffee, and when McGland said, "No, but thanks a lot," he left. "I'll look in on you in the morning, Gowan. We might rip a chop if you're free for lunch. Meanwhile, if you need anything I'm in number 20. Good night. Good night, Miss Spofford." He closed the door quietly behind him.

"He's a nice bloke," McGland said. "I recommend him highly."

Geneva rose and finished tidying the room. She dropped the whiskey bottle into the wastebasket and emptied ashtrays into it. She glanced twice at the other ashes in it, but asked no questions. The telephone, still dangling on its cord, she restored to its cradle. McGland smelled her as she bent to accomplish this, and closed his eyes. Why should the breath of morning come to him now, a bit of human scrap quite prepared to consign itself to the junkheap?

"Don't do all that," he said when he heard the tinkle of hangers in the clothes closet. "Your grandmother will be turning up here if she finds you gone."

"I thought you found my family quaint."

"They think I'm a viper."

"You are. And it's not part of your charm. Why haven't you telephoned? You haven't called me since that evening. I should think you would after — what happened."

"I promised not to. It's a point of honor."

"I appreciate your chivalry toward my grandmother," she said dryly.

McGland turned over in his mind a piece of moral book-keeping. Geneva had, in a rush of uncontrollable feminine emotion, given herself to him because she'd thought he had been trying to kill himself. In the confusion, he had lost his own head too, and taken something under false pretenses. Now, however, he had tried to kill himself, so didn't that square him?

She sat down, after swinging the armchair about so she would face him directly, if not he her. She seemed to sense the wheels of self-justification turning in his mind, and to have resolved to have none of it.

"What happened a couple of weeks ago was a mistake. But that's not the point — I mean regrets and all about what's past. The point is you might have known I'd be worried sick . . ."

"Worried?" he said in a dry voice.

"Yes. That you might try to kill yourself again. Nobody at the Springers' knew where you were, or at least they wouldn't say."

"Forget about me. I'm a dirty rotten worthless no-good low-down swine."

"Men can be so conceited. Anyhow, I found out where you were through overhearing Mrs. Punck. So Grandma's the unsuspecting go-between." Geneva paused, and shifted a little in the chair so that she did not face him quite as squarely. She sat sideways, her knees together and both feet to the left of the chair. "Gowan, have you ever been interested in a home? Or is that too hairy to ask?"

This girl had changed, McGland thought to himself. That first evening, she had talked with the kind of slang-slinging put-on worldliness that had made him want to say aloud, "Come now, that's not your style." She had obviously been trying it on for size. The vocabulary, half real life, half soaked up from the authors of the hour, was applied like a kind of verbal cosmetics. Once, he remembered, she had put two fingers to each temple, like a fake medium in a trance. That was all changed now — now she was herself with that simple combination of bashfulness and hostility that old Spofford had re-marked about her. That habit of giving you what-for while looking at the floor. But then, he had only thought, "Why can't American girls be themselves? Why can't people be them-selves?"

An involuntary belch escaped McGland now, which made him quickly recover his Falstaff-at-Elsinore pose. He did this by half-hooding his eyes and gazing just past her at the wall be-hind her. "I consider the home an invasion of privacy," he said.

"Yes, I heard you say that once before. It was witty the first time, and probably witty now too, though I'm not exactly in the mood for quips."

"You've been making them yourself. The way you say them they rhyme with whips."

"Well, I'm sorry about that." She raised her eyes to look at him. He was turned half in profile, and the corner of his mouth was slightly raised up in a faint grin, which suggested that air of crooked and lazy wickedness that is seen in the side views of crocodiles. She said without further preliminary:

"Gowan, I'm worried about a friend of mine. She thinks she's in trouble and doesn't know what to do. I thought you might know something to take. She's done everything. Jumped off tables, gone bowling, horseback riding and whatnot."

"And all of these methods have proved abortive?"

"Gowan, you certainly have got some sense of humor." Her eyes now met his squarely, in a faint smile. A deep, clear hazel in color, the largest, probably, that he had ever seen, they seemed to dilate even further as he looked into them, like bulbs lighting up, deepening the crazy beauty of that face. "Later I may laugh, but not now."

"'Can't the bloke marry her?"

"He's married already. Not very securely, but there is a wife in the background."

"Maybe he'll get a divorce. Meanwhile she should go to a doctor. Any one. Even the family doctor is often able and will-ing to make the right connection. The profession is more flexible and — common-sensical about those things than people generally think."

She rose and walked to the desk in the corner, where there was a fresh bottle of whiskey. She screwed the cap off and looked around for something in which to pour a drink. "You'll find a clean glass in the bathroom I think," he said. "Wrapped in one of those sanitary wrappers."

He could hear her tear the sterilized casing from it, pour whiskey in, and run some tap water. She walked back into the room and stood drinking. She rolled an eye at him as she gulped. Still holding the glass, she walked to the back, raised the Venetian blind and slid the window up. The sound of swimmers splashing in the pool behind the motel could be heard. She bent to look out, accentuating the full, strong sweep of her loins, those thighs like the pillars of a temple. He felt a spurt of rage at the thought of that primordial innocence on which evil is so often visited. He felt quite sincere in this, thinking them both alike victims of some eternal mischance. He experienced one vast, last plummet of yearning, the desire to reach out and take her yet. Resisting it was perhaps the single act of self-mastery he had ever performed in his life.

"It may be a false alarm," he said.

"I keep telling her that."

"Is she in school with you?"

"Yes. Due to go back in a few weeks."

"Don't they have those nonresident terms, where you stay out for a semester and do what you want? What do they call them?"

"Service quarters."

"Well, it's something to think about."

"It certainly is."

McGland doffed the icebag, as though he were yet tipping his hat in some ornate, chivalric homage to courageous womanhood, and got up. "It'll all come out all right I know. You tell her that. Now look, I've got a wad of cash I wish you'd take and keep for me. Three or four hundred it must be." He got his wallet from his coat and began to empty it into her bag. She turned from the window and said rather sharply, "Don't be silly. I don't want this."

"Well, I do. And I'll lose it or go through the whole wad in a day or two if I keep on at this rate. You mind it for me. If I hide it in a corner somewhere I'll forget where it is. It's some royalty money, and I don't want to blow it on another bender. We'll go have dinner. I'll keep in touch."

When she had gone, the bills safe in her bag, he stood a moment on the porch watching her drive off. As she drew out onto the Post Road, she turned to see if he were there, saw him and waved. He waved back. The other physical distractions having subsided, he could feel the pain in his jaw again, tolling his knell. He said softly to himself, "Christ, if my love were in my arms, and I in my bed again." The car was out of sight.

Inside, with the door shut and the blinds drawn again, he reviewed once more his moral bookkeeping with this new entry in it, and closed that ledger for good. There was more reason for his departure now, not less. His remaining would serve Geneva more poorly than his going. That would be even truer if matters did not clear up for her. No father at all was better than a father drunken and broken. He would give the child a heritage, provided he were not around to soil it. Better a dead poet than a live dog.

That thought through, he walked the room a bit, reflecting one last time on his conclusion. He paused in his wanderings among the furniture to turn the television set on. He might wait for a sign. Like most unbelievers he was very superstitious, and often interpreted trivial coincidences as calls to act, or rather, waited for trivial coincidences to propel him on a predetermined course of action. He could wait for a sign.

Seated in the armchair he watched a Western, an episode in a family serial, a late movie. Midway that his head began to nod. He was startled from a doze by an advertisement. It was a dentifrice commercial of which the scene was a gay public waterside with a diving board, where, against a spoken liturgy of reassurance, only the young and beautiful, their smiles flashing like wielded knives, tumbled divinely through the summer air.

He got the orthopedic harness off the closet shelf and detached from it the rope part. He made a check of the door and the draperies to make sure they were fully shut. In the middle of the room was a chandelier, which he now appraised. Evidently this part of the motel had been built around an old inn of which they had preserved as many features as possible, and the stout chandelier was one. At least it looked stout. It was not lit; the only illumination in the room now came from the television set. He turned that off. The room was not quite in darkness; sufficient light seeped in around the door and through the draperies from the front porch for McGland to see what he was doing. He got the straightback chair from the desk and set it under the chandelier. He climbed up on it with the rope in his hand. He tied one end of the rope around the sturdy main trunk of the light fixture and knotted it tightly three times. He gave a few tugs to test it. It seemed solid enough.

As he knotted the bottom end of the rope into a noose, he found himself remembering the story of the amaranth flower. He was not thinking of the real life plant — of which he had often picked a variant called love-lies-bleeding — but the mythical bloom of the poets, which according to legend never fades. That was because, in the belief of the ancients, the flower sprang from the seed of a hanged man. Did one really experience such a paroxysm in his final throes? It was a pretty story anyway.

He drew the loop snug and, almost curious, kicked the chair out from under him.

twenty-three

"YOU SAY AN OUNCE of prevention is worth a pound of what?"

The mirth had gone out of these routines for Spofford. But his sarcasm as such had become more open now, like a lanced wound, and there was no teasing in it, not even of Mrs. Punck herself — only a dense, diffuse resentment of everything and everybody. Things had backfired in a way and to an extent that he had hardly envisioned and certainly not deserved.

"What did you say it's worth a pound of? I didn't quite catch that."

Mrs. Punck did not raise her eyes from what she was crocheting, in a parlor chair past which Spofford paced. "Never mind that," she replied. "I know you've been mocking me. I'm on to that. I'm not going to repeat it."

"Don't you think we have enough doilies for this house?"

"This one isn't for this house."

Spofford stood with his back to Mrs. Punck before a framed photograph on the parlor wall at which he had once often gazed, but not in some time recently. It was a picture of his Uncle Emanuel's football team, one of the first seriously organized outfits of that kind in this part of the country. It was the 1881 squad of a state agricultural college to which he had gone — the only member of his family who had been educated, up till Geneva. The figures, somewhat ferociously lined up in their formal positions, were yellow and faded now, but he could make out his Uncle Emanuel, grimacing as he had done in real life when Spofford was a boy, his dense shock of black hair as Spofford remembered it too. He resembled Spofford's father. Though temperamentally quite different — Emanuel had been run over by a train when he was fifty — the two shared the Spofford damn-the-torpedoes attitude. Here he was savagely exemplifying the role of quarterback as it was then understood, in a getup that had not been any longer in serious use since practically the date of the picture.

He wore a uniform to the sides of the pants of which were sewn leather handles, by means of which his teammates had picked him up and hurled him bodily over the scrimmage line to the other side, often for gains of several yards. Those were the days before there were any rules. People had been regularly killed in football games until, apparently, Teddy Roosevelt had got mad and threatened to put a stop to the whole thing unless some control was exercised by means of rules imposed on the sport from within. Rules were what had been sorely needed; there was no doubt about that. Yet in the images inherent in that picture — the fierce bearded athletes, his uncle hurtling forever through space into enemy territory — resided, for Spofford, the principle of a lost hardihood. Something had gone out of people, that was certain. So why, if that were his mood, did he take it out on Mrs. Punck, who typified in her vestigial way some of the principles mourned? Because his emotions were scrambled, that's why, and his thoughts in a state of continual scrimmage themselves, and he could not control them. He glared at her hostilely. He thought of his far, forlorn bond with the commuters, tenuous at best, now broken forever.

Mare came in and sat down, going quietly toward a chair like someone in charge of a meeting about to start and that had been waiting for her. Spofford began to leave the room but she detained him by putting out a foot over which he would have tripped had he continued his attempted exit.

"I never thought I'd live to see the day," she said, opening what was clearly to be another grim family conference.

"Oh, let's not open that can of peas again. I'll go talk to Mc-Gland. I'm going to talk to that guy. I tried to reach him a pile of times. I'll see you all later, but I mean don't sort of all sit there dying at me. I know we're in a pool of blood, but at least don't make things any worse than they are."

"Wait a minute. What are you going to tell him?"

"A thing or two. Why, that he's got to do right by her, some way, somehow. We don't know exactly how, but right. What else?"

"Up the social ladder means down the moral one," said Mrs. Punck with unabating acumen. "I've always said it." She spoke without interrupting her crocheting; indeed, it had speeded up. "It's this culture. Meet the right people and you're bound to do the wrong things. I've always said it."

"So don't say it no more," Spofford retorted. He wondered to himself how Rappaport stood it. But he knew perfectly well how Rappaport stood it. A kind, affectionate wink at Spofford, in the course of Mrs. Punck's cozy philosophizing, said it clearly enough: we take people as they are, with charity and if necessary amused affection; we ride the punches; we enjoy what we have in the best and most human way we should. The knowledge that Rappaport was getting the good out of everything along those lines in the sunset of his life irritated the hell out of Spofford — an irritation with himself. Had he let something slip through his fingers? His vexation was not lessened by the sight of the chairman of the meeting walking and yelling around the room now — a Crazy Woman. "We should of stuck to what we decided first! No chickens to commuters. *But none!*"

"Oh, let's not have the Ride of the Valkyries this time, shall we, darling? Let's not stand there shrieking like Brünnhilde. I mean McGland's marriage doesn't mean anything. He as much as told me he was getting a divorce. I didn't realize what he meant at the time because I didn't know he was married, but looking back on it now I realize that's what he meant. So for all intents and purposes we can consider him a single man. A little old for Geneva, in his thirties, but single. The only question is, where do we go from there? Let's decide on a course of action. Geneva must like him or she wouldn't have had that much to do with him."

"Well, I don't," Mare said, suddenly stopping behind a chair and gripping its top. "And I don't want any part of him."

Mrs. Punck stopped her crocheting to look at her, and Spofford came a step back into the room from the doorway where he had been hovering with his hat in his hand. "What do you mean?" he asked.

"Just that. I won't have my daughter marrying somebody who'd get her in trouble."

Spofford spun away, clapping a hand to his head. "Oh, my *God!*" he said. "Are we going crackers on top of it here, so we can't think straight about — I mean is this hysteria, or what? *He's responsible.*"

"No he ain't responsible, is just what I'm trying to say. A girl deserves better than a man who'd get her into trouble."

"Oh, my God! What sort of Alice in Wonderland logic is this?" Spofford turned to appeal to Mrs. Punck, who only answered, crocheting again, "My daughter can make fine points." As though an unsuspected subtlety had been found lurking in a family thought to be elementary.

"A man who'd get a girl in the family way ain't husband material," Mare went on, "and I don't want him for no son-in-law."

Mrs. Punck's needle flew while Spofford now began to nod to himself, as though trying to pump from his inner self the understanding necessary for the grasp of these nuances. "What about the child then?" he asked.

"I'll have it," said Mare, lighting a cigarette.

He nodded again, or yet, in a finality of befuddlement, of sheer bottomless uncomprehension of women and their ways, hoping that by pretending to understand it he would understand it. Mrs. Punck, hooking up a strand of thread with her pinkie, understood. But then she had probably had a glass of sherry. She seemed uncommonly flushed.

"We'll go away in the winter and live in Florida, for my health we will say first, or for a much-needed vacation. Geneva can take her off-campus semester — they all have to have one of those learning-through-living semesters. While we're there, I'll have the child, which we'll all then come back with. I'm not too old."

"That will be the story we'll give out," Spofford told Mrs. Punck, taking hold. "Next point, the matter of who'll take care of the chicken farm while they're away."

"You and Ma," Mare said. "George will be here some of the time, but for some of it he'll be in Florida with me. When he is, you two'll hold the fort."

"Won't people talk about that?" Spofford said, trying to wink at Mrs. Punck. She refused to have her attention distracted, however. "Two unmarried people under the same roof alone?"

"I may be married by that time," Mrs. Punck said, without raising her head. "And out of the house. So you'll be under the roof alone. And while you are, you might fix it. It leaks like a sieve."

Mare brought her two fists down on the back of the chair and became a Crazy Woman again. "Not now, Ma!" she said. "We can't go into that now. Later maybe, when this other has all cleared up. But *not now*."

Spofford found himself galloping toward town, with no clear idea why he was going there — except that he should do some thinking before talking to McGland. It would have been wrong to say he was depressed. His mind hummed. There was no doubt that calamity had a way of keying you up. It seemed always out of chaos that new order was brought. Chaos was not just something over which the spirit of God had once creatively brooded, and then no more. Oh, no. Chaos was here to stay, for us to brood over each time anew, with, and possibly even for, God; to bring to our lives and to life in general ever fresh forms out of that which was Without Form and Void. The very notion of their family being plowed over by a poet was as exhilarating as the circumstances themselves were unsettling. It was crazy-making. In a twinkling they had all been transformed into different people, all their molecules rearranged, like *But* said. Everything was relative. He should subscribe. He should even join the National Semantics Association. As recently as last spring he had been a man stagnating on the brink of senility. Now he was on fire. McGland had only one fault — he was worthless. How many pillars of society free of that particular flaw could hold a candle to him on other counts?

Once the charge sent through him by this course of thought had spent itself, however, the immediate facts again settled in the pit of his stomach. He would have to face McGland.

Finding a library book on the seat beside him, which he had meant to return the day before but neglected to, he decided to stop in and take it back now. Ella Shook got behind the desk when she saw him come in.

"Morning, Ella. Saw you at the *Freud* movie the other night. Like it?"

"Yes. Yes, I enjoyed it. It was very instructive."

"I thought the wedding scene, where Freud got married, was especially interesting. You probably noticed that Old World custom he observed, where the groom steps on a wineglass and smashes it as part of the ceremony."

"Yes, I remember that. It's an old folk custom."

"Course it's a defloration symbol."

"Out."

"Freud himself probably didn't realize the significance of it at the time. That was well before he —"

"*Out I say.*"

"Fine, and then I'll go straight to the Board of Trustees and tell them intellectual discussions ain't allowed in the libary no more."

"You do that." She sighed and dropped her hands on the desk. "Look, Frank Spofford. We're all glad when people get a new lease on life and broaden their horizons with art and literature, but you've become an absolute pest. You're driving everybody crazy all over town, private citizens and public officials alike, while you live a little."

"I aim to do all of that I can before I shovel off this mortal coil."

"You do that, but not in here. Now I have the right to bar any person from this building whom I consider a public nuisance, and I hereby declare you a public nuisance. Effective this morning, you will be allowed in here to return books, draw new ones, and get out. Nothing more. You are to keep your mouth shut and your nose out of the better magazines. Is that quite clear? I should think you'd be a little less rambunctious this morning, considering your poet friend is dead."

"What!"

"Hanged himself in the motel. It just came over the radio this morning."

That was how Spofford learned about it. When Geneva did, she had a miscarriage. Nor was that all — for the death of a poet was not so ill a wind as to blow no more good than that. When Dr. Rappaport was telephoned he came running, and took care of matters with such a blend of skill, solicitude and discretion that no one among the Spoffords could now welcome him into the family with anything but open arms. He was a member of it well before he and Mrs. Punck were formally married — Spofford himself found him a member of it when he hurried into the house, half an hour later. He remained to become an ever more deeply rooted member of it in the course of the family conferences that followed the immediate resolution of that crisis, his opinion widely sought after and respected. Because the Spoffords were far from out of the McGland legend. Indeed, they had only begun to be stuck with it, judging from the descent on the farmhouse of journalists who had got wind

265

of something they could hardly have been expected not to pursue. Mare took over now, and when she spoke they knew it was with the voice of authority.

"My girl's been plucked·from the burning — pulled back from the fire just in time, and I aim to keep it that way," she said. "Pa done us no good, Ma done us no good. I'll handle it from here on in, and the rest of you will keep in the background. I want Geneva's name kept *absolutely and positively out of this thing.*"

"I'd keep it out," said Spofford, who was itching to talk to the reporters.

"They got wind he had some connection with a woman member of this family," she went on, ignoring him. "That much is clear from the reporters. I can tell they know, even the mealymouthed ones. They're sniffing around and they'll leave no stone unturned. No use in our denying it. There was a woman — so a woman they'll get. In other words, everything will proceed according to the plan we agreed on before the other blew over. That it was me he was mixed up with."

"Oh, my God."

Mare quietly brushed down some crumbs from the front of her dress, for they were all sitting around the big kitchen table having tea and some Banbury tarts Mrs. Punck had made. Mrs. Punck drank her tea with rather an air, as befitted a family with a literary side, not to mention a doctor about to come into it — and ignoring for the moment that one of them had a breaking and entering rap hanging over him.

"What you say sounds a little wild, Mary, but probably just wild enough to make sense in the circumstances," Dr. Rappaport said. They knew he wasn't through from the way he frowned into his cup with his gentle, burning eyes. He seemed to be admiring the old family china even as he put his mind to the more immediate problem. "Just what is it you object to about Emil?" Mrs. Punck had once asked Spofford, and he had answered, "If he just wouldn't always look like Bernard Berenson appreciating something. There's a famous picture of Berenson standing in an art gallery contemplating stuff. It's a posed picture, so he *knows* he's supposed to just stand there and ap-

266

preciate away, while we appreciate how he does it. Rappaport has got something of that in him. Notice how he's always admiring something around here? He admires everything we've got — the horsehair sofa, those old andirons, that Currier and Ives print. Your Banbury tarts." "And me," Mrs. Punck had said, and added, "And you too. He thinks you're a scream."

"McGland's was a wild talent. He lived a wild life, had a wild death, and now I suppose keeping astride this rather wild tiger we've gotten aboard calls for wild measures. Mary, just who have been after you?"

"Well, besides the newspaper reporters, there's *Life Magazine* going to do a spread of him, and I'm also granting *Time* a interview. They don't want to overlook anyone whose beau he might have been, the way it looks. So instead of simmering down around here it looks as though they've only just begun to boil. And I repeat again, with me watching ·the pot this time. That a car outside?"

Mare herself rose and walked to the window to see what had drawn up in the driveway. There was a spring in her step familiar to Spofford as that of someone embarking on a new life. He had seen it in Mrs. Punck. Mare turned around after a glance outside.

"Reporter?" Mrs. Punck asked.

"No. It's that young Englishman who's writing a book about him. Who visited us that night. The one with the eyes like chocolate carmels. You go see if you can help George in the barn, Pa. I'll go upstairs and change into something decent. Skedaddle, all. There's a heap to do."

"To do," said Mrs. Punck, pushing back her chair with a will.

267

MOPWORTH

twenty-four

FOR AS FAR BACK AS he could remember, Alvin Mopworth had liked girls. He had liked them so much, from such an early age, that he soon earned for himself the expectedly derisive nicknames from more normal boys in the English schools among which he was successively shunted in the effort to cure him of his weakness. The taunts were whispered in the classroom and shouted at him from street corners where he could be seen passing in the company of some pretty little classmate, carrying her books. It all began in London.

His concerned mother, a designer for a fashionable milliner in the West End, sent him to a private school in Switzerland, in hopes of correcting his obsession in fresh surroundings and a healthy outdoor environment, but it did no good. He continued to seek out the company of little girls, again carrying their books when he was not strapping on their skis for them or buckling them into their iceskates. "He was always rather an odd boy," said a motherly marquise who witnessed his removal from that school to still another, this time in Somerset.

There, one day, his mother took him out on a picnic, hoping to air her anxieties to him in a heart-to-heart talk.

"Why aren't you romping about with the rest of the boys?" she asked.

"I'd rather the other," he said.

His mother shut her eyes, as though flinching under strains of discordant music. "The Battle of Waterloo was won on the playing fields of Eton," she said. "Pray God England hasn't another war."

"If she does I shall try for the Air Force."

"To impress the girls with your uniform and brass buttons, no doubt."

"I say, this ground's a bit damp here, Mother. Why must we eat sandwiches in a field?"

"Because that's what a picnic is," his mother explained, closing her eyes again. "Eating sandwiches in a field."

Why must we eat sandwiches in a field? Smiling a little to himself, Mopworth remembered the incident now as he crossed the Spoffords' walk. Marching toward the house (with that brisk, erect stride he had indeed learned in a hitch in the R.A.F.), he had caught, between the barns and chickenhouses, a glimpse of pastureland behind the farm, and that had no doubt stirred the recollection. Perhaps the white paddock fence beyond it had something to do with it too, because they'd had to climb one to find a place on which to spread their picnic lunch. Hadn't a bull hovered threateningly in the background, like a raincloud? And hadn't he made a joke about the rather modish toreador slacks Mum had had on? They'd laughed heartily together at that, except for Mum.

It was at Somerset that he had in any case for the first time given Mum some reassurance. Instead of whacking about with girls that year he had joined the Dramatics Club and won a leading role in the class production of *As You Like It*, acquitting himself with such credit as Rosalind that Mum had gone both nights in a delirium of pride, pleased by this sign that he was participating in school activities and being one of the gang. This was in 1950. His mother, then long widowed, had suddenly married again, a retired manufacturer with whom she now lived in Mayfair. They and Mopworth rarely corresponded any more.

The bent for acting steered him into radio and television after his graduation from college. It was a good livelihood, but after the first excitement it settled down into merely that. He cast about for something more "emotionally rewarding," while sensing vaguely that only something like writing or painting would genuinely suffice to that end. He wrote some light verse, selling a few pieces here and there. Nothing much. Meanwhile the occupational environment supplied unending rounds of pretty girls, whom he pursued on a scale rendering him, once again, suspect in the eyes of his contemporaries — this time on intellectual grounds.

We know today that everything is the opposite of what it seems. Thus lavish tipping conceals a niggardly nature, filial devotion the wish to do one's parents in, and sexual athleticism a basic doubt of one's masculinity. The shadow of overcompensation fell early across Mopworth's youth, because of this great jolly keen yen for girls, but the really grave doubt of his sexual adequacy had its beginnings at a party in Chelsea where he found himself messing about with two women at once — or so nearly so as made no difference in the reckoning. It was the party where McGland had wound up the bender touched off by the discovery that he was to be dropped from the cast of the Tuttles. It all happened after McGland had left with the dark baggage he had picked up there. Much to Mopworth's relief, for relations between them had been strained in those first days, not relaxed as they were to become later when Mopworth was no longer acting and McGland was riding high as a literary lion.

Mopworth had been in a canoodle with a tall brunette in a red dress, who was wearing a perfume so heady that when he went out onto the terrace for a breath of air later he carried her spoor with him. Because the girl with whom he started a canoodle out there drew back at one point and, sniffing, asked, "What's that you're wearing? Bellodgia?" Mopworth had had to admit that he didn't know; that the fragrance adhering to him had been picked up in a previous canoodle, inside.

"Well, wear it in health," the second girl said. "Because you're not admitting — you're bragging — and when a man does that it's for a damn good reason."

"What?"

"He's got to prove something he isn't."

"'I'm not trying to prove anything. I just want a spot of the old slap and tickle. No harm in that surely. Come on, give us a kiss."

The girl's name was Peggy Schotzinoff — there was no doubt about it — and she was a dancer in a ballet troupe. They were exponents, not of the classic ballet, but the more modern variety of which the dances, spastic, vital, often American-influenced, are concerned with the depiction of contemporary phenomena such as slum clearance or the installation of high tension wires through valleys in which people have hitherto lived in peace.

A gramophone had started up inside, and Mopworth said, "Then give us a dance." After he had propelled her for half a chorus about the gravel floor of the terrace (enough for him to confirm privately the legend that ballet dancers are poor ballroom ones), Peggy Schotzinoff leaned back away from him a bit and said with a smile, "You're very graceful," adding suggestively to the onus under which Mopworth now already labored. He knew that she would blab about this. He shrugged and wagged his shoulders in an exaggerated, almost oafish, fashion, to indicate that her remark was not unqualifiedly true, or indicated at best a merely primitive zest for rhythm. He hadn't really wanted to see this baggage again, or anyhow not much, but wishing to redeem himself he plowed ahead in the only manner open to him under the circumstances. "Are you free for tomorrow night? We can have dinner and then go up to my place for a spot of heavy breathing."

"You do go at one."

"Well then, later in the week."

They did eventually dine, and afterward went to Mopworth's flat for a brandy. There, after some strenuous importunities in shirtsleeves, he was forced back with an understanding laugh. "Don't struggle so *hard*, Alvin."

"It seems to me you're the one who's struggling."

"No, I don't mean that way. I mean don't fight so hard to prove what you feel this need to. That you're a man."

"I don't want to prove anything. I just want to go to bed with you."

"You see?"

"You'll hate yourself in the morning."

Mopworth rang up the baggage of whose essence he had reeked in the first instance, when all this had gotten started, but by the time she could have dinner with him, which was a good month later, word had gotten around in this rather knowledgeable set that Mopworth was racing his motor, and why. In the cab after dinner, he seized her in a passionate embrace and began to devour her with kisses, gobbling her throat, her bare arms and shoulders hungrily. She wriggled free of his grasp after a moment and sat back in her corner to tidy herself.

"We all admire the way you're fighting homosexuality, Alvin," she said, drawing her lip down as she applied lipstick to it.

Mopworth nodded, looking out the window as he recovered his wind. "We'll go up to my place and talk about it."

Perception in these matters was, if anything, even further advanced in the United States, and, of course, most acute in that part of it to which his pursuit of McGland eventually took him. Thanks to some there who had known him in London, or had known of him through mutual friends, his reputation preceded him everywhere he went in the purlieus of literary New York and its environs — to be eventually watered by his own conduct. It was a vicious circle. It was to define and color his pursuit of Geneva Spofford. Before he could get to her, though, it appeared he must contend with the very formidable roadblock thrown in the way in the form of her mother, who received him when he called at the farm after McGland's death. After a few preliminary words, he asked after Geneva.

"She don't feel good," Mrs. Spofford said, watching him pace.

"I know. Cut up after the news. It must have been a shock to her."

"Why to her more than the rest of us?"

"Well, after all —" Flustered, Mopworth realized he had stumbled on a naturally sensitive point. "I mean we both saw him only the night before. It's all so awful."

"What's all so awful?"

"Death and all that. So dashed absolute."

"Were you all together?"

"Not actually," Mopworth said, marking where his feet fell in the pattern of the rug he systematically traversed, as though its design were some sort of maze which if properly followed would bring him out to daylight. "We just happened to sort of converge, you see, at poor Gowan's."

"The motel?"

"Yes." He made a vague gesture of belittlement of the fact, shrugging off what his very shrug caused to germinate the faster. Mrs. Spofford waited until his labyrinthine passages about the surface of the rug had him marching straight toward the chair in which she sat. She then said, as he swerved to avoid her:

"If you want to know what she visited him in his room for, I can tell you. It was to try to break it up between us two."

Mopworth had become familiar with, indeed addicted to, those American comic strips in which consternation among the central characters is depicted by liberal interpolations of the word "gulp," as well as by a quantity of nuts and bolts flying graphically in all directions in the thought-balloons over their heads. What he answered now might have been rendered: "Between — gulp — you?" Nuts and bolts.

"Gowan McGland and me. He chased everybody, I knew that, but it didn't make no difference. Well, Geneva went to ask him not to see me any more, because it would only lead to heartache."

"I see. That comes as rather a stunner to me," said Mopworth, touching his breast pocket to make sure he had his notebook with him. "Why are you telling me all this?"

"If you want to talk about it, I think it might be better if we went somewheres else. I'd rather not be overheard here."

"I quite understand how you feel. Maybe we can find a nice quiet pub where we can have a pint or two."

Maybe he should never have gotten into this at all, Mopworth thought as he followed Mrs. Spofford into Indelicato's. Maybe he should have taken a heave at fiction instead. He might by now have a novel finished, even published. Something worthwhile too, a novel of social analysis or protest. One of those books about sensitive chaps who can hear their father hawking and spitting in the next room. Well, too late for that now, he thought as he threaded his way among the tables toward one in the corner. But up what byways the life of a Boswell took you! That McGland certainly got around. How had he beat the Proving Something rap anyway? Probably because he had the Tortured Artist thing going for him, and the pigeon-holers can't put you in but one pigeonhole at a time.

Seated at the table with a firm grasp of his stein, Mopworth tried to listen attentively as the woman went on about how she couldn't talk about it. She let drop key phrases like "give each other something" and "unhappy boy at heart," key phrases that unlocked no doors, while Mopworth turned over in his mind the possibility of a chapter on geniuses who had had mistresses from the lower orders, that he might sell first as an article. Let's see, there was Rossetti with his cockney model, Dowson with his waitress, van Gogh and the chit he gave his ear to, and now McGland with this good woman of radiant health, maternal solidity and sandy coloring. Such women no doubt appeased that nostalgia for the primitive that haunts overintellectual man. God knew he needed some side money, Mopworth. The expense of feeding these informants was well-nigh ruinous; his advance had run out and appeals for more expense allowance were eliciting sharp squawks from London. He must try to horse some money out of an American publisher. Let's see, there was Brahms and his prostitutes, and didn't Moussorgsky spend a lot of time whacking about with tarts? Lucky chaps to be born before psychoanalysis, too. Mopworth always found himself coming back to the problem of beating that rap.

Being seen about with the likes of Mrs. Spofford did little to get him off — it fitted too well into the angle with which the pigeonholers cut off your escape from that quarter: the proverbial gravitation of jessies to older and dowdier women who "posed no threat," etc., especially if they were married, etc.

It took Mopworth some few interviews to suspect that there was less here than met the ear — a smoke screen no doubt to shield her daughter from the research attendant on public curiosity? Not that Mary Spofford needed him to take her out, or remained dowdy for long. She gave up the men's trousers for women's trousers, and for dresses of flattering color and design, the mackinaws for belted tweed coats. She was seen in the company of New York journalists and photographers, all on expense accounts and all vying with each other in the restaurants to which she might be taken in hopes of pumping more from her than the repeated "We were just friends," spoken in a manner guaranteed to leave the opposite impression.

No one was let near Geneva, who was in any event soon packed off to Wycliffe for her final year. The story on McGland appeared in *Life*, with a spread showing comparative landscape shots of Scotland and Connecticut, countries in which the poet had begun and ended his life, respectively. There was one of Mary Punck Spofford in a green sweater and scarf, her hair cropped and dyed gold, smiling against the flowers and white Leghorns of the farm "among whose simple folk the driven artist had found friendship and a measure of peace in his last days."

With the publication of the article the Spoffords were no longer simple, and their own peace was at an end. Geneva was asked everywhere on the strength of her mother's widely known liaison with McGland, and her family were pointed out on the streets of Woodsmoke. The Spoffords now had a kind of aggregate chic, in the special aura of which each of the individual members moved. Harry Pycraft, his motel now a landmark, pestered Spofford to come and have a nip with him again. He finally did. In Pycraft's office he was shown a fattening scrapbook which included a newspaper feature picturing the Dew Drop Inn along with the ship from which Hart Crane had jumped, the house in which Vachel Lindsay had drunk the disinfectant, and other comparable cultural attractions. The visit was interrupted by a party of pilgrims who had motored out from New York, for whom Pycraft excused himself to go show them room number 23. Spofford left the office and never went back there again.

He did not resent Mare's appropriation of the limelight, from which he was in any case far from wholly excluded. He was discernible in the background of her *Life* picture, scowling into the sunlight in a tweed jacket and cap, and he was widely mentioned in Woodsmoke gossip as the companion with whom McGland had gone pub-crawling, getting into brawls now, of course, a matter of police record. The breaking and entering indictment seemed least of the adventures of a certified eccentric and bohemian.

Thus that prestige the Spoffords had never enjoyed by reason of their being old Yankee stock — hardworking, sober, frugal — was now showered on them as principals in a legend. Scandal made them what virtue could not: people who mattered. A date with Geneva was the goal of every blade at Amherst and other nearby schools; an invitation to her house a prize to which only the privileged dared aspire. That Christmas she turned up with her roommate, Nectar Schmidt.

Spofford met them at the railroad station in his rig, wearing the goggles and white driving coat he had acquired for the old-car gymkhana at the country club (in which he was now up for membership). Nectar, a short girl with cropped black hair and a habit of twitching her nose in a manner that made her dark glasses jump, saw him instantly as the mixed contemporary type of which she fancied herself one: the blend of the intellectual and the colloquial, a capacity for the artistic combined with the discriminating nostalgia for junk. She loved this car they bounced home in, with the "Antique" license it now sported. Her parents were divorced and she made her home with her brother in Pennsylvania. This was the holiday invitation she had wanted. She looked past Geneva, who was seated in the middle, studied Spofford a moment with a gravity in no way lessened by the nervous twitch of her nose that often accompanied her sober contemplation of something, and remarked that his profile reminded her of their history professor.

"Your grandfather would pry shoot me if he could meet Timken," she said. "But I mean just Timken's face, before he opens his mouth?"

"Grandpa's pry more intelligent," Geneva said. Though radically dissimilar in appearance and temperament, the girls resembled one another in many ways, due to Geneva's habit of modeling herself on the more worldly girls she met, at the moment Nectar Schmidt. Her own speech was liberally sprinkled with this slurred rendering of "probably," a word which rarely if ever has all its syllables pronounced in any case.

"Timken's pry the least interesting professor there, ackshy," Nectar said. "I mean all he can do is harp on *knowing* something about the subject. In class the other day he ranted and raved about how few people know what a centurion is. I mean do you, Mr. Spofford?"

"I think it's a mythological creature, like a satyr."

"That's the way I feel about it," said Nectar, who had no doubt this humor was intentional, like all the other amusing solecisms the old fellow got off.

She decided he was one of the most fabulous things going, trailed at very little distance by Geneva's mother — who was by now accustomed to the word fabulous and beginning to use it herself. The woman called Mrs. Punck seemed a little hazier, a little harder to place here. Put her down as a quaint touch of the kind that can be accommodated by people secure in their status, like the Currier and Ives print one hangs on one's wall because one knows better, or expressions like "ain't" and "stood in bed" which are all right to use because one knows better than to do so. A form of slumming, they are, conscious barbarisms whereby the mind revitalizes itself from below. These were all things Spofford had once tried to drum into Mrs. Punck, who now planned to marry Dr. Rappaport in the spring and move into his house in the Hollow. As for George, he took one look at Nectar and went and hid in the barn, where he remained for the rest of the afternoon stacking bags of feed. Nectar's first impressions were little subject to verification anyway, since the two girls rarely saw the family. The minute they arrived the telephone rang, and the whirl of holiday parties was on.

Tad Springer called to ask Geneva to the annual Holly Ball at the country club. His mother had spent the day prodding him into it. Geneva agreed provided a date were got for Nectar Schmidt. Before Tad could report back after a canvass of his available friends, Mopworth rang up to invite Geneva out and was dragooned for Nectar. He agreed in order to get to see Geneva, whom he tried to date in the course of his first dance with her at the ball. "Well all right, if we can get somebody for Nectar," Geneva had to say again.

"Wouldn't that be a sticky switch? I mean I'm with her *here*."

"I guess. I'll have to think about it."

Later that evening, flushed with punch, Mopworth took Geneva's hand in the lounge to which they had strayed from the dance floor for a breather. She tried to turn it off by moving on toward a window which looked out on a view of the golf course, frozen under moonlight. Since this involved edging round behind a clump of potted palms, Mopworth took it as a quest for seclusion, and tried to kiss her. "How about a spot of the good old will toward men?" he said. "You're divine. Aren't you glad?"

Nectar noticed both the brief but significant absence in which this occurred, and the smudge of red on Mopworth's jawbone, and, her perceptions fired to twice their normal acumen by personal injury, she minced no words in her verdict on Mopworth as she and Geneva lay in bed together that night holding their post-mortem on the ball. "He's pry a fag," she said.

"You mean because . . . ?" Geneva let her response hang fire till she saw where her own sagacity was expected to lead her. She had no wish to appear wanting in that quality prized above all others by her generation, the ability to see through people. Many of her crucial reactions awaited the cues from Nectar, who would, herself, never be caught on the naïve side.

"He left me for you, and you for the Endicott piece. You saw him bearing down with *her*, didn't you? I don't know what else in skirts he chased after that. Anybody gunning his engine at that rate has reasons."

"What do you think of Tad?"

"He's sweet but kind of weak. The sort of man who could go either way in the end, as a husband. I mean a joy around the house because he's so good-natured, or a poop because he's got no starch. Well, that's about it. He needs a little more lemon in him." Nectar bounced over and lay with her back to Geneva, a position that, in these wee-hour post-mortems, usually presaged an intimate cross-examination. "Are you two supposed to be a team?"

"Not especially. People are such contradictions, aren't they? I wish I had your sharp insight into them, Nectar. I have no idea what people are like. It's at the bottom of my insecurity

I think." Geneva took pride in her insecurity, which she and Nectar had turned and examined from every angle, like a precious stone. Between them they built it up, they polished it. Geneva bounced over on her own side and said suddenly, "Would you like to date Tad? Because go ahead, Nectar. I'll fix it up. See what comes out of that?"

"What can we lose?" said Nectar.

That arrangement was made for the New Year's Eve party the Springers gave. Tad invited Geneva to it when at the last minute it was decided he might ask some of his contemporaries to an affair his parents were giving for theirs. Learning Mopworth had already dated her for that night, Tad agreed to pair off with Nectar Schmidt in order that they might all be together again.

The experiment aimed at mixing the two generations resulted in the elders being rather put on their good behavior. Along with the usual quota of students going steady, dancing only with one another, etc., was a fair sprinkling of campus conservatives in the matter of politics. There was one Goldwaterite, a Wesleyan boy, whose opinions were too reactionary even for some of the older Republicans. An argument between him and the graying Beauseigneur took up the first hour. These samplings of the young were relieved only by a few intellectual bums — what old Spofford called Harvard beats.

"Nobody's having any fun," C.B.S. protested to Bobsy, aside. "Where did we get all these wet blankets? I thought you were supposed to have fun at parties. Or is that a quaint predilection of mine? Correct me if I am mistaken." Beauseigneur, at his elbow, nodded agreement with these general complaints. Both men sulked under their funny hats, which were cone-shaped and secured by elastic straps under their thickening chins. They were both holding highballs in tumblers of hobbed milk glass, which C.B.S. had been browbeaten into collecting as a means of relieving the strain of business life, and both seemed genuinely disturbed at having to see the old year out discussing fundamentals.

"When we were young we had some gumption, it seems to

me," Beauseigneur said. "We were radicals. I wouldn't give a dime for a youngster who isn't a radical, for a while."

"Run along to the game room then," said Bobsy, watching her son and the Goldwaterite in serious conversation with Geneva Spofford and another girl.

"I'm not one now — a radical I mean," Beauseigneur persisted, "but I do consider myself a liberal, stockbroker or not. I'm a liberal Republican. *He*," he continued, pointing at the Wesleyan student, "is one of those Republicans who are giving the party a black eye. Who don't seem to realize that it began *as a liberal party*. Why, we were sponsoring social legislation before the Democrats ever heard of it. But I think the important thing, the thing that gives me pause about the younger generation, is that the element of *rebellion* is missing. We all revolted against our parents."

"Because they were conservatives," Bobsy said. "We're liberals and bohemians, so to revolt against us our children have to be stuffy. Nothing could be more natural. *Their* children — your grandchildren, Beau — will be like us again. So run along and have your fun, you and C.B.S. There's a new electric pinball machine downstairs."

Thoroughly depressed by the intrusion of the grandparent theme, the two men trooped off to the game room.

An even worse pall had settled on the gathering there. Some of the owlish young had found their way to it, including another campus reactionary who was giving Haxby a bad time about the Kennedy administration, drawing him into a support of it so far in excess of anything he seriously adhered to, or would ten minutes ago have dreamed himself capable of espousing, that he scarcely knew whom he hated the more, the boy or himself. Seen from behind, Haxby presented a picture of controlled hostility which his face would have confirmed. His stocky trunk was held stiffly erect up to his neck, which bulged red over the collar of his dinner jacket. One hand also gripped a milk glass tumbler filled with whiskey and soda. The other arm hung at his side, the hand alternately doubled into a fist and held with one finger pointing straight to the floor, like the barrel of a pistol. While he debated with the boy he watched his wife and the young Englishman named Mopworth. They were the only ones at the new pinball machine, but the Englishman was using it as a desk to write down something in a notebook that Lucille was telling him. It was toward the latter pair that the two newcomers made their way. "Get this party off the *ground*," C.B.S. was saying. "Right," Beauseigneur echoed, following his host to the pinball machine. They advanced on it with the air of gangsters about to appropriate it for the failure of the owner to pony up a specified amount of protection money. "Could we trouble you for this, if you're not using it?" C.B.S. said. "Of course," said Mopworth, and led Lucille Haxby off to a corner where there was an unoccupied leather sofa. But before they sat down, Lucille made some excuse about freshening her drink and darted off through the crowd and upstairs, Mopworth after her. Haxby followed all this with his eyes while the youth he was stuck with elucidated his views on the malfunction of liberalism since Roosevelt.

Since research for *McGland in America* consisted principally of retracing the erotic swath cut by the poet down the Eastern seaboard, Mopworth found himself pursuing, week after week, the same women McGland had done, for journalistic reasons. Notebook in pocket he tried to pump the poet's "conquests" without letting on he knew there had been anything between them but just friendship. "I understand you're one of those who met him socially," was his gambit, or sometimes he would say "culturally." In the case of a few chatterboxes with their hearts set on a place in the McGland legend, this was a bung drawn from a brimming barrel, but it sealed the mouths of those with any real secrets. Mopworth soon learned to tell the difference. The number of the latter to be seen at one of Bobsy Springer's parties was more than might have been thought possible, and they all avoided Mopworth like the plague, for the word was out that he was at work on a book. He suspended his chase of Lucille Haxby until after midnight, in hopes that copious draughts of champagne and a round of "Auld Lang Syne," sung with hands linked, might loosen her tongue.

The result was that he spent even less time with Geneva

than, at the Holly Ball, he had with Nectar Schmidt. Which gave Nectar all the data she needed to nail down her diagnosis. She assured Geneva, again as they lay in bed holding their post-mortem, that she now had Mopworth taped.

The thing that made him chase everything in skirts was a *basic hostility toward women.* By promiscuous pursuit, he made *them* look promiscuous, and thus unworthy of pursuit. "And that flamenco dance he does every time he's cross," she said. Now Geneva had never actually seen Mopworth stamp his foot, but she could vividly see him doing it now, under Nectar's analytical spell, and striking a dozen other attitudes as well. "Oh, he's pry trying to fight it, in his way, I don't deny that, but there it is." Mopworth disposed of, Geneva turned the discussion to Tad.

"How do you like him now? After tonight?"

"He's O.K. Fine."

"You two danced a lot."

"He's a good dancer."

"Does he want to see you again?"

"Let's talk about it in the morning. I'm absy exhausted."

twenty-five

THAT HE WAS UNDER a cloud was, by this time, well borne in on Mopworth, who now made his fatal mistake. He tried to clear himself.

He forgot that vigorous or prolonged refutation or denial of a charge cloaks the inner recognition of its truth. He followed the girls back to Wycliffe College after the holidays. True, the print of McGland's cloven hoof led there; but after learning all there was to learn of the shambles McGland had made of a certain faculty reception following a reading, Mopworth had no reportorial reason whatever to stay in town, but stayed on anyway to date the girls. Geneva first. He took her to the most expensive restaurant in town and ordered a bottle of vintage claret to go with their roast beef.

"Are you sure you can afford this, Alvin?"

"Why do you keep asking me that wherever I take you? If we must be crass about it, the English publisher has kicked in with some more advance and I've now got an American one. The McGland bandwagon gets jollier by the day. But I do want to do justice to Gowan. Did he really make those passes at the President's wife? What's apocryphal and what isn't? Every time I spot a new suspect she takes a powder."

"You were very fond of him, weren't you?"

"Weren't you?"

"Why do you say that?"

"Oh, God, must we have this *game?* Everyone knows that research on Gowan consists in little more than picking up his amorous spoor. Oh, don't *cry.*"

"You're cruel."

"I am no such thing. I'm simply trying to get some facts. Surely you can tell me once and for all whether there was anything between you. Obviously I shan't use real names."

"There was nothing between us."

"That was what you went to his room to tell him the night I was there?"

"Alvin. Don't you see this voyeur role you're playing? Vicariously reliving his —"

"Piezoelectricity," Mopworth said. He had gone insane, kicking his feet about in all directions under the table like a skater having them go beneath him, to the peril of all. When Geneva looked at him in surprise and said "What?" he did not repeat the word. It was simply one that came back to him from physics lab in schooldays, a term for electricity produced by pressure, as in a crystal subjected to compression along a certain axis. He had only used it as a sort of expletive anyway. "Your mother," he said quietly, rearranging the silver around his untouched plate. "When did it start between them?"

"You can leave my mother out of it too, I should imagine. She's suffered enough."

"Of all the women I've talked to, she seems to be the one most of all to be feeling no pain," Mopworth retorted. "I've decided her story's been made up of whole cloth to throw them off your scent. How am I doing?"

"Well, there are plenty of other women you can 'interview,' as I suppose you must call it. I noticed you had a good time chasing Lucille Haxby on New Year's Eve."

"I had to chase her. She took a powder every time she saw me coming."

"That's the second time you've used that expression tonight. What does it mean?"

"It's underworld slang for vamoose, scram. Geneva, you seem to have an amazing lack of familiarity with your own argot. The other night you didn't know what a patsy was. It's part of your sweetness. Innocence," he said, smiling richly at her across the table.

Geneva remained unwon by this. She frowned into her own plate and said, "What about Bobsy Springer? Are you making any headway with her?"

"Let's keep this up. There's nothing better than cold roast beef. Not that we're likely to get to that, either."

"I'm sorry, but don't you see, Alvin?" Geneva leaned an elbow on the table to regard him, and Mopworth wailed inwardly at the recognition of the tableau that was coming. Chief among her attitudes was this one apparently derived from magazine advertisements for port wine. They showed a girl sitting at a table with an elbow thus cocked, her chin in her hand, in which a cigarette smokes, her head inclined to one side while she converses with her companion, usually an older man. "Writing this book is a way of vicariously reliving Gowan's sex life, and in so doing identifying yourself with him. He's your — your —"

"Surrogate," said Mopworth, trying to satirize the opposition by supplying their words for them, as he sometimes now did. "Through him I play the rake, re-enacting the adventures of Don Juan with none of the risks."

"And in so doing express your inverted affection for him."

Mopworth grasped the edge of the table firmly in both hands, as though he were going to overturn its contents into her lap. Before executing this extreme measure, however, he got hold of himself, remembering just in time the significance of self-defense. Or was it in time? He was in a war you could not win, in the hands of a regime that shot all its prisoners after a fair trial. And he was in America, where all this had been brought to perfection.

Well, instead of protesting he would play it cool. He would *not even ignore them*. He would amble through the whole damn thing like Henry Fonda, and afterwards take her out for a ride in the country, in a densely wooded section as they said in the tabloids, and there stuff her damned breasts into his mouth, first the one, then the other. That would be later. Now, with a rather pleasant, two-can-play-at-this-game little smile, his brown eyes twinkling mischievously, he said, "Could your reaction to my simple inquiries indicate there *was* more between you than you admit?"

"No, because I'm not the only one who says all this. Nectar says it too."

Blabbermouth, he thought. He made a date with her.

"But I'm not *criticizing* you when I say it. Don't you see that, Alvin? Can't you get that through your head?" Nectar Schmidt said patiently. "You're the one who thinks there's any onus attached to being that way."

Mopworth toyed with the picture always evoked by the term "onus attached." It was vaguely sickroom in feeling, and was some thingamajig with a loathsome little aperture in it, encircled by a sleazy suggestion of fuzz, dangling by a string from a shapeless object held in someone's hand.

"So you *have* been saying things about me. I've sensed it. I've felt it."

"You mean you have a keen intuition?"

Mopworth again grasped the edge of the table and this time came even closer to overturning it into his companion's lap. Jolly good show that would be, to clinch the case against him, wouldn't it? He reminded himself again that this was Mental Health country, and one should expect to be driven crazy by a certain amount of this type of thing. This was their line of goods. Again, he must roll with the punches. He must *not care*. He must be amused, and very little of that. He knew what he

288

would do when this evening was over, when this whole business was concluded and wrapped up. He would go away somewhere where he was not known and for a solid week do nothing but howl like a dog.

He said, "No, Nectar, I don't. I'm rather a poor judge of character, actually. Not like you lot. Geneva told me you've been saying these things."

"That's rather a catty thing to do," Nectar said, spearing a forkful of salad.

"I suppose. You mean Geneva's talking about you behind your back."

"No. You talking about her behind hers."

"Piezoelectricity!" Mopworth's voice, cracked though it was, brought the waiter at a trot to ask if anything were wrong. He said there wasn't and waved him away. Nectar glanced up at him with her head still bent over her salad. He said, "Where were we?"

"Talking behind people's backs. Do you do it about all the women you go out with? Will you say things about me later? You see, Alvin," Nectar went instructively on, looking earnestly at him now and executing the little twitch of her nose that made her glasses jump (why did she wear dark glasses in *here* where there was scarcely enough light to eat with the naked eye?), "you do have these hostilities toward us. Instead of denying it you should admit it — clear the air. Face up to it squarely and see what there is to be done about it. You see the way you're twisting your napkin? Whose neck are you wringing?"

"Yours."

"All right. Fine. That's better." Nectar paused, her point made, to let it sink in. While she did so she took a sip of her wine. "The thing is that I don't *judge* you when I say those things. We all have a dash of the opposite in us, women of the masculine, men of the feminine. It's nothing to be ashamed of." He stuffed her into a culvert, after sending a whiff of piezoelectricity through her, wedging her well in out of sight among the dirt and leaves so no one would discover the body, as she went on in what was suddenly a more intimate, or at least personal, tone. "Ackshy, it's pry that counterstrain in myself that makes me cotton to you."

"Is that what you're doing?' Mopworth said, shooting a glance at the door.

"Yes. Masculine women tend toward feminine men, and vice versa."

"Yes, I see. I know," said Mopworth, falling to his food.

He now had to admit that he Harbored Resentment Toward Women. There was no use denying it. It was growing by leaps and bounds — every time he talked to one of them it seemed. God but this was a tough course! If you'd told Mopworth that before the summer was over he would physically attack a woman he would have laughed in your face. Yet he knew how deep-seated his hostility was becoming, and how urgent the need to do something about it. To bloody well tidy himself up.

He spent all that spring interviewing people, driving from city to city as the job required. By mid-June, when the commencements were over and the graduates had returned to their homes, he had worked himself back down to Woodsmoke, and so he rang Geneva up. They had a skein of spaghetti and a bottle of Chianti at Indelicato's.

He had decided absolutely on a mood of light jollity, and so he took her hands across the table and said, "My God, they're like ice. What school did you go to? No, let me guess. You can always tell women's colleges by the temperature of their hands. Hot moist palms, Sarah Lawrence. The erratic creative daemon. Medium cool for Radcliffe, and room temperature for the all-around Smith type." She smiled wanly, in no mood for jokes. The great eyes dropped hostilely, the full red mouth compressed itself. "Come on, buck up, how about a spot of the old American camaraderie? Drink up and we'll go on a bun."

"What's a bun?"

"You don't know what it means to take a powder. You don't know what a patsy is. And now you don't know what bun means. I tell you you're overeducated."

She smiled rather tautly again, picking at the straw around the wine bottle. "And now what to do with myself."

"Ah, yes, that." Mopworth leaned back, wary and sympathetic both. They had stumbled onto the national crisis: what American women were to do with their liberated minds and opened vistas occupied half the magazines and a growing swarm of social anthropologists. "We must have a good talk about that later. But a bun is a bender, a toot. Come on, drink up. I think the secret of Indelicato's Chiantis is that he hangs them down there among the provolone cheeses. Then knock'd back, knock'd back! We cannot bag Truth sober, but with clubbed feet and muddled wits mayhap we'll stumble on't."

"Why are you always trying to get me tight?"

"The better to loosen you up, my dear. Mmbah-hah-ha. Mmbwah-hah-ha. Happy, darling? This wine is supposed to loosen your tongue. Is it doing that?"

"Yes, and a few of my teeth, too."

"That's the ticket, laugh at our troubles! We'll have another bottle. Boohwah-hah-hah."

In spirit, Mopworth slipped his hand down her blue-and-white checked gingham dress, till under his palms he could feel her breasts put forth their buds. They would flutter like caught doves in his grasp, they would strut like pouters . . .

After dinner he drove to the beach. They looked out across the darkening water in the silence that followed when he shut the engine off. He dropped an arm along the back of the seat, and drew her head toward him till he could smell the fragrance of her hair, newly washed and bound with a yellow ribbon. He turned her by the chin and kissed her.

"Why so sad, prithee why so sad?" he said.

"Why must you always break into poetry at serious moments? Are you afraid of feeling?" He was so baffled by this that all he could say was, "I see what you mean."

"Now that I'm graduated what *shall* I do with myself? What's it all for?"

Mopworth hunched his shoulders and sighed toward the everlasting sea. "I'm afraid I can't help you there. I'm not Margaret

Mead." This announcement seemed so to depress her that he found himself saying quietly, suddenly quite like a horse tout slipping somebody a good tip out of the side of his mouth, "Come along with me through New York, New Jersey and parts of Pennsylvania." He had a good bit of interviewing to do there.

"Will you be seeing Nectar? She lives in Gettysburg."

"I may. But how about it? I'm very fond of you, Geneva."

She lit a cigarette from a match he had ready for her before she had shaken it from its pack. He watched her lean forward and kiss the cork tip, leaving no doubt a red stain on it in the dark. "Alvin, how old are you?"

"On for thirty. 'Time, you old gypsy man, will you not stay, put up your caravan just for one day —?' "

"Why is it you've never married?"

Turning his head slightly away in the gloom, Mopworth bit an imaginary fly out of the air. It was a gesture he had learned from her grandfather, old Spofford, whom he had once seen do this when exasperated or at his wits' end, like a harried old dog. He then engaged in another bit of pantomime freely and openly, having decided to take the offensive. Cranking an imaginary phonograph, or perhaps sausage machine, to suggest the mechanical nature of the platitudes in which romance here seemed to have become enmeshed, he said, "Because I don't want to face the responsibility of loving one woman, I fear the involvements and the problems this would pose . . ."

Geneva, who was gazing out her window and had not noticed the action, or detected the irony in his voice, nodded thoughtfully and continued, "It's too much of a challenge. God knows you're not alone in hesitating to take the final mature step. There are lots like you. Lots. Of both sexes."

Mopworth now made the decision of his life. Since he could obviously not lick 'em, he decided to join 'em. That was it in a nutshell. He swiveled about a bit on the seat, as though he were impaled on a spindle there and trying to make the best of it. Then, gripping the steering wheel in both hands, as though they were taking a turn at breakneck speed rather than sitting quietly in the dusk by the seaside, he said: "Mightn't it be that your constant unmasking of me masks a deep-seated fear of being unmasked yourself?"

It was so simple, as religious conversions are said in the end to be by those who surrender their souls up to God after a hopeless struggle. He got the hang of it instantly, with no trouble whatsoever. He was suddenly talking the language of the natives, with a fluency that made him feel a naturalized citizen overnight, and not a foreigner any longer at all.

"So you're the one with the hostility," he went on. "A hostility toward men based on a . . . on a . . ." Here he momentarily faltered, but Geneva readily supplied the words for which he was groping. "A fear of them. Yes, that's right, Alvin. A fear, or at least hesitancy, based in turn on a doubt of my adequacy in a love situation."

Mopworth's first surprise derived from the belief that she was engaging in self-criticism. Nothing of the kind. In America such self-inventories were not admissions of faults at all but claims to complexity. Basic insecurities and feelings of insufficiency and the like were all degrees of intricacy on which the natives preened themselves; bandying the terms was part of courtship. This was all far less developed in England than here, where women were cherished not for their beauty and virtue, as was once the case, so much as for the resonance of their problems and the subtlety of their needs. Mopworth had inklings of this now. Geneva Spofford had given herself to only one man, a man in dire straits. She had rushed in to save him (at least so she thought) at a crucial moment, and her surrender was the only means at her disposal by which to lure him back to life. Mopworth had no knowledge of the scene, but he was given its gist, or its moral, in what Geneva now told him as she summed herself up for him in the crowded darkness of the Volkswagen: "I suppose what I need is a man who needs me. I have got to have that." The confession was like having been given a glimpse of her thigh, or the touch of her breast — if not the sight of her naked.

Like a knight-errant pondering the promises and perils of the country through which he wanders, Mopworth pushed on down to New York and then into New Jersey and Pennsylvania, reflecting on everything Geneva had told him and wondering what lay in store for him in Gettysburg. For he had decided to drive the forty miles he had to go out of his way to visit Nectar Schmidt. Sex life in America was beginning to fascinate him.

twenty-six

AS HE NEARED GETTYSBURG, Mopworth became disturbed by certain thoughts he had been having relative to Nectar Schmidt. These were not just idle notions but minutely constructed malicious scenarios worked out in great detail, in which he imagined various misfortunes that might befall her, that she especially would not like. They had a single theme. They all involved failures of expectation, of which the common theme was that she be "brought down a peg or two." (Americans made so much of status.) The futures he worked out for Nectar, often lying in bed in some motel or musing behind the wheel of the Volkswagen on long motors, were thus in essence reversals of the jolly forecasts of class prophecies.

Mopworth imagined, now, that she did not make a brilliant match at all, of the kind to which she no doubt confidently looked forward as her due, but married instead a sod who fizzled out completely. He made this sod, to whom he gave the name Herkimer Stoat, the head of a failing button factory which he inherited from his father but soon ran into the ground thanks to plain ineptitude and the inability to handle people. He said "From where I sit" and "Can do." That Nectar was spoiled and extravagant went without saying, and that only hastened their inevitable decline. They went from city to city, the Stoats, carrying their dwindling belongings in scuffed suitcases secured with twine, finally trying their luck with a dry-goods store in like McKeesport which Nectar attended to while Stoat peddled some sort of rubbish from door to door. Mopworth put her in a house dress in a pocket of which she kept change — the few spools of thread and yard or two of scallop trim which they sold a day requiring no cash register — and had them living in two rooms behind the store. They were open Thursdays and Saturdays until nine.

Mopworth came to with a start, ashamed of the clarity of detail with which all this was worked out. How could a chap as nice as he be such a bastard? Was he devising these scenarios of his own free will, or was some nasty agency over which he had no control turning them out inside his head without his real consent or genuine participation? He was, at all events, in Gettysburg, and he stopped at a public phone booth to call Nectar, with whom he had been in touch along the route, and notify her of his arrival. She told him to come right out, giving him directions for getting to her house from where he was.

The house was modern in the now more or less hidebound sense of that term. A rectangle of redwood and glass perched on a rock ledge, it was approached by a dirt road that coiled like a length of intestine around a steep hill. It was owned by her brother, with whom Nectar had lived since the divorce and dispersal of her parents. Miles owned a record shop in town, run for him by a manager, as he himself shrank from human contact and was physically unable to wait on trade. It was Miles who brought matters to a head between Mopworth and Nectar, because he drove Mopworth absolutely and completely out of his mind in the course of a single evening.

Miles typified, at its final, untenable extreme, the malady of self-consciousness, with its attendant horror of the obvious. His inability to wait on customers was only one example of the exquisite pitch to which this quality had in him become developed. He could not say "What's yours?" or "Can I do anything for you?" He could say "Hello" or "Goodbye" only with the greatest difficulty, usually with averted eyes and a flustered smile. "Merry Christmas" he could not utter. The thing was simply out of the question. He usually hid in the house till the holidays were over, in his room when that was invaded by well-wishers. If some circumstance absolutely required his emergence and exposed him in the street to a neighbor or acquaintance advancing with extended hand, his anguish usually infected the other and successfully aborted the ceremony. Wishing somebody a happy birthday was equally out of the question, and as for having to say "So nice to have met you," or "I hope you slept well," these ordeals simply palsied his tongue. It was for this reason that having a guest in the house, necessitating as it did any number of such direct attritions, left him shattered — and often the guest as well. If physically touched, Miles would recoil as though shot.

He was not in when Mopworth arrived, about four in the afternoon. The house was flooded with music which Mopworth had begun to hear halfway up the drive. It came from a phonograph Nectar made no move to turn off, or even down, so they sat exchanging their first gossip amid billows of dissonance of an extremely advanced order. Both the turntable on which they originated and the speakers from which they issued were concealed, at least from Mopworth, who cast vain glances into all corners of the long living room in search of these sources. No part of the room offered any refuge since there was a pair of stereophonic speakers at either end of it, in keeping with the ideal of high fidelity enthusiasts, to give the listener the illusion of *being inside the sound.* When Nectar went to the bar to fix them their second drink — a move that consisted in little more than turning her back on him for a second, as the house was an assemblage of "areas" rather than formally divided rooms — Mopworth went into the kitchen on the pretext of admiring the place. The music came through unseen louvers there too. He wandered back into the living room after noting that a stew was simmering on the stove.

The house was one of those of which the architect's dream seems to be that of making the finished product resemble as closely as possible the blueprints for it. It was constructed of what are, often belligerently, called "honest materials." The walls were of bare brick, relieved only by an occasional unframed specimen of those canvases that seem not so much to have been painted as puked; the chairs were the string-bottomed kind the very sight of which can raise hysterical welts on the rumps of some beholders; the fireplace tools stood in a milk can. The ottoman supplementing the chair to which Mopworth returned was a portion of tree-stump — oak he was told after inquiries which led Nectar to believe he was admiring it. The shape of the chair called for an occupancy so nearly supine that he had to raise his head every time he took a drink in order to keep from dribbling whiskey down his shirt front, like an invalid sipping tea in bed.

"Who wrote this?" Mopworth asked, pointing thumbs toward both ends of the room. Nectar's reply was drowned out by an increase of the din about which he had inquired.

At five o'clock the front door burst open and a pale youth with colorless eyes and flying straw hair entered. He plunged into the house as the timid swimmer plunges into water, after hesitating on the bank for several minutes. He had, indeed, stood at the door for some time before plowing through it, having noticed the car in the drive. It is by such sudden musterings of their will that unsociable egos often give a first impression of great gregariousness. He came straight on in, to get it over with.

"Ah, here's Miles," Nectar said. "Miles, this is Alvin Mopworth."

Mopworth tried to shake the other's hand, but it was twitched free of his grasp in the nick of time, like a goldfish he had tried unsuccessfully to scoop from a tank. Stripping himself of his coat, which Nectar hung up somewhere, Miles made for the bar and poured himself a drink. He stood there taking gulps from his glass with obvious discomfiture. Pauses in the conversation were excruciating. He began to walk around the room, and once when he passed Mopworth's chair he suddenly raised his arm, as though he were going to punch Mopworth in the nose for having come. Sensing that the burden of making the host feel at home here lay squarely at the door of the guest, Mopworth again jerked his thumbs two ways toward the ruthless loudspeakers and asked, "Who wrote this music?" Miles said a name, then seized a record envelope from a table and thrust it at Mopworth, pointing out some copy on the back of it that he might find instructive:

"In his Montevideo days the composer became tantalized by the possibility of expressing in tonal anarchy something of the challenge inherent in utter Chaos. If over the systematically mangled motifs of the adagio movement there broods the unmistakable *Geist* of decay — the phosphorescent shimmer of corruption painted by the flutes, the answering, nauseated bleat of the oboes — the subsequent andante undertakes the re-assembly of resulting chromatic debris. A tentative, narcissistic whimper from the violins, suggesting a last invitation to *Welt-schmerz*, is shouldered aside by a belch from the brasses, rude yet reaffirming . . ."

Mopworth prolonged his immersion in this statement, fearing that to raise his head would be to reveal his outrage. The composer's name was Quichimi — a good name, too, for the state induced by his music. Provided it *was* accented on the second syllable. This racket was giving him the quichimies. Yes, he had the screaming quichimies. He was getting drunk, a sobering thought in itself . . .

With relief he saw Miles disappear into a study at the end of the living room where by now it had developed the turn-table was. Nectar had made a trip or two there, to add a few LP's to the automatic spindle. Mopworth hoped the purpose of this one was to shut the phonograph off. No such luck. He could see Miles, in a blessed interval of silence, shuffling through a stack of albums for replenishment. When Nectar excused herself for a look at the stew in the kitchen, Mopworth found himself momentarily alone. He flung himself on the couch with a moan of protest. He wanted to clamp a cushion to each ear, to pull down the dung-colored draperies and wind them around his head until he knew no more. He must pull himself together. He would show them all what decent music was. "The new concerto is coming along," he would write to Clara von Hoffmanstahl in 1823, "but I can really no longer bear the strain of these constant public recitals, for which ill health equips me less and less. I warn all! I coughed up blood again last night, nearly a quart, my liebchen, my vogel. Again that pest Bruno plagues me for another 'triumph' in Vienna — for what? To line his pockets and send me to a pauper's grave. How I long for the peace of your arms, and twilight over the Strudelstrasse. Yes, when this beast is put down, the verrücht third movement, I fly to your side, and then God willing . . ."

"Dinner'll pry be an hour or more."

Conversation became a matter of reading lips. How could a nervous wreck like Miles stand it anyway? That was the paradox. Perhaps the very noise formed a kind of protective wall around him. The final record did at last come to an end, and the silence that followed was bliss, though Miles himself continued to give Mopworth the quichimies. One method Miles had of sheathing himself from subjects of even a remotely emotional content was to lapse into dialect at the first threat of their approach. "I dinna dream ye were callin' on ma sister serious, mon," he remarked of Mopworth's having driven this distance to see her. The guise of a Scotsman was dropped for that of a Southern plantation owner when, in response to something Nectar said of Mopworth's present research labors, he said, "Ah had no idea yawl were a writin' man, suh." All this while he nervously gulped down whiskey on the rocks, as though the institution of the cocktail hour drove him to drink. Mopworth too continued to drink more than he should; regrettably, because the wine Miles served with the stew was superb and he was unable to do justice to it. It was a Burgundy called Musigny which Mopworth had not hitherto tasted.

All more or less pleasantly numbed by dinner, they settled down again in the living room. Nectar sat on the couch with some knitting. Glimpses of her legs, tucked up under her bright plaid skirt, made Mopworth wish Miles would go. But Miles couldn't. The inability to say good night was of a piece with the inability to say hello — a painful extension of the trouble people universally have in simply getting up and out. Mopworth solved the problem by rising to turn in himself, hoping that when he came back out of his room, half an hour later, Miles would be gone. He was. Nectar was still curled up on the couch knitting. He stood watching her in pajamas and robe. It was a red silk dressing gown with a heraldic emblem on the breast pocket and broad lapels, which made him resemble a profligate emperor. He struck an attitude under one of the framed throwups.

"Running up a sock or two, are we?"

"Yes, for Miles." She held up a tubular fragment of wool, in which some suggestion of geometric design was beginning to take shape. "He's very fussy about fit." She knitted a few stitches, peering at her work with that studious intentness so characteristic of her, and which was by no means restricted to people. The lamplight shone on her cropped black hair. Her nose gave a jump, this time without jogging any smoked glasses for she was not wearing them. "You don't like him."

"Nonsense. Why do you say that?"

"I feel it. You resist him, pry out of some sort of resentment."

"Oh, no. Not at all. I may have trouble talking to him as freely as a bloke might wish to, but that's because he's so high-strung," Mopworth said, deciding that the best answer was to tell the truth, if a partial, or modified, truth.

"Why do you say that?"

The comment seemed perfectly self-explanatory to Mopworth, as though he had said that her skirt was plaid and the sock she was knitting red. "Isn't he?"

"I've never noticed it, speshy."

"Pry because you're used to it." He had lapsed into a sudden involuntary imitation of her way of talking, which he hoped had passed unnoticed, or, if noticed, would not be taken as malicious. He must watch that. As an actor he had often kept himself sharp by impersonating other people's diction, as a musician practices scales. He had on several occasions — in fact that day alone in the car — mimicked Nectar's speech, whose peculiar slurrings and elisions fascinated him. She ran the constituent vowels in a sentence into bunched arrangements of her own, that were completely arbitrary like a child's.

"Used to what?"

Mopworth's fists clenched themselves in the pockets of his robe as he now imitated Spofford. He bit a fly out of the air. He knew the heads-I-win-tails-you-lose nature of any such argument with this woman. But there was nothing to do but plow ahead in the hope that maybe this time a chap wouldn't hang himself. "The way he shrinks from human contact."

Nectar knitted a few more stitches, and then, raising her dark eyes, she gave him an understanding smile. "Has it occurred to you that it may be you who shrink from human contact? That you're simply projecting into him what you experience in yourself — a hyper-response to another man in the room?"

Mopworth had it that she and this Stoat character lost even the dry-goods store to which they had come, so that Nectar had to peddle homemade doughnuts door to door, eking out in this way a meager living which was supplemented by Christmas baskets from the church and a turkey at Thanksgiving from the local what did they call them here? Ward heelers.

He turned and faced Nectar squarely, albeit from the far end of the room to which he had now stalked, and said: "I wish now I had stayed in a motel."

"Why?"

"So you could visit me," he said, completely reversing his intended implication because saying as much as he had served somehow to ease his resentment and even induce a kind of remorse.

"You're visiting me."

"It's not the same thing. I wish we were alone, Nectar."

"We are. Miles has gone out for a drive. He won't be back for hours."

Indignation in some curious way stoked his desire, the two becoming progressively mixed, or mutually nourishing. Or was it so curious? After all, they were both classified as passions. And hadn't Conrad said in *Victory* or somewhere that the sex bond is based on antagonism as much as love? Get that "based on." Not interrupted by, or complicated with — *based on.*

"So we're alone."

"I see what you mean. Speaking of Miles," he said, sitting down beside her on the couch, "could it be that we're breeding too fine an organism?"

"I know what you mean. Yes, he's a boy of almost ethereal sensitivity."

"Man. Not boy. Could it be you continue to regard him as a boy the more easily to regard yourself as a girl? Rather than a woman?" Delighted again to find he was getting the hang of this Yankee business, and back in the swim with it, he added with zest, "And thus avoid sexual responsibility yourself?" He reached for her hand, which she drew back sharply. Realizing that he had gone too far, he went still farther so as to appear to be kidding. "Electra," he said with a good-natured grin.

She set the knitting on a table.

"This is serious," she said.

"Why?"

"You lash out at me as a way of diverting attention from yourself."

"Why the hell shouldn't I?" Mopworth said, anger now taking the lead in his mixed emotions again, like a horse breaking out of a bunched field for a bit. "I mean divert attention from myself. I have nothing to hide. So why the devil — I mean, besides I was joking."

"What better way of cloaking a serious charge? You know you're vulnerable, and the best defense is a good offense. And I find what you say offensive all right, Alvin."

"Oh, rot! I'm not lashing out at anybody. It all started when I hinted at something that's actually plain as day to any objective observer, and so I'll say it outright now. That your brother gets on a bloke's nerves. I can't stand him. There, that lay the cards honestly and simply on the table, right side up and no dissimulation? I can't stand him. I'm not criticizing him by saying that, and I'm sure he'll say the same thing about me. We just get on one another's nerves."

"What you say figures."

"Why?"

"Hate is the best way of repressing its opposite."

Flesh and blood could stand just so much. Seizing her by the shoulders with both hands, he shook her till the couch springs shrieked beneath them. She bounced violently in his grasp, like a life-size rubber object. His clutch shifted from her shoulders to her throat, round which his fingers tightened. "Stop psychoanalyzing me!" he shouted. "Stop it, do you hear! Stop, stop, stop it! All of you!"

He paused, one knee on the couch, in the pose in which Othello is seen smothering Desdemona in illustrations of Shakespeare. Nectar wriggled free of his relaxing grasp and moved away from him. She did not run away, or even rise, but sat on the end of the couch, away from him, tidying herself. She watched him as, still standing with one knee on the couch, he stared at the floor, his arms hanging loose at his sides.

"Would you like me to give you the name of a good doctor?"

Mopworth turned away and nodded once, or seemed to. His eyes were glazed and he was breathing heavily.

"Because now I'm really worried about you, Alvin. You seem to be more hostile every time we meet."

Mopworth now gave a shake of his head, like a dazed boxer coming to. "Hostile schmostile," he said, trying to pull himself together and recover at least a measure of his dignity. "You wanted me to get violent. To attack you. Of course. It would prove your point. Well, I'll not give you the satisfaction." He managed a wry smile over his shoulder and said, "Except maybe to tear that pretty dress off your back."

"That won't be necessary."

Before his astonished eyes, she rose, unzipped the dress and pulled it over her head. She laid it across the back of a chair. She removed her underthings and then her shoes and stockings. Then she lay down on the couch and said: "Take me."

"Where to?" Mopworth said, hedging.

"Make love to me. Go in and win. Here's your chance to prove I'm wrong about you, if I am, and you're right."

He stood hesitantly over the couch, looking down at her. He pulled uncertainly at a jowl. "This isn't the way."

"Why not?"

"A man needs cooperation."

"What do you call this?"

"It's not the same thing. Not this type of attitude."

"Take your clothes off. We'll be alone for a long time. I know that. Come and master me."

Mopworth shook his head again, this time in genuine concern for her.

"You always have to be the dominant one, Nectar. It's not right in you. I say it for your own good. Ah, how you must hate men," he said. Though undeniably acute, that still wasn't a strong enough finish for his point. He needed something sharper, some last, spearing rejoinder. A phrase from a magazine feature on the Ordeal of the American Female which he had recently seen swam into his mind. "You're an emasculating woman," he said.

"And what kind of man are you?" she called as he turned away.

"I don't know," he said, shaking his head. "I just . . . don't know any more . . . I'm all mixed up."

"Then don't criticize my brother."

With that she rose, rather in the manner of one who has made her own point, and proceeded to dress again as though nothing had happened, which in a sense was the case. Mopworth circled the room in a dull rage, inspecting things in it he had not noticed before, or that he had not fully absorbed, his anger gorging itself on one or another of the framed upchucks. He paused and regarded with a kind of malevolent glee the milk can from the neck of which the fire tongs and other hearth implements protruded.

"Has anyone in your family ever owned a dairy farm, or worked in a creamery?" he asked.

"What on earth are you talking about?"

"This milk can. The whole house is done in such honest materials, as you call them, that I figured one of you must have worked in a cow barn, or had some such bit of background."

"Alvin, perhaps you'd best go."

"Perhaps I had."

He was dressed, packed and out of the house inside of fifteen minutes, and in another five speeding down the highway. He did a hundred miles that night before turning in at a motel.

He was determined to get back to Woodsmoke before Geneva could get a letter from Nectar, or even a telephone call. She *must hear his side of it first*. She *would* hear his side of it first he vowed, gritting his teeth as he took a banked turn at seventy miles an hour on the deserted highway. He had done right in declining such a gambit, had he not? What man could possibly have given a proper account of himself under circumstances so aimed at discommoding him? That girl was crazy, and if he didn't steer clear of her he would wind up in the bin himself. Had he already gone round the bend? His ears burned with chagrin, so he must still have possession of his faculties. That scene back at the house would in due course join the half-dozen episodes the memory of which made him draw his pillow across his face and moan into it. For the moment he tried to put it out of his mind with a roll call of the girls to whom he had made love, truly and happily, each as should be — she the fragile vessel possessed, he the possessor, the truly ravishing male, not effete but jolly well robust, primitive even, Pithecanthropus erectus you might say . . .

But as he lay sleepless in a motel bed at two A.M. his confidence seeped away, his doubt returned. The one ebbed as the other flowed. He had not suspected himself capable of such vehemence, driven to it though he had been. The beast that sleeps in all of us (dozing lightly in some) had certainly wanted out, back there in that awful house. Had very nearly gotten loose, too. There was no mistake about it: *at that moment his fingers had wanted to close round that soft white throat.* "I am a murderer," he said aloud to himself in the darkness, hoping by exaggeration to make the whole thing something that could be laughed at. "I wanted to throttle the breath out of that woman, drag the body out into the yard and under cover of darkness bury it in a shallow grave. Now I am alone in a strange motel, with people fleeing past me at sixty miles an hour on a Godforsaken highway in the black American night."

Since he did not fall into the proverbial "troubled sleep" till daylight, he stayed in bed until noon, and didn't reach Connecticut until nightfall — too late to phone Geneva except to say where he was and ask her to dinner the following evening. Pinching the phone cord in two fingers, he held his breath and steeled his nerves for refusal, or some sort of hesitation, but she agreed quite readily. Nor was there anything odd in her manner when she said, "Fine, Alvin. Sevenish?" He said in a "natural" voice that he had seen Nectar Schmidt and so on.

They went to Indelicato's, and again Geneva picked pensively at the wicker sheath around the Chianti bottle. At last, after two glasses of the wine, she said, looking into her plate of lasagna, "Nectar telephoned me last night right after you did. I gathered there was some sort of drama." So she had got there first with her story after all.

He swallowed what he had in his mouth and with a nod remarked casually, "I could wring her neck."

"So I gather."

"Oh, come now. She's letting that Grand Guignol imagination of hers run away with her. What else did she say?"

"She seems to think you need help."

"What I don't need is Nectar. I want very much never to see Nectar again as long as I live, and that seems to me the first step both on the road toward mental health and, if I may say so, on the road toward you too, what? Little more wine?" he said, with an odd laugh.

"Did everything sort of — go blank?"

"No. Everything suddenly went quite clear. *She has got to go.*"

Geneva became earnest, leaning farther toward him, so that the end of her scarf, loosely knotted like a Girl Scout's around the collar of her middy blouse, dangled dangerously close to her lasagna. "Don't you see, Alvin, that your attempted rape of Nectar was just another expression of your rage at being unable to feel any desire for her? It's so simple. You can't love a woman so you hate her. This hate, which includes hatred of yourself, explodes in an attack of physical violence that —"

Mopworth wasn't listening. The most overwhelming sense of reassurance was flooding him. At the first mention of the word "rape" he had looked up hopefully from his own plate. He was a sex criminal — what a relief! — and not a murderer at all. All this in a latent, or potential, sense, of course, but that was not the point. One thing at a time and everything by stages. The point for the moment was that a perfectly normal impulse had gotten out of hand, not an abnormal one; carried out, it would have meant the forced physical possession of his victim, not her extinction. He felt, somehow, restored to the human community again.

"Do you suppose that's what I was up to?" he asked wistfully. "You seem so much better at sorting these things out than I, Geneva, and I mean it would give a chap something to go along on, to take hold of, if he thought he were capable of rape —"

"Of course I wasn't there, but that's the way it seems to me, knowing you as I do, Alvin. There are of course normal emotions mixed up in all crimes of passion. Distortions of them, in a sense."

Mopworth took further heart from the term "crime of passion," for the kindred implication of the primitive at work in him, rather than the effete, which was of a piece with the feeling of being a respectable member of the human race again that had been inspired by the word "rape." Perhaps a satisfactory balance of the two could somehow yet be brought about, and he be made whole again. But he knew that his problem, though put in a more encouraging light, was not therefore more simple. No, it was a knotty business, this getting straightened around, this having insight. What he could do was work his way out of the hole he found himself in by the one gleam of light he had been vouchsafed, the one rope thrown down to him in the pit in which he had lain: that he had behaved like a sex fiend. Nobody could take that away from him.

Impulsively, he reached out and took Geneva's hand. He felt it warm in his, first acquiescent, then responsive, returning the pressure. She smiled, and though, typically, the great golden eyes dropped their deferential gaze to the table, he knew both the smile and the gaze were for him.

The emotions that thronged his breast were abruptly routed by an incident that illustrated fate's knack for invading crucial moments with the most grotesque coincidences — indeed, perhaps, for directing them.

The table at which they were sitting was in the downstairs bar where McGland and Spofford had had their run-in with the local hooligans. Similarly, the smattering of types consequent on the commuters "discovering" this originally workmen's hangout was again in evidence in the night's trade. At the bar were a middle-aged woman in a soiled trench coat and a hussar's hat, and her companion, a thickset man with a red neck which overflowed his shirt collar and that of the black leather jacket he wore above well-pressed tan slacks. In a pause in their own conversation, Mopworth and Geneva listened to that of the other couple, conducted in voices that would have been impossible not to overhear. The man was explaining the meaning of the term "laissez faire" to the woman. "David Niven has got it. George Sanders. Actors like that," he said. "Means suave stuff. Man of the world." There was an exchange of arch references to himself, after which he laughed and put his arm around her in a great bear hug. The woman nearly fell off the seat in his direction. They laughed and had more fun about that.

"Well," Mopworth observed to Geneva, "there's no doubt *he's* heterosexual."

His remark had the misfortune of falling into a sudden silence, and the man heard it. He turned from the bar, gave Mopworth a look, and came over. It was only a few steps to their table.

"Was you referrin' to me, bud?"

"Why, yes," Mopworth answered with a pleasant smile, rising. "I just said you were heterosexual."

"That's what I thought." The man gave his trousers a hitch and his chest swelled up like a blowfish. "Care to back up them insinuations with a little action, and maybe see if there's some truth in them?"

"Apparently you misunderstand the term." Mopworth laughed good-naturedly at their little contretemps, at the same time evaluating the inch of forehead, or less, that separated the other's tar-black hair from his caterpillar eyebrows. "It simply means that in your case things are exactly as they seem. A canoodle going with every confidence in self, nothing to prove, and with great laissez faire I might add —"

"Hell business is that of yours? Hell do you think you are anyway, coming around here giving people angles on theirself? I'm jist as normal as you any day, as I said I'm ready to step outside and prove. Or stay right here if you'd rather." He gave his belt another truculent hitch.

"But of course! That's precisely the gist of my —"

"Look, bud, I don't care to hear any more about this particular wrinkle tonight, see. If you're so sure you're in the clear about all them fancy names your sort likes to go around calling people to show they're educated, maybe you're ready for that little demonstration. Or maybe if I flatten that pretty nose of yours you won't have so much trouble keeping it out of other people's business."

Here Geneva began a gesture of protest at the same time that Indelicato, who had been momentarily attending to something in the main dining room overhead, bustled back down from the stairway behind the bar. He shouldered his way between the disputants. "Now, now, what's all this about?" he said, holding them apart like a referee. "What's it this time, Jake?"

"He said I was heterosexual."

Indelicato turned to Mopworth. "That right?"

"Why, yes, as a matter of fact I did," Mopworth said, "a term the meaning of which he evidently does not — Let me explain. It refers to the normal erotic makeup of either male or female —"

"Now I warn you, bud." Jake moved a step closer with a force that made light of the obstruction between them, namely Indelicato.

"Now listen, Jake," Indelicato said, trying to squeeze his way back between the two, "he don't mean no harm by that. Nobody's a hundred per cent normal or adjusted is what they figure these days, is all the fellow probably means to infer." Indelicato had evidently been educating himself in these matters, either by reading or by diligent eavesdropping on the clientele newly dignifying his place. "*We've all got a dash of that in us is all I'm sure he's trying to get at.*" Indelicato turned to Mopworth again. "That right? You mean Jake here is *partly* heterosexual, just like everybody else."

Mopworth shook his head, laughing patiently still. "No. This chap is clearly *all* that. No ifs, ands or buts. *But* the thing I'm trying to get through his —" An involuntary glance at the other's cranium only made matters worse.

"Why, you —"

With an angry growl he let fly with a swing that missed Indelicato as narrowly as it did Mopworth. Indelicato dug in for a last attempt to separate the two and, finding this beyond his means, said, perhaps out of a long-standing exasperation,

"Oh, all right! If you guys want to mix it up go on outside! I've had enough of it in here. I'm sick and tired of all these brawls and misunderstandings I'm getting in here lately. I've had it. This place is getting a bad name, I don't know why, I don't think I got it coming to me. But go on outside if you want to mix it up. I give up."

"That suits me," said Jake. "Unless he's afraid of getting them pearly whites knocked down his throat."

Mopworth made a gesture of despair like Indelicato's, then took the other by the arm and led him through the door, still trying to explain the meaning of the term that was causing all the confusion. His words were lost in the general hubbub, for as Geneva was trying to restrain Mopworth, the woman in the hussar's hat was tugging, though less hysterically, at her own man's sleeve, and in the wake of these trooped several interested diners. Mopworth, who was forcibly struck by his opponent's resemblance to an ape as he hunched forward through the door, had his own reasons for what the majority took to be suicidal folly.

Among his habits had long been one of scrupulous daily exercise. When in New York, he always worked out with barbells and wall pulleys in the gymnasium of a health club to which he belonged, as he had in London. He occasionally went a round or two with the retired prizefighter the New York club kept around for members interested in learning something of "the manly art of self-defense." He had concealed these habits as being far too wide open to interpretation as narcissistic desires to cut a figure — to cultivate a masculine ideal that he did not inwardly feel he measured up to.

In any case, he easily evaded not only the first wild swing into which the ape threw himself the instant they had squared off in the parking lot, after handing their jackets to their women, but most of those that followed too. Good footwork and the knack of finely timed ducking sufficed to elude the intended haymakers, which wore out no one but the ape himself. Once or twice the ape stumbled into the ring of spectators encircling them. After each such fiasco, he would put his guard up again and hunch menacingly in for a fresh try, snorting and wiping his mouth with the back of his hand. His murderous expression made Mopworth laugh — though Mopworth prudently did not try to move in for any blows of his own. His first act on arising in the morning was always to limber up before an open bedroom window, where he would alternately squat on his heels and rise again, squat and rise, arms extended before him. Sometimes he would fold his arms and vary this with a Russian dance. Defending himself against the ape seemed at times little more than an adroit recapitulation of this calisthenic — squatting in time to insure the passage of the lullabyers over his head, bobbing erect to collect himself for the next.

Tiring after several minutes of these inconclusive maneuvers, his adversary presently tripped and fell down, provoking a gale of laughter from the crowd. This enraged him, and he suddenly shifted his tactics from boxing to those of simple rough-and-tumble. Lowering his head, he charged like a bull, butting Mopworth in the stomach with a sudden lunge that sent them both rolling in the dirt. They fetched up against the front tire of an automobile, their arms flailing and their legs kicking. It had degenerated into a complete dogfight, with the ape finally on top of Mopworth and pummeling him about the face and body. A shout of protest from the onlookers and cries of "Let him up! Fight fair!" was followed by the sight of Geneva suddenly breaking out of the ring of the spectators and beating the ape about the head with both of *her* fists. "Get up, you brute! You coward, get off of him and fight fair!" Stung, perhaps, more by her taunts than by her blows, he did. The two faced one another again with fists cocked, this time with a difference. Mopworth was genuinely enraged for the first time in the entire episode. He took the offensive now, and with a speed that gave him the advantage of complete surprise. First he feinted a left to the body that lowered the other's guard, and then with lightning speed brought his right up from the ground in a terrific uppercut that sent the ape reeling back against the car, down whose chromium-plated slopes he slid to a sitting position. In the course of his descent, he struck the back of his head, either on the radiator grillwork or the Mercury-like figurine that crowned it. Whichever it was proved to be an unexpected ally to Mopworth, for the ape sat there with a dazed expression that drew a cry of alarm from his woman. She knelt down beside him and began to rub the back of his head. Concerned himself, Mopworth started forward to make solicitous inquiries, but felt himself jerked abruptly back by the arm.

It was Geneva. "Get into the car," she said. "Here's your coat. I'll go in and pay the bill. I'll be right out."

"But —"

"Do as I say," she ordered through her teeth. She wheeled him about and gave him a start toward where the car was.

He climbed in, tossing his coat into the back seat. He waited for Geneva behind the wheel. She was no more than two minutes. "Can you drive?" He nodded, coughing. "Then hurry. Let's get out of here. No, let me drive. You're in no shape to." She got out, came round the other side and got in behind the wheel as he shoved over.

She headed for the beach. After shutting off the engine, she took one look at him and said, "Give me your handkerchief." She climbed out and walked to the shore. In the darkness he could see her stooping to dip the handkerchief in the water. She brought it back dripping, and, in the illumination from the dome light, wiped the grime from his face and tenderly dabbed a cut on his lip which was still trickling blood. "You —" she began. She did not finish, leaving unclear whether an epithet or an endearment had been intended. She completed her ministrations by suddenly dropping the handkerchief and taking his rumpled head in both her hands. She was sobbing.

Sympathetically, Mopworth reached into her blouse and drew forth a white breast. He kissed it reverently, putting his lips to its hard bud with a moan of joy. "How beautiful, how beautiful," he said, babbling the word over and over.

"You poor, bumbling, blundering sap. What will ever happen to you?"

"Nothing if — What I mean is, something has, right now, if this can possibly mean as much to you as it does to me. Geneva, I need you. I feel as though I've been kicked by a mule into paradise. Don't kick me out again."

These were well-chosen words. She stroked his hair with an

urgent, unaccustomed possessiveness. Mopworth knew it was not as simple as all this. The sudden turn in his fortune made him realize well enough the pivot on which Geneva's own emotions revolved. More than he needed her, he clearly divined, did she need his need of her. He for his part no doubt needed her need of his need of — God, where would it all end! Now, at least, it was begun.

"Geneva, could it be you and me?"

"Oh, my God," she sobbed tentatively.

They became formally engaged to be married toward the end of that winter. Nectar Schmidt got her announcement in the spring.

twenty-seven

"WHY DO PEOPLE EXPECT to be happily married when they are not individually happy? You go on so in America about marital contentment. Every magazine has an article with Nine Keys to it, or Seven Steps, as though the quest had any more sense to it, or any more hope of fulfillment, than the search for El Dorado. In no other country is this really juvenile ideal so naïvely held out — and with what failure! How do you expect mankind to be happy in pairs when it is miserable separately?"

So Gowan McGland had said in an interview in the New York *Times* and several other papers, as well as on a number of occasions from the lecture platform. Mopworth was now recording it once more in the manuscript of *McGland in America.*

The book was going poorly. Marital responsibilities and impediments were the least of the reasons. The women he interviewed remained stubbornly divided between the clams with secrets and chatterboxes wanting to get into the act. Mopworth now quite understood the nuisance regularly put up with by police trying to solve crimes, that of fake and crank confessions. He even had to pick his way with a skeptical eye among McGland's own surviving statements about his exploits, though these, to do him justice, were never in the nature of braggadocio, but rather of comments, theories and *obiter dicta* concerning the opposite sex. (Mopworth had thought of entitling the work *McGland on Women*, but doubted it would get by the censors.) Nor was suspect garrulity confined to the Don Juan side of the legend. Harry Pycraft, that Post Road host, grew daily more glib in his claims of generosity toward penniless and early divined genius, which Mopworth knew very well to be false having stayed at the Dew Drop Inn when McGland did. He had overheard at least one brisk dun for the rent money.

Standing at the window with his hands in his pockets, Mopworth had a vision of the day when *he* would be interviewed by the press on the publication of his book. He had some mots all ready. "What I hate about writing is the paperwork." And: "A writer is like the pencil he uses. He must be worn down to be kept sharp." Suddenly he seized a magazine with a short story in it that he particularly admired and began beating it into insensibility against the edge of his desk. Tedium, funk and rage composed in equal parts the sum of his attitude toward what he was doing, taking the stage by turns. "Why did he go and kill himself?" He asked the question rhetorically, knowing too well the burden he must soon shoulder of undertaking to answer it seriously. No book on McGland with any pretense to respectability could duck it. It was the knowledge of his utter unfitness for that climactic task that made him pospone it by dawdling and puttering over the elements preliminary to it. Thus he would pop off here to check some fact, there to run down another clam (or talking machine), or bury himself for weeks at a time in the local library, reading up on the "contemporary literary scene" in the name of thoroughness! He was thoroughly bogged down — that was as far as thoroughness went. How could anybody cogently theorize about suicide anyway? Could McGland himself, were he to return to this earth for an hour, make the exact state of mind under which he had taken leave of it comprehensible to another man? He, Mopworth, could not now even clearly recall what had gone on inside his own head during his brief flurry as a sex maniac. He hadn't the slightest idea what he had been thinking at the time. Not the slightest. It was all a blank.

Staring down at the sheet of paper in the typewriter over which he stood, hands in pockets again, he toyed with the idea of opening dramatically with Gowan's end in the motel room, then switching back to his boyhood in Scotland and thence steadily forward to the tragedy again, in an attempt to explain it in terms of what lay between. Instead an idea for a couplet began to form in his mind:

> The minute I find something's done in flashback
> I want to rush right out and demand my cashback.

He typed it straight off and sent it to the *Saturday Review*.

His English and American advances were both about run out, as well as what he'd socked away from those few lucrative years in London when he'd been in such great demand as a Silly Ass type on the telly, and kept dashing from studio to studio; and being now a father as well as a husband, he needed other sources of income while he finished the book. Turning out light verse brought in precious little, God knew, and Mopworth faced a decision: whether to go back to television acting. Which would make him a commuter, for he and Geneva had settled in Woodsmoke.

They lived in a rented house in Punch Bowl Hollow, and to get the couplet in the day's post he trotted through a light snow between picture windows to Vineyard Road, where all the subdivision's mailboxes stood in a long row. He slipped the letter into theirs, between the Beauseigneurs' and the Wolmars', clapped the lid shut and raised the flag.

As he started up the private road again he heard a loud backfire followed by an insistent honking, and, turning, saw Spofford leaning out of his flivver squeezing the bulb of the horn with a gauntleted hand. In place of his familiar duster he wore today a more rational topcoat, but he did have on the goggles, which he pushed up onto his forehead. "Hop in and ride along to New Haven," he said. "I have to see my lawyer."

"Jolly idea, but this snow . . ."

"Won't amount to anything. I can smell real snow. This is just dandruff. So O.K., I'll drive you home first to tell Geneva you'll be gone for the afternoon. If I get through in time maybe we can get tickets to that new musical. Mrs. Punck won't go. She has this thing about appearances."

What tempted Mopworth was the interviewing he might get in on the way. The old man had more under his bonnet about McGland than anyone else around, at least about the crucial Connecticut days, but he doled it out the merest scrap at a time, to conserve his importance to the legend and also, Mopworth liked to think, to protract the hours of comradely drinking now apparently central to Spofford's conception of the literary life. He talked just enough to make you come back for more — not that he wasn't welcome on his own any time he wanted to visit his granddaughter and, now, great-grandson, Mike Mopworth.

Curiosity about Spofford, in fact, had grown until it sometimes eclipsed Mopworth's interest in McGland. The man was a puzzle in as many ways as he was a pest. Why, for one thing, did he continue to call the woman Mrs. Punck long after she had become Mrs. Rappaport? Let alone imagine she would pop off to the theater with him under the circumstances. Perhaps merely the gesture of asking her sufficed to express the idea of casual living which had somehow gotten lodged in his head. How, for another thing, had he managed to beat the breaking and entering rap? After two continuances in the town court, the indictment had been quashed and the whole case suddenly and mysteriously dropped. What had happened? From vague hints dropped by Spofford it was to be suspected that he had managed it himself by some twist more devious than any lawyer had at his disposal. Blackmail even? That possibility was not to be ruled out. The man knew more about everybody in Woodsmoke than, often, their own intimates did. Mopworth was banking on his itch to brag as a means of worming the facts out of him at last. Maybe today would be the day.

They were soon sailing down the Merritt Parkway at thirty miles an hour (Spofford having refused to hear of their taking Mopworth's Volkswagen) while Spofford went on about how his old lawyer had died and his son had moved to New Haven. Spofford had preferred leaving his business with the son to finding another attorney in Woodsmoke. "Mrs. Punck keeps after me to switch to hers, but I don't like him," he said.

"Why do you keep calling her Mrs. Punck?" Mopworth asked.

"For old times' sake. We all like to think back on the days that are no more, when we were single. That's married life."

A rather fuzzy and elliptical answer at best, the analysis of which Mopworth presently abandoned. His most ticklish question was delayed to coincide with their leaving the Parkway, when the complications of navigating a dense flow of traffic into New Haven might suddenly throw Spofford off his mental guard. It squandered what could be Mopworth's last chance for a confidence on this outing, on something really having nothing to do with literary research, but his curiosity had got the better of him. "It's none of my business, really, I know. But if you don't mind saying, how did you ever get those charges dropped?"

"What charges?" Spofford asked with an innocence that made Mopworth roll his eyes toward the side curtain with the torn isinglass that offered their sole protection from the cold. Its mate was either gone or in hopeless tatters, for there was none on Spofford's side, and they shouted to one another above the wind. Though the snow had stopped the wind was rising. Mopworth had brought no gloves and sat hunched down with his hands in his topcoat pockets. "You know — that bloke whose window you broke. Dr. Wolmar."

It was a Saturday on which Yale had a home game, and to the sound of the motor as well as the gusts above which conversation had to be conducted was added that of streams of stadium-bound cars honking impatiently at the obstruction in the road. Their occupants streaked past, when oncoming traffic permitted, with glances either annoyed or amused. There were no connoisseurs out today. Mopworth frequently closed his eyes, or averted them to the isinglass, in which the gash was widening noticeably. One corner of the side curtain had become unhooked and was flapping in the breeze.

"I'm going to tell you something I've never told anybody else," Spofford said when they had turned off onto a less traveled thoroughfare. It was a side street, indeed almost deserted. Spofford either knew his way around New Haven very well or they were lost. "I've kept my ears open in the years I've lived in Woodsmoke. Note that I say ears, not eyes, because I'm not one of your voyeurs they call them now days. You've overheard conversations you felt no guilt about overhearing? Embarrassed or uneasy maybe, yes, but not guilt."

"Constantly," Mopworth said, to encourage him.

"The open windows where I sometimes stood, it was to listen, not look. I only say this to nip any misunderstanding in the bud. You've got a good, fair mind, without no murky corners or damp subcellars, one thing and another, so far as a man can figure out, and besides," Spofford said, loudly and after clearing his throat with what seemed a fit of irritation, fidgeting behind the wheel, "I want to reveal a confidence to you to show that I like you in the family."

"Why, that's one of the nicest —"

"Oh, the hell with that. The thing is, I am not a Paul Pry and I do not deal in gossip. But I do think that people are entitled to my undivided attention."

"I understand you perfectly."

"Maybe you do and maybe you don't. Here's what I'm trying to say. When you have enough on people to hang them is when mercy sets in, and you want to give them another chance. But what they tell you won't clear them — only what you overhear. Unguarded moments. We owe each other that curiosity. All right then. So once, when I was on my way home from the Wolmars' after sitting for them, I passed their bedroom window and heard a conversation going on between those two that only a man dead in his heart, with no more interest in his own kind, could not stop to listen to. It was a argument, never mind what about. At the height of it, Dr. Wolmar, who up to then hadn't seemed mad at all, at least not crazy mad, took off his pants and flung them in his wife's face. There was nothing mean or vicious in it, nothing worse than what people constantly do to one another, in fact a lot milder than some of the tales I could unfold. It was more like emphasizing a point that hadn't ought to been emphasized quite that much. I don't judge the man. How does that famous remark of Spinoza's go?"

"Neither to weep nor to laugh, but to understand," said

Mopworth, who was wondering how Spofford understood that the trousers had been pitched if he'd only been listening and not looking. Perhaps in these vigils he had from time to time glanced in the window to clarify to himself some point in the colloquy?

"That's right. Well, you're a writer, is another reason I tell you these things. You should be interested in human nature. It's all grist for the mill."

"I appreciate that," Mopworth said. "But what has this to do with your trial? Indictment rather. That got quashed." The Spoffords themselves all said "squashed."

"I'm coming to that now. You see, the whole point in legal proceedings is that people have something 'on' you. Society has something on you and feels it should do something about it. Well, I had something on my accuser that was a damn sight worse than what he had on me. Worse than breaking and entering — at least *my* breaking and entering. Because that had a moral purpose. It wasn't to steal anything at all, but to find out something in his notes about a patient of his that I had a moral right to know about. Don't ask me who, because that part I won't tell you. But I know you believe me just as Wolmar believed me though I refused to tell *him* who the patient was — because by that time I didn't need the information no more. Things had changed. It was none of his goddam business but these psychiatrists can't help prying I guess. So he wouldn't bring his weight to bear to get the case squashed. So I had to play my trump card. I had to use my club. I took him aside one day and says, 'If you don't use your influence to get this thing squashed I'll tell everybody somebody threw their britches in somebody's face. Again we don't mention no names.' That did it." Spofford removed his hands from the wheel to execute a gesture at some fool motorist in traffic again so dense that Mopworth chose to close his eyes once more. Through some apparent shortcut they were back on the main drag — they were being passed by the same cars all over again, the occupants glaring a second time as they disappeared at speeds not to be gainsaid.

Mopworth asked: "But how could a private citizen get the

authorities to drop what was a criminal and not a civil charge? He wasn't the plaintiff. Did he have you —?" Mopworth did not know what folly had brought him to the brink of the word "certified," at which, of course, he shied. "Did he have some such right in the eyes of the law?"

"No. Just as a local pillar he had the case thrun out. A few wires pulled behind the scenes can do this where the defendant is himself not a real criminal but a person of standing. Status I guess is the word for that now days. Well, here we are. I hope I won't be too long."

Spofford was a good forty-five minutes talking to his lawyer. While waiting in the car Mopworth worked out a quatrain inspired by Spofford's pronunciation of "status," with the long "a," which struck him as itself suggesting one of the two groups into which the very word could be taken as a shibboleth dividing people:

> *None will ever dare high-hat us*
> *If we but pronounce it status;*
> *But they'll be bound to underrate us*
> *If we persist in saying status.*

Without the poem, which didn't seem to him very good after he had jotted it down, to occupy him, Mopworth felt the cold in the open flivver, and spent the rest of his wait in a nearby bar from a window of which Spofford's return could be noted. When he saw him emerge from the office building he ran out and beckoned him across the street for a drink. It was now too late to think about a matinee, and after a quick whiskey they set out on their homeward journey. This was marked by two incidents.

The single side curtain, which had been flapping ever more ominously in the wind finally tore free of its moorings altogether and vanished in a gust behind them. Spofford jammed on the brake and they got out to search for it. They finally located it beside the road some fifty yards back. Spofford stowed it in the rear compartment for possible repairs, and they continued on.

Hitchhikers were a common sight along the road, and they

thought nothing of the short figure, buttoned up tight in a dark overcoat, whom they saw flagging a ride when they were about halfway home. Spofford very nearly did not recognize Dr. Rappaport, but he spotted the black bag just as they flashed by, and slammed to a stop again. Dr. Rappaport climbed in between them with expressions of gratitude, clapping his mittened hands together after he had settled his bag on his knees.

"What brings you out this way, Emil?" Spofford asked.

"I had a consultation out of town." Rappaport did not specify what town, and Spofford wondered if it were New Haven, and why Mrs. Punck hadn't mentioned it. "I was called in by a doctor friend of mine on a case that rather puzzled him. He wanted a second opinion. So I went up early this morning. It's nothing serious, I'm glad to say. Well! This is a lucky break for me." He looked from one to the other of his companions with his pleasant smile.

Mopworth had sprung out to give him the middle seat, not to retain the outer for himself, which would have been an advantage only in a closed automobile, but courteously to yield what, in this case, was the warmer position. They were all a good deal snugger now. Dr. Rappaport had earlier in the day been dosing a patient with muscle spasm, and he smelled agreeably of wintergreen. Mopworth slumped down and listened to the older men discuss something Rappaport and Mrs. Punck were particularly interested in — the formation of a local chapter of the Council of Christians and Jews. Spofford was rather acid in his opinion of a woman named Mrs. Stern, who was being considered for president.

"She's not the right sort for a ticklish position, take it from me," he said. "She has this strong prejudice against anti-Semites, and this ain't a case where you fight fire with fire."

Rappaport was so delighted with this that he sat shaking with laughter. He even nudged Mopworth with an elbow as he said, "Prejudiced against anti-Semites, I like that, Frank," he said. "That's wonderful." Spofford pulled the gas lever down all the way, till the car was wide open. One of the curious things about Rappaport was the complete unpredictability of his laughter. You never knew when he was going to be amused, or what would amuse him, and his covert chuckles were more disconcerting than his open outbursts. "Yes, I can see Mrs. Stern's vibrations are all wrong. She'll have to go."

It had turned quite cold when they reached Woodsmoke, and Dr. Rappaport surmised they would all be glad to get home to their respective kitchens. "They're the thing, as I'm glad to see modern architects getting back to realizing. Frank, I believe Eunice has a stew going, you're more than welcome to take a bite with us. There'll be plenty, and I have a bottle of good Burgundy I want to open. Wine is one of the things Eunice and I don't have in common, and I don't like to drink a whole bottle myself. How about it?"

"Well, all right," Spofford said, after a hypocritical hesitation. "We'll drop Alvin off first then, and I can phone from your place that I shan't be home."

The scene that greeted Mopworth when he got home himself was one of harried domesticity indeed.

It was being enacted in the kitchen by which he entered, Rappaport's notions about the revival of traditional cheer there notwithstanding. Geneva stood in a central serving "island," as architects call them, trying out a new beef casserole for which she was reading from not one but three cookbooks, all spread out open before her on a sort of prop shelf, like a speaker's lectern. Her hair was disordered and her apron, a short-length tunic ending in a horizontal row of pockets like a carpenter's apron, was smudged with flour and other foodstuffs, as well as crammed with an extraordinary number of implements — perhaps even a small hammer for pounding flour into the strips of flesh disposed about her for convenience in a half-circle. Mike was crying in his pen in one corner of the room; he had apparently just pitched one of his playing blocks into the hooded fireplace. There was no fire going, and the block lay among the gray ashes. Geneva was drinking from an Old-Fashioned as he entered, her head bent over one of the cookbooks. The general picture would have been a perfect illustration for one of those magazine articles dealing with the Ordeal of the American Woman, bearing a caption like "The Hoax of the

Feminine Mystique" or "Educated — for What?" This was so hilariously the case that Mopworth could not resist a smile, which he tried to pass off as one of pleasure at being home again. The serving island was so circular and centered so exactly in the kitchen as to resemble the Information Desk in Grand Central Station. Mopworth walked up to it like a passenger with a question to ask.

"What are you doing, darling?"

"Oh, for Christ's sake!" Geneva said. "Waiting for a streetcar. Where have you been?"

"Well, actually I'm home early, rather, if you remember my saying we might stay for the matinee. Gramps was in great form, he —"

"Oh, Christ, pick that child up before I pound some flour into both of *you*."

"Right you are!"

Mopworth made one of his observations about married life. Marriage was the fabulous invalid the theater had once been. The same doom was continually predicted for it, while it continued miraculously to survive. One got into the habit of introspection about one's own. One started and ended each day appraising it in terms of the experts' diagnoses; one assessed the shared moments of it like one taking a patient's pulse. The conclusion Mopworth now drew about it was based on a sizable span of daily experience, now for the first time recognized in terms of a general principle. It was that the woman determined the weather in the house. From her came permission to laugh, instruction to brood, the cue for fun or woe. As he stepped in the door Mopworth realized that the first thing he did was, not greet Geneva, but read her face to determine how she should be greeted. He consulted her face like this many times a day, as one consults a barometer, to see what kind of day or evening it will be. He had done this now, he remarked to himself for the first time, for well over a year.

Was it true of all marriages, or only marriages like his, in which the man is the acquiescent type wanting only peace in the house? Was it more true now than it had once been? Or more true in America than elsewhere? That woman calls the ever-changing emotional tunes to which one dances, was that a universal fact accepted abroad without fuss and only exaggerated in a country where emancipation was bearing its first disillusioning fruits, like early returns in a doubtful election? Mopworth understood that theirs was a pivotal generation. With them the institution of marriage might stand or fall. Quick divorces and as speedy remarriages were bringing about a way of life for which the anthropologists already had a name: serial polygamy. Several wives or husbands, only in succession rather than simultaneously. There was a bloke in town who had already had five wives, whom they had discussed at a family Thanksgiving dinner at the farmhouse. Most of them marveled that a man could have that many mates. Mrs. Punck had made the most notable comment (which had made Rappaport nearly choke on his turkey with laughter). She had said: "He's just not the marrying kind."

The needle tonight seemed to waver between Stormy and Change. On the far side of Change was, in any case, that portion of the barometer devoted to Fair. He knew that the slightest shift in circumstance — success with the casserole, a bit of bracing gossip — might save the evening. He swooped Mike up and disappeared to change him. The end of Mike's caterwauling, then gurgling contentment after his bottle, went far toward composing the house. The casserole safely in the oven, Mopworth fixed them both drinks, giving Geneva a fresh glass for hers. Glutted with milk, Mike rolled over and went to sleep in his crib. Returning to the living room, Mopworth remembered the Burgundy Rappaport had invited Spofford to share with him, and he decided to open the last bottle of a case of Musigny he had extravagantly bought. It was the wine Miles Schmidt had put him onto, and he groaned at the memory of that evening as he hurried downstairs to fetch it. "This dinner is going to deserve the best," he said as he opened it, a good hour before dinner, to let it "expand" as the experts urged. Watching him from the living room couch with her drink, Geneva seemed to brighten. He was setting the table with their good silver when she suddenly sprang to her feet and said, "Oh, I want to show you the door prizes I got for Wednesday. My turn to have the bridge bunch in." She pulled a self-deprecating mouth when she said this. Geneva liked to play bridge, but Mopworth was a dolt at the game and so evenings of it with other couples were out: she had to resort to afternoons with the ladies.

"Swell!"

The purchases Geneva opened for display on one end of the dining table were two. They were a small ceramic dish with a humorous inscription giving rise to the belief that it was a coaster, and a poodle dog in low relief with a hole in its head indicating him to be a wall plaque. "We keep giving a booby prize as well as a main prize," she said. "Custom and superstition."

Mopworth admired them companionably a moment. They stood side by side, holding their drinks. He fingered the prizes with his free hand. "Very nice. Quite cute really, both of them." He gazed at them a moment longer, smiling and nodding. Then he asked: "Which is which?"

The evening lay in tatters at their feet. He knew that the instant the words were out of his mouth. He deserved the booby prize himself! Geneva turned in silence and walked into the kitchen.

He stood in the doorway watching as she looked into the oven to see how the casserole was coming. He had his work cut out for him, all right. Over his shoulder he glanced back into the dining room at the objects still lying in their wrappings on the table. He stole hurriedly back while she was gone and reinspected them, in hopes of discerning some clue to their relative worth, perhaps price tags on their undersides. But there were none. "Damn," he said under his breath. He overturned the boxes in which they still reposed. No price markings on the bottom of them either. He muttered an even stronger oath. Hearing the oven door close he shot on tiptoe into the living room (marked off from this by a five-foot combination fernery and bookcase which served as a "room divider"), where he was to be seen lighting a cigarette and gazing out the picture window, which gave on one identical to it across the road.

325

By now he had some rough kind of plan hammered out in his head.

"Sorry my little joke misfired." He drew the draperies, having seen the head of the house appear in the other window, a chap named Dumbrowski whom he couldn't stand. Dumbrowski was the author of a succession of widely read (but unreadable) novels that were said to make pots. The closing swirl of fabric cut short an intended greeting over there.

"Joke?" Geneva seemed to want to believe it.

"Of course joke." He simulated surprise. "You mean you thought I was serious? Come now, ducks." He drifted toward the dining table, where he fingered again the awards. "It's actually an old gag. Didn't we see a sketch based on that on television once?" he said, fabricating. "Or maybe I was alone that night. You were pregnant. Mike all right?" An urgent appraisal of the materials of which the objects were constructed told him nothing. Both seemed earthenware, enameled in bright colors.

"Is this cloisonné?" he asked rather fulsomely, hefting one in either hand in a manner intended to confuse her as to which was meant.

"The *dog?*" The stress of the word, as if in surprise, suggested it must be the meaner of the two items, and he tacked for harbor accordingly.

"No, silly, this one. The coaster."

"Coaster! Is that all it looks like to you? Something to set a glass of beer on?"

"What is it then? Is it a tray for pins? Is it one of these things women burn perfume in? Is it —" he raised his eyes, like one taking stabs in a guessing game — "a kind of trivet?"

"If you can't tell it's an ashtray maybe it had better go back. I mean that should be just too simple." Her anger seemed to have shifted from him to her purchase, or rather to have broadened out to include it — small progress in either case.

"Of course. An ashtray. How stupid of me." Mopworth recovered on the word something of his now slightly eroded British accent, saying "schewpid" with an exaggerated richness that seemed to restore to the object some of its lost prestige.

"Maybe you don't think it's good enough to put ashes in."

"Of course I think it's good enough to put ashes in." What a quagmire all this was! What he had said was "And I said you *were* fit to sleep with pigs." He brought the rout of meaning to a conclusion by executing a sort of caper and saying self-deprecatingly:

As the husband is, the wife is: thou art mated to a clown,
And the grossness of his nature will have weight to drag thee down.

Mopworth was glad now that he had gone at the guessing game at the rate he had. It made it harder for her to doubt that he had been kidding all along. Everything pointed to her wanting to believe that, at least on the surface. Perhaps in that case she would pursue the matter no further, preserving her doubt in order to save her pride. "Another drink?"

"Which is which?"

"What?"

"Which is the main prize and which is the booby, if it was all only a joke?" She sat down and crossed her legs. "Well? I realize women take everything personally, especially insults, so make it good."

Mopworth drew a deep breath. Then with that now familiar sensation of taking a corner on two wheels he said, "The poodle."

"The poodle is what?"

"The booby."

She took a cigarette from a box on the table. He extended a flame. "Well?" he said.

"You'll never know."

Then that was to be his punishment — never to know. He was to be consigned to a kind of hell such as might be devised by an existentialist writer of adroit stage comedies, in which the characters, unworthy of any profounder doom, are left to dangle in one another's presence in a petty but eternal uncertainty.

He fixed them both fresh drinks and brought them to the cocktail table. Now he began that peculiar, measured sort of pacing that was so characteristic of him, that McGland had noticed in the Chelsea flat where they had first met, when the Tuttles had gone telly. It was not quite marching, neither was it quite anything else, as though he had been told a long time ago as a child to pick up his feet and had done so ever since. Even his normal walk had a faint touch of this prancing to it. He paced to the far end of the room, turned on the sole of one foot and came back again. Sometimes he went off at a slight angle to alter the regularity of this repetition. His hands were in his pants pockets, and he looked at the carpet as he walked. At last his pacing became more measured.

"I just want to throw this thought out to you," he said. "My original question — what started all this brouhaha — might be regarded as implying *not* that you can't tell the main prize from the booby, but that you can't tell the booby from the main. A different kettle of fish altogether. The booby's too good, is the idea. I just want to throw that thought out to you for what it's worth. Now how do you feel about it, ducks?"

"Let's have dinner. And don't open the wine. It's much too good a bottle to waste on a night like this."

But he had already opened it, of course, so he poured it while Geneva dished the dinner. The casserole was superb, and he said so. Geneva said as she watched him pour her second glass of Burgundy, "I paid four dollars and fifty cents for that prize, and our rule is never to go over two."

"Oh, really?" Mopworth marched back to his end of the table with the bottle. "And what's your minimum on the booby? Have a floor on that, do you, sweets, just as you have a ceiling on the main?"

"Oh, stop jabbering like an idiot."

"Right!"

Mopworth wanted only peace. To pursue that he sought, only and always, to please. He cleared the table and washed the dishes, according to a now fairly established pattern, this time finishing what remained of the wine and even having a little brandy before pitching in, however. He was a cotquean, like every up-to-date husband, especially among the more well-to-do, or at least sophisticated, levels, where the passing of the servant

328

might be more readily mourned than among the working classes. He had stumbled on the word in the dictionary while looking up something else entirely. "A man who busies himself with affairs properly feminine," was the definition of a cotquean. He had never heard of the word before. But every husband was one now, apparently. Mopworth did not necessarily resent the fact, or begrudge the time and effort devoted to this estate; it was after all a dreary nuisance and why should a woman be expected to put up with it without protest? He did feel a faint sense of demoralization, however. But it was a price he was willing to pay for that domestic stability in which alone the pleasures and satisfactions of married life might be pursued.

He went upstairs to the bedroom when he had finished tidying up, to assess the possibility of cultivating some of those.

Geneva lay in bed with a book spreadeagled on her stomach, staring across her feet toward the opposite wall. He got into pajamas and struck the same attitude, so that they resembled in their formal positions two supine caryatids supporting together the solemn and ponderous entablature of matrimony. He knew that she was planning to cry. Unless before that happened her emotions found an alternative relief — say, airing them to another woman. The exchanges of wedded conferences among housewives, at once cozy and bloodcurdling, represented a sorority Mopworth could neither fathom nor buck, and more than vaguely feared. Men had their trade unionism, God knew, their club ancedotes and their bar-car camaraderie, but its lore concerned women to whom they were *not* married. They did not sit and over their whiskies deplore the wives of their bosoms, as the ladies apparently did the husbands of theirs, sometimes humorously, sometimes damn well not. Mopworth prayed God the phone would not ring, or that if it did it would not be Minnie Dumbrowski across the way. Geneva owed her something in return for Minnie's account of Jack's interlude with a girl who popped out of smoker cakes.

"Only hostility toward the woman as a woman could make a man make a remark like that."

"It just slipped out."

"All the more significant."

"But it wasn't *intended* to be derisive. I didn't *know* it was. It was simply an inadvertent sort of remark. Question, rather," he corrected from the other bed, lolling over onto an elbow. "Because you keep calling it a remark, which is significant on your part. It shows that basically you *want* a man to be hostile — or you want to believe he was hostile — because it satisfies a hostility within you. And since the war between the sexes and all that seems to be part of the normal kit and kaboodle, or so we've come to accept, why pick on any one specific reflection of it as being so awful? I mean if you're going to make a federal case out of it . . ."

"This was more than just that. This was the malice of a certain kind of masculine temperament, toward the opposite sex. Only a man who hated women at bottom would be capable of a remark like that."

"Question."

"It was a remark, in essence. It was just a question in form. Its purpose was to ridicule something a wife had brought home. I think you ought to see these things for what they are, Alvin, if you ever want to get straightened around. You resent me as a man naturally would resent a woman who saved him from homosexuality."

Mopworth resumed gazing sluggishly at the far wall across his turned-up toes. He waited for the moment when the dispute was ended and he could start reading. He was deep in a good book he wanted to get back to. There was an unspecifiable, but clearly minimum, span of silence after which one might safely judge it to be the end of a wrangle and not a pause in it, and turn to private concerns without a breach of decency. Instinct told you when that moment was reached. He watched the second hand swim around the face of the electric clock on the dresser. One minute, two. When it again reached its zenith he would pick up his book. It did. He opened the book stealthily and began to read. Geneva threw her legs suddenly over the side of the bed and reached for the blue leather address book beside the telephone on her table.

"I'm going to call Nectar."

Mopworth let his head fall over the side of the bed, where, hanging out of sight between it and the wall, he resembled a passenger sick at sea. Hidden from view there, he cursed, gnashed his teeth, clenched his fists, and silently groaned. He rose before they had been put through to Gettysburg and went into the living room to avoid hearing any of the actual conversation. He was pacing there when he heard its upshot.

He walked the shag rug in bare feet, his robe hanging open, smoking cigarettes. Once he peered through the draperies to the Dumbrowskis' house across the street. He resembled a participant in an amateur theatrical peeking through the stage curtain at the audience. For here you came to regard your neighbors quite as audiences, spectators of your life, a condition scarcely relieved by the sense of your being witness to theirs. What did he care whether Jack Dumbrowski had a fling with a tart in a smoker cake, except that it indicated an extra dividend from those rotten novels of his — something they made economically possible?

Mopworth worked out a downfall for him. He had it that Dumbrowski picked up a nail from one of the tarts, and that his wife left him. Purged and remorseful, he wandered from place to place trying to make a new life for himself, fetching up at last in Pennsylvania, where he met Nectar Schmidt, and they got married. Good! Goody goody gumdrop. Each was what the other deserved. She introduced just enough perception into his work for Dumbrowski's next book to be a mess — too good for the cretins that had hitherto constituted his audience and not good enough for the readers who made a solid literary reputation — and they sank into dire poverty. They were last seen in, oh, Terre Haute, Indiana, where Nectar tried again to bring in a little money selling doughnuts door to door, the snow descending everywhere quietly, through the roof and onto the floor of the unheated single room in which Dumbrowski, the knack of writing a good bad book forever lost to him, and plugging away at another bad good book —

"Well, that was nice." Geneva entered the room a good

ten minutes after him, also barefoot. Her mood seemed to have cleared, and she wore a smile.

"Couldn't begin to catch up on all the things we have to chin about," she said. "But it was good talking to her again, and guess what. Nectar's coming to pay us a visit. We've set the week end of the twelfth."

Mopworth closed his eyes and rolled the balls behind their lids till he was nauseated. When he opened them again it was to stare at his hands, which lay in his lap with the fingers intertwined, like interlocked spikes in one of those novelty-shop puzzles which cannot be disentangled, tug as one will, unless one knows the secret, when they separate with ridiculous ease. He gazed at them for a long time after his wife went back to bed, without moving.

twenty-eight

THE TRAIN BRINGING Nectar Schmidt to Woodsmoke was half an hour late and Mopworth, down to meet her with the Volkswagen, killed the time in a bar across the street from the station. He had two beers and a thing called a meatball grinder, which some failure of the faculty of disgust enabled him to eat. It seemed to consist of two, or possibly three, boiled golfballs obscenely lurking in a loaf of bread longitudinally sawn. He doubted that Indelicato would have had it about, or that it was authentically Italian at all. It was to be numbered, in any case, among the hazards of life in contemporary America.

These were many, both physical and spiritual, but he liked to think he was doing as well as most of the natives with whom he found himself flying fraternally over the obstacle course, and possibly better than some. He was still married, though the institution was widely considered no longer to work. People continued to go in for it because there was nothing better, and besides one has invested all that pother in courtship, from which there is no place to go but forward. The whole thing was like one of those plays of which one has read bad reviews but to which one has already bought tickets. One goes anyway. One muddles through.

His marriage had more pluses than minuses. He had one fine boy and another on the way. At least Mrs. Punck said it would be a boy because Geneva was carrying it broad and flat rather than narrow and projecting. Of course the experts would have to be let make what they would of the overproduction. He could already hear Nectar, after learning that this pregnancy was the result of his impetuous wooing one night when Geneva was caught unprepared. He tried it on for size. "There are men who need to turn their wives into child-bearing slaves," he said aloud. It did not really convince him and it only alarmed the bartender, who could not distinguish what he said but saw that he had a customer talking to himself. Talking and, what was worse, laughing. There was only one satisfactory refuge from all this theory about sex, and that was its practice. Too bad you had to climb out of the sack and face the whole damned business of getting on with women all over again. Did women suspect it was in the sheer need to get away from *them* that one buried one's face in their bosoms, one's self in them?

The train could be heard rumbling in, and Mopworth paid and hurried across the street, a fragment of paper napkin snagged in the vest over which he buttoned his coat as he trotted.

Nectar was standing on the platform looking around for a familiar face. Mopworth spied on her for a bit from behind a man with massive shoulders in a red lumberjack shirt. She was dressed in a spruce brown suit flecked with darker nubs, like flakes of tobacco that wanted brushing off. She had on her dark glasses, in which she looked a little furtive, like someone hoping to be mistaken for a celebrity. She had let her black hair grow and it hung to one side, that on which she inclined her head in that gaze of spurious sincerity, the list further emphasized by the weight of the grip in her hand. It looked very heavy, as though it contained enough clothing for a month's stay. Mopworth gave another unstable cackle. The grip was new and of smart blue leather, not at all like the wicker satchels secured with twine with which he had been visualizing her walking the streets of the city in poverty. He watched her for a moment longer from behind the fat man, sagging at the knees a little to keep out of sight. Then he danced through the crowd sideways with one arm upraised, shrieking gaily: "Nectar!"

"Hello, Alvin."

Gossip tides us over the first constraint of a reunion, and Mopworth used theirs to feed Nectar some straight lines he had prepared, to see how closely her answers would conform to those he had mentally predicted.

"Fine . . . Fine . . . Yes, she married Dr. Rappaport, and do you know what? Old Spofford keeps calling her Mrs. Punck."

"It's pry his way of denying it. I think he was interested, though they don't speak the same language."

But were not these victories Pyrrhic, in that the very game he played with her secretly proved her charge? How did his amusement differ from the glazed malice of those porcelain chaps who more honestly ran in packs? What at the first crack of hello was he erecting against her but that seething masculinity posed now also at times, and secretly, against Geneva? What was happening to marriage that each could now be but the other's outer landscape? That during mealtimes and even bedtime each must vanish into a private country packed with emotional contraband? Where were the sweet participants of verse and song — gone with the "yesteryears" that drifted like whiffs of old sachet through the lines of Mrs. Punck's "favorites." Love itself was coming apart like the spines and covers of the crumbling heirlooms she got down from the shelf or took along on sitting jobs. What was behind the human botch of mating? Did it lie deep in some failure of animal nature, or was the culprit the squiggling ego, subtly dividing what flesh would join together? And how, even were he to find an answer to all these things, could he relate them to any comprehension of Gowan McGland? On what rock had *he* broken? Or had he simply hanged separately because we no longer hang together? And had he died — or lived, like all of us — with fragments of antique verse yet caught in his mind, like a kite in the branches of a tree? We long to "share" experience. Yet each of us lies in darkness with his few private scraps of treasure, like those Etruscan warriors of old who were said to be buried with their nostrils stuffed with precious stones.

"We're going to the Dumbrowskis' tonight, you know," was one of Geneva's first statements on their arrival home. Mopworth disliked his noting that though she spoke to him she said it for Nectar's benefit, a girlish desire to show her old roommate how they lived, something of the gay tissue of their lives. "You're coming along of course, Nectar. I just talked to Minnie on the phone, and it's all set."

Set, too, was Mopworth's jaw as he thought again of the six solid hours of conversation to which we maniacally commit ourselves when we accept a dinner invitation. Who do we think we *are?* he thought as he carried Nectar's luggage to the guest room, tramping on the carpet to suggest to himself the barren wastes of dialogue across which they must again slog side by side with Jack Dumbrowski. Why their two households had begun to exchange invitations was one of the mysteries of a social system administered by women, which Mopworth did not feel equipped to discuss. He secretly bewailed what he had quickly perceived to be one of the curses of the suburbs: the perfect negative correlation (as the statisticians called it) between friendship and social life. The two had nothing to do with one another, as they still might, say, in such benighted back reaches as Cedar Rapids or Stoke on Trent.

"I've never read any of his books," Nectar was telling Geneva over their first drink when he returned.

"Of course you haven't," Mopworth said. "What you admit is that you *have* read Jack Dumbrowski. *That's* a confession."

"Why do you say that, Alvin?" Mopworth knew Geneva was trying to telegraph him a warning to shut up, but he perversely avoided her eye. Instead he watched Nectar, who was having a spot of sport with Mike. Sitting on the floor saying "Kitchy koo" through the slats of the playpen, she looked really quite absurd.

"They're full of characters saying 'You mean —?' to one another," he said. "And that junky lyrical 'somewhere' writers stick in for atmosphere. 'Somewhere a bird sang,' or 'Somewhere a screen door twanged,' or 'Somewhere a woman's laughter broke the stillness of the night.' You know the sort of thing I mean, Nectar."

Nectar gave him a laughing nod over her shoulder. A sense of complicity with her began to dissolve his dread of her visit. He might have an ally in the war with Geneva over Dumbrowski. A belief that it might all be yet all right leaped up within him. It was partly the drink he was himself putting down, partly hope springing eternal, and though it had involved for the moment nothing more than her single laugh and the lamplight sliding along the silk scarf at her throat, it seemed enough for an evening, and possibly a lifetime. His attempted rape, or murder, of her seemed never to have occurred. It was one with all the dust we collectively and willingly sweep under the rug. His spirits rose, he turned to face Geneva with a smile. "Come on now, ducks, you're being much too polite. You don't like his novels any more than I do. They're not *written*. And of course I don't mean Nectar won't find nice *people* at their parties."

Geneva laughed. "Well, that's right. None of *his* readers." Then they all laughed together, and Mopworth, proud of his wife's pleasantry, went on: "He has these tens of thousands of readers, you see, Nectar, but nobody's ever *heard* of him. He's got no *reputation*."

Geneva shook her head, deploring their amusement with a smile at the floor, then changed the subject while Mopworth took the glass out of her hand to refill it. They were all quite gay by the time the sitter arrived. This turned out to be no less than Spofford, bundled in a plaid overcoat and with the earflaps of his tweed cap down as far as he could get them.

"Hello, all," he said. "Cold snap's started. Had your car checked, Alvin? Well, well, Nectar."

Leaving Spofford behind in the house made Mopworth rather uneasy, for he was by now able to surmise the manner in which Spofford had passed the time in the homes of others for whom he had sat. Mopworth had never expressed this misgiving to Geneva, as it would have meant betraying a confidence, so he bore the anxiety himself. He confined his objection to Spofford as a sitter to complaints that he could press no payment on him — disingenuously, because they were as glad to have the money as Spofford was of the chance to perform his great-grandparent's role. Still, the thought of Spofford's knowing as much about them as he did about the Wolmars and the Wilcoxes and whoever else's premises he had scoured was a chilling thought. Therefore Mopworth kept all letters and private documents in a locked drawer, in a study itself locked (let the old poop make what he wanted of that if he tried the door). His mind was further relieved tonight by Spofford's asking whether it was all right if he asked Emil Rappaport to drop in for a game of chess. "By all means, and help yourselves to the whiskey," Mopworth said.

He put it out of his mind as he left the house and made for the one across the road, still filling Nectar in on their host as he bundled his two women along over the frozen ruts that lay between. "Richness of characterization is obtained by saying 'part of her' all the time. Part of her wanted so-and-so, while another part of her wanted such-and-such." "Alvin!" Geneva scolded as they hurried up the walk. They were all laughing through chattering teeth when the door opened and Dumbrowski himself spread wide his arms for Geneva to run into.

"Come you in, one and all! Ah, and the extra dividend as promised," he said, shaking Nectar's hand in both of his. His green eyes darted from face to face like dragonflies over the surface of a pond. "Alvin. Glad to see you. Come join the throng."

He was wearing a plaid jacket with black silk lapels, on one of which was a stain of grease which Mopworth found enormously encouraging. A sort of postscript to his reddish hair grew in a small bit of beard on the top of his chin, parted, its ends twisted into spears and possibly waxed. But that was the grooming normally given a mustache, was it not? Are we not correct in this assumption? Then why —?

"Minnie, some more guests! Minniehaha!"

Minnie was almost as tall as Jack, but a good deal thinner. Bent shoulders and a pale face consumed by the strain of getting a counterfeit passed in the world as a true coin made her seem half her size. They had no children, but she had that look characteristic of women burdened with husbands to whom they must play second fiddle, which sometimes curiously resembles that of women worn out with childbearing. She had to sustain a hoax that Jack was a "hell of a swell egg" as well as a good writer, twin delusions still dear to himself but through which she herself may have begun to see. For lately the strain was beginning to tell; she had taken to unburdening herself to Geneva, at whose round front she enviously glanced. All this in turn made Mopworth privy to Dumbrowski's seamy side. Minniehaha still pretended to believe that he had his little amorous indulgences coming to him — might even require them for vigor and verisimilitude in his work — but made no bones about the wear and tear of being his wife. She admitted he was selfish. The discovery that he was an ass remained yet to be made — perhaps never would be made, in keeping with those protections to the ego all women must maintain in marriage. Mopworth was touched by her valor, which in his heart he knew all wives shared, to some degree at least. Most women do their best to help us pass for men in the world, he thought.

The living room into which their host bulldozed them with outspread arms was a cheerfully crackling congestion. Mopworth's eye instantly picked out Tad Springer, who spotted them coming in at the same moment. He smiled uncertainly first, then waved them over to meet his girl.

She was a spruce little redhead named Marjorie Ormsby. The last name rang a bell for Mopworth. It was when memory had supplied the "Dr." before it that he recalled the dentist bill that had come to McGland's motel posthumously. Somewhere in Mopworth's mass of notes was a reminder to pay a call on the sender. Whatever for? To leave no stone unturned. Dr. Ormsby was one of the last persons to see McGland alive, and while the advantage shed little light in Mopworth's case it might be different in Ormsby's. He might offer a clue to the mystery — or he might not. Perhaps nothing would, or there was no mystery. "Play the man, stand up and end you, when your sickness is your soul," was Housman's terse advice, on which McGland may as tersely have acted. Or the motive may have been closer to that fear of death that Byron ironically finds the more common one for suicide — a fear to which the deed certainly brings an end. Or maybe a combination of both. Or something else unsuspected, buried forever with the victim.

No such extremity, at any rate, would beset the dentist's daughter. Her laughter bubbled like a spring, and on her finger sparkled a stone whose significance Tad happily confirmed. Then Geneva did one of those unpremeditated, uncharacteristic things that endeared her to Mopworth. She linked arms with both of them and brought them all three together in an impulsive congratulatory hug. They seemed so propitiously gay together, and Mopworth felt so good for them, and also for Minnie, who beamed on the scene. He was proud of the way Geneva looked. She wore a red wool dress that made no bones about her condition. Pregnancy can be sexually stirring, however disfiguring women may find it. He wanted to thrust his hand down her low neckline as though he had never seen her before. Sensing a vibration at his elbow, he turned and saw Dumbrowski's eyes fixed on the same attraction. They were bright with lust, and there was a loose, lupine expression about the mouth. Dumbrowski jerked his glance away and heartily demanded orders for drinks. Minniehaha bustled off to fill them, leaving him to play host in the more creative sense.

Hearing that Tad had a job in a brokerage office and that the engaged pair planned to live in New York, Dumbrowski launched a ringing eulogy of that metropolis, which met his standards entirely and which he would never live far from. He spoke truculently, as though someone had expressed a contrary preference. He then made a typical gambit. "Speaking of backgrounds," he said, "do you know that I was born and raised on a farm?"

Now, there was nothing Mopworth could more easily believe than that this man had rustic origins. But the information was offered with such implicit faith that his hearers would find it incredible that they automatically protested it as such, with assurances of their surprise at learning that anyone so citified as he had ever tilled the soil, let alone in Kansas, and so on. A murmur to that effect went round the group, to which Mopworth contributed a half-hearted mumble as courtesy required.

"Well, people who haven't lived close to the elements, I mean in some form or other, be it land, sea or the deep woods or what have you, lack something," he said, and whether intentionally or otherwise, his eye rested for an instant on Mopworth.

Mopworth reduced his income to a mere trickle, still coming in from paperback reprints of the good bad books, but the bad good ones he was trying to write while, let's see, where were we, while Nectar brought in a few dollars selling baked goods from door to door, these got progressively worse. Mopworth moved to a chair when the group broke up, and did a little work on the chronicle. He had it that the two wrongdoers sat at their evening meal, and as they shared their humble repast Dumbrowski told her about his day in New York. He had been in to see his lawyers, Slewfox and Basketwhat, about collecting royalties from the Russian editions of his works, which was a laugh because the Russians had only published them to show what a cultural wasteland America was and had no intention of acknowledging the pirated versions, let alone pony over hard rubles for . . .

Mopworth was a little ashamed of himself when he saw the lavish buffet to which they were in due course herded. He ate his lap supper beside Marjorie Ormsby, with whom he then shot three games of pool in the game room downstairs before they relinquished the table to others. Then he found himself upstairs again, alone in his old chair. He sat there a moment taking the party in.

Through an open door he saw one of those gay little groups that for some reason always collect in the kitchen at large parties. At its center was Dumbrowski himself, one arm around Geneva, another around Nectar. One need not peer into windows in order to spy on people. Every moment of our lives is an unguarded one if there is someone watching of whom we are not aware. Then a gesture, a glance or a twist of expression may let slip a secret far more denuding to the spirit than the removal of a garment to the body. Dumbrowski now made one of his habitual motions. It was to raise one shoulder as he spoke, in the kind of semi-shrug by which detachment is affected, or notice given that one does not oneself take too seriously the matter about which one is talking. This was not the plowboy but the Easterner synthetically overlaid on it, through which the plowboy was all too transparently visible. It was a mannerism Dumbrowski had picked up east of Chicago, certainly. Another was that of lightly smoothing down his back hair with a hand in which a cigarette smoked, a gesture possibly acquired from playwrights he had seen dining at the Algonquin.

Mopworth sensed something on his left. Turning his head slightly he saw Minniehaha in a nearby chair, watching the same scene. Her shoulders drooped and the smile she had worn was gone from her face, like a mask dropped. One hand lay palm upward in her lap. She heaved a sigh, such as one might have thought an expression of contentment did one not know otherwise. Poor Minniehaha, sinking under burdens of which that spuriously affectionate nickname was the least. Yet perhaps she was at least momentarily content that the buffet she had fixed had been so heartily devoured and that the party was humming along as it was.

Mopworth returned his gaze to the kitchen, where Geneva had suddenly become the center of attention. She looked oddly unfamiliar, gesturing airily with a highball as she told a story.

"Well, so the minute Alvin got home I hauled them out, you see, both of them, and showed them to him — anxious for the master's opinion, you see." She sipped at her glass while the others waited, a circle of expectant grins. "He looked at them a second, nodded. 'Mm hm,' he said, 'very nice.' Pause. Then he said: 'Which is the main prize and which is the booby?'"

A burst of laughter greeted the finish, causing her to flush with pleasure like a young girl who has just given a fine account of herself in a schoolroom recitation. Dumbrowski laid his head back and guffawed, at the same time giving the girls an extra squeeze. Perhaps he had a third arm lurking somewhere in the melee, for Kitty Sweeney threw him an odd glance. Mopworth turned to see Minnie smiling. Feeling a feverish glow, he rose and went over. "Freshen your drink?" he asked.

Minnie looked down at her glass, seemingly surprised not so much that it was empty as by the fact she was holding one at all. "I guess not now . . . Well, gee." She reconsidered. "Well, all right, maybe I'll have another. It's rye and water."

"Swell."

Mopworth marched through the company toward the kitchen sink, disorganizing its ranks somewhat. All the bottles were on a counter there. He mixed the highball slowly, so as to eavesdrop a moment on Dumbrowski, who was holding forth on anti-American sentiment as he had encountered it abroad. How the subject had so quickly gotten round to that was impossible to say; but it was one of those switches Dumbrowski could manage in a twinkling toward topics on which he was informed.

"The British hate us for obvious reasons. England has sunk to a second-rate power and she can't stand it. Oh, sorry, Alvin. But, you know, I always think of you as an American."

"That's how I think of you, too, Jack."

When Mopworth turned from the tap after drawing water for Minnie's highball, a corner of Dumbrowski's mouth was hooked up into a taut grin, and there was a curl to one nostril. Nectar said quickly, "I hear you made a very mean crack to Geneva about her bridge prizes, Alvin."

"Guilty," Mopworth said. "I don't see how they stand us, Jack."

Now Mopworth did something else foolhardy. He stepped once more into their midst, as one walking deliberately into a thorny hedge, and kissed Geneva on the cheek, pausing to murmur into her ear, "I think you're wonderful." Her eyes shone, and she smelled like a hot flower. She was riding the crest of one of those waves of pure joy in which she was as anxious to please as, in their troughs, she was powerless to do so. She glanced from one to the other of the two men in a mute plea for them to make peace. Mopworth did not stop to note the results in Dumbrowski's case. As he carried the highball to

342

Minnie, still sitting alone in her chair like a neglected guest, he heard Geneva say behind him, "When are you going to read us that chapter of the new book you promised, Jack?"

Mopworth wanted to wring her neck. He would have groaned openly had he not been bearing down on Minniehaha with the highball. Geneva was not engaging in peacemaking, but in capitulation. Indeed, in betrayal. Or had she forgotten that the favor she was asking her host was something her husband found, of all bores on earth, the most galling? At any rate, thanks to her overflowing heart they were in all likelihood about to be subjected to another chapter of the dreaded Work in Progress. The evening began its precipitate descent. Dumbrowski modestly refused, and what with one thing and another the chairs were presently being pushed into a circle and the congregation formed.

Mopworth fortified himself as he had done against Nectar's arrival: by drafting a hasty checklist of the clichés to be expected in order to keep a sort of box score on his predictions. Thus a rapid mental review of Dumbrowski's literary offenses would include those already noted together with comparable effects. There would be the innumerable "You mean — ?s," the junky atmospheric "somewhere," that "part of her" business, plus the host of descriptive stencils like "a thickset man with beetling brows" and "a small birdlike woman." Oh, and that "as if in a dream" locution which appeared on every page, alternating with the likes of "his senses swam in a mist." Such lyric touches were intended to relieve a style obviously regarded as earthy, as typifying the school of brutal realism. Thus the general narrative itself abounded in sentences like "With a bellow of mingled rage and pain Dumbrowski came at him," and "Behind him he could hear Dumbrowski's heavy breathing," and "A savage grin contorted Dumbrowski's simian features." Mopworth always dubbed in the author's name as he rehearsed his literary offenses.

He was now almost eager for the reading to begin so as to get his box score under way. "We're all crazy to listen to you, Jack," he said as he hurried for the best chair in the room. This was one at the very back of the group, behind a split-leaf rhododendron which concealed the paper and pencil in his lap, with which he could make his tallies unobserved. He saw Geneva and Nectar take seats near the front. He was dismayed by one thing. He had the hiccups, as he often did after eating and drinking heavily. A bout of them was usually of short duration, and if this threatened to become a source of embarrassment there was an exit through which he could conveniently slip. As an extra precautionary measure he had ready a wadded handkerchief. Dumbrowski had returned from his study and was frowning into a sheaf of manuscrift through his reading glasses.

Dumbrowski was certainly a big bruiser, Mopworth noted as the former got himself set in the armchair in which he faced the expectant audience. His shoulders were too broad, his arms too long, and his hair needed some judicious cutting, like his books. As he frowned at the pages he chewed on a pipe, about which there was still some doubt whether he would keep it lit or let it go out. He prefaced the reading by telling them something about the theme of the book and giving, also, a synopsis of the action preceding the excerpt chosen. This was a story, he said, about a burned-out boxer who signs up for one last fight in an attempt to get enough money to marry a woman he is in love with, who has three children by a former husband. He is not only badly beaten but critically injured, so that he is rushed to the hospital immediately following the bout.

" 'Stramaglia knew that he lay dying,' " Dumbrowski read, in a voice that was low and modulated, yet vibrant with respect for the material. " 'Part of him wanted to die. Part of him wanted to live — desperately. A grimace of pain contorted his handsomely rough-hewn face, the features of which were touched with something at once brute and tender.' "

The "at once" thing — he had forgotten that one, Mopworth thought as his pencil flew in its tally of the bromides, now falling thick and fast. He made merely a single stroke for each, but even so it was a job keeping up — and then the damned hiccups, which he had thought about to subside, suddenly resumed. A woman in the row ahead of him turned around and glared. Mopworth dropped the pencil for the handkerchief,

344

stuffing it into his mouth like a gag. It muffled the sounds slightly, but that was all.

"'A great weariness assailed him,'" Dumbrowski was continuing. "'Somewhere a car backfired, and then he heard children calling in the street below his window. A cart rattled distantly in the corridor. Then he was dimly aware that the door of his room had opened and someone was sitting in the chair beside his bed. He knew without opening his eyes that it was Constanza. He smiled drowsily and put out his hand.'"

A hush had fallen across the room as, in a pregnant pause of more than usual duration, Dumbrowski took a last suck on his cold pipe and set it aside in order to give full attention to his reading, which was gripping his hearers. One thing he did have, or rather two. He had a resonant voice and a certain knack for giving his own lines the expression exactly suited to them. Mopworth himself had to hand it to him. He admitted to himself that, on television say, the story might be done with a good deal of dramatic tension, hammy of course, but effective nonetheless. He found himself caught up in the emotion generated among the audience, and forgot his pencil and paper. As the reading continued he became genuinely affected.

"'"Constanza, I have a request to make that may seem strange to you," Stramaglia whispered thickly from the pillow, "but would you . . . would you bring me my gloves? I'd like to die with them on."'"

A snicker escaped Mopworth at the same time that a sob caught in his throat. In addition, he still wasn't over the hiccups, so that the resulting eructation, and the moment to which it led, was one of great confusion indeed. Everyone turned to look at him. Dumbrowski himself raised his head, in time to see Mopworth slide down out of sight behind the rhododendron. Dumbrowski resumed reading quickly, in an effort to recover what he could of the spell that he had been weaving. Fortunately, he was near the end of the chapter, or of the section he had chosen to read, for things were never quite the same after that.

Presently he was putting the pages of the manuscript together and then to one side on a table, to a ripple of compliments and handclapping. Mopworth joined in, applauding more vigorously than the rest and mumbling sounds that were unintelligible but vigorously favorable in tone, and which he supplemented by appreciative nods and glances around that nobody saw. By the time his facial play had run out, people were getting up and glaring at him. Dumbrowski rose too, smiling gratefully, and said, "Well so! Thanks for listening, and now on with the dance!" He set briskly to work replenishing drinks.

Mopworth ducked into the kitchen ahead of him and poured a great dollop of whiskey into the first glass he saw and ran out the back door with it. The "breezeway" was a bit of architectural bastardy whose very name he loathed, but he was thankful for the garage to which this one led. He stood in its cool, oil-smelling darkness, just the right compromise between the flushed heat of the congested house and the cold outdoors. He waited there looking through the side window to his own house, where he could see the comfortable figures of Spofford and Rappaport bent over a chessboard. They looked very happy there, under a cloud of tobacco smoke. The two old fellows seemed to have found a lot in common. Mopworth wished he were with them, sipping whiskey and watching the game, with Ravel going softly on the gramophone.

Taking a drink from his glass here he found it to be Scotch, rather than the bourbon he had thought he was pouring. He knew that he had made rather a mess of things. He had got Dumbrowski's goat, but good. Now it was only a question of time till the undercurrent of animosity between them, so long implied or concealed, must break through into open hostility. Yet though he and he alone had mucked matters up tonight, it would only be to Minniehaha that he would ever, ever, ever apologize — and hadn't she been the one to throw him a tiny taut smile of sympathy and understanding at his embarrassment? A smile, even, of sly complicity?

When he girded himself and went back into the house, Dumbrowski initiated his revenge before he could get a word out.

"Well, Alvin, how is *your* book coming? Going to read us a

chapter of it? Turn about's fair play, you know," he boomed jovially above the crowd.

Mopworth knew that to be derisive. Oh, how he knew it! Dumbrowski was quite aware that the book was getting nowhere, and recalling the fact to mind was his way of expressing contempt both for the projected work and for the pretensions to a more "literary" realm than that exemplified by his own popular, never well reviewed novels. He never missed a chance to take a dig at either the book or Mopworth's friend McGland, whose poetry he enjoyed deflating by the simple expedient of taking it down from the shelf and reading it aloud. Behind all this was the natural resentment of the provincial for the intellectual. He got in his most telling thrusts by those references which emphasized best the shakiness of Mopworth's claim to the latter life.

Feeling increasingly isolated by all this, Mopworth circled about, drinking and spoiling for a fight. He avoided Geneva's glances, by midnight more anxious than reproachful. Once, out of the tail of his eye, he saw, or thought he saw, Dumbrowski smiling in his direction as he whispered something to Marjorie Ormsby. What was he telling her? How far out of bounds had whatever rot was going around about him become? "Behind him he could hear Dumbrowski's heavy breathing," he whispered derisively to himself in retaliation. "Somewhere a loon called. You mean —?"

It was toward one o'clock, when the party was boiling noisily toward its climax, that Dumbrowski gave him what he took to be *casus belli*, and on what could not have been more clean-cut grounds.

He found himself standing behind Dumbrowski and a dapper but gloomy-looking man from Greenwich, whose name he hadn't caught. As he paused there, it was borne in on Mopworth that they were discussing Geneva, whom they were watching as she chatted away to several people in the vicinity. Her naked shoulders caught the lamplight, and her bosom heaved with laughter under the deep-cut dress. The two men nodded and smiled appreciatively. Then Dumbrowski said something Mopworth caught only fragmentarily but that, under

347

the din, seemed to have something to do with someone's being "picked up without any trouble."

Mopworth took a long pull on his drink and pushed his way over just as the other man made off. "All right, Dumbrowski," he said, "I heard that."

"Heard what? What? Heard what?"

"What you just said. Shall we step outside?"

Dumbrowski coughed in a rather flustered fashion, and looked down at Mopworth's glass. "Don't you think you've had about enough, old boy?" he asked.

"More than enough. Just slip out through the terrace, shall we? Don't want to create a scene in here, you know."

"I'm sure I don't know what the devil you're talking about."

"I think you know what I'm talking about, Dumbrowski."

Dumbrowski paused and returned the other's narrowed gaze. "You hate my guts, don't you?"

"I would if you had any. You get 'em, I'll hate 'em."

"Why you —" Dumbrowski's fists opened and shut at his sides, and he spoke through clenched teeth. He managed to control himself. "Look, I've got guests to think about, and besides you're too drunk for the code to let a guy haul off on you. But you come back here tomorrow any time you wish, and by God —"

"How's first thing in the morning?"

"That's fine with me."

"I'll be here with bells on," Mopworth said. "That's a promise."

twenty-nine

MOPWORTH AWOKE the next day, Sunday, about eleven o'clock. His head felt like a rock, as though in the intervening hours of sleep all organic matter had been adroitly extracted from his skull and replaced with cement. His mouth had a taste both metallic and ashen. When he moved his eyes, the contents of the room became like the objects in a cinema film being run at slow speed.

This condition cleared after a time, and he began to raise himself, joint by joint, onto his elbows. From below came a steady low murmur of voices, suggesting by their tone something of the snug camaraderie of two women exchanging confidences. They seemed to be in the kitchen. Once he thought he caught the word "him," and another time "basically." He dropped back on the pillow again.

He lapsed into a troubled doze in which he dreamed that he was alone in a telephone booth on a remote stretch of highway, fumbling for a coin to fit one of the three slots on the box. There was the sense of having to be put through to someone whose identity was not clear but over whose whereabouts there hovered the vague need of transatlantic connections. He awoke abruptly, as though by volition and out of the sense of urgent requirement remaining from his dream, and sat up. He reminded himself that the best way out of a hangover was to fight one's way out of it. He climbed slowly out of bed and picked his way to the bathroom, where he put first his hands, then his head, under the cold water tap.

After this calculatedly administered shock he felt better. He combed his wet locks, modifying by a good half the caricature that confronted him in the glass. Sunshine was pouring in the window. Glancing out, he saw the trim figure of Pussy Beauseigneur on one of her walks. In her wake capered a small dog, and judging by the short tweed coat that sufficed her it had not turned bitterly cold. Behind the Beattys' house their Angora cat was rolling on its back on the dead grass. Were the treetops swaying or was he? The confused fragments of last night had by now reassembled themselves into a coherent, though uninviting, whole, and he recalled the key to the episode which had climaxed his own part in it: "Fists at dawn." It was by now, of course, closer to noon.

He dressed before joining the ladies. He found them in the kitchen as expected, smoking cigarettes over dishes littered with the stubs of predecessors. The companionate murmur came to a halt at his approach, and as he entered they turned to take him in.

"Good morning," he said.

"What's morning about it?" Geneva said.

Smiling, the boy fell dead. Smiling, the two women watched him proceed to the electric percolator plugged in at the sideboard. "Anybody want any more?"

"Yes, I'd like some," Nectar said. They were both in dressing gowns, Nectar's a watered blue silk, Geneva's a multicolored Paisley that he had bought her, half-zipped the way he liked to see it in the morning. Any other morning, that is, but this. Now it reminded him of the state of war in which he operated. They had, in view of his drunken incapacity to do so, not discussed the ruckus at the party on their return home last night. He expected to be quizzed about it now, but he had no more stomach than they for the post-mortems.

"What was all that about between you and Jack?" Geneva asked when he had poured coffee for all of them.

"You'd be surprised," he said, glancing down at her open throat. His relish easily converted itself into censure.

"No, I mean go on, what was it all about?"

"Nothing." He took his coffee and a cinnamon bun into the living room, carrying the bun in his mouth, like a dog. He sat there eating and listening to the silence in the kitchen.

"Was it about the accident you had during the reading?" Geneva called. "What was that funny noise you made?"

"It arose out of that," he answered through the wall. "You might say that the mood it created between us was not exactly conducive to, oh, the hell with it. Some other time."

The women set down their cups on well imaginable exchanges of warning signs, and rose and went upstairs to the nursery. It was now from that end of the house that the conspiratorial murmurs floated down to him. He forgot them presently in the need to reappraise his own position and decide on a course of action.

The tangle of considerations in which he was enmeshed was complex. It was ostensibly in the cause of chivalry that he had taken exception to what he had heard — that he had enacted the casual modern-day equivalent of handing someone your card. Yet the woman whose honor he was defending had invited the innuendo which had provoked him, thereby proving herself no less at fault than the offender; he might have made the same or a similar remark himself had it been another man's wife *he* was looking at. He was for all that even madder than he might have been had the issue been clear-cut — pique with the woman who extenuated the offender's offense increasing the steam he could only blow off by punching the offender in the nose. In conclusion, he could not let the woman know it was for her he was behaving like a ruffian. It would be a breach of the very code he was upholding. God!

"Code." Hadn't Dumbrowski used that word? Yes. He had forborne punching Mopworth's nose then and there because Mopworth had been three sheets to the wind and in no condition to defend himself. Therefore honor required that for Dumbrowski's sake also he must proceed under the "Fists at dawn" flag, because Dumbrowski had coming to him the chance to sock Mopworth in the nose, too. The demands of honor had got shifted around.

After a glass of orange juice and two more cups of coffee he buttoned his coat and slipped quietly out the front door. He stood on the step a moment, letting the cool air brace him further. The Dumbrowskis' house looked blank and silent. There was probably no one stirring there, on second thought. He would make it later. He was about to turn around and go back inside when the draperies across the way flew apart and Minnie, also in a dressing gown, sprang into view. She gave a start of surprise at the sight of him, then waved. He crossed the street and went over.

She was holding the door open for him when he arrived.

"Hello, Alvin."

"Good morning, Minnie." He extended the Sunday paper, which he had picked up off the mat. "That was quite a party. I didn't have a chance to thank you properly. I'm afraid I left under . . ."

"That's all right. Come in and have some coffee. You look like the wrath of God."

She closed the door as he walked on into the parlor. The room had all the hideous disorder of the morning after. Heaped ashtrays spilled over onto tables stained with food and drink, dirty napkins lay everywhere. He began to pick a few of them up off the floor.

"I won't have any coffee, Minnie, thanks. I've come on some other matter."

"What?"

"Is Jack up?"

"Not yet." She threw a worried glance up the staircase, then at him. "Who's apologizing to whom this time?"

"Well, we more or less arranged to meet this morning. You'll see. I'll wait for him to come down — say fifteen minutes or so — and while I'm doing it I'll just help you tidy up."

"Oh, never mind all that now. I'll do it later." She stood unhappily in her green wrapper, beneath the hem of which two crimson pajama legs protruded. "You and Jack had words."

"Yes."

"I don't see why anybody goes to these parties. There must be some sacrificial, or ritualistic —" She groped for the right explanatory bit of jargon which she might somewhere in the past have heard or read, and which might shed some light on this particular aspect of the human puzzle, but could not recall it. And just at that moment she was cut off by a sound on the stair.

There was a scuffle of footsteps and Dumbrowski's head, his face mangled with sleep and an icebag on his rumpled red hair, appeared above the newel post on the landing turn. "Whah's sa ma?" he muttered thickly (like one of his own characters).

Mopworth stepped over and presented himself in clear view on the living room floor.

"Hello, Jack. We had a little sort of date for this morning. Remember?"

"Oh, yeah."

"I can come back later, of course, if now isn't convenient. No hurry."

"No, that's all right. Get it over with," Dumbrowski mumbled, and shuffled back upstairs, settling the icebag on his head.

"I'll give you time to freshen up, and one thing and another."

When Dumbrowski had disappeared, Mopworth turned to see Minnie sitting in the chair in which he had noticed her last night, the hand overturned in her lap again, looking as woebegone as ever. "You going to have a fight?"

"That's the general idea, I'm afraid, Minniehaha."

"What about?"

"I'm afraid I can't say. It's between us."

She raised her eyes from the floor. "He used to do a little boxing," she warned him.

"So have I. Still do as a matter of fact."

"I suppose there's nothing I can do to stop it."

"I'm afraid not."

She sighed and rose. "Well, I'm going into the kitchen and have that coffee, if you'll excuse me. You'll find magazines and things there."

"Right."

He sat near the window where the sun was streaming in, paging through a popular women's magazine. Unable to concentrate on any of the articles, he glanced at the photographs and illustrations accompanying them, and at some of the captions and titles. He was aware of rattled kitchenware, and muffled sounds overhead. Once Minnie marched through carrying a steaming cup of coffee and a doughnut on a plate. "He can run a mile without stopping," she said, pausing. "You've seen him trotting by on the road."

"Many, many times indeed."

She continued on up.

For the third time that morning he heard suggestive murmurs in distant rooms. The conversation was low but urgent, rising to a volume that once or twice almost enabled him to make out a word, but not quite. Minnie came down and returned silently to the kitchen.

Ten minutes or so later, Dumbrowski descended in a black turtleneck sweater and denim slacks. Above the trim and pugilistic aspect of his body, however, his face looked as though he had been pulled through a hedge backwards, resembling Mopworth in this respect, of course. Setting the magazine aside,

Mopworth repeated his offer to let this go until some other time.

"No, let's get it over with," Dumbrowski said doggedly.

He led the way through the kitchen, where Minnie did not glance up from her coffee, and around to a spot behind the garage where they were concealed from view. Mopworth took off his coat, under which he had a heavy flannel shirt. They squared away on a width of lawn screened from the house by a clump of birches, from which the ground they stood on fell away to a small pond in which the Dumbrowskis had once kept goldfish.

They circled one another for a minute or two, their guards up, edging about for the advantage. There was no doubt what that consisted in on that steep incline: it consisted in remaining above one's opponent. It was for that reason that the alternating shifts in their arrangement found them presently very nearly among the birches. It was essential that something be done to break the ice.

"This has been brewing for a long time," Mopworth said as they sparred.

"It was bound to come to a head," Dumbrowski agreed. He cocked his forearm — the right — a bit, and Mopworth stiffened his own guard, at the same time thrusting out his chest to give that impression of pectoral strength that is always suggested in photographs of prizefighters. He thought of Stramaglia, the dying protagonist of last night's fictional work.

"We don't cotton to one another, you and I," he said. "And there you have it."

"What's the use pretending otherwise? You don't like my stuff. I know that."

"It's not my dish of tea."

"I hate that expression," Dumbrowski replied with unexpected violence. "So mincing and, oh, I don't know — la-de-da. So —"

"Finicky?" Mopworth suggested, helpfully.

"That's not strong enough. The word I'm looking for —" The intention to heap further obloquy on the other was interrupted when Dumbrowski stumbled on a stone, very nearly losing his balance. He recovered it and said, "Why don't you come right out and say what you think? Not that I don't know what your dish of tea *is*. All that English lot! Bowen and Firbank and what's his name — Compton Burnett." He continued to reel off a string of contemporary British novelists who did, with uncanny accuracy, reflect Mopworth's private reading preferences, though to the best of his knowledge he had never discussed them with Dumbrowski. Having his taste thus impugned made Mopworth bristle, and he nearly said, forgetting the circumstances, "Care to step outside and repeat that?" "Lint pickers! Eyebrow combers!" Dumbrowski exclaimed in a sudden burst of spirit. "All those hemidemisemiquavers!"

Mopworth recognized well enough the rage of the popular hack whom critical approval has bypassed. Dumbrowski *was* one of those authors read by hundreds of thousands, but of whom no one has ever heard. Oh, he knew what was in Dumbrowski's craw all right! But that did not spare him the comparable sting of having his *goût* as a reader under attack. Now he felt the urgent need to strike a blow.

"It's better than burly realism," he retorted hotly. "And all that sex you chaps slather on to prove nothing more than that you've got hair on your prose. And all that 'somewhere' crud, and that 'as if in a dream' routine. Yes, indeed, make mine English!"

That did it. Dumbrowski stood like an animal stunned by a surprise blow. Then, his head lowered, he came at his adversary with a bellow of mingled rage and pain.

"Bellow of mingled rage and pain." Hmm, where had that —?

Mopworth met this first charge by adroitly stepping aside, letting his adversary go by as bullfighters let bulls go by them, in certain passes. The result was that, deprived of his target, Dumbrowski stumbled on in his plunge and really lost his balance, sprawling headlong among the birches. He got to his feet and came for Mopworth again. Mopworth at the same moment lunged forward to meet him, and they came together, their arms flailing. Neither used what boxing skill he had, perhaps because their physical condition dulled the will to fight and left them reluctant for anything but the series of clinches into which their exertions flung them. Presently Mopworth tripped on a stone, stumbling against Dumbrowski, and, interlocked, they danced down the incline toward the goldfish pond. They fetched up short of it only because, at the climax of their career down the grass, they clumsily pulled one another down in a jumble of arms and legs. This had the effect of converting the encounter into a wrestling match, and by an accident of the terrain in Mopworth's favor he landed on top, but so near the water that any attempt to improve their positions might have spelled disaster for both of them. So he sat there on Dumbrowski's chest for a bit.

"This will teach you to speak lightly of a woman's name," Mopworth panted.

" 'Diculous." Dumbrowski brought the word out between gasps of his own. "Never understood this — fussing over a — compliment paid a — woman."

"Compliment?"

Dumbrowski nodded. "Only told Feversham be — sure go talk to *her* if he wanted picking up."

"You mean —?" Mopworth said.

Dumbrowski nodded again. "Feversham was depressed. So I told him to go talk to Geneva. She picks you right up. Has that pizzazz. Always thought so. Great fun. At least appreciate your taste in *that.*"

Mopworth climbed off of him. He turned away and dropped leadenly to the grass, in a sitting position. He knew well enough now what was happening, and he offered no resistance. He was helpless against what was dawning on him. Behind him he could hear Dumbrowski's heavy breathing. Somewhere a car backfired, shattering the Sabbath midday stillness. As if in a dream, he gave his head a shake and said, "It was all a ghastly mistake."

"I'll accept that."

He could hear him getting to his feet now. When Dumbrowski spanked the dirt from his clothes, it was as if the blows stung Mopworth's cheeks. But when he turned to look up over his shoulder, Dumbrowski's face was twisted in a grin of forgiving triumph.

Dumbrowski knew that he had won; in his eyes there was that quiet knowledge. There is no point in my resisting the rest of it either, Mopworth told himself. How part of me hates him while more of me hates myself. How I rise, as if in a trance, to dust off my own clothes. And how, at last now, Dumbrowski, his breathing still stertorous beside me, is steering me up the lawn to the house and even into it, my arm in his viselike grip.

"Wash up in there," Dumbrowski said, not unkindly. "Then come back into the kitchen for some coffee."

Minnie came in, appraising them both apprehensively. "Well?"

"Nothing. Misunderstanding. Apologies all around. Coffee all around. Forget it. We'll never mention the episode again."

They sat hunched up over their cups of strong black coffee, the two men, their arms along the table, facing each other in a new understanding that needed no words. Each treasured within him the satisfaction of having stood up to the other, yet respected the other for having done the same. Somewhere a clock struck — once — and Mopworth told Dumbrowski that he had to go. He rose, shook hands, and took his leave.

As he strode across the road to his own house, he knew a strange peace — the peace of a man who has faced up to what courage and chivalry demanded, and not flinched. He knew it was the same with Dumbrowski. They had passed the acid test. They would never speak of this again, yet they were strangely cleansed. Part of Mopworth regretted the incident — always would — but another, deeper part of him would always prize it for the challenge that had come out of it . . . a challenge met. Somewhere a duck quacked. The air was like wine. It was with a high heart that he opened his own front door — to see the two women sitting on the living room couch together in serious conversation. They looked up expectantly when he entered.

The worst of the battle still lay ahead of him.

thirty

"SOMETIMES I WRITE DRUNK and revise sober, and sometimes I write sober and revise drunk."

Mopworth was hammering out a paragraph recalling things McGland had told reporters. What reporters might ask Mopworth himself and the answers he would give on the publication of *Madder Music* (his new title) were a constant distraction, and he tried to banish them from his mind. He was groping for a unifying thread to the paragraph which the quoted pleasantries themselves lacked, save in the collective uncertainty as to how seriously they could be taken. The drunk-sober system, as McGland's recipe for a balance of the Dionysian and Apollonian ingredients necessary to art, cast grave doubt on itself. And Mopworth could not decide whether it belonged in a chapter on his working habits or his drinking.

As Mopworth copied the statement from the newspaper clipping into the manuscript, he remembered Tad Springer's fiancée and her dentist father. With a growl of self-rebuff he pulled his appointment calendar toward him and on the page for the coming Saturday almost viciously scribbled himself a reminder, "Seen Dr. Ormsby *yet?*"

Doubt as to how he must frame his inquiries made him resist certain interviews. What on earth would he ask Dr. Ormsby? Would he barge in cold and inquire on behalf of posterity what work McGland had had done on his mouth that day, then whether he had "seemed in good spirits," etc.? Here an idea struck Mopworth. It was time for a checkup in his own case. Why not make an appointment for one, then as he sat in the chair bring the subject round casually. Of course. Why hadn't he thought of it before? He looked up Dr. Ormsby's number straight away.

As he picked up the phone and was about to dial, he heard a voice on the extension. Minnie Dumbrowski was saying,

"— thing a complete misunderstanding, you see. Can you guess from that what it was?"

"What do you mean?" Geneva asked.

"What Alvin *thought* Jack had said." Minnie laughed. "It's kind of — well, Jack was saying to —"

"Just a sec, Minnie. Is there someone else on your line?"

Mopworth set the phone down and ran to the window, where he stood gnashing his teeth and swearing. He had thought the party incident — the memory of which made him want to put his head inside the pillowcase at night — closed. Here it was being reopened by one woman in a blithe oblivion of how it might be taken by the other. So little do supposed friends realize what a shambles an innocent remark may make of another's household. Instinct told Mopworth the facts of the case bore the seeds of a sequel brisker than the original episode. With Nectar still in the house his misunderstanding of what Dumbrowski had said to the other guest was certain to be found "significant." Even without her, Geneva by now possessed the necessary sagacity on her own.

The hope that Geneva might be taking the whole thing as amusedly as Minnie made him want to listen; fear that she might not be deterred him; so that he stood immobilized at the window for perhaps ten minutes, staring out. He could see the roof of the Spofford farmhouse, and a corner of the bedroom that had been Geneva's. What had she been like as a small girl? In the distance was a patch of hazy blue that was the Sound, and, nearer by, the crossroads where little Peter Craig had been run over by the Bloodmobile. He was fortunately doing well. The weather had remained clear. The sky hung like a blue bell over the world. Somewhere a — oh, to hell with all that! He turned and, quickly but without making any noise, picked up the phone. Only the dial tone met his ear. He set the phone down and, as quietly, opened the door of his study and thrust his head into the passage. Downstairs could be heard the eternal murmur of sorority. He listened till he heard what he hoped was a low little laugh from the guest. Were they chatting like dormitory roommates again, and was it all going to be all right? He tiptoed into the corridor, past the bedroom doors, and stood at the head of the short flight of stairs leading down into the vestibule.

"He pry wanted to think that was what Jack said, and that's why he misunderstood him. We often hear what we want to hear."

Mopworth turned and instead of going back to his study went into their bedroom, closing the door behind him with a loud bang. He removed his coat and, holding it by the collar, began to flail his unmade bed with it. He had been doing this for a few seconds when he heard footsteps approaching up the stairs. He quickly dropped his coat on a chair and began to make the bed. Geneva entered. She closed the door quietly behind her and stood watching him with folded arms.

"Why are you doing that?"

"Ask her. How should I know? Isn't that what we've got her for, to explain everything to us? Not only what we're doing but why we do it? The sort of things we have in mind?"

"Then it was you on the extension."

"Togetherness."

"And you heard Minnie tell me the whole story. So now we all know. Not just us but the whole neighborhood — what you think of your wife."

"What do I think of her?" he asked, tucking in the foot-end of a sheet with lethal care.

"That she goes around dressed like a hussy."

Undoing his work, yanking the sheet this way and that till it came loose from its corners, he said, "I did not think that. I was defending you against a man who thought so, or I thought thought so."

"It's the same thing. We make slips by hearing things wrong just as much as by saying them, and it's just as significant. So that you let escape your opinion of me, and by so doing humiliate me in public."

"When is Nectar going home?" He was holding the sheet by its end, as though he were going to tear it slowly and methodically into strips, quite calmly.

"She's only been here three days."

"She evidently hasn't heard the Chinese proverb about guests and fish."

"Alvin, you're really impossible."

He dropped the sheet and lay down on the bed after she had walked out again. He could hear her angry stride being modulated for re-entry into the living room downstairs. He put the end of a lighted cigarette into his nose and inhaled it through one nostril, pressing the other shut with his finger. He had practiced this feat off and on, and could now almost perform it without gasping and spluttering. He would soon be able to amuse Mike with it, and perhaps even have it in shape for use in polite society. Remaining on the bed, he picked the sheet up off the floor and began to see how much of it he could stuff into his mouth. He heard the voices growing louder downstairs and presently gayer, as the two turned to other subjects.

Mopworth opened his door after a while and left it open, being able to reach the knob without getting up. They were discussing former schoolmates and what had happened to them so far. Periodically the conversation was interrupted by requests from Nectar as to where she could find cooking ingredients and utensils in the kitchen, in a manner that left no doubt she was fixing dinner for them. They were downing martinis at a great clip. He went back to his study, but couldn't work. He finally took a shower, dressed again and marched downstairs. Nectar was standing in the kitchen "island" with a cooking fork in her hand, describing a movie she had been to with a man with his leg in a cast. They were both laughing loudly. They had forgotten all about him.

Two or three drinks and he had caught up with them. For the chicken cacciatore it developed was under way, he opened a bottle of claret. By the time dinner coffee was reached they were all feeling fairly relaxed and mellow. As he stirred a lump of sugar into his cup, Mopworth decided this was as good a time as any to air the matter on his mind.

"I understand my little set-to of the other night has been processed, labeled and stamped," he said. "May I be permitted to say a few words in my defense?"

"Defense? But who's been attacking you, Alvin?" Nectar cast

a wondering look at Geneva, who returned it with a shrug as she lifted her own cup. Geneva's manner had, in its effect on Mopworth, the same blend of baffled relief as had her gay narration, at the Dumbrowskis', of the bridge prize crisis which had at the time of its occurrence been so harrowing an ordeal. At such moments he felt the whole human scene, particularly its sexual relations, to be a vast mare's nest of which the less sense one tried to make the better. He was determined, however, to plow forward with the subject in hand.

"If a man is accused of harboring views of his wife against which he has actually been defending her, mistakenly or otherwise, then I no longer know the meaning of the term chivalry."

"Alvin." Nectar closed her eyes, which were really rather nice shut, just as her mouth was. "Alvin, I didn't say," she answered in a tone suggesting that under the sealed lids the eyeballs were pry rolling upward into her head, "I didn't say that you harbored the opinion in question, only that believing another man did momentarily satisfied something within you. And I'm not judging you for it."

"No? Well, then it's high time you did. Why aren't you judging all these things? What kind of a world is this where we find all these dreadful things in one another and then don't judge them, don't condemn them? I'm alarmed. I mean I genuinely am."

"But why?"

"Why? Because it shows a grievous lack of standards, that's why. If that's your opinion, then you should have nothing more to do with me. Go whole hog. If these are your estimates of me, I insist on being thought ill of. That's the least I would expect."

"I refuse to condemn you."

"Then I must ask you to leave my house. I hold certain moral standards which I expect to be observed under my roof." Mopworth tried to make all this as jolly as possible. "When man was thought to be a little lower than the angels he was quickly censored for the slightest offense. Now everything about him is regarded as a cesspool but nothing is deplored. There are no standards!" Mopworth flung out both arms and rose.

"Now you're playing the Victorian paterfamilias, pry in order to counterbalance the other."

"What other?"

"That you secretly want your wife to be compromised by loose tongues. Now wait! Every man has this sort of double image of a woman. Part of him wants her profaned, along with the other part of him that's glorifying her. Sex is an emotion that has given rise to both the tenderest love poetry and the lowliest ditties. Part of him —"

" 'Part of him.' God, Nectar, you're beginning to sound like a character in one of Jack Dumbrowski's books."

Here Nectar appealed to Geneva, who was sitting with her chin in her hand, holding her cup by its ear but not lifting it. Her big eyes gazed into the cooling coffee. "You see how you lash out in all directions? Nothing more proves what people say about you — and are sincerely trying to help you with, Alvin — than all this — this hostility you absy throw around in all directions. Why do you think you do?"

"I don't know, but I didn't used to. I didn't in London, or Somerset, or Switzerland. It started here, with people telling me I have this hostility. If you tell a chap he's sick long enough he'll get sick. I think we're all fugitives from mental health. The next time somebody comes to the door collecting for mental health I'm going to ask whether he's for or against."

Nectar had to keep turning in her chair to keep up her end of the conversation, for he had begun to pace now, picking up his feet again like the lad Epaminondas, who had been told by his mother in the old tale, "Be careful how you walk on those eggs, Epaminondas."

"Now you're just being facetious. The proper study of mankind is still man, and when we say you have this hostility toward women, why don't you stop and try to appraise yourself in that light, instead of responding with more hostility that only proves the point? Why can't we be honest with each other?"

Mopworth turned, a gleam in his eye. "Say, I like the plural sound of that. Is turn about fair play? May I take a whack at being honest with you?"

Geneva raised her eyes in alarm, but Nectar laid a restraining hand on her wrist. "Of course, Alvin, go ahead."

They watched him pour three brandies, which he set down on the table. He took a gulp of his, watching Nectar. Geneva shifted carefully on her chair.

"Very well," he said. "I think you're a man-hating, sexually frustrated, potential Lesbian oral cannibal with a slightly sadistic streak — and I'm not criticizing you when I say that."

The silence that followed was one in which his words echoed like the report of a whip that had been cracked in sport but had caught somebody on the cheek. "I hope for your sake you're drunk, Alvin." But Nectar shook her head at Geneva again and said, in a voice lower than her normal tone, "No, no. Think nothing of it. I'm glad it happened. It clears the air between us."

Mopworth, whose face felt like frozen rubber, manipulated his features into an expression appropriate to the gasp which he managed to bring out. "What? You mean you think I meant that?" He looked from the one to the other. "You don't see I'm only trying to show you how ridiculous all this is?"

He remembered, too late, that that made no difference. Even true, it made no difference under the rules by which they now lived, namely that everything was revelatory, jokes and hoaxes most of all. No, you could not beat the rap. The prosecution could rest. All they need do was sit back and watch you dangle from the rope by which you had hanged yourself.

In view of this, Nectar could regard him with satisfaction as she sipped her brandy, saying as she set it down, "We're all trying to help you, Alvin. You know that. But the first step to getting yourself straightened around is recognizing what's awry. I think if there were doubt in your mind that you have antagonism, that outburst should take care of it. But go on and accept that that's part of human nature. Man is a mixture of *opposites*. It's no disgrace to have your share of it. We *all* have a dash in us of what Geneva's doing her best to help you out of, and beautifully. You're making progress. That's the important thing. It's nothing to be ashamed of. It's *all*, after all, *sex*."

"And a man who likes women is already half perverted," he

said, nodding as he foraged for cigarettes. He found a fresh pack in a box on the coffee table. His statement was neither agreed nor disagreed with, and the women rose to clear the table, with great compliments from Geneva on the dinner, which Mopworth seconded. He had turned his thoughts to Dumbrowski. Did he now have another potato to peel with Jack, or should he forget the whole damn business? He was thinking about it when he learned that the Dumbrowskis were going to drop in for a drink after dinner. That had been arranged with Minniehaha in the course of the telephone chat.

Dumbrowski entered carrying two advance copies of his forthcoming book, *The Smell of Jasmine*. One was autographed to the Mopworths, the other to Nectar. He wore this time a red sweater with a shawl collar, in which he stood watching them read their respective inscriptions, with suitable exclamations of pleasure over the book, the jacket, and so on.

"When is it coming out?" Nectar asked.

"Pub date is two months from today," Jack said, accepting a brandy from Alvin. "Ah, the antifreeze. Welcome little potion this night. Thank you, Alvin my boy. Sit you doon." He was very expansive, his voice more resonant than usual, his smile broader, perhaps in the general determination to be big about everything. Not a word of their squabble was mentioned again. They all had brandies or liqueurs in hand now, and Mopworth offered a toast to the success of the book.

"Any offers from Hollywood?"

"A few of the Western carp are nibbling, but no bites as yet." Jack seemed to address his answer to Nectar although it was Mopworth who had asked the question. Nectar, still paging through her copy, said, "Two months. I didn't realize publishers got them out so early."

"Gives them plenty of time for advance promotion. I'm glad I've got a hardboiled merchant for a publisher. Review copies have been out well over a month already. And of course bookstores don't observe pub date. I've seen mine on sale weeks before."

Now, Mopworth knew that reviewers sold copies of books

they didn't want to keep to secondhand dealers, for prices that netted them a tidy little side income. A chap he knew who did short blurb notices for a magazine had told him you could get a third of the list price if you got rid of them fast enough. Mopworth worked out a fine installment of the continuing Dumbrowski chronicle around that gimmick, as Dumbrowski called all narrative pivots. (The failure of Friar Laurence's letters to reach Romeo in time was a gimmick.)

He had it that several critics had already glanced at *The Smell of Jasmine*, and finding it stank had chucked it onto the slag pile, for bundling up and carting off to the used dealers. These are even less conscientious about deadlines than regular bookstores — being, in fact, unaware of their existence. Thus it was that Dumbrowski, browsing along on Sixth Avenue one day, found his book on sale three weeks before pub date in a *secondhand store*. To find one's novel disposed of even before it is out is a nasty shock indeed, and a serious crackup was the result. He took to his bed, never to rise again. Nectar fixed him chicken soup and milk toast, but he seldom touched any food. He never recovered — neither did he die. As an escape from this perpetual burden she had a brief affair with an automobile salesman. Mopworth gave him snaggle teeth and a tendency to hives. He was married too, and they met in dingy bars on side streets (pub dates) and one day . . .

"Alvin? Help Jack with the phonograph, will you? The turntable speed lever is tricky, Jack, and Alvin knows how to set it. We must get it fixed."

Jack had also brought along a recording of a new comedian he wanted everyone to hear. Everyone enjoyed him, but he and Nectar expressed a special appreciation that became a kind of bond between them. After the rest had drifted off into conversation, they sat on the floor in front of the phonograph and played parts of it a second time. Mopworth wound up in a chair about midway between them and the other two women, who chatted on the couch together about the theater. Mopworth had difficulty keeping his eyes off the pair on the floor. They sat with their hands behind them, leaning back braced on their arms, wearing smiles of alert discernment that broke into laughter at the high points, or especially relished parts, of the comedian's monologue. He noted that their hands were a few inches apart on the carpet.

Mopworth jerked his head away and made a resolute effort to screw his attention into Geneva's and Minnie's conversation, which had to do with Not Getting into New York Enough. That one. After a few moments, however, he reached to a low table for his brandy and was powerless to check a glance in the other direction. The two were in the act of exchanging one of their smiling nods of appreciation, which this time, he thought, Jack seemed to prolong and subtly alter into a speculative, or suggestive, gaze at Nectar. Jack then reached for an ashtray, and when he reassumed his former position his hand came to rest a mere inch from Nectar's.

Again Mopworth hauled his eyes away. This is unhealthy, he told himself. You should get out more, mix with other voyeurs. Your peer group, so to speak. Christ! had he drunk too much again? He cleared his throat and called himself to order. He jumped to his feet to light Geneva's cigarette for her, pausing also to set fire to Minnie's when Minnie decided to join her. When he strolled back to his chair, clinking the lighter shut and pocketing it, Jack had curled a little finger around Nectar's. They were laughing heartily at the record just then, as though the development had occurred without their knowledge or sanction. Mopworth sat in his chair brushing and blowing cigarette ashes off his shirt front as though he had caught fire. His eye flicked out of control again to the right. Jack had put his whole hand on top of Nectar's. She overturned hers, still absorbed in the record and reaching for her drink with the other, and took his grasp.

Mopworth thought this a little eerie. Had there been a kind of clairvoyance in those ridiculous "installments" of his? He had an aunt who would have gone farther. She belonged to an occult Eastern sect which held that the realities of life are willed by our thoughts. That would be going too far. Nevertheless, his idle ruminations had been apparently woven out of materials which something within him had detected as compatible, and quite capable of transformation into actual fact.

And here he was being punished by having to watch it all burgeon under his very nose, in his own house. He must have other thoughts, and quickly.

He was relieved, therefore, to note a stir which indicated the pair were breaking up and coming to join the others. His relief was short-lived however. For before they separated, he saw Jack begin a murmured exchange the exact words of which were inaudible but of which the gist could be inferred. Their expressions left no doubt of its nature. He said something in a low voice, Nectar nodded, and they came over, Jack looking like the cat with canary feathers on his whiskers. A rendezvous had been made — or at least some agreement reached for its future contraction.

The Dumbrowskis left about midnight. Mopworth saw them to the door and down the flagstone walk to the road. The night was clear and cold. The stars hung like baubles from an invisible tree. Somewhere a twig snapped. Perhaps the one he had picked up and was mangling in his clenched fists? Yes, it was. He pondered again the mystery of sexual privilege, then and after he had gone to bed, leaving the two women to chat for half an hour as they tidied up. It was all a puzzle. First there had been that snark McGland writing his own ticket in rumpled tweeds and seedy linen, now across the way there was apparently a road-show version of the same thing, while he, Mopworth, a model of grooming, oh, not that he wanted anyone but his wife, but there it was just the same — that curious female fancy for the ogre. He was not interesting, not abrasive, not creative. He lacked color. He was perfect, but that was about all you could say for him.

He wondered how they would be together. Then what Nectar might tell Jack about him, and made a movement as if in physical pain. He pulled the pillow out from under him and put his head inside the pillowcase and moaned into it. He would show them all yet. "I can no longer," he would write to Frieda Meyerhoff in 1810, "without respite bear the strain of composing the libretto for the new operatic score, which I am determined to do in rhymed couplets. When does Hugo go to Dresden? Have me then, make the fountains of my spirit flow again . . ."

This was a mere two years before he was to make his famous 1812 overture to Josephine . . . von — von —

"What are you doing in there?"

"I was just . . ." He emerged and watched Geneva close the bedroom door. He sat up, for a last moment's companionship while she got ready for the night. She disliked coming up and finding him asleep, and having to retire alone. She did not immediately begin to undress, but sat on her bed, facing him.

"Well, that was rather out of left field," she said.

"What?"

"Nectar thinks she'll leave tomorrow. She says she has so many things to do in New York she should stay there a few days before going on home."

"What things?"

"Oh, shopping and one thing and another. She may even look for a job."

"Well, go to bed. Or what I mean is, come to bed. You're round as the world, aren't you, darling?"

thirty-one

"WELL, GUESS WHAT."

Geneva had entered the study after his "Come in," following her knock. He called it out rather gruffly, not because the interruption annoyed him but because of the deference with which she rapped, which seemed to imply that she considered himself a genius who Must Not Be Disturbed — a species of fourflusher with which the local woods were full. Dumbrowski Must Not Be Disturbed. There were others. He was fed up with these self-fanciers who made their wives creep into their studies, leave a sandwich on a tray and creep out again, like servants. It had never occurred to him that his wife might be trying to build him up with this gingerly show of importance around the house. He did try to sift out other elements in it. Was he angry with Geneva, or with Dumbrowski, or with himself? Was it his frustration, turned outward on innocent targets, that *Madder*

369

Music was again bogged down? No, damn it, he would stick by his view that these things could be appraised without recourse to subreasons and byreasons. Another human presence as such does not disturb a man who is *really* concentrating, certainly not that of one's wife. Why, he wrote whole sentences in his head while she talked at dinner, or while he washed the dishes or bathed little Mike. Molnar had written his plays in a public café, while Faulkner had been able to write on horseback. Or was it while leaning against a horse?

Geneva sat on a chair the way she had on the side of her bed a few weeks ago. He divined by her manner some gossip of a special order, like a four-star bulletin. It was that expression of mingled portent and expectancy, the latter being the obvious readiness to relish his own reaction when it came.

"Guess what."

"What?"

He let her take her time, since he had a pretty good idea what it was she was going to spring.

"Nectar and Jack are having an affair."

"What!" He might as well keep his hand in at acting. God knew he might have to fall back on it for a living soon enough. "Geneva, what in heaven's name are you saying? When did you find this out?" The sight of her swollen body made him more than normally intent on pleasing her about this. "Who told you?"

"Alice Carter. She ran into them at the Biltmore having lunch, and their expressions left no doubt. She knows Nectar too, you know, and probably wormed it out of her. Nectar'd naturally be more sort of sticky about telling us because we'd feel, well, rotten about it."

"Only on Minniehaha's account. Poor Minniehaha."

"I might have wondered why she stayed on in New York. She really isn't looking for a job. Haven't you? Wondered about that I mean?"

Mopworth tipped back in his swivel chair and laced his fingers behind his head. "Like to go in and see Nectar? Have a good chin-chin? Maybe you could get her around to coughing up what gives. I mean I think you deserve to know, and you're due for a day in town."

"Could you —?" She cast an all-embracing glance around at the house.

"Of course. I'll hold the fort. Stay the day, for dinner even."

"You're a lamb."

"No, pig, I'm afraid. There'll be the usual fee."

"I don't suppose you can wait till tonight?"

"Tonight too."

"You *are* a pig. Well, all right, come on."

Mopworth enjoyed her days in town almost as much as she did. Long absences are clairvoyant of our final solitude, but short ones have their own felicity, like pauses in music. He was perfectly happy cleaning the house, bathing and feeding Mike, and then doing a bit of carpentry on a kitchen cabinet with drawers that wanted planing. And he was free for a while of *Madder Music,* that dreadful bore whose problems were proliferating in all directions. He must now see McGland's widow, rumored to be in New York working on television scripts.

While Mike napped he worked out for an hour with the barbells and punching bag in the small corner of the basement he had fitted out as a gymnasium. And he developed another episode of the chronicle. He had recovered from the first spooky uneasiness that had cowed him into abandoning it, and instead a growing sense of the evildoers' guilt stung him into fresh ingenuity in working out comeuppances. If he had voodoo powers he ought to use them.

He saw Nectar, then, trundling a wire cart down a supermarket aisle. She had now been married two and a half years, to a sod still nebulous in conception. She pulled one by the hand, had another riding in among the groceries, and was great with a third. She wore a tacky coat with an imitation fur collar, and looked tired. She was worn out with childbearing. Then a social worker came and gave her some plain talk about contraceptives. "We are breeding from the bottom again," the sociologist said, "which is the perennial trouble. The upper classes, the people who *should* mate, don't." She left some leaflets on the subject which she hoped would be read and seriously digested.

In the middle of the afternoon he had an unexpected caller. Minnie Dumbrowski dropped in, and, finding Geneva out, accepted Mopworth's cordial invitation to join him in a cup of tea. He was slightly embarrassed at his appearance, because, deciding to be secure in his masculinity, he had tied on a house apron. They laughed as he took it off and excused himself to go brew the tea. Minnie looked as though she did not want tea, and had in fact imbibed large quantities of what she did want. She drank half the cup of oolong Mopworth fixed, then abruptly asked for a drink. As he handed it to her she broke down. "Jack's got another girl. Some one in New York. I don't know who. Do you?"

She watched him alertly as he answered, "Gee, Minnie, no, I don't. I'm sorry."

"Are you sure?"

"Of course. How should I know? Jack's no — We're not close friends. As you well know."

"Yes. I just thought . . . Well, never mind."

She looked so sad that he wished she would burst into tears and relieve herself. But she didn't. Hers was not the serviceable feminine hysteria that boils over but the simmering misery of the chronically wronged. And as he saw her, sitting there, he thought the real wrong against her was not physical but spiritual. Far worse than Dumbrowski's shabby infidelities was the conviction into which he had bamboozled her, that he had a right to them. Blazing with anger, Mopworth longed to tell her that she was not married to a free spirit requiring elbow room and ever-expanding horizons, but to a cheap two-timer. But he suspected she needed the rationalization as a prop to her own ego.

It took him therefore quite by surprise to hear her bring out rather calmly: "I'm thinking of leaving him."

"I would." The words floated out as easily as her own, over the dark inner reminder to himself to rein himself in, that one did not in this world glibly advise rupture. He shocked himself. Ignoring himself, he went on, "These things are always hard, but what you're putting up with is harder. I quite like you,

Minnie, and it hurts me to see you playing second fiddle to . . ." He did not finish the sentence, letting its unspoken conclusion hang suggestively in the air.

"You can never tell about marriages," Minnie said, getting the subject momentarily off her own by speaking in large generalities. "Some that start off with a bang turn sour in a year. Others with two strikes on them have smooth sailing for life." She was mixing her metaphors rhapsodically. "I envy you yours, despite the bumps and grinds I know you've had, like everybody else." Mopworth had to put his hand to his mouth, in a meaningless pose. The bumps and grinds of life! Good God, there was a solecism worthy of Mrs. Punck. He thought that he would break into an uncontrollable smile even while his heart bled. "And I dare say it's worked out fine for you, helping to solve your problem and all. You've come through wonderfully. Looking at you now nobody'd ever think there had been anything wrong. Everyone is gratified at a cure like that. Everyone instinctively roots for it."

"You can get married again, Minnie," Mopworth said, after a copious pull on his own drink, now no longer tea either. "You're relatively young yet. You can't be over thirty," he said, knowing she was thirty-five. "And maybe you'll have children with someone else," he went brazenly on. He was always surprised at the intimacies that so easily sprouted here. This sort of thing would never be tolerated in the British Isles. "Sometimes sterility — you'll forgive me for bringing up freely a subject you bring up freely yourself, otherwise I wouldn't dream of — but you know as well as I do that sterility is often the man's. No, you're not too old to have children. Not by a long chalk."

"You make me feel better already, Alvin. This was what I needed. We women let our hair down with one another all the time, but I never realized before — it's somehow much better with a man. More . . . Could I have another one of these?"

She had become quite mellow by the time he saw her to the door, about five o'clock. That was ten minutes before Geneva phoned from New York to say that she was still in Nectar's flat — Nectar had a small place on the East Side — and to ask would he mind her staying in to dinner. She and Nectar had loads to talk about. Mopworth told her by all means to stay in, and as late as she wanted. Everything here was fine, and after feeding Mike supper he would forage among the tinned goods for himself. She could not have heard Mike bawling in his playpen above the sound of phonograph music audible to him in Nectar's flat, in volume reminiscent of the Quichimi concoction going in Nectar's house in Gettysburg that time. Geneva sounded a little high, but happy. What was this curious excitement with which the news of a broken home was invariably greeted by that sex whose very overriding emotion was the instinct to build one?

It was midnight when Geneva came in. Mopworth had fallen asleep over a book on the couch, but he heard the car and scrambled to his feet to greet her in the garage. She seemed a little sobered down now, or perhaps her excitement had worn off, or she was tired from the train trip. But she told him what she had learned as they retired.

"It's quite serious. Jack's thinking of leaving Minnie."

"Not if she gets the idea first. She was here this afternoon, and she's about had it."

Geneva turned from the closet where she was hanging up her dress, and looked at him with accusation. "'Minnie was here today? Why didn't you tell me?"

"I just did. Anyhow, she knows all about it — except who the woman is. I didn't tell her that. Though I suppose she'll find out soon enough."

Geneva finished hanging up her dress, then nudged her shoes into the closet with her feet. She pulled her slip over her head and sat down to peel off her stockings. Mopworth dropped to his knee to undo her garter clasps for her and draw the stockings down himself, but she remained cool to this devotional. Her thoughts were elsewhere.

"Minnie was never right for Jack," she said with a rather truculent sigh. "She's sweet but — well, the country cousin type, isn't she? Minnie is basically a small-town girl and will always basically remain a small-town girl."

374

"She's never lived in a small town. She was born in Detroit. She lived there all her life until she moved East."

"Oh, Alvin, I didn't mean that literally. Of course I know she was born and raised in Detroit. I mean she's that *type*."

"Which may make this harder for her to take than a more sophisticated woman. She'll have to find out soon enough who the other woman is, and I don't fancy that. Do you?" He rose and watched her walk, naked, into the bathroom. "Well, maybe she'll forgive us once she's rid of that sod."

"Why do you hate him so? He's not all that bad. Oh, I don't exactly *like* him, but he has his points. Nectar says he's a very ardent lover. Very — physical. You've taken a real scunner to him, I mean out of all proportion is what I'm trying to say."

Mopworth could not let this pass. He must tell Geneva the facts before she developed too misguided a loyalty about this thing. He owed it to her — as well, perhaps, as a measure of rebuke.

"It was under our auspices that this little caper got started, you know. And not in their house, either, in ours. I saw what was probably the first pass he made at her, downstairs the night they came with that record. Under my very eyes, and yours too if you'd had them open. Couldn't you see that canoodle he pulled under the pretext of sitting by the phonograph? Why should you defend anybody who abuses your hospitality like that?"

There was a brief silence. Then Geneva reappeared in the bathroom doorway, toothbrush in hand. Her look was now definitely charged with accusation. "You mean you knew what was going on all this time and didn't tell me?"

Mopworth raised his arms and let them fall at his sides. The mood between them had palpably curdled. Nevertheless he undressed and climbed into her bed.

She gave him a single glance when she saw him there, then went to check Mike in his crib across the hall. When she snapped the lights out and came to bed she backed into it. He settled the covers up around them, drawing his hand under. He ran his fingers gently up and down her spine, then let his hand slide to rest on her thigh. The next move was that carefully calculated, qualified pressure which was made to seem inadvertent but was intended to test the likelihood of her being persuaded round on her back. She stiffened, edging away from him.

"Minnie dropped in and came right out with it? Just like that?"

"I think she wanted my blessing, about leaving Jack I mean. I had that feeling."

Geneva raised her head around. Her back remained firmly turned to him. "*What* did you say? *Leave* him?"

"I gave it to her, of course. My blessing I mean. I told her she deserved a live-in husband, maybe some kids. That'll leave Jack and Nectar free for each other. It's best that way. They were meant for each other." He was powerless to keep from adding, "That way they won't spoil two families."

The prospects for making love, hitherto dim, were now hopeless. Nevertheless he could not resist one more try at drawing her about. She met his movements with a gesture of denial brusquer than any before. "You think a woman is a pancake, or a damned phonograph record, to be turned over when you want, don't you?"

"Oh, I wouldn't say that, ducks. What's the matter?"

"I feel such a fool."

"Why?"

"You knew what was going on all the time and didn't tell me. Men can be such deceivers."

thirty-two

WHEN MIKE'S BROTHER, Amos, was born, Mopworth sent up to Geneva's hospital room an enormous bouquet of carnations with a card on which was written a limerick in honor of the event. He often composed limericks for special occasions, some of them bawdy, but not all. It read:

> *I know it's ungrateful to grouse*
> *With such a remarkable spouse,*

> *But now you've a little*
> *More room in your middle*
> *There's none left at all in the house.*

Soon afterward they moved into a big Victorian place on the other side of town, far from Punch Bowl Hollow. Mopworth now broke down and took on some television acting, as the maniacal rental and other economic pressures compelled. He was promptly typed — the Silly Ass Englishman again — which always assured him a few roles but prevented his getting many. That suited him perfectly. He did not want to be commuting to New York while he wrote in his spare time, he wanted to write while he acted on the side.

This though *Madder Music* was getting to be a joke even to himself. How long had he been at it now? Over three years. However, he plunged back into long-suspended labors on it by abruptly making an appointment to have his teeth cleaned. He had put off calling Dr. Ormsby's office all this time, but now he did it and went, and after the woman assistant had cleaned his teeth and taken the X-rays, he sat back in the chair with a magazine she gave him to wait for the doctor himself to come in and read the negatives. Five minutes later the plates were being held up and squinted at by a cherubic little man whom Mopworth now remembered having seen about town in tweed jackets with his tummy encased in a Tattersall vest. He clattered some tools lightly about in Mopworth's mouth and said, "Only the one weeny cavity. Miss O'Connell will give you an appointment."

"Just a moment." Mopworth climbed out of the chair with the bib still around his neck, to check the doctor's exit. He waited till the nurse had removed it and gone herself. "I'm a friend of Gowan McGland's. In fact I'm writing a book about him. Does the name ring a bell?"

"Of course."

"It seems he was in here the day before he died. You were one of the last people to see him alive. Can you tell me anything about that visit? How did he seem to you? Was there anything . . . ?"

Dr. Ormsby gave him a moment's prolonged regard. Then he took him by the arm and through the door with such haste that Mopworth thought he was being given the bum's rush. Instead he was steered into the consulting room and waved to a leather chair. Dr. Ormsby took the one behind the desk. He said:

"I've thought about McGland a lot and often wished I might have someone to compare notes with. To really talk to about him. But if it's for publication it's no go. I mean I couldn't consent to be quoted."

"Please put your mind at ease about that. I'll be absolutely discreet. Look, let's do this. Let's say you tell me what you can, but I won't say anything you don't want. I'll show you everything for your approval, and I'll never quote you by name without your express permission. How's that?"

"That seems safe enough." Ormsby frowned out the window a few moments, as though collecting his thoughts. "What I had to tell McGland was that he was going to lose all his teeth. Now that's a nasty shock to anybody, but especially to your — oh, I won't use such a silly term as ladies' man, though I gather that's what he was. God knows — Well, let's not get off into that. But what I want to say is, there is a kind of person to whom the very thought of toothlessness is so horrible as to be absolutely unbearable. I've had to break the bad news often enough to know the type. And it's the type — man or woman — who don't act up about it but sit there quietly. They've climbed into that hole and pulled the hole in after them. Despair. I can spot it every time. It's the ego that won't let you see itself naked. I've studied this and read about it. They usually manage to keep the whole thing a secret — that's part of it. I'll bet you never knew McGland suffered the agonies of hell over his teeth. That half his waking thoughts were, How long will this bridge hold out? Did you?"

"I never knew he wore a bridge."

"You see. So closely he guarded his secret. And you can be sure he envied you that smile with the sickness unto death. There's more to this than vanity. Psychiatrists tell us teeth are linked with virility in the masculine mind, that they stand for that in dreams too. The fear of losing them is like the fear of castration. In our journals nowadays we're being gravely warned about pulling little boys' teeth, I mean how we go about it. They seem to equate it with castration. I know there's too many of these words around but sometimes they're valid. This may be one of those times. I say may. The fact that he went home and killed himself after hearing the verdict and the sentence is suggestive, not conclusive. And it may have only been the occasion, or one of a number of causes. The roots of suicide aren't clean-cut like the roots of a tooth, that you can see clearly on an X-ray. No. No, they're deep and tangled, twisted and twined so hopelessly together you can never make head or tail of them."

After this outpouring Dr. Ormsby suddenly stopped and scrutinized the caller again. He seemed to have dropped the subject entirely when he said, "You say your name is Mopworth? That's been ringing a bell too, and now I remember where I heard it mentioned. You know my daughter Marjorie. She married Tad Springer."

"I do indeed. An enchanting girl. She must make you happy."

"Yes. Or unhappy, leaving home. My wife is dead. I live alone." Mopworth was trying to frame some adequate response to this when the doctor cut the need short by instantly resuming the conversation on its preceding track. "Marjorie's young life hasn't been all beer and skittles, as you English say. I guess you're English." Through Mopworth's simpering admission of this the doctor drove on, "When she was fourteen she had a friend, a boy in her class, who went out in the barn and shot himself after — well, could you guess?"

"Of course not."

"After working all evening on a model airplane with his father. He was the most brilliant boy in the class. I said along with everybody else, 'The most brilliant boy in the class, all A's, his future before him,' et cetera, et cetera. Later I learned that's statistically among the most common set of circumstances for a suicide — a brilliant male adolescent, one parent this, the other that, in the spring of the year when a man's fancy and what have you." Here Dr. Ormsby picked up a blotter and tapped the desk with its edge for emphasis. "Do you know what the most frequent cause of death is among adolescent boys? Suicide. Do you know why the rate is less for girls?"

"No, why?" Mopworth's hand, closed round his notebook, itched in his pocket, but he wisely refrained from drawing it out for fear that the sight of it might abruptly stanch this monologue. He had struck oil here, all right, if he worked it properly. This clearly consisted in giving the good doctor his head and then sorting out what was relevant later. "Why is it less among girls?"

"They let off steam. Get it out of their system by throwing hysterical fits, getting up and stalking away from the dinner table. Our tantrums sometimes save us, you know. But boys tend more to keep things bottled up in their system, till *kabloom.*"

The voice of a woman could be heard in the outer reception room complaining about the length of her wait. Apparently missing the timely humor of this, Dr. Ormsby sprang to his tiny feet with a glance at the wall clock. "Well, Mrs. Halsey is grumbling away out there. Besides . . ." Here he turned and paced away from Mopworth, looking at the floor and pulling thoughtfully on his lower lip. "Besides if I chatter away to you much longer I might spill another angle on this that came up in the course of McGland's visit, and that's really none of my business any more than it is yours. It may have no bearing on the case at all, pure speculation, and putting it in a book might be what you British call a bit thick. Well, nice to meet you. Miss O'Connell will fix you up with that appointment on your way out."

Mopworth hesitated for only an instant. He sensed clearly enough the eagerness to talk pulsing behind the prudence that restrained the doctor now, like floodwater threatening a levee. He said: "It might be interesting to continue our conversation over a drink sometime."

"That might be nice. Lunch gets to be rushed around here, but if you're ever free for dinner. As I say, I spend more evenings than I like to dining alone."

"How about Indelicato's tomorrow at eight?"

"That would be fine. I like Italian food."

With a napkin tucked around his rosy chin Dr. Ormsby did his justice to a plate of lasagna and some red wine. After spumoni and coffee he pulled the napkin off and laughingly agreed to a brandy. He was wearing one of his gayer waistcoats, which he loosened with a groan of contentment. Mopworth decided now was the time to make his pitch for the information hitherto held to be top secret.

"What was it you meant when you spoke of something else coming up in the course of McGland's visit? Even if it has no bearing on the subject, one likes to be thorough about his research. I mean just for the sake of checking it off."

Dr. Ormsby's eyes sparkled as he turned to watch two women enter and settle themselves at an adjoining table. He certainly seemed suitably glutted and demoralized to talk, and he did. But he frowned as he prefaced his words with a warning.

"This is strictly confidential, at least as of now, you understand." Mopworth repeated his promise to publish nothing without permission. "All right then," Dr. Ormsby said, wadding in his fingers the wrapper of a cigar he had lighted, and fixing his eyes on that. "It was just that a few days before he came to me, someone had pulled a tooth next to the one I said was a goner, and on which a bridge *might* have been hung for a while at least. There was something odd about the whole thing. I know dentists are notorious for criticizing their predecessors' work, so you can take what I say with a grain of salt, but it seems to me it was pulling *that* one that rendered our lion toothless. I don't see how the other man could not have known that. McGland's story was that the man had realized it was perfectly sound, but pulled it because its position jeopardized the one *I* said had to go. Now, we sometimes give up one tooth to save another, but not a sound one to save one that anybody with a diploma could see was on its last legs. Only the grossest incompetent could make a blunder like that." Dr. Ormsby's manner sharpened after this prolonged recitation of the facts, and he now looked attentively at Mopworth. "Do you by any chance know who his dentist was?"

A thought had struck Mopworth that sent an odd chill up his spine. He said, "No, I don't. If he had any regular one. He was on the move a great deal of course in his last years. I know he was socially acquainted with a man who practices in New York. Lives in Greenwich. He's called Dr. Haxby."

Ormsby waved the suggestion aside. "No, Haxby's one of the most brilliant men in the field. He would never make a boner like that."

The chill went up Mopworth's spine again. It was the turn of his own head in the direction of the two women that touched off the connection in his mind. Instinct was doing his thinking for him, for one of the women looked a little like Lucille Haxby —ash blonde and willowy, just slightly stooped, sadly pretty with narrow gray eyes. Other associations flew into place among the shuttles whirring away in his brain: how one had always heard Haxby referred to as "insanely jealous," how one guessed from bits and pieces put together that McGland's affair with Lucille had flamed up to its full height just before his end — some full-time romanticists even rumoring it to be its cause — and how firmly Lucille had refused to talk.

Mopworth slept very little that night. His mind lashed about in ceaseless speculation. Could the term insanely jealous be taken quite literally? Could such a temperament, inflamed by the humiliation that is really central to jealousy, prompt such a man to take the vengeance open to him when he found his rival at his mercy in that chair? It was hard to believe. Yet why any harder than that your next-door neighbor had shot his rival with a gun, or his wife, or both, as good folk wake up daily to discover? Those clenching fists of Haxby's which Mopworth now remembered, those grinding jaws and cold blue eyes, they might not be capable of sighting down a gun barrel and pulling a trigger, but they might of a subtler, less detectable crime. If you read about such a thing happening in a small town in South America you could believe it. Why not here?

He said nothing to Geneva that night about what he had learned. But about two o'clock the next afternoon, fortified by a few stiff drinks and wondering whether he were going mad himself, he got up enough nerve to telephone Haxby's New York office and ask for someone in charge of appointments. He was turned over to a Miss Woolsey. He asked her whether she could tell him if McGland had received dental attention there at any time during the two-week period which he specified. She said just a moment, she would have to dig out the appointment book in question. He heard a drawer slide open and some pages turned. Then after about five minutes' wait her voice again.

"Yes. One visit, on the sixteenth."

The next question up to Mopworth was crucial. He pondered it pacing the floor of his study with another stiff drink in his hand. Had he the gall to get Haxby on the line and query him personally? Gall or not, he would have to. He plucked the phone from its cradle and this time put in a person-to-person call.

"Oh, Mopworth, yes, of course," came that wiry nasal voice, exaggerated by the electrical connection. "You're doing that book on McGland. How's it coming?"

"Nothing to brag about. But that's what I was calling in reference to. I was just checking a few facts, routine things that have no real bearing on anything, but that the biographer has to take up anyway. People like to read these 'human' touches, you know, like those trivial things Jefferson listed in his ledger and what Disraeli ate for breakfast. You know the sort of thing I mean. I believe McGland went to you and the thing I was wondering whether you'd confirm — Uh, well, this is a bit sticky, so feel free to refuse if you want. But there is this notion that McGland never paid his bills. Was that your experience?"

"Oh, I never charged him for what I did. I was glad to do it. I wouldn't have dreamed of sending him anything for that."

"I see. Well, thank you very much. That answers my question as far as you're concerned." Mopworth calculated his next words to a hair's-breadth. Very casually, as though he were about to ring off and the question were a mere afterthought, he asked, "I don't suppose he had much of anything done? Or do you recall?"

"I pulled a tooth for him. Checked over the rest."

"Oh, yes. Remember what was wrong with it? I know it's the hell of a bore, but it's these little touches — I hope you don't mind?"

"Not at all. It was abscessed."

"Did you try to save it? I mean I have one myself that seems to be tuning up," Mopworth threw in with a laugh, "and I hope I can bank on what I hear, that you chaps can do wonders these days —"

"Oh, yes. I did all I could. Treated it for some time, but it was no use. Too much gum decline there anyway as I remember."

"Several visits I suppose?"

"Yes, or a few. I don't recall exactly. But it was clearly hopeless, so I pulled it."

"I see." Mopworth, who had been standing all this time, and who now felt beads of perspiration beginning to form on his brow, turned to look out the window as he said: "You don't normally pull teeth, do you?"

"What do you mean?"

"Don't dentists of your, well, standing usually turn that over to extractionists?"

"Normally, yes, but once in a while we make an exception. If there's reason to do it right away, or the patient wants it over with. I was perfectly willing to do it."

"Thank you. That's all I need to know. Please give my best to Mrs. Haxby. Goodbye."

Mopworth stood at the window for half an hour or more, feeling as though the top of his head were about to blow off. Haxby had killed McGland. That was the simple sum of matters. The few lies in his account clinched it. The deed may have been aimed only at maiming the lion, but it had led to his end, and in any case had been done with murder in the doer's heart, so he was guilty of murder, if not in the first degree then in the second or third, or of manslaughter; or if of nothing legally definable as such then of its moral equivalent. The fact remained: Haxby was a killer. There he was in his New York office with his fancy practice and his national reputation, filling cavities and fitting inlays with a hand as red as Macbeth's.

These thoughts brought in their train one scarcely less appalling. Now that he, Mopworth, had the solution to the

384

mystery of McGland, what could he do with it? Nothing. He could not so much as hint at it in the book without all hell breaking loose around his head. The first thing a publisher would do with a charge or an insinuation so sensational would be to check the facts, and their trail would lead first of all straight to Dr. Ormsby, whose confidence had been solemnly guaranteed, then on to Haxby, who would sue to a fare-thee-well. The discrepancy about the number of visits could be taken care of by destroying the back appointment calendar, leaving only Mopworth's word about the telephone conversation, which was next to worthless. The girl who had found a record of only the one visit would probably not recall the conversation clearly enough for her testimony to cut any ice. For the rest there was not a shred of evidence — the urnful of ashes reposing in the little Scottish village "between the snarling river and the mumbling sea," all that remained of McGland, would tell no tales. The end result would be a whopping libel suit, even if Mopworth used fictitious names to protect the guilty.

Having pursued these facts to their grim conclusion, Mopworth went downstairs to tell his wife. He found her ironing in the basement.

"My God," she said, "are you sure?"

She set the iron on its metal trivet and pulled the plug out. They went upstairs and had a drink while Mopworth paced the living room floor. He took Amos for a ride over his shoulder, so it shouldn't be a total loss.

"I can't believe it any more than you can, but there it is. I thought I was at work on a biography, but it turns out to be a murder mystery. Which now I can't write. I've uncovered the perfect crime." He stopped to evaluate a light in Geneva's eye which he thought he recognized. "Now look," he said sharply. "You're not to breathe a word of this to a soul. *Not to a soul.*"

"Oh, I won't. But why . . . ?"

"Because we can't talk about it any more than I can write about it, that's why. Now, Geneva, don't make me regret I let you in on this. Gossip would be worse than a book, because in that case *I'd* be sued rather than the publisher."

"Well, you're not in England now, you know, where I

understand people sue at the drop of a hat. Oh, don't worry. I'll not talk." Her expression turned from sobriety to alarm. "What did you mean you can't write it now?"

"Because that's the heart of it, and not to be able to write it would break my heart." He gave her Amos and flung himself into a chair, wondering if his dramatics weren't a bit excessive; partly the overflow of an inner relief at being free of a long oppressive burden, one whose size — or rather the degree to which he'd fallen short of it — had been long demoralizing. Equally demoralizing was the look that came into Geneva's eyes, with its hint that she was reading his mind.

"Alvin, you aren't rationalizing a secret wish to drop it?"

"Really!" he said, twice as vexed by this as he would have been had there been no foundation for it. He flung his legs out farther and rolled his head about. "That's the hell of a thing to chuck at a chap at a time like this. Just when the bottom falls out of everything, I mean then to insinuate that a bloke wants the excuse to bail out. Shouldn't he get a little more understanding from his wife than that?"

"I suppose." She sighed humorously at him across Amos's back and said, "Men want their wives to be understanding. That's not the same as being understood, is it? In fact if you understand a person is when it sometimes gets hard to be understanding."

"That's fine, keep spinning fine distinctions. Keep flinging nuances at a chap as he disappears into the Pit."

"I'm sorry." Across Amos's back she continued to regard him, if not more sympathetically, at least with increasing alarm. But he had to twitch about and bring a fist into a palm to keep it that way. Why? Why in God's name had he to behave like a man in a crisis when a crisis was what he was in? Why did you have to *act out* what you were going through, in order to be believed?

Marriage is corrupting. It is based on the most ticklishly maintained emotional advantages themselves dependent on the eternal practice of diplomacy, which is more than half chicanery. Anyhow, here he was having to fake the truth. He had to chew the scenery, as it were, to get a rise out of his wife. Presently his resentment at having to twitch about had him twitching about quite naturally. In part, he felt his over-all resentment justified by the fact that he didn't really know himself whether he wanted to drop *Madder Music*, or how badly. And if he didn't know, how could Geneva? The thing needed a Nectar Schmidt. She could have pointed out that he had pry bitten off more than he could, with professional ease, chew. That much had to be admitted. It did not mean that he would have chickened out had this upheaval not occurred, or that he was using it as a ruse for doing so.

The paralysis into which Mopworth was thrown by the development continued for weeks. Never had he known such a profound and immobilizing funk.

He paced the floor of his study, chewing on a succession of pipes, of which he had accumulated quite a rack in the process of trying to effect a transition in his smoking habit from cigarettes, pausing briefly to fling a dart at a board he had nailed up on one wall, or to scratch off a few lines of light verse that came to nothing. There were times he wished he drank on something more than the modest scale he did. Good binges must at least have the merit of temporarily ventilating those prone to them, of, so to speak, emotionally worming you. His mood spread through the house, infecting Geneva, whose temper shortened until there was very little left of that indeed. She finally burst out with the suggestion that he go rent a study outside somewhere if that was the way he was going to act — a proposal at which he gave an odd laugh in view of the trouble they had meeting expenses as it was. When they were put to it to scrape together the rent money the first of the month, she sometimes wondered if they oughtn't buy. It was in the midst of this trying period that they received an unexpected telephone call from Minnie, who had fresh domestic developments of her own to report.

The Dumbrowskis had been divorced and Jack had promptly married Nectar Schmidt. No more promptly, however, than Minnie had a widower from her home town, into whom she had run in New York one day when he happened to be there for a business convention. No greater change from Jack could have been imagined, or wished, for her (the Mopworths had indirectly heard) than this hardware salesman, kind as a woodcutter in a fairy tale and utterly devoted to Minnie, whom he had borne in triumph back to their native Detroit. Now the two were in New York again for a few days, this time for a lodge convention. She was dying to bring him out to Woodsmoke for a visit. The women arranged one for the next afternoon.

The transformation in Minnie took the Mopworths so unawares that they had to get acquainted with her all over again before they could possibly begin to absorb her husband. She was twenty pounds heavier, her voice an octave higher, and her hair a bright yellow. An armful of bracelets tinkled merrily as she gestured away, smoking cigarettes in a holder and picking bits of lint from her husband's coatsleeve. Some finally released individuality, or independence, some long-suppressed feminine essence seemed literally to squirt from her in every direction, like juice from a bitten apple. The same gossip that had once consisted in bills of particulars about Jack was now devoted to praise of Harry, and the intimacy of her revelations made the Mopworths quail.

"He's given me a sex life of my *own* for a change," she said, clattering back on high heels from the kitchen, where she had gone herself to add a little more water to her highball. "He's the first man I've ever had a you-know-what with. I don't care who knows." Mopworth thought she was having a nervous breakdown, or had gone off her chump, but it was only sudden happiness. Still it was a lowering business. He himself laughed nervously from time to time even while appalled. "A man should know how to play *tunes* on a woman. Draw melodies from her, like a musician playing a harp. That's a good lover, giving not just taking. Oh, he's one in a million."

The object of this eulogy sat with his big pink head on the back of the couch on which he comfortably slumped, smiling sleepily, his eyes closed, as though life were not a rat race at all but some wearing jollification from which he was snatching a few minutes' respite preparatory to its resumption, of which he also lazily dreamed. A large convention badge, evidently affixed to his lapel for the duration of the sessions, had his name,

Harry Plewes, on a card attached to it. The badge itself was a white button decorated with the mystic sign of his fraternity, from which hung a blue silk ribbon, as though he had just won first prize in a hog contest and were resting from the strain of being exhibited. He and Minnie kept nudging one another at things that were said, as though everything were related to some complex network of private jokes between them. A reference Mopworth made to the town's recent purchase of the local country club, aimed at changing the subject from that of Plewes's virtues as a husband, brought a skirmish of elbows and an exchange of smiles between them, perhaps pertaining to some jointly relished goings-on at their own country club back home. "I used to tell Effie Sticky —" Plewes began, and choked half to death with laughter as a shove from Minnie cut the allusion short, as perhaps too ribald even for this conversation. Some minutes later, when the talk had again briefly undergone a change of theme, Plewes said suddenly into a pause, "Effie won't be free on Saturday, but she'll be reasonable," and opened his eyes long enough to wink at Mopworth.

Mopworth got up and ran into the kitchen, remaining there for some time. He fixed a mess of crackers and cheese while he tried to sort out his impressions, which had been coming too fast and too vividly for ready absorption. What it came down to was staying there alone for a bit to think about Plewes. He thought Plewes might be brought into focus better without the physical distraction of his actual presence. Perhaps brought into focus as a type? He saw that the hog comparison would not do. Plewes was himself more like a great piece of human fruit about to burst with good will, or a bomb about to explode with it, leaving everything within a certain radius a shambles. Mopworth had never before met anyone who was all heart, though he knew such people existed. Heart burst from Plewes's shirt collar, from his vest buttons and even from the seat of his trousers. As Mopworth was running through this course of thought, the kitchen door swung open and Plewes himself sailed in. Highball in hand, he came smiling to Mopworth's side and laid an arm on his shoulder. He stood there watching him spread cheese on crackers, so that they resembled a pair of conventioneers in a hotel room, out for a good time and a few laughs.

"Ever hear the one about the bwah hee her and the hee haw bwah?" he seemed to say, giving off an alarming vibration. Mopworth shook with laughter, but it was not his own. It was Plewes's laughter, for Plewes had him firmly in his clutch. Mopworth was himself solemn as a judge. "No, I don't believe I have." The fear struck Mopworth like an icy current that the other might have no intention of catching the early evening train back as originally planned at all, but would stay the night. What if Plewes wanted to get drunk, expanding his present sociability in proportion? They would have stewed heart for dinner and grilled heart for breakfast if their guests ever took such a thing into their heads.

"There was this egg salesman . . ."

Mopworth stopped what he was doing and, remaining bent over, the knife with which he was spreading a cracker frozen in its position, looked in desperation to the side of him away from Plewes. He fixed his eye on something bright lying on a chair. There was no rescue there, however. It was a phonograph record on the envelope of which was a picture of Fritz Reiner, the conductor, sitting inexplicably alone with his baton in a field of knee-high grass.

Midway the story, Minnie clattered in to remind Plewes that they had a banquet to get back to and that they would have to dash for the train as it was. In his ecstatic relief Mopworth flung an arm around Plewes and implored him to stay, but they could not, they had to make this train. He sustained this spasm of camaraderie as he raced them to the station in the Volkswagen, shouting into the back seat where Plewes sat his hope that they would call again next time they came East.

Minnie wondered aloud whether they should look up Jack and Nectar while they were in New York, to show there were no hard feelings, and to trot out Plewes. Mopworth now became hysterical. The idea of such a confrontation was so exhilarating that he spent the rest of the trip doing all he could to insure it. "They're in the Village, now if you can't find them in the book you phone Geneva for their number and address, do you hear? Oh, that's a wonderful idea! You must by all means do it."

The train was standing in the station when he shot to a stop and rushed round to help pull Plewes out of the back seat, into which he had with difficulty been wedged. By the time he had bundled them onto the platform the train was starting up. Plewes pushed Minnie onto the last coach but one, still trying through clouds of steam to get in what he had "told Effie Sticky." Mopworth did not hear. He was too busy pushing Plewes on in turn, like a furniture mover shoving a piano up a flight of stairs single-handed. Minnie stood in the coach vestibule calling down some last-minute remark Mopworth couldn't make out. He responded by shouting, "They live on Bleecker Street, that's it!" He galloped alongside for nearly the length of the platform. "Don't you forget to go look them up now!"

Driving back, his breathing gradually subsiding to normal and his composure returning, Mopworth tried to reconstruct from memory the events he had just been through, and could not. He felt that he had never been through anything quite like it, in the sense of its being simultaneously shattering and bracing. The change in Minnie could be simply enough explained by the principle of reaction, which understandably enough drives divorced parties toward mates as unlike their predecessors as possible, and changes them commensurately in the process, but Plewes! It was amazing how a man could be both a grotesque and a type. He couldn't wait to get home and compare notes with Geneva.

When he walked into the house, however, he saw that the prospects for any such cheerful exchange of impressions were not good. His heart fell at the sight of her sitting by the window, drink in hand, wearing that brooding, excluding expression he had come to know and fear, a sign that something unhappy and turbid had unexpectedly been stirred up from the depths of her spirit. The obvious comments on what they had just seen were passed, while he waited for her to reveal what was on her mind.

"Maybe we ought to move to the city," she said, at last.

"Why? So we can come out to the suburbs and see people like us?" He smiled at Amos, whom he had scooped from his pen and now held by his chubby trunk in midair till he had provoked a wet grin.

"They have fun."

"They seemed to have it popping out here to the country. And they must live in the suburbs themselves if they belong to a country club. I finally figured out that what he probably told Effie Sticky —"

"Why do you always change the subject when I bring up things like this? I'm sure it's a husband's cross to have to hear his wife dish up her gripes, but what have I got out here? Just stop and think about it a minute, Alvin. What, really? Except a house and family."

"It's all I've got."

"You have your work." Mopworth let this go, aside from a glance he exchanged with himself in a wall glass in passing. "You see, that's all the difference. And when a woman — anyhow an educated woman of today — doesn't have that, or some equivalent *outlet*, or life *like* it with which to *be* somebody, she doesn't have enough. I mean *fatally* not enough. There isn't even any social life worth the name. Tad and Marjorie, yes, but that's only partial. She and I aren't friends, we're not wired for each other. I can't sit with her over drinks or lunch and feel that kindred spirit thing that's so desperately important *with someone*. And with Nectar gone, I mean in the sense of being out of one another's life, and now even Minnie, who do I have? Nobody. It's one of those inventory times when a woman wants to cut her throat."

"Well, let's move to the city," he said, depositing Amos back in the pen. "By all means. We've got two kids, just what drives people out of New York *to* the suburbs, but what the hell. I mean I don't want you to be unhappy."

"Well, I am," she said, walking to the bar to refill her glass. "If there's anything you can know with certainty, you can know that. Oh, Christ! And all I can think of is those lines from the poets like 'Men must work and women must weep.' And then you do want to cut your throat."

Mopworth had found it not in the nature of marriage for the one to be able to cheer the other when it was needed. High spirits are not infectious, only low. She would make him miserable, he could not make her happy. Married life is always lived on the lower of two emotional levels, as it is on the lesser of two intellectual ones. There was only one small consolation open to him when she lay resolutely with her back turned, as he had known she would when he slipped into her bed to offer what balm he could. He could then put an arm around her and fall asleep, as he liked, with a breast in his hand.

But he could not sleep, and about one o'clock he extricated himself carefully from the bed, slipped on a robe and went down to the kitchen, where he fixed himself a grilled cheese sandwich by warming it between two flatirons, as Geneva had once hilariously told him she and Nectar had used to do when they were roommates back at school.

thirty-three

WHEN AMOS WAS two years old and Mike three and a half, the Mopworths made plans for a long week end in New York in which a holiday in town would be combined with apartment hunting. Since they had no live-in help it involved moving sitters in bag and baggage for the four days in question — specifically the Rappaports, who would not hear of their hiring outsiders for a job they were only too glad to take on themselves. They briskly and even resentfully spurned all payment, other than such presents as the Mopworths brought back from town, usually a bottle of vintage Burgundy for Dr. Rappaport, a cardigan or a scarf for Mrs. Punck. "We know what a struggle it is for young people, financially speaking-wise," said Mrs. Punck, who was making great strides with her own English.

There was a great two-way banging of luggage as the elders came in and the Mopworths went out, toward the waiting flivver in which Spofford had just delivered Mrs. Punck (as one involuntarily went on thinking of her despite all mental reminders that it was no longer her name) and would now drive the Mopworths to the station. Rappaport had gone on a house call ideally convenient for a return on foot through the intervening woodlot where he loved to ramble, having discovered a family of pheasants and other naturalistic delights in it, but he had faithfully promised to be on hand for the Mopworths' departure. There was still a quarter-hour's time, so they all sat down in the kitchen for a cup of mid-morning coffee. Mrs. Punck kept scanning the woods through the window, clucking impatiently when it yielded no sight of Emil.

"Maybe he thinks punctuality is the thief of time," said Spofford, playfully undoing the bow of her apron.

"I would take exception to half the remarks you make, Frank Spofford, if I didn't consider the source."

"In this case it's Oscar Wilde. He said punctuality is the thief of time."

"Well, he's got it wrong. It's procrastination." Mrs. Punck turned from the window, repulsing with a slap Spofford's attempt to retie the bow and doing so herself. "If you're going to hang around here make yourself useful. Go check the boys in the back yard. You know," she said to Geneva, who sat on the edge of her chair, looking, as she sipped her coffee in a blue tweed suit, like a guest in the house rather than its mistress, "Amos is accident-prone."

These new clichés which she picked up from everyone now, including the young housewife to whom she was giving them back, sounded, on Mrs. Punck's lips, centuries old, a part of immemorial folk wisdom. She spoke of people's being accident-prone or having a basic insecurity as she once had (and still did) of their being their own worst enemy and generous to a fault. She was, of course, slowly but steadily absorbing a good deal of the more modern vocabulary from Rappaport, adopting from his example many words and phrases she had resisted in Spofford, whose rise was still remembered as too meteoric, and much of whose "crazy talk" she still deplored. "She's got a thing about me," Spofford would say, managing to combine in this way a kind of knowledgeable amusement with Mrs. Punck and an indication of offhand intimacy with her; even hinting at a sort of Design for Living relationship between her and him and Rappaport. To which there was, within the limits of sociability, a peculiar validity. For he was always on hand at the Rappaports', playing chess with Emil while Mrs. Punck spent the evening sewing or going over the minutes or the ledgers of the amazing number of organizations of which she was secretary or treasurer.

All this went through Mopworth's mind as he watched them with one eye on the clock, and listened to their chatter and their ribbing. There would be three people holding the fort while they were gone, not two, for it was a certainty that Spofford would be hanging about most of the time in their absence. Spofford no longer hired out as a gardener except for the two families he continued to give a day a week, the Beauseigneurs and the Wilcoxes, so the hours often hung heavy on his hands. As, indeed, they did on Rappaport's — now to be seen emerging from the woodlot judging from Mrs. Punck's exclamation at the window. It interrupted an account of the fresh crisis into which the Society of Christians and Jews had been plunged by the departure of the chapter's president. Mrs. Punck herself was its treasurer.

"Why don't you put me up?" Spofford said. He gulped down the last of his coffee with loud noises and a great bobbing of his Adam's apple. "I'd make a good president. I'm completely without prejudice, for one thing."

"Are you, Grandpa?" said Geneva, who could remember when he pronounced the word "pre-judas." She was twitting him as a last-minute way of making Mrs. Punck (on whom most of the care of the house would devolve) feel good. "Can you honestly say you're without prejudice?"

"Of course. I hate everybody regardless of race, creed or color."

"You think he's kidding?" said Mrs. Punck. "George Lowry

says there's a theory you were baptized with lemon juice, Frank."

"He should talk, after that speech he gave at the town meeting against frills on the school budget. He thinks the scholars should have hardtack and water for lunch."

"I agree with you there, not that it affects his opinion of you. It takes a thief to catch a thief."

"To catch a what? I don't believe I quite —"

"You know George Lowry's daughter, don't you, Geneva and Alvin?" said Mrs. Punck, ignoring this. "Polly Wood? Isn't she in the social swim here now?"

"She tries to be, Grandma, too hard I guess is the trouble. She's really rather sad," Geneva answered, in a tone corresponding to this truth, and consulting Mopworth with a glance. "She sort of puts driftwood all around the house and gives parties with themes?"

"She's trying to live down her old man, who's about your father's age, honey, or a little older," said Spofford. "He's an authentic oddball, actually. He begins with the crust when he eats a piece of pie. I've seen him at the diner. And smells everything before he eats it. Mrs. Lowry says he smells everything he wears too. Fact. He'll smell a shirt before he puts it on."

"He has to be the dominant one," said Mrs. Punck.

"Course his brother Andrew is worse. He's one for the book. He walks in and out of the supermarkets with his hands up, to declare that the storekeepers are all robbers."

"How can he walk out of them that way if he buys anything?" Mopworth asked. "How can he hold the bundles?"

"He's crazy. It wouldn't be exaggerating to go that far, would you say, Mrs. Punck? I mean here — he spends part of every day in a Barcalounger with his legs up in the air, just like a business executive, only not to save his heart. No. It's to keep the sediment out of his feet. He thinks we have sediment in our blood, just like wine in a bottle, and it will settle down in our feet if we let it. I've heard the story, though it's probably apocalyptic, that he walks around the house on his hands and knees because in evolution our whole bag of insides were developed to hang down from our back, and that the sudden upright position raised hell with all our organs and makes them sag and get dislocated and one thing and another, especially in women. Fact is I've heard that theory expressed by scientific men, not just crackpots, and they advise the quadruped position for as much a period every day as you can get in. Well, anyhow, there's Andrew Lowry, climbing up and down the stairs on all fours, like a dog."

"The town's changing," said Mrs. Punck. She put her cup down and turned. "Well, Emil, at last?"

Rappaport called "Hello, all!" from the door, which he was hardly more than inside of than he was borne back out of it on a general tide of exits — for it was time to go.

The Mopworths thought better of saying goodbye to the two boys, who were playing contentedly under an apple tree, for fear of provoking protests and even possibly tears. The house itself screened their actual departure in the flivver. The Rappaports stood in the dooryard waving goodbye, the one in summer serge, the other in an apron, recalling a specific Currier and Ives print, though of course the young people were speeding away from the old homestead rather than toward it.

The instant the bellboy was out of their hotel room with his fat tip, Mopworth rang room service for drinks. Geneva kicked her shoes off and sat back on the bed to watch the television. She laughed in response to Mopworth's look of humorous inquiry and said, "Just because it's here I guess. Or because we are. I'm so excited I don't know where to begin. That the way you feel?"

"I sure do. We had cabin fever. Bad thing for couples, make no mistake about that. Get away together more and people won't be getting away from one another so much." He set briskly to work unpacking.

She turned the set off when their drinks arrived, and after the first relishing gulp of her Old-Fashioned she settled herself on the bed again and said, "I think I'll phone Nectar now and let her know we're here."

It was just like home.

Mopworth listened as he drew forth dresses and trousers and

hung them in the closet, reconstructing the conversation from the half of it audible to him as a monologue. Dumbrowski was apparently about to fly West to work on the script for a movie being made of *The Smell of Jasmine,* so if they all wanted to dine together it must be tonight. Mopworth's spirits soared: they would see them only once, then, and have that part over with in a matter of hours. In his elation he flourished aloft a silk undergarment of Geneva's which he held to his cheek like a degenerate. He gave his "moronic whinny" as he nuzzled it. In explanation of her laugh she said, "Alvin's horsing around. I guess we've both been stir crazy and didn't know it." He savored the soft texture of the material lasciviously against the skin of his hands, while she asked Nectar to repeat what she had just answered. Mopworth gave off his antics and returned to the work of unpacking. Geneva wound up the conversation after arranging that Nectar and Jack would pick them up at the hotel at seven.

"Nectar agrees with what I just said. She says cabin fever is one of the worst things in a marriage, she knows that by now. They're both glad Jack's flying West. People have to get away from one another once in a while."

"I can understand how she feels." The principle made little sense personally to Mopworth, who had been trying unsuccessfully to court his wife for weeks at home, but who could see that in the release and stimulation of a hotel room the situation would change overnight, so to speak, from what it was there. Getting away together *was* a form of getting away from one another.

So far from having come down in the world, as Mopworth had envisioned in the chronicle, the Dumbrowskis had distinctly risen in it. Neither made any secret of the sum *Jasmine* had fetched in Hollywood, or the fee Jack was getting for his work on the script. He promptly took the evening into his own hands, overriding Mopworth's proposal of Lüchow's by herding them into a cab and directing the driver to a little Italian restaurant in the Fifties he knew they would like. In the creeping taxi, Mopworth began some deft probing aimed at determining whether the Pleweses had ever descended on the Dumbrowskis, learning to his disappointment that they had not.

Mopworth was quite resigned to Jack's tyranny once he had tasted the food to which it led. They all acceded to his suggestion of shrimps Arnaud, spaghetti with clam sauce and veal scaloppine. He affected a worldly, even bored, air, through which could nevertheless be discerned the pleasure he took in the ice he cut here at Luigi's. At the same time his speech was studded with contractions like "Could be" and "Will try," which are associated with a far less urbane world than that of which he imagined himself a part, namely the world of business and promotion. He warned them early on that he would have to leave at ten o'clock to see his agent (from whom he may have acquired the habit of sentences devoid of subjects and predicates) for some last-minute briefing about the Hollywood deal. He would do his best to rejoin them later in hopes they could all "tuck in a brandy somewhere."

It was then that Mopworth suddenly remembered something his own agent, Schlumber, had urgently advised, about a possible part for him in a new television serial for which the cast auditions were to start in the morning. Something — perhaps Dumbrowski's contention just then with a single strand of spaghetti — had recalled Schlumber's, "The early bird will get this worm, baby, and it's fat. The serial's a combination of droaring room comedy and cozy family stuff that'll get a sponsor in a month and run for a decade. Some new writer I never heard of. The show's got a Silly Ass Englishman who's a shoo-in for you, so you be there at ten A.M. sharp, Studio G at N.B.C."

As the evening wore on, Mopworth found himself looking forward to the audition.

When he walked into Studio G behind Schlumber, next morning, he saw at first nothing but the mess of boxes, wires and floodlights that give such rooms the look of ill-run warehouses. Then he spotted in a corner the producer of the script, for whom he had worked, sitting in a huddle with a woman who was unmistakably its author. There hovered about her a vague air of familiarity: something about the way she scribbled in her copy on a crossed leg, the tweed coat caught up loosely about her shoulders, the hair like winter sunlight which lay across her cheek. When she tossed up her head to fling the hair out of her eye, Mopworth recognized McGland's widow.

"Edith!"

"Alvin!" She rose to wring his hand, dropping the script on her chair.

Schlumber stood beaming at the scene. "You two know each other?"

Mopworth introduced Edith Chipps — the name under which she had continued to write — explaining that they had worked together on the London B.B.C. When he noticed the producer turning to greet some new arrivals, Schlumber ducked to permit the old friends a word of reunion. It was rather strained.

They sat on folding chairs, not quite facing one another. Edith kept nervously drawing her slipping coat onto her shoulders, and accepted a cigarette from Mopworth, and then his light, with a flustered air.

"Let's get the embarrassment over with, shall we?" he said. "Why didn't you answer my letters? I must have written half a dozen."

"Oh, I've meant to, Alvin. But I've been all over the world, you know — Sydney, Rome, Dublin — and they've had to catch up with me."

"It couldn't take them two years."

"I figured I'd run into you and we could talk about it. It's so sticky writing about your marriage to someone."

"All you had to do was say so. Not that you look very happy talking about it either. So let's forget it."

"How's the book going?"

"Chugging along," he lied.

She frowned at the floor and said: "I can't talk about Gowan."

"Of course. All you'd had to do was dash me off a note saying so and I'd have understood."

"I know I can't because I've tried. With that other chap."

"Who?" Mopworth asked with a chill of apprehension.

"Didn't you know someone else is writing a book about him? Noel Graham — that editor who first published his poems and has that packet of screaming letters. I hear they're sort of rushing it through . . . But of course it'll be nothing like your warm thing, Alvin. Just a critical biography."

Mopworth looked toward the group of actors gathering for the tryouts at the other end of the studio. He was numb, as though some protective, no doubt delusive, husk had fallen from him, leaving him naked and frozen. He had continued with the book after all, or rather resumed it on recovering from the shock that had made him momentarily lose heart, deciding that the biography could survive the loss of that chapter, however essential, indeed climactic, the real-life elements of it on which he had stumbled. What the public didn't know wouldn't hurt them. The main problem was to maintain some confidence in his own credentials as a biographer. Now he was back in the groove again, only to be sent reeling from a far more serious blow. How would his poor thing look in the wake of a full-dress biography by Noel Graham?

He could guess Edith's opinion of his qualifications in that light. Were he to look back suddenly now, the thin scarlet lips might be found curled in a smile of sympathy that would be little better than outright scorn. He hated the pitying hand she laid on his wrist as she said, "We'll talk about it later. Look, Alvin, you don't have to read for this Algie part. Not for me. You know that. It's yours if you want it. Of course hang about if you like, to get a line on the script. And then couldn't we have some lunch when we break? What about it? I've so wanted to talk to you. You must excuse me now."

Mopworth stayed to skim over a copy of the script and to listen to a few of the tryout readings, but found it easier to walk about the streets alone. He had coffee in one place, a drink in another. He windowshopped down Fifth Avenue, scarcely knowing what detained his gaze. He wandered back to the studio around twelve-thirty to find them knocking off for lunch, and Edith really looking around for him. She smiled and came over, snatching her coat from a chair.

"Jesus," she whispered as they went out, "of all the cheesy British accents. Let's go to that — No, I can't take any more people breathing down my neck. These restaurants are awful at noon. Let's have a sandwich in my room. I'm right here at the Gotham. Do you mind?"

"Of course not."

Edith stretched out on the bed in stocking feet, with an Old-Fashioned in one hand and a cigarette in the other, while Mopworth varnished with mayonnaise the chicken sandwiches for which neither showed any real zest. He was aware of her blue eyes following him about the table at which he officiated as though he were host, which he was, to the extent of having insisted on paying the check. She had combed out her pale hair, then smoothed it down with a brush, but the face it framed retained the ravages of a harrying morning, perhaps a harrying life. Into its evenly molded features had been etched, since he had last seen her, lines that brought out, so to speak, her shrew's side. They softened gradually in repose, and even, at certain favorable angles which she no doubt knew and culti-vated, vanished altogether. They seemed to soften, too, when she forgot her own professional fret and focused on Mopworth an expression of brooding concern. He knew that her solicitude for him and his project was far from disinterested; nevertheless she followed his own glum abstraction with a certain wary compassion, wriggling her toes in her stocking feet and sigh-ing for them both. Mopworth took all this with a grain of salt, his cynicism deepened by the subtle hunch that there was more to her part in all this than she was letting on, and that he would learn more about it in due course. Meanwhile he could not be expected to be unmindful of her long legs, one of them drawn up, so that a fold of her blue dress fell away to reveal a width of silken thigh just above the knee. She was completely unconscious of this, as she held her glass on the crown of the knee and sighed up at the ceiling. At such moments the Beauty and the Shrew blended together in her face, and you saw what you might on canvas had the Pre-Raphaelites painted bitches. As he poured himself a glass of beer from one of the two bottles they had ordered, Mopworth thought wryly to himself that Edith ran up and down her emotional octave so regularly that any man who could have her for a month would probably know what McGland's life with her had been like without troubling to ask. Perhaps he would not abandon the book after all . . .

As if divining the secret track of his thoughts, she said rather suddenly from the bed, "Why don't you say something?"

Alone in a room with a beautiful wasp, Mopworth had already a sense of the precise intimacy on which he had a moment ago been ruminating.

"After all I don't see what call you have to make me feel guilty. Should I have told you earlier Noel Graham was doing his book?"

Mopworth took protracted gulps of his beer and walked the room, holding his tongue like a man making clear his determination not to pick a quarrel, or to have one picked. The scuff of a passing footstep in the corridor reminded him where they were.

"Need you drop yours because of it I mean? Noel would give his eyeteeth to know about Gowan what you do. As would I, to tell the truth!" she added with suddenly sardonic force. "McGland in America. Christ, how sick I am of being asked how 'I felt about it.' As though we hadn't been as good as divorced for — I can't even think how many years. What did you find out about him? Isn't research half scavenging, I mean doesn't it make you feel like a garbage collector half the time? Did he sleep with just absolutely everybody?"

"Anybody who would go to bed with him, Edith," Mopworth said quite matter-of-factly, sitting down in the same manner on this one. It was the better to hand her the second of three Old-Fashioneds sent up at once, of which she had disposed of one. She passed the empty glass to him as he gave her the full. She drank, raising her head on the pillow. "He was pretty carnivorous then?"

"He was that, as you don't need me to tell you." Mopworth laughed as he recalled aloud: "This is the way it always is. The interview gets turned around and people start asking me about Gowan. They're very curious about him." She lay, disposed to his regard, with her legs straight out and her feet crossed. Her head was crooked up against the two wadded pillows, this being a double bed. The counterpane was becoming a bit rucked up from all these maneuvers. She had evidently been in some tropical clime recently, judging from her deep tan, almost mahogany in shade, really too dark for her fair hair and blue eyes. "How many would you say he had affairs with?" she asked, looking past his shoulder at the far wall.

"I don't keep score. I mean I'm not a detective, though you often do feel like a scavenger, as you say, mucking about in somebody else's past. Eight or ten that I know of, so it may be more like a couple of dozen all told."

"What a ram," she said without humor. "What would you say the women were like? Can you tell me about any of them? Could you introduce me to any?"

"Are you writing a book too?" Mopworth laughed.

He need hardly have. That was the secret at which he had guessed from her shifting, if not shifty, manner. She figured now was as good a time as any to make the admission.

"As a matter of fact I am," she said. She then went on in her defense: "I mean all these books about Gowan. Why? I mean books and articles and this to-do. And the whole legend thing. Who would have thought? How do these things get started? Why is some one writer boomed over all the rest, when some as good or maybe even better are ignored? How starved we must be for another Byron to start grooming him for the role the instant he turns up. Hang the mantle on him and shove him onstage! Never mind whether the mantle fits or he's right for the part."

"In other words he wasn't any legend to you."

"Oh, Alvin, what a dull thing to say. No man is a hero to his valet or his wife? You must be pulling my leg. The thing is, however much you know someone and like them, the world's view can't be yours. Public life is one thing, private life another. They're absolutely two different things. We shared a private one. In that you know one another inside out. In all the details. There are no secrets."

"In that case maybe you can tell me something about his teeth. Did he stew over them quite a bit?"

"Teeth? He didn't have any trouble with his teeth that I know of. He took good care of them — always popping off to the dentist to have them checked. Why do you bring that up?"

"How many had he lost?"

"None that I know of, though I think a few of them were capped do you call it? Why are you asking me all this non-sense?"

"Why do you think he killed himself?"

"What's that got to do with it? How you do skip around."

"Well, why did he? What's your theory?"

"That's a large order — usually an impossible one. There's never any simple answer. Why does anyone? We all have it in us. I sometimes feel that way myself. Don't you?"

"Yes," said Mopworth, lying in order to preserve, if possible to further, the mood of confidence and frankness that was unexpectedly springing up between them, and that might reward cultivation in some hitherto unsuspected fashion. Edith took a hurried swallow, spilling a drop on her breast above her dress. Mopworth blotted it with his handkerchief while she went on: "But to get back to my book, haven't I a right to my innings? Aren't I entitled to my say?"

"Why do you say 'say'? Who's said anything against you?"

"He must have told you what I was like," she said, sliding her eyes away.

"He never once mentioned you. He never said a mumbling word about you that I ever remember. Everything I know about you is firsthand. And everything I shall come to know."

There was a silence during which she rather demurely digested his sentiment, or rather the tone into which he had unex-pectedly dropped while stating it. He said even more softly: "You needn't fear anything I might say, Edith. Or any competi-tion for that matter. I'm thinking of chucking the book."

"Oh, Alvin, surely not?" she said, hopefully. The pout of sympathy with which she regarded him, sliding up a little against the headboard, was really too much. Still, he had little cause for amusement, since his own hypocrisy was growing like a mushroom. The sight of the sad expression he presented in his turn made her reach up and lay a hand feelingly on his shoulder. Like a man bowing to the inevitable, he bowed his head — till his cheek came to rest on her bosom. She uttered a soft, rather sensuous little chuckle of rebuke or something,

405

and gave his hair a good-natured tousle. After some moments of silence — though he could hear her heart thumping with such clarity that he was reminded of how French doctors had always been able to conduct examinations without the aid of a stethoscope — she shifted his head over a bit. It was an adjustment made for comfort, not in the interest of admonition or rebuff. She did not shove it away, she simply set it to one side, like a dish. He became cross-eyed looking at the demarcation on her skin where the sun tan ended.

He now heaved a sigh subject to various constructions: whether he were expressing fatigue and defeat at the hands of fate in an unequal struggle, deploring his own movements in a philosophical fashion, or setting an amorous tone in which further advances could be prepared, was left wholly in doubt. He preferred for the time being having his motives open to misinterpretation even by himself. So they lay awhile, Edith holding her glass in midair so it would not drip on Mopworth's head, Mopworth's arm across her body, the hand on the other side of her still clutching his glass of beer. He made a slight movement aimed at easing the strain of their positions, which brought his lips against her throat.

"Not today."

It sounded so much like a housewife speaking to a door-to-door salesman that Mopworth could only answer, like a rejected peddler, "Some other time?"

He then came up for air with such directness and such a grin on his face that he might have been satirizing them in precisely such terms — leaving that avenue open to himself. The smile was sufficiently satirical to imply that she had read into his actions a degree of intention he had not himself had in mind their conveying, yet charming enough to seize any hope of progress in that direction that she herself might care to hold out.

She swung her feet off the bed and thrust them into her shoes. "We have to get back to the studio, or I do. I assume you do want the part?"

"Of course, Edith."

"Well, I want you, and so does Westerly. Then we'll be

seeing plenty of each other. You do understand it's five days a week. You won't be in every episode, naturally, but it'll mean a full-time job." She glanced at her traveling clock on the dresser and said, "Oh, it's not two-thirty yet. We needn't pop this minute. Maybe you'd care to listen to a few pages of this? I'll read it aloud. Eat your sandwich while I do, go on."

He thought she meant the first script of the serial, but it was the manuscript of her book she dug out of a grip. It was while listening to a chapter of A Welsh Idyll that Mopworth touched bottom. It was good — burning, immediate, a picture of a man he couldn't have written in a thousand years. Impressionistic, erratic, full of gaps and errors, it nevertheless ran through its subject with a wild brilliance all its own. It made what he was doing look slick and sick. After Graham's no doubt scholarly critical appraisal and this woman's flamboyant memoir, what could he possibly publish that wouldn't be ridiculous by comparison?

He left the Gotham for the studio, and the studio for his own hotel, feeling gored, bled empty — but disabused. What had the old chapel hymn said? "And the burden of my heart rolled away." His emotions were curiously like that blend of leadenness and lightness that marks the early stages of intoxication. Yes, he was liquidating a delusion as well as a dream. And now, finally and for good, he would no longer have to worry about the damned book — except how to square things with his publishers. Maybe he could turn over his notes to them for use by a likelier choice, if not return their advances from the fat income with which he was about to be showered. He had let go. The stone was off him. He was exhausted but free. He wasn't a writer, he was a television actor, and a jolly good one within his limits.

thirty-four

HE HAD BEEN in the hotel room a good two hours before Geneva showed up, shortly before six, looking tired and harried. She had been out since early morning with a real estate agent. A day among choked streets made worse by the filth and din of demolition had shown her how uninhabitable New York now was; glimpses of a few apartments how exorbitant anything they needed would be. Even Woodsmoke's insane rentals looked good from here, and so did Woodsmoke. She had been in cabs longer stationary than in motion, and had twice gotten something in her eye. The second time had required the services of a nearby optometrist. She was both grim and edgy, and Mopworth wisely threw no more cold water on a project for which she had taken the aggressive, and must be left the initiative of abandoning. When she asked where he had been all day he sat down on the tub in which she lay soaking and told her.

"Went after this new serial, *Mr. and Mrs. Wallop*, as I told you, and it was the damnedest thing. You know who's writing it? Edith Chipps. Gowan's widow. Like old times on the B.B.C. She wants to live in this country for a while."

"What's she like?"

"Pretty, but a bit of a tartar in her way. But the script looks good, from what I saw and heard. Everyone's keen on it. The part's mine if I want it, is the real news, and I've decided I want it. It'll start sustaining, of course, but no one has any doubt we'll have a sponsor in a month."

"But if it's daily won't you have to commute?"

"Not if we move to New York. We can set aside, say, three hundred a month for rent. That be enough do you think from what you saw today?"

"From what I saw today I don't ever want to live in New York. It's horrible, Alvin. I mean the old joke about shall we walk or do we have time to take a cab, it's *true*. No, I'm absolutely discouraged about the whole thing."

"Then we'll start living a little in the country. Better house, maybe buy or even build — how about that? A maid for you of course. And *lots* more trips into the city."

He bent to kiss her while she lathered a leg. When he sat up again she said: "How about your book? Doing the show and rehearsing every day for the next will be a full-time job. You can't write along with that, can you? How will you ever finish it at that rate?"

It was here that Mopworth committed the second of his really major deceptions. He pretended, or at least encouraged the belief, that he was giving up his career as a writer for her and his family. This put her squarely in his moral debt, an advantage which he rationalized by telling himself it was long overdue, and the only means by which he could get his desserts as a husband. And perhaps it was. Marriage *is* corrupting, he thought to himself with redoubled emphasis. In the complex, hundredfold daily emotional transactions of which it was formed, shrewd bargaining was inevitable — with dishonesty close on the heels of that. Mopworth's beef in a nutshell was that he was not appreciated. For think. He did his own work and a third of his wife's, dropped his moods to attend to hers, ministered to her humors and humored her wishes — and it was all taken for granted. In common with her generation she took as a matter of course an amount of distaff drudgery by the male that would have appalled a previous. How often had he not dropped his broom or fled the sink at the sight of Spofford or the Rappaports coming up the drive, to save both their faces. Once Spofford had caught him vacuuming and asked in surprise, "Geneva sick?" He had mumbled some such excuse for her, and himself. He did not mind playing the scullion for an hour or two a day, to share that much of what any intelligent woman must rightly consider a grinding and possibly degrading bore. What he minded was its being expected. He had tried by parody to calibrate the exact degree to which it was, but his irony was wasted. "I've finished the dishes. Is there anything else?" She had answered, "Have you bathed Amos?" He had saluted smartly and withdrawn, to see to that.

In saddling her with a moral obligation that was trumped up, as a means of exacting a respect not forthcoming from legitimate devotions, he was only following the example set by Geneva herself — not that it was original with her. Women habitually exaggerated their "day" in order to elicit a response very possibly commensurate with the facts, which might otherwise be denied them from men fagged out themselves. Geneva would falsify the offenses of some woman she disliked, or to whom she had momentarily taken a scunner, in order to make him share a grievance that, bored or wearied with women's rivalries, malices and social politics, he might otherwise have shirked. These things were all part of the diplomacy of marriage, where one had sometimes to lie in order to survive, or shout to be heard. Even lovers instinctively act on Talleyrand's dictum that God gave people tongues in order that they might conceal their thoughts. Geneva lied to survive and she shouted in order to be heard. In making personal hay of his end as a writer, Mopworth was lying to survive and shouting to be heard as a husband.

To keep the sense of his sacrifice green, and her gratitude warm, Mopworth next began to exaggerate the trials of commuting — though God knew they were bad enough on what was now a bankrupt railroad. The trains were late, dirty and falling apart. Sometimes they were so late they were early; that is, as you loitered toward the platform expecting the usual wait for the eight-something, you suddenly found yourself sprinting for the seven-something, rattling in an hour behind schedule. Wearying enough in summer, the delays were outright hardships in the winter, for the station at Woodsmoke was unheated. Then one had a choice of standing in a packed shed breathing air partially warmed by human bodies but polluted by tobacco smoke and deprived of ventilation by closed doors, or freezing in the open. If the wait was long, one usually alternated between the two, pacing the platform in overshoes and muffler till that no longer seemed preferable to what one had just forsaken for it, and one went back for another spell in the fetid shed. There was always someone breaking the un-written law against sociability in the morning, and to avoid these Mopworth stood in a corner with his back to the room, like an animal in a stall. If in winter there was next the danger of drawing an unheated coach, in summer there was that of sitting in one in which the air conditioner was on the blink. The rates went up as the service declined, and the maintenance stopped altogether. Seats that broke were not repaired; their parts lay in the aisles like scrap metal. The windows were patched with tape and opaque with filth. The washrooms were often such as to make the question of where one performed one's mission academic. Indeed, Mopworth once opened a door to one to find a passenger, an elderly gentleman, urinating on the floor in a towering rage. "Maybe now they'll —" Mopworth heard before hastily clapping the door shut again. There were mice.

To these ordeals must be added that of actual physical danger, for the broken windows were the result of stones hurled through them from mischievous boys on the track — or, as at least one arrest proved, degenerate adults. Glass was being shattered in this way at regular intervals, and once a woman two seats ahead of Mopworth had had to be removed at a way station to be treated for cuts and bruises. Mopworth always took a seat at a window already cracked and taped, or patched with card-board, banking on the Law of Probability to reduce the likeli-hood of another rock coming in that one again before it came in another. He took the additional precaution of pulling the shade down (if there was one) which sometimes provoked glares from seatmates who thus had their reading light cut off. Newspapers being rattled and throats cleared became a customary sound effect in these daily travels.

Mopworth remembered the psychiatrist they had quoted to McGland at the Spofford farmhouse following the ruckus at Indelicato's and the police station sequel the night he'd first met Geneva — how long ago it seemed now! — the psychiatrist who held that commuters secretly wanted to suffer these trials as the last chance they offered softening modern man to show something of the spunk of the pioneers. Sweltering or freezing on sidings while hotboxes were fixed and luxurious luncheon appointments washed out supposedly served this end. Perhaps there was some truth in the theory. Suburban men certainly played up the rigors of their lot, when they were not playing them down — which came to the same thing — gradually building up a humorous folklore. "I can take the seven A.M. out of Stamford and be in New York in time for lunch." Still, Mopworth himself found that, at least in the extreme form in which they were publicized, these hardships were the exception. It was junk you rode on, but, often for long stretches, fairly punctual junk. For the rest, he could use the hour's ride to study his script, read a book, or catch up on his sleep, the last especially when they were stalled by mechanical breakdown for any length of time. And at the end of his cityward journey there awaited him pleasant work with amusing people. And sometimes, in the afternoons, an hour in the arms of Edith Chipps.

His affair with her moved forward quite simply and naturally from its tentative beginnings, with none of the agonies or soul-searchings celebrated by novelists vying with one another to portray the inner torment of their subjects; certainly nothing of that famous American by-product of sex, guilt. Adultery made Mopworth if anything a better husband. Mellowed by pleasure, thankful for it (his ego of course soothed by the sense of romantic conquest), he went home a more kind and generous man, twice as willing to deserve the gratitude on deposit for him there by "pitching in" after dinner and bathing the children. "Another woman," or man, is low on the list of causes for divorce. Infidelity has probably stabilized more marriages than it has shaken. It is from its discovery that the trouble arises.

It was the other, the inner strains and corrosions to which his marriage as such was subject, that began, after this spell of fair weather, again to manifest themselves.

There was no housework for either of them once they had the maid on which Mopworth insisted the instant the commercial hopes for the serial began to materialize and their income to leap from next to nothing to anywhere from two to five hundred dollars a week, depending on how much free lance work he got in addition to his role on *The Wallops*. Whenever the maids quit (for there was the proverbial procession of them) the house was flung back into chaos worse than before, for Geneva had now enrolled in a couple of education courses in a nearby university in the hope of regaining her intellectual bearings by going into teaching of some sort. She took a job helping out in a local nursery school run by a woman she knew. Having to drop these studies and this work for days on end while she found and broke in another domestic sent her into emotional tailspins that naturally affected the entire family. Once during a solid month of such shambles she came close to a nervous breakdown. The beds in that interval went unmade, the house unswept, they dined from cartons fetched from the Chinese Gardens and Indelicato's. In the course of that crisis Mopworth got Edith to write him out of the script for a week while he took over the house. Then each afternoon at two he would drop what he was doing and tune in *The Wallops*, the entertainment at which housewives the country over were said to refresh and renew themselves for fifteen minutes every day. His dramatic counterpart, Algie, was referred to as being "off on a short cruise," for which Mopworth, dustcloth in hand or slumped in a striped bottlewasher's apron, could only envy him. Toward the end of the week another maid was found, but the victory had an unforeseen result. Troubles grimmer than those from which they were extricated sprang from this episode in the lives of the Mopworths.

thirty-five

WORD THAT THE employment agency had found help arrived about three o'clock that Friday afternoon. Geneva was not yet home from school, but Mike was. He was in the playroom, gluing together a model car. He was now five. Amos, three and a half, was napping. The minute he heard from the agency, Mopworth rang up Edith in New York to tell her it was all right to write him back into the script.

He telephoned from his study, now little used except for reading and rehearsing, but always available for the acquisition of solitude as such, for Geneva or himself. He did not hear Geneva come in the front door of the house. As she dropped her armload of books on a living room table, she suddenly remembered she must call the shoe store about some snowboots that had been ordered for Mike. After checking Mike's whereabouts with a greeting shouted down the basement stairs, and learning from him that his brother was still asleep, she moved to do this. She picked up the downstairs extension in time to hear Edith's voice using an endearment about which, casual though it was, there could be no mistake. Upstairs, Mopworth froze at the sound of the connection opening on the line and then quickly closing again, as the extension was put down. He drew the conversation to an end and hurried downstairs, praying desperately that he would find Mike waiting at the phone to call one of his friends, but steeled for horror. Geneva was sitting in a living room chair, waiting for him. Her face was pale.

"Are you sleeping with her?"

"Oh, come now."

"I heard what she called you."

"Everybody does that in the theater. It doesn't mean anything."

"Not like that."

She sat with her knees together, leaning slightly forward with her palms joined together, like a swimmer about to dive into some immaterial substance occupying the space directly in front of her. She was staring straight down to the floor.

"Don't lie to me on top of it, is all I ask. My self-respect has taken enough of a beating in this marriage. I'll think more of you, and of myself, if you simply tell me the truth. Do you sleep with her?"

"In the middle of the day?"

"Why not? What's wrong with that? It's done all the time."

"In that case there can be no harm in admitting it. Nothing

much wrong with it if everybody does it." He was tramping rhythmically about the room again, this time treading the grapes of wrath. Still his face was not altogether drained of that old clean-cut boyish look, the look of someone eager to please and to be well liked. He might have been about to burst into a recitation of "Boots, boots!" for the benefit of some elderly visitor.

"I think it unforgivable of you to be clever at a time like this, to twist my words around. Why don't you tell me straight out? Have you slept with her?"

"Not a wink," he answered, marching.

"There was no mistaking the tone of her voice. That kind of 'darling' can mean only one thing."

"I hear it little enough in this house."

"Are we going to be brilliant or are we going to be honest? Need you be cruel as well as unfaithful?"

"Why is it that every time a man defends himself to a woman he's cruel? Why is that?"

She breathed deeply and looked away, though otherwise remaining exactly as she was in the chair. She sat stiffly, almost primly. "I guess it was only a question of time till you did this to me," she said. "You had to prove you were a man without me."

It was always doubtful up to the last split fraction of a second whether Mopworth would meet contention listlessly or with vigor. There was so much to be said for either method, since neither had any effect. He hardly knew himself what the reaction would be till it set in, often of its own accord, so finely conditioned had his reflexes become, so delicately balanced between opposing possibilities of equal futility. Sometimes a sentence apathetically begun would take on a sudden violence.

He now stopped, flung his arms into the air and exclaimed, "Oh, Jesus Christ and God Almighty and I don't know what all! Why does a chap always have to be 'proving' something? Why would he have to be doing this 'to' you? Can't you sleep with a woman just because you want to?"

"Then you admit it's true."

"I deny everything. I take the Fifth Amendment."

"Don't be a silly ass. You admit it by your behavior. And by your hysterical denial you admit my interpretation is right. You had to hit out at me in some way, Alvin," she said instructively, almost pedagogically. She had the patience of someone with a dull pupil.

She rose and went to a cigarette box. She took from it a package of Marlboros — for some reason she always left them in their original containers when filling the boxes — shook one out, dropped the package back into the box and closed the lid. By this time Mopworth had ready a trembling flame.

"I guess this is a rap you can't beat," he said. "I can see that now. It's no use bucking the system. A man can't want to sleep with a woman just because he wants to sleep with her. The simple cry of the flesh and all. No. That's out. Plain sexual appetite for its own sake — like plain hunger for food — is no longer possible. A lady-killer today is automatically tagged as undersexed."

"I might have known you'd do this to me, sooner or later. You had to."

"I did?"

She nodded solemnly. "Your ego required it."

The languor into which he had begun to lapse suddenly reversed itself again as he followed her back to her chair. Before she could sit down in it, he seized her by the arm and whirled her around. "I'm not doing it *to* you! *I'm just doing it*. Can't you get anything as simple as that through your —"

"Thick head?" she said with a grin, glancing with satisfaction at the hand squeezing her arm. He was hurting her nicely. Everything was going her way. "Go on, get in your animosities. Lash out at me in the way you want to. Get all the malice off your chest. Unbottle your hatred. It'll clear the air between us. And don't feel too bad about the spectacle you're making of yourself. It's human nature to resent someone who's done something for us. We always hate our benefactor. It was only a question of time till you did something to me that both hits out at me as a woman and gives you identity as a man. And with Gowan's wife. Of course, I see it all now. That completes it for you, doesn't it? I hadn't expected such a neat pattern,

416

that tucks in so many angles for you. You've shared the same woman with him. That makes you really as good as Gowan himself."

This drove Mopworth to a retort for which he was so instantly sorry that he felt himself actually regretting it as it emerged. Yet at the same time it created the moment toward which they must all along have been blindly forging their way, step by step and day by day, the intolerable, obligatory focus toward which everything had led, and which it was imperative they face. He blurted out: "Well, I've often wondered if we hadn't shared the same woman before Edith Chipps."

It was in the next split second that the tide of battle hung in the balance. The wild throb and sway of Geneva's own emotions must be the decisive factor. He had just slashed her in a manner that would have proved her accusations as nothing else could, and had she taken a moment to reflect, she might have kept silent and, by preserving her grievance, secured her case. Being woman as well as human, however, she preferred another kind of triumph — or the emotions boiling up within her required it. The discovery of his infidelity had wounded her pride, and the only balm available in the white heat of the moment was to scream at her betrayer, "Well, make no mistake about that! He had me before you did! In case you think you're the only pebble on the beach, lover boy!"

It was like a blow on the face, silencing them both. Geneva looked no less than Mopworth as though she had been physically struck. They stood facing one another in a balance of fury which rapidly cooled to the same stunned, frozen embarrassment for both. After a moment, they turned silently and simultaneously away from one another, like exhausted assailants between whom a draw has been declared. Mopworth turned to the bar and fixed drinks — which neither of them touched. They avoided one another's eyes in a common shame. Neither had any advantage: they were both wrongdoers now.

The subject was never mentioned again. A weird, unearthly peace settled over the house, like one of those sultry unnatural lights that fall just before summer sunsets, when everything hangs in a suspension so prolonged it seems it must be eternal.

They were both spent, yet curiously purged: as though the sheer fact that there was nothing more to say for themselves guaranteed their saying nothing more to each other. An armistice had settled on them without its being declared, or even hoped for. It saved their marriage — for the time being.

It remained for an act of outright chivalry to deal the final blow to that.

thirty-six

MOPWORTH GAVE UP EDITH, who scarcely pined away, being in any case ripe for the attention of another member of the company. With the new maid all that could have been hoped, the household ran smoothly once again. Geneva was free for both her trips to the nearby campus and the two hours a day she helped at the nursery school — in which Amos was now enrolled. Along with her spirits she recovered the humor with which she had always been at least periodically able to brighten domestic life. If humor is the word, for it was really an acid kind of wit, often a shot fired in the war between the sexes. But at its best, Mopworth knew, more deserving of the name of wit than the quipping tomfoolery and lighthearted horseplay that were his own contribution to the gaiety of the hearth. Often it had a kind of surrealist quality, however dry and wry. Late one night, for example, they were lying in their respective beds reading when there was audible in the distance a series of reports, like gunfire, followed by a kind of outcry, unmistakably feminine.

"What was that?" Mopworth said.

"Some poor woman shot her husband."

The maid being a jewel, the Mopworths decided it was time for another week end in New York.

This one gave early promise of being more eventful than any they'd had there before. The hotel had a telephone message waiting for them when they arrived. It was from Nectar, who had known they were coming in. Geneva called her back the instant they were settled in their room, to learn some un-expected news.

Jack had left her. Or, more accurately, had just informed her by letter that he would not return from Hollywood, to which he had recently again gone, ostensibly to make some changes in the script of his movie, actually to see a bit actress for whom he had fallen the first time, and whom he had in the interval been secretly spending time with on visits of her own East. The passion, he now stated by registered mail, had turned out to be conclusive. He would give Nectar any kind of divorce she wanted.

"Congratulate her for me," Mopworth said. "I think she's well rid of him."

"Do you mind if I go over and hold her hand? It's some-thing a woman wants to talk out with another woman. And don't you have theater tickets to pick up?"

"Fine, but get back in time for an early dinner now. It's an eight o'clock curtain."

Sobering though the news was, Geneva could not be expected to be uninfected by its drama. No woman is divorce-proof; a breakup stirs her as much as a marriage. Throughout the evening Geneva's mood was one of subdued excitement. She returned breathlessly at ten minutes after seven, too late for a proper dinner before the show. They would have supper afterward, meanwhile fortifying themselves with a candy snack picked up in the hotel lobby on the way out. Throughout the entertainment, a musical, Mopworth stole glances at Geneva. She laughed at the jokes and responded to the tunes, but she was distinctly preoccupied by a crisis more vital to her than any unfolding on the stage.

Afterward they went to a place called the Flamingo, where they both suddenly found themselves with appetites of a sort to which night club food is hardly adequate. Even by night club standards, the portions of fried chicken they were served were scant to say the least. Flushed by the three martinis they had drunk while waiting for it, Geneva found herself with the courage to complain. "Of course, madam," the waiter, a tall man with a hatchet face, said, and marched toward the kitchen to get them some more.

A scene now unfolded for which Mopworth could scarcely believe his eyes. He had just raised a glass of beer when the waiter returned from the kitchen carrying on a huge platter enough fried chicken to feed an army. He set this down before them, said, "Will this be sufficient?" and withdrew.

They were sitting side by side at one of a line of white leather banquettes. Another row of them ran parallel to it on the other side of the room. The small stage for the floor show was to their right. They were squarely in the middle of their row, in full view of most of the restaurant. After the shock of the initial surprise, a cold rage flooded Mopworth's veins, like a current of ice water. This sensation turned instantly to one of fierce heat as he sensed the line of amused smiles on either side and across from them. His cheeks burned, his head throbbed. He would have been prepared for surly response from the waiter, or one of crisp discourtesy — could even have seen some slight justification for it under prevailing standards ("After all one doesn't go to a night club for food"). But this act of deliberate and calculated humiliation — comparable to the practice followed in an expensive French restaurant of which he'd heard, of rolling a movable blackboard up to your table with the prices of the entrees on them, when you asked about that on finding them absent from the menu — left him so sick with horror that he scarcely knew what to do, or what he was doing. He stared, stupefied, at the mountain of food on the platter: a gross heap of legs, wings and breasts like something in a nightmare.

By now everyone was looking. The floor show was to go on in ten minutes, but there would be no spectacle like this. Mopworth tried to say something to Geneva, but his tongue stuck to the roof of his mouth. He raised his bent head to glance at her. A brave smile on her face was followed by a pathetically humorous sigh as, like one "being a good sport" and going along with a joke, she thrust her fork with mock zest into a piece of chicken and put it on her plate — for there was not even a serving fork on the platter! This, if anything, increased his horror. Primly, she cut off a bite and tucked it into her mouth. She took another bite, then another. How could he simply sit here and watch this? It was like standing by and watching your wife violated. He did not know how much longer he could endure it, nor yet quite what he could do about it. His chest constricted, as though a clamp were tightening around it; the pulsing in his ears made him fear his head would explode. Glancing down the row of faces, which made him think of spectators in a Roman amphitheater, he saw a man with thinning blond hair whisper something to his wife, a woman with a high hair-do and a mink stole. He could bear no more. Rising to his feet, he suddenly grasped the table on its underside and with a furious heave overturned it.

Sections of cooked poultry flew in every conceivable direction. The platter itself, which was round, tumbled onto its rim and rolled under a table on the other side of the room, like a hubcap from a speeding car. A drumstick bounced toward a waiter who was going by just at that moment, and who sprang nimbly out of the way. A wing came to rest against the toe of a black patent-leather shoe under another table. Nor was the fried chicken of course all there was to the story. Vegetables, salad, assorted relishes, and water and liquor glasses all joined the shambles. Great brown glops of gravy from the gravy boat stained the carpeting, on which also a ball of mashed potatoes landed miraculously intact, like a snowball. The ketchup bottle, for which they had asked in a previous request, contributed a vivid spout of gore to the general result.

"Come on," Mopworth said. Standing stiffly a moment to let the lady precede him, he marched out in her wake.

The next sixty seconds were a sensation like that of evacuating a dream. It was like what one undergoes when one half realizes one is asleep and dreaming, and wishes one would wake up. Flight was checked by a wait of nearly that length at the cloakroom. The girl on duty, oblivious of the drama from which she had been screened by a lobby wall, set down a magazine she had been reading and rose to pick up the claim check Mopworth had slapped down. With great deliberation she consulted it and vanished to fetch his clothes. Had it been only a hat

Mopworth would have fled through the door (as Geneva already had) without bothering to redeem it, but it was cold and he was wearing an overcoat too. He snatched these wraps from the surprised beauty and hurried out, leaving a dollar bill on the salver.

Geneva was standing at the curb beside a militarist in a frogged coat, who by dint of furious blowing on a whistle produced a cab. Mopworth climbed into it behind Geneva, and after parting with another bill managed to wrest jurisdiction of the taxi door, which was held firmly from the other side until this exchange had taken place. He called out the name of their hotel, and they were presently speeding through the night traffic.

Neither spoke until they were well upstairs in their room. By that time Mopworth's breathing had returned to something like normal, though his voice was thin and strained.

"Did you ever see anything like it?"

"No, I never did."

They sat on opposite sides of the bed, their backs to one another, more by Geneva's choice than his. He reached around and tried to take her hand. "I'm sorry, darling."

"I should think you would be," she said, withdrawing it.

He was to be thrown into a second astonishment while scarcely recovered from the first. He watched uncomprehendingly as she rose and went to hang up her coat. "What do you mean?"

"I have never, *never* been so humiliated in my life."

"That's why I did what I did. I'm sure there was a better way, but it's all I could think of at the moment."

"No, that's not what I mean. What you did was the real humiliation."

He shook his head, like a dazed prizefighter. "What are you talking about? I don't understand."

"Because you don't want to understand. How you can sit there and think I can ever, ever forgive you for putting me through that shattering horror is something *I* will never, never understand."

"But it was the waiter who — It's evidently a technique they have for people who expect to — to —"

"That was bad enough. What you did was worse. Infinitely worse. I thought I'd die! I wish I would." She clenched her fists and beat them against the sides of her head. "I wish I were dead! Did you know that Bill Hoffritz was there? In the — in the audience?"

"I don't even know who he is."

"He's an old friend of the Dumbrowskis'. Nectar knows him. The advertising man. He'll probably tell her the whole story."

"Now let's not get off the subject," Mopworth said, with dogged spirit. "Let's state the factors. You ask for a decent helping of food, after the measly portions we get. A reasonable enough request, only you're not supposed to make it. You are embarrassed. I try to show what I think of that. Chivvying a lady. Humiliating a lady. In public. I refuse to stand for it. I avenge her. I — call it what you want. *I hit back.* Blindly, I'm so insane with rage —"

"You're insane with rage at me."

"No."

"Yes. You pretend it's rage at the restaurant, but that's just a guise. It's secretly at me. For putting you into such a situation."

"That's not true. Oh, I might later when we're alone ask you what you did a thing like that for, expecting a square meal in a night club, that's not what people go to them for —"

"There, you see?" she said, pointing a finger at him. "You admit it. It's out now. You can never take it back. You resent me for making a spectacle of us in public. But bad as that is, or mistaken as it is, it'll pass. In fact people were starting to go back to their own dinners, and one or two of them were annoyed for us. Bill Hoffritz was probably one of them. He shook his head, I saw him. So in another minute it would all have blown over. But no, you didn't want that. You couldn't pass up a chance to punish me by causing a scene worse than the one we were in, by humiliating me much, much more, by making a public spectacle of me no one would miss. *You had to rub it in.* And all under the handy guise of chivalry. Oh!"

"Here we go again," Mopworth said, dropping his hands to his sides.

"No, Alvin, here we don't go again. Here we stop."

He saw that she had reached into the closet and was getting her coat out again.

"This does it. This I can never live down. Not in a hundred years. It's no use. No, don't come near me, it's no use. This is it. I'm going."

"Where are you going?"

"Somewhere, anywhere. To Nectar's. She'll be up yet. I need a drink. Somebody to talk to. Any somebody."

Mopworth continued his movement away from the bed, dropping into a chair at the far side of the room. She paused at the door on her way out.

"*Now* will you do something about yourself? Now will you see somebody? Somebody who might be able to help you? Because you'll admit after tonight that you need it."

Mopworth moved his head in a way that could have been interpreted as a nod of assent, or as a kind of weary shake of it from side to side. He didn't know which it meant, really, or care one way or another. It was accompanied by a shrug.

"Not that I can see it's doing us any good any more, now. It's for your own good that I suggest it, if you're cracking up. As far as we're concerned, I can't imagine picking up the pieces any more. Not after this."

Mopworth remained in the chair after she had gone, he couldn't have said how long, staring at the wall. He still had his overcoat on. After a while he telephoned down for a drink. While waiting for it to come, he removed his overcoat, and then he started to take off his shoes, but the lace on one of them became snagged. He spent a long time sitting in the chair, picking at the knot. At last he gave it up and just sat there in the chair, waiting for his drink to arrive.

thirty-seven

FROM THE WINDOW of his upper-floor room in the Woodsmoke Sanitarium, Mopworth could see, across a short, wavering level of treetops, to the distant barnyard where George Spofford was picking his way among stray hens with a bag of feed on his shoulder. He vanished into a barn, and then the kitchen door opened and old Spofford came out. He stood gazing around a few moments, then went down the stairs in response to a call from his son, who beckoned to him from the barn. The pecking chickens cleared a path for him too. It all looked very peaceful out there. The weather had turned warm. The late morning sun streamed through the grilled window at which Mopworth stood.

Presently he turned back to Geneva, who was sitting rather stiffly in a straightback chair, her eyes fixed on the floor. The easy chair was unoccupied.

"Do your parents sell to restaurants or only to people?"

"We used to sell to the Main Street Grill, but that was a long time ago. No, not to restaurants that I know of, any more."

"Guess what we had for supper last night." He gave a peculiar laugh, not expecting an answer. Geneva rose nervously and stood at the window, but with her back to the view. Not facing him either, she said in a tense but resolute voice: "This is no good, Alvin."

"But you wanted me to get help."

"Not on this scale. And it's not what you came here for anyway. This is just a trick to make me keep from going through with it. Oh, I can see your mind working away. How could she leave him at a time like that, him in a sanitarium, et cetera. Well, it won't work. You're clever, but I can see through this one."

"Yes, but the children."

"We've been through that too, and I'm convinced my view of all that is right. Now *is* the best time to call it quits, when they *are* young and don't realize. It's later that'll be bound to be upsetting. And anyhow, I've never believed it better to keep children in a disharmonious house than to put them through a divorce. That's the lesser evil. The worst victims aren't the ones of broken homes, as we call them, but prisoners in ones that ought to be. Besides, children are tough."

Mopworth sighed and flapped his arms once. He lay down on the bed width-wise, his head propped against the wall and his legs dangling over the side. He wore a fielder's glove into which from time to time he slapped a ball, to deepen the pocket. "What will you do?"

"Nectar and I are going to open a school for disturbed children."

Mopworth drew a deep breath and held it till his senses reeled. He let it out with a long, "Pwaah," and said, "Well, there'll be no want of them. You should do a brisk business."

"I think it inexcusable of you to throw that at me in terms of our own situation," Geneva retorted with spirit. "Ours are in damn good shape, everything considered, and you know it, though of course there is the worry about Amos's attention span. He keeps falling asleep in Basic Relaxation. But all in all we're luckier than most parents, and should be grateful."

"That's what I meant," he said, slapping the ball into the pocket of the glove with growing boredom. "There's a great need."

"All right then." By her tone Geneva seemed pacified, but her eyes flashed as she went on, "It seems to me that when somebody is trying to do something useful about all the trouble in the world, only a little something in a little corner of it, but *something* — not to mention that this is the field in which your wife has been trying to carve out a little niche for herself, the profession toward which she's been hacking her way in her spare time — the least you can do is wish them well."

"Of course I do. I'm sorry. You know that. Where will you set up shop?"

"We're not sure yet whether here or in New York. Here would be good because there's nothing like it within a radius of several towns, and I'm known a little here because of my working in the nursery school. But New York might be better because of the courses we want to take for the specialties we want to go into. I now have my teaching certificate, and could stay at the university here for more studies, but Nectar thinks they have more to offer at Columbia. We'd like to talk it over with you later. We want your advice, of course."

"I wish you'd stop treating me as an individual in my own right," Mopworth said, clawing an orange. He had put the ball and glove aside. "Nothing is more irritating than that." He poked a segment of orange into his mouth.

"I want all this to be amicable," Geneva warned him tartly. She watched him spit a few pips on the floor, brushing some from the counterpane. "There'll be financial things to settle, which people can manage to be adult and civilized about."

He blew out a mouthful of scrap. "Not me."

"So I repeat, Alvin, I *am* going through with it. My bringing you this basket of fruit in no way means I approve of your being here, or don't see through your tricks. You're foxy, but it isn't going to work. And don't expect me to bring the boys here to see you. That's one stop you're not going to pull. I've got to go now. I'll see you later. Goodbye, Alvin."

So now he would have to throw the whole business in reverse, he thought after she had gone, use all the ingenuity he had employed to get admitted to the place in extricating himself from it. Dr. Wolmar wasn't going to like that, and therefore it wasn't going to be easy. Being now a director of the sanitarium, he was likely to take special exception to having the institution played fast and loose with, considering the waiting list they had. Even more would he resent being personally made a fool of.

Mopworth had not been long immersed in these ruminations when he was summoned by their object himself, for a talk. Eating the last segment of orange, he went downstairs to Wolmar's office.

"Well, how are we today?" Wolmar asked in his dense Bavarian accent.

"Fine. And how are we?"

Mopworth had decided on amiability, but the problem was

just how much. As Wolmar consulted a dossier on him to which Geneva had contributed heavily despite her disapproval, Mopworth assessed him. Wolmar had given him a broad smile which doubled his resemblance to a duck. Any resemblance to an animal for some reason increases when we smile — perhaps because the futility of trying to shake off a similarity by claiming our human estate is exposed. Wolmar's bill of a nose seemed to flatten out farther every time his lip rose. So vivid was the illusion that when he opened his mouth to speak you were surprised he did not quack instead of talk in a normal tone. This point became an obsession with Mopworth, who at the same time, became uneasy over his obsessive concentration on it.

"You have a history of sexual difficulty," Wolmar failed to quack. "Zis hostility toward women. Would you care to talk about it?"

"No, I'd rather you did. Say anything that comes into your head *however insignificant it may seem at the moment*. Even if it seems to you to have no bearing on the subject."

"Are you at home with women?"

"Occasionally, when their husbands are away." Mopworth did not mention his attempted rape, which, heavily as it would have weighed in his favor on general principles, would have worked against his immediate purpose — to get out of here as soon as possible now that it apparently wasn't going to do him any good as far as keeping his wife was concerned.

Wolmar smiled again, reading in his notes a moment. Then he didn't quack: "Evidently you don't want to commit yourself." Mopworth looked around with a significant gesture at his surroundings and gave his odd laugh. Just at that moment the interview was interrupted by the ringing of one of three phones on Wolmar's desk. It took very few words on Wolmar's end to reveal it as a call from home. Mopworth rose and walked to the window, where he stood looking out at the grounds for the duration of the conversation.

"Yes . . . Yes . . . *Natürlich.* No, I couldn't get three together. Two are on the aisle in the fourth row. The single is farther back but O.K. I take it and you and Lotte can have the pair . . . What? No, it's not *Rosenkavalier*, it's *Die Fledermaus*."

Mopworth could conjure the formidable figure of Mrs. Wolmar, taking her constitutional in even the coldest weather. He remembered from the days in Punch Bowl Hollow how impatient she would seem with the winding lanes of the subdivision as, bundled in tweeds and a head shawl, sometimes swinging a stick cut from a tree, she would strike out for open country. She was occasionally accompanied by Wolmar, more frequently by another woman whom inquiries had revealed to be Wolmar's unmarried sister. She had come over from Germany a few years ago, apparently to stay, judging from the third ticket making the odd lot Wolmar had had to obtain for the performance of *Die Fledermaus*.

Mopworth turned from the window, spurning the apologies murmured by Wolmar on hanging up, and asked after Mrs. Wolmar. "And your charming sister," Mopworth inquired, not sure of this adjective for the second of the Valkyries seen striding in bitter weather up Vineyard Road, "is she still with you?"

"Lotte? Yes. She lives wiz us. We are all opera happy. And Strauss crazy in particular. Well so! We get on wiz ze interview."

Mopworth answered as he was expected to the routine questions put to him, his attention now firmly fixed on something else. A plan for deliverance had sprung full-orbed into his mind, with no conscious or systematic thought of his own it seemed. Nor did he waste any time in putting it into action.

Within the hour he was seated at the desk in his room, writing to Lotte Wolmar:

"My lebkuchen: I must speak to you if only by this miserable pen and ink. I find things unendurable. The score for the new opera goes poorly. The strain under which in the summer of '98 I composed the bulk of *Der Schweinhund* is nothing compared to that under which I continually groan with *Nix Verstehe*. But you were there then, ah, that summer at Wiesbaden, my schneken, my vogel . . . "

He wrote a succession of these notes on house stationery, in his own hand. He was banking on that for detection, having had to submit a specimen of his handwriting for analysis on admission. This was one diagostic measure for which, as a matter of fact, Mopworth had some respect. What more accurately offered a graph of the individual nervous system than this trail of ink which flowed with the minute exactness of a cardiogram itself? The trick was to read it back. He had no idea how good the graphologist here was, but at least there was a sample of his handwriting on file against which to check the letters. The question was how long it would take them to solve what was going on under their noses, for he posted the notes freely in the sanitarium mail drop. He made occasional seeming attempts to disguise his handwriting, and he signed all the letters by a pet name, Your Munchkin. Though he was not a hundred per cent sure of what he was doing, he knew that essential to it was the appearance that the writer was trying to conceal his identity.

The missives he supplemented by sending to their object an occasional parcel of goodies. The first contained a few artificial flowers taken from a vase in the main lounge, a Hershey bar, a couple of tangerines and a bottle of Seven-Up. There was a covering allusion to the packet in his next billet-doux: "I wish, my pfeffernüsse, I could add to these protestations of my regard some more appropriate tangible evidence, but can only manage the poor offerings which you will in due course receive. This place is a madhouse! Who can work in such surroundings, with such distractions! Still I struggle night and day with the damnable first act . . ."

The contents of the parcels declined, depending on the accessibility of the lounges, kitchen pantry, storeroom and other quarters from which he scrounged them. The second contained a dogeared copy of *McCall's*, a paper weight and a head of lettuce. Next followed a ballpoint pen and a bag of walnuts. At least something was being done, according to a plan that had boldness and imagination, of a kind likely to undercut all that nonsense about being "ready to go home." To aid the authorities, who proved rather slow in solving the case, he would drop subtle hints. He would walk the corridors humming tunes with his eyes closed, like someone experimentally revolving a motif in his head. Once he sat in his room with the door open, bowing an imaginary cello.

"My opening!" he wrote at last. "What do you think has supplied the inspiration? Nothing less than this verdammdte plumbing. I know now that the introductory theme of *Nix Verstehe* will be a sustained orchestral monotone, like the howling in the walls when a bathtub tap is left open in another room (you will remember the inn at Wiesbaden, my strudel). The opening note of Wagner's *Rienzi* is a prolonged trumpet note that is crescendoed and then diminuendoed. Every horn player fears that note. Well, the whole orchestra will fear the opening measures of *Nix Verstehe*, I promise you, yes and the audience too . . ."

After two and half weeks, the door of his room flew open one morning, Wolmar stepped inside, pointed through it and failed to quack: "Out!"

"Why?"

"Out I say! I want you packed and out of this building inside of an hour."

"But why?"

"I think we have the right to choose the sort of person we want in this place. You're sick! You need help."

Mopworth dug his suitcase out of the closet and dropped it on the bed. He began throwing shirts and socks into it at a great rate. "Don't you want to keep me awhile for observation?" he said. "Don't you need a few mmbahahaha to give the place mmbahohoho." He gave the peal of maniacal laughter for which he had once or twice been called on in his career as a professional actor. It rang down the corridor.

Wolmar quickly shut the door. He dabbed his forehead with a handkerchief. He was sweating. "Get out of here," he repeated in a terrified whisper.

"What if I refuse?"

"Then I shall not hesitate to use restraint, sir."

The thought of a mental patient being bundled into a straitjacket to hustle him *out* of a place, rather than into it, so appealed to Mopworth's sense of dramatic values that for a moment he was tempted to toy a little with the threat of this measure. But prudence moved him instead to finish with his packing and get out while the going was good. He signed the papers that he had been assured would be ready and waiting for him in the front office, and inside of an hour and a half he was walking, suitcase in hand, down the road toward the Spofford farm.

He didn't want to see the whole family — just old Spofford — and so he stopped in a wayside booth and telephoned him. Luckily the old man was home. He told Mopworth to sit tight where he was, he would be along in a jiffy to pick him up. Mopworth had been sitting in the open booth watching for only five minutes when he heard, then saw, the Ford rounding a bend in the road. Spofford stopped precisely beside the booth and grinned out at him.

"Have a good rest?"

"Very."

"Hop in. We'll have a bite at Indelicato's."

Since Spofford had visited Mopworth several times in the sanitarium, and knew from their rather frank conversations all that was going on, there was no need for them to discuss it now. Spofford took nobody's "side." He listened impartially to both Geneva's and Mopworth's, having made up his mind firmly from the start to have no opinions and certainly to make no judgments. Not that either talked as much as he had hoped, which rather cheated his curiosity and left his full tolerance undisplayed. When they had settled down at Indelicato's behind stiff whiskies, he said, as though he knew enormously more than he did, "We have to try to be understanding. It's the least we can do, especially when we don't understand. Now let's talk about something else. What'll you do?"

"I'm going back to New York. If my family do."

Mopworth died hard. He did move back there once it was established that Geneva would. He drifted from job to job for over a year after *The Wallops* went off the air when Edith abandoned it to work on her book in California, but he was able to earn a livelihood for himself with his free lance work, and so contribute substantially to the support of the children.

432

Though Geneva had custody of them he saw them regularly and even often. They were his reason for not returning to London, as within him he longed to do. They were his tie with America. Geneva and Nectar eventually opened their school in an old house on the West Side of Manhattan, remodeled so they could use the lower floor for classrooms, the upper as living quarters. The two continued taking specialized courses of study in their chosen field, Geneva attending N.Y.U. while Nectar went to Columbia, enrolling in classes which alternated their absences from the school, so that one of them would always be on hand. They did their homework together, evenings, reading their books and discussing them in the large front bedroom which they shared.

Mopworth remained at loose ends, and sometimes his heart bled for England. He had long since stopped turning out light verse. Once in an especially restless interval he was tempted to try his hand at serious poetry. "When in the peristaltic clutch of love," he wrote, and not only tore it into shreds but threw them on the floor and jumped on them, as though stamping out a flame that must not be let spread.

What *was* behind the human botch of mating? He had puzzled too often and in vain over that one to think he could ever solve it now even as a victim. All one knew was that it seemed to get worse from generation to generation, as the gulf between the sexes widened until it threatened to become fatal. Was there something inherent in the sex bond itself that made a mate an adversary? Or was Mind the culprit, the overintellectualization of what should remain an emotional and instinctive link? Was it a failure to be romantic — a refusal to embrace the illusion to which nature invites us, and which we circumvent to our cost? Not even the poets romanticized women any more. Who would any longer regard their breasts as doves, or their hands as lilies? But did women themselves any longer invite such comparisons, women with their shirts and slacks, their well-stocked minds and their rude language, and the other competitive proofs of their equality with men? And this din of talk about their Ordeal. What a racket they had going, what a lobby they controlled. They now had a corps of trained anthropologists filling the magazines with the discovery that housework is tedious, as though office work were anything else. Was housework any more stultifying than the clerical tasks to which their husbands daily set forth without benefit of journalists advertising their lot or psychologists mourning it? Well, perhaps that wasn't quite fair: the offices and factories looked good from the kitchen but not the kitchen from the offices and factories . . . But here he was again churning away at a subject he had decided there was no point in churning away at. One thing was certain. When it comes to sex we talk a good game, but that's about all. We're no better off with our freedom than the Victorians were with their tyranny. Ours seems a world in which the Individual prospers at the expense of the Pair. Maybe the price of the one is the decline of the other.

In any case, there's an eternal truth, for male and female alike. It's only the privileged who complain.

One day a review of *A Welsh Idyll* shot off the page of a newspaper and hit him square between the eyes. It was a glowing notice. He bought the book, and read it with admiration and despair. An old dream gave a last flicker of pain, and died. For weeks his spirit was like a bed of ashes, faintly stirred by sight of bookstore window displays or scraps of praise heard in conversation. For the memoir was a success, and Edith herself came to New York on a tide of publicity. As he hoped and feared, he ran into her one evening at a party. The flush of triumph and a hearty tan combined to give her face a rather frenetic glow, which nearly made Mopworth laugh, but she did look beautiful in a long blue gown, her hair now swept up in royal style from behind and secured by a flamboyant comb edged with a row of seed pearls.

"Alvin. Just the man I want to see. I've got an idea for a new serial with a swell part in it for you."

"Buffoon type. I didn't think you'd bother with mundane things like television any more, Edith. The book is beautiful, of course."

"Oh, thanks, Alvin. But it's only a critical success, and I'll never write another. And what if it sells fifty thousand? No, we've still got to make a living, haven't we?"

They found a free corner in which to sit and catch up on one another. Mopworth had of course the more to relate. Edith hadn't known of any marital difficulties and was surprised to learn of his divorce — or at least she expressed surprise. Then she sized him up with an arch smile, a twinkle in her eye. "Another woman?"

"You could say that."

"Don't tell me it's your wife's best friend."

"Well, yes," Mopworth said. "As a matter of fact it is."

They were engulfed just then by a fresh wave of well-wishers bearing down on Edith to congratulate her, ruling out all further hope of clarifying the matter for the time being.

There were about ten people in all at that end of the room, and, having crystallized as a group by chance, they remained intact as one for nearly the rest of the evening. They formed, it turned out, a core whose conversation proved infectious, toward whose animated circle other guests gravitated, individually or in pairs, till finally there was a single, prolonged dialogue going.

It was toward midnight that the discussion got around to the subject of sex. Several there seemed to know something about it. One was a journalist who wrote on various aspects of the topic for the popular magazines, and two were instructors at local colleges. Everyone drank a great deal and everyone had a very good time.

They sat far into the night, talking about love.